ANIMUS

POLLY J. MORDANT

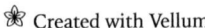

AS ALWAYS, TO MY DEAR HUSBAND, MALCOLM, MY INSPIRATION.

ALSO TO MY DEAREST DAUGHTERS, BETH AND LUCY, WITHOUT WHOSE SUPPORT THIS COULD NEVER HAVE BEEN WRITTEN.

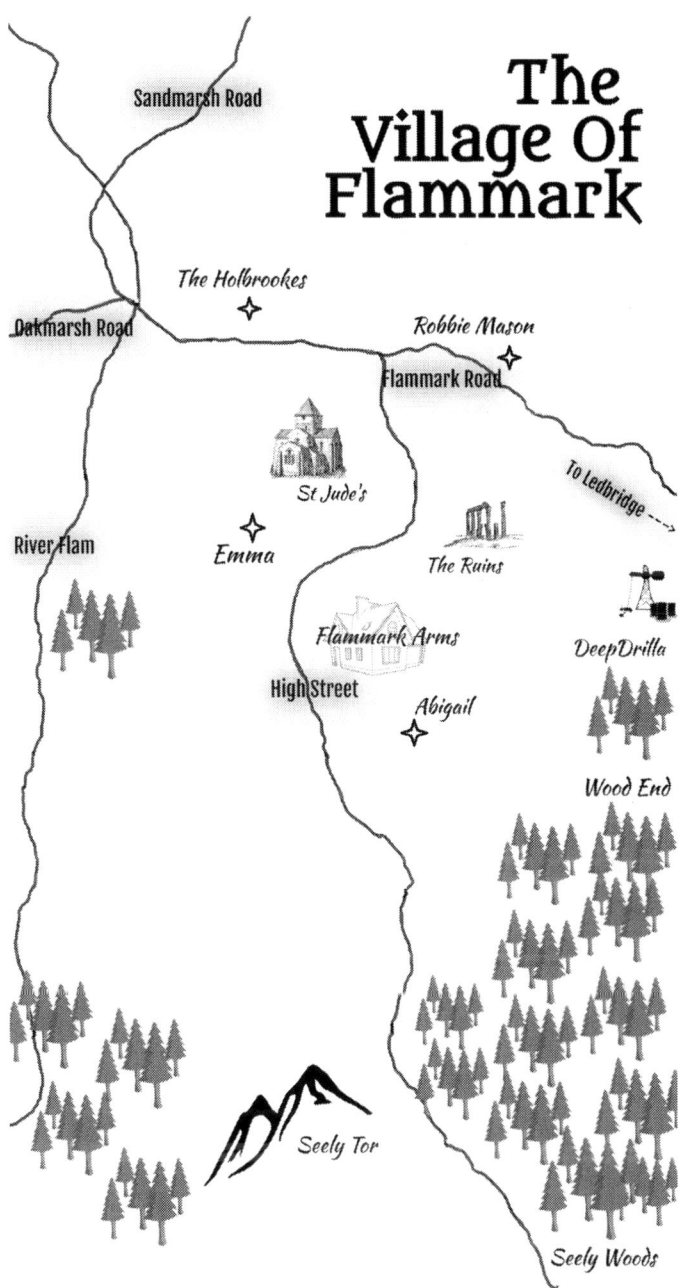

The
Village Of
Flammark

Sandmarsh Road

The Holbrookes

Oakmarsh Road

Robbie Mason

Flammark Road

St Jude's

To Ledbridge

River Flam

Emma

The Ruins

DeepDrilla

Flammark Arms

High Street

Abigail

Wood End

Seely Tor

Seely Woods

❦ I ❦

ARRIVAL

Deep down, moving yet unformed within the mantle of the earth, its spirit fingers never rest.

Always pushing, struggling upwards, inch by inch it gains its ground. Born of fire, seasoned by stone, no element can thwart its slow advance.

Though centuries have passed, they are as blinks of an eye to the ghastly vapour. Determined, forever patient, it reaches the half-fused rock of the earth's upper mantle. No need to push here. Gentle penetrations are all the dark essence needs to snake through its viscosity and find the quickest route to the outer crust.

Now hard. Much harder. Igneous formations impede its progress—push it back, sometimes by miles, until it can find softer seams. Then on it creeps. Implacable. Undeterred. Exploring every crevice, fingering every flaw and fissure, it continues its slow, inexorable climb.

Soon—if such a word can mean anything to something so primal, so ancient—its rocky cradle gives way to more permeable stone, easier to infiltrate. Perceptions quickening, it senses an elemental change, one not felt since the Removal.

It stills its excitement. With miles yet to go, this is not the time to lose control.

Insinuation second nature to it now, it continues its blind assault on the rock, around the granites, through the basalts, shales and sandstones, drawn by a familiar magnetism which directs it, influences it.

Arrival is imminent. Anticipation charges every tendril of its being. Soon it will Become again; will take form and substance to breathe what it craves and yearns.

The final push comes harder than expected; some unanticipated obstruction in its path. Not a rock. Something else forbids its entrance. It has to find another.

Time. More time. Will its journey never be over?

A fault! Unexpected, miles deep, opens the way to familiar seams.

Caressing the cracks, it courses freely now, scrambling to freedom in a final rush of energy that releases it upwards and out. Birthing in misty white curls of essence, the vapour coalesces; shimmers in the precious, life-giving air.

At last!

The arms of the breeze encircle and lift him. Whisking and spiralling, they blow him into life. Within its embrace, he throbs with the beat of a newfound heart, powering lungs that expel his first breath to the skies. A skeleton follows, organs next—oh, the feel of skin!Soon he can hear the wind that carries him, sees the stars above him, sighs as his feet touch the precious earth below him, as he is set down in all his nakedness.

One last fragment of essence can never be incorporated. Holding out his arms, he is wound in a cloak and given his staff and precious sphere.

With which he stands on the rock that bore him: a craggy outcrop overlooking some kind of settlement. Lights from a source unfamiliar to him twinkle along wide pathways, illuminating structures occurring with such frequency they could only serve as one thing: dwellings.

He lifts his chin, interrogates the air, understands what he has to do. Filling his lungs, he raises his staff and, attuning, smashes it down on the granite.

The sound shock cracks the air like a whip.

Reverberating all the way back to the blazing centre of the earth.

DISTURBED

Though the sunrise promised yet another brilliant summer's day, Emma struggled to swing her leaden legs out of bed. A skittering noise had pierced the druggy fug caused by an extra sleeping tablet. God knows how long it'd been going on. Since in came from the window, it took only seconds to understand the sound. She had no doubt who caused it: someone who knew how much loud knocks at the door still terrified her.

Someone who'd left home without her bloody mobile phone. Again.

Finally managing to disentangle herself from a sea of bedclothes, Emma shuffled to the window and peered between half-drawn curtains down into her pocket-handkerchief garden. Just as she thought. Abigail. Stooping, loading up another fistful of soil, the girl dropped it as soon as she heard Emma's tap on the glass. With an unabashed grin, she brushed her hands together and gave a thumbs-up before pointing to the front door.

No one had died, then.

Grabbing her kimono robe, Emma made her way downstairs and, after fumbling with the locks, opened the door.

"At last!" Abigail cried, sailing past. "I thought you'd never wake up!" She paused as Emma checked the landscape before running the bolts again. "Still using those as well as a key?"

"I haven't been able to shake the habit. I'm glad you remembered not to bang."

Leading the way into the kitchen, Emma yawned. "Before you tell me what brings you here at—what is it?—half past five in the morning—I need coffee. What's the herb of the day?"

Abigail thought coffee the drink of the Devil, and tea not much better. She preferred the more eccentric concoctions of the Herbal Tea Company, which Emma hadn't found inconvenient at all, that is until she'd ordered an assortment that came in a lovely glass-topped wooden case. It looked great on her worktop, even if she only opened it when her friend came round.

"Oh, I dunno. Something with chamomile. It'll calm me down."

Emma said nothing as she made the drinks. No stranger to Abby's missions, at silly o'clock she could have done without this one, whatever it might be. Her drugged sleep having made not the slightest impact on her exhaustion, she indulged a vain hope that all her friend wanted was a listening ear.

Abigail said, "You're looking tired."

"And this surprises you?" replied Emma, chortling. "Being untimely ripped from bed doesn't help. Especially when I hoped to get a lie-in. It is Saturday, after all."

"It's more than that, though, isn't it?" Abigail replied, perceptions as spot-on as ever. "Still getting those dreams? It's been … what? Eight months now?"

"Thereabouts. I'd been doing okay, but lately they've been back with a vengeance." Emma gave an involuntary shudder. "Last night's was really bad."

"Why don't you go and see someone? Maybe Will? I know he's your best friend and all that, but he's a priest, he's used to dealing with emotional stuff. Or why not find a professional, some kind of counsellor or … or even a shrink. There must be one in Sandmarsh you could talk to? Robbie could maybe refer you; that's what doctors do, you know."

"Nope. I've already shared most of it with Will. And I don't want anyone playing about inside my head. You of all people should know that."

"I s'pose."

Emma brought the drinks to the table and slumped down on a chair. "You're right, I may well have to do something. I can't keep turning up to the surgery like this." She yawned again. "I feel weary. Spaced out. Reception's busier than ever and I had to take a Mogadon in the hope I could get some rest this weekend. I just wish I could get Ben out of my mind. Things might have turned out so differently if—"

"No point, Emma, trust me. You'll never know the complete story behind why the curse chose him. Never. All you know is he's gone and that's that. You've got to move on."

Fine words from one so young. How old was she now? Nineteen? Yet Abigail had been marked by her own troubled past, so her advice couldn't easily be ignored. The girl had come through it all okay, though, thriving in her junior's job at the salon.

So why couldn't she?

Abigail cocked an eyebrow at Emma over her steaming teacup. "What about Westen?"

Emma returned her look in silence. Good question.

"I thought you and he had a thing. I mean, all right, he … killed Ben, but—"

"I know, I know. He had to—line of duty and all that. I don't blame him—" She smiled at Abigail's knowing regard. "Honestly I don't. At least not anymore. He did the right thing. Probably the best outcome for Ben too, given all his injuries."

"So?"

"So, nothing. I went with Westen to the Flammark Arms a few times. I know he comes over as a bit …"

"… insensitive?"

Despite herself, Emma chortled. "I know I used to think that, but he isn't really. He's interesting and witty and down-to-earth. He knows how much I went through with Ben and beneath all that … hardness, there's kindness. Patience." Emma sighed. "I'll never be able to tell him the whole story about what happened last year, so I'm not sure a relationship with Westen can ever be on the cards. There are too many things I'll always have to keep from him, and that's not fair. To either of us. So … yes, it's not going anywhere."

Yet even as the words were uttered, part of her didn't wholly believe them. She did genuinely believe Ben was better off dead; no compelling reason why Westen shouldn't think he'd been anything other than a crazed psychopath on the rampage. So why couldn't she commit? Maybe she hadn't forgiven Westen for shooting him, or maybe she hadn't forgiven herself. After all, she'd been the primary target of the Blaxton curse, not Ben.

"Anyway," she said, with a little shake of her head, "you didn't come here at this ungodly hour to talk about my love life, or lack of. What's up?"

The only sign that Abigail had not begun the day in her usual manner lay in the fact that, though her long blue-black hair had been brushed, she'd left home without threading it into its usual braids and beaded ornaments. No make-up, either. Something definitely exercised her. An all-too-familiar air possessed her—a kind of brittle excitement—that lent fire to her violet-blue eyes. It made Emma dread what was coming next.

Abigail leaned forward. "Did you hear anything last night? Feel anything?"

"Like what?"

"Oh, I dunno. Like an earthquake, maybe? Just a tiny one, but—"

Emma could have laughed. It had been years since her earth moved.

"No, nothing. After the nightmare, I tossed and turned until about half-one then I took the Moggie." She bowed her head and lowered her voice for the shame of it. "Two actually. After that I slept through, not that I feel any better for it. What time are we talking about?"

"Two-ish?"

Emma shook her head. Took a sip of coffee.

"At first I thought it was the frackers."

"What, that company out in Ledbridge? What's it called … Godzilla or something?"

"*Deep*Drilla, you dafty!" Abigail chuckled. "Good one, though. I'll nick that."

"I thought they'd stopped. Isn't there supposed to be an embargo on any more fracking? Since all that trouble in—where was it?—Blackpool?"

"Yeah. That was a while ago now, but … Godzilla—I really love that name—are still camped out, together with all their gubbins. I think they're waiting to see if the government will change its mind. Remember, drilling has been suspended, not banned. They could start up again. I hope not. Once they've gone, maybe we could replant all the acres of woodland they destroyed when they set up the site. Bastards."

"So … you think they've been drilling on the sly? Surely that's not possible. They'd be monitored."

Abigail shrugged. "Dunno. But I'm going to find out. Thing is …"

"Go on …"

"Well, as I said, my first thoughts went straight to Godzilla. Before the shaking began, I heard this massive crack. Like the lash of a whip or a … a … an electrical charge or something. I didn't sense it coming from Ledbridge. Felt much closer to home." With a dramatic flourish, she pushed her hair back off her shoulders, and action which wafted a sudden burst of patchouli scent. "Emma, I think it came from Seely Tor."

"Wow, that near? You sure?" Emma put her cup down, light dawning. "Hang on, you're not talking about 'feeling' as in the way we lesser mortals do, are you? This is your 'Sight' thing, right?"

Abigail moved her head slowly up and down, the excitement in her eyes growing wilder. "I've been trying to pinpoint it. Sat for ages in front of my orb. It showed me nothing but mist."

"Perhaps there was nothing to see?"

"Possibly." She wrinkled her nose. "Actually, it's a bit difficult to admit, but I've not been all that successful with it. I can't seem to get a connection. I wish Gabby had taught me how to work it before she left. Having said that, last night was the first time I got anything from it. I suppose even mist is a sign of progress!"

Emma nodded, wondering where the conversation was heading.

"I know it's dead early," Abigail continued, a wheedling tone edging into her voice, "but I have to get to the salon for half-eight and I haven't even done my own hair properly. I'm dying to get to the Tor and have a look and wondered—"

"—if I'd go with you." Emma smiled, dying inside.

But why the hell not? It wasn't as if she had anything else to do, and a walk up the Tor might be just what she needed.

She drained her cup. "Okay. Give me twenty minutes."

❧ 3 ❧

STUCK

Superintendent Peter Piper must have cursed the day his parents bestowed on him a moniker so unfortunate that every friend or colleague—apparently even his wife—would feel moved to call him Pecker. Westen had come across some tricky nicknames in his time, but the ones that took a pop at a copper's manhood were the worst.

Thinking about it, maybe that's why Pecker was such an irritable bastard.

Though not an unfair bastard. Contrary to the assortment of clichéd police procedurals the majority of the great British public seemed to watch on their televisions, in real life, senior officers didn't generally get where they were without playing a reasonably straight bat. The qualified respect his squad had for the super bore this out, adding to Westen's general foreboding that something must be seriously up to be called in for a personal interview at seven o-fucking-clock on a rare Saturday off. Ten minutes in, his worst fears were being confirmed.

"The decision about your promotion request came through last thing yesterday." Either through annoyance or embarrassment, Pecker's face reddened as he gripped Westen's file. "It's out of the question, I'm afraid, Jamie. Out of the bloody question. It should come as no surprise, but there we are."

"May I ask for a reason?" asked Westen, his temper already on the rise. "Sir."

"Don't take that tone with me. You know well enough why. That business last year. You must have known you'd blown your chances. Jesus, man, your conduct triggered a full-blown enquiry!"

"Spell it out for me, if you would, sir. Again."

Pecker sighed and leant forward, holding Westen's gaze.

"Jamie, you took—stole—a gun from a retired Inspector's house. As if interfering with that crime scene wasn't enough, you fired on an unarmed—not to mention an unclothed—suspect." He moved back slightly, flicking the file with the back of his hand. "It's all here. The statement from the Blake woman confirmed it. By the time you arrived at her home, Ben Cregan held no weapon, and in her opinion no longer presented any danger. Christ, man, according to her you didn't even issue a warning."

"How many times to I have to go over it?" Weste spoke through gritted teeth. "Cregan was a madman. Seriously out of control. He killed the Holbrooke and his wife in the vilest way possible. One of ours, sir. It couldn't be clearer that he intended to do the same to the two women. When I arrived at Em—Miss Blake's residence, he'd immobilised both her and Abigail Chater and was on the attack. He'd taken the doctor, too, remember. Robert Mason."

Westen pressed his lips together, knowing he should dial it down. He could never be called an emotional man; not much threw him. Yet he replayed that night over and over. How he'd turned up at Clearview Cottage, seen Cregan through a gap in the blinds, arching his back, cock erect, his cut and bloody mouth grinning like a maniac. As if he was about to beat his fucking chest.

That's when he saw the flash of steel.

"With what exactly?" Pecker asked. "He carried no weapon and the injuries he'd given himself were so extreme, in Savage's opinion—and we have to take the word of a senior pathologist—he wouldn't have survived the night. Christ man, at the post-mortem Cregan weighed less than eight bloody stone. Savage's report makes harrowing reading."

The super sat back as he took a breath. "Jesus Christ, Westen, you were lucky to get away with a few weeks' gardening leave. I had a hell of a job persuading the chief constable not to take your badge. If it hadn't been for the Blake woman making a personal appeal to the CC, you wouldn't be sitting there now." He smacked the file again. "But not before he marked your card. So, any hopes you may have regarding any forthcoming promotion are dead in the water. You're pissing in the wind."

Westen worked his jaw, railing internally at the decision. He'd saved lives that night. If he had the choice he'd do it all again. How many times did he have to say it? "He *was* armed, sir. He had a scalpel."

"Not by the time you shot him, Jamie."

Barely keeping calm, Westen ploughed on. "By the time I gained entry, I didn't know he'd dropped it. All I saw was this mad fucker—who not twelve hours earlier had eviscerated Holly and his wife—determined to visit the same fate on Emma Blake and the girl. I had no time. No choice." And after he had thrown Cregan's lifeless, pathetic body off her, and freed the Chater girl, he'd returned to Emma, held her while he calmed her terrified screams. Even now his breath hitched as he remembered how she hadn't let him go until the rest of his team arrived.

"You completely ballsed it up, Westen. Didn't you?"

He blew out a sigh. Yes. Made a complete fucking mess of everything. He'd arrived at Sandmarsh last year as a young Inspector, not two years in the rank and with a spotless record, lured with the promise of a decent ladder to climb. Now he was being forced to tread water until he could reverse opinion and, hopefully, mitigate the blot in his file.

Worth reminding Pecker. "Sir. With all due respect, I took my current position after DI Holbrooke's retirement on the given expectation that it would fast-track to a suitable promotion."

Pecker laughed, a grim, mirthless cough of a thing. "That was then."

As if wanting to move the conversation on, Pecker sighed. "Look, Jamie, I like you. Your team likes you and you have an excellent clean-up rate. But upstairs don't approve of your methods. You're abrasive and you rub them up the wrong way." He closed the file and set it aside. "We'll have to put up with each other for a bit longer, I'm afraid."

Silence filled the room as Westen contemplated his situation. He'd known he was chancing it the moment he picked up Holly's gun. In any other circumstances he'd have been drummed out of the force, had it not been for the savagery of Cregan's attack on Holbrooke and the level of danger to the two hostages.

"Want my advice?" Pecker asked.

Like hell he did. "Of course, sir."

"Keep your head down. You're in purdah. Another year, maybe, and your situation may well look very different. Suck it up. You're still young." He cracked a smile. "Ish. Moves are afoot. You never know, something might come your way sooner if you get your act together." He polished his nails on his jacket. "Erm ... I've been approached for a spot of special duty."

"Oh?"

"Need to keep things close to the chest for now. Don't get too excited, it won't be for a few months. I'm waiting on a decision from the Met. I'm due in London in a few hours, hence why we're talking now. I don't know when I'll get back."

"Not so secret if the Met's involved. County lines, is it?"

"No, drugs don't interest me. It never bloody stops. Once you get rid of one gang there's always another waiting in the wings. It's … something else. Something big. But now's not the time to share. You'll know soon enough."

Westen wanted to thump something or someone. Pecker would do. It wasn't that he disliked the man, just that he'd been the one to show him how far he'd fallen. He didn't do failure, had never seen himself as one of those disillusioned coppers—always at odds, railing at the machine, self-destructive. He was good at his job. No, he was fucking *great* at his job. But though he couldn't have changed anything about the way he handled the Ben Cregan case, deep down he knew why the brass couldn't swallow the outcome.

"So, that's it then. I'm stuck."

"For now, Westen, for now. But you know how it is in this game. Things can change fast."

❦ 4 ❧

SEELY TOR

Although Seely Tor lay only a half-hour walk away from Clearview Cottage, they took Emma's jeep. Abigail hadn't wanted to risk being late for work.

Once at the plateau, Emma made the turn onto the stretch of rough grass that acted as the Tor's car park and switched off the engine, pausing to take in the view before getting out. This early in the morning, it lay before the two women more stunningly compelling than ever, and they couldn't help but share a quiet moment as they gazed through the windscreen at the panoramic vista of Flammark —and beyond to Sandmarsh—the needle-spire of its cathedral piercing its way through the cloudscape.

So beautiful.

As she clambered out of the car, Emma felt a huge onrush of relief. Out of the cottage her memories lost the capacity to haunt her. She could breathe again.

Maybe Clearview was the problem. Perhaps she should move out, try a fresh start somewhere else altogether. It hadn't been the first time she'd wrestled with the idea, but in the end, knew she'd reject it. There'd been enough running away, and she'd promised herself time to regroup, grow new roots. Her heart sank at the thought of leaving the cottage, despite the horrific memories that lived there with her.

Emma loved it, pure and simple, and was more than grateful Will had offered her the tenancy for as long as she wanted it. Being there meant she could be near him, easily able to pop across the green to the church or the vicarage for succour or a chinwag. Forged by the horrific events of last year, their friendship could not be any closer. It would stay that way forever, for she knew with a bone-deep certainty that only a calamity would force Will to move from the place where he grew up.

She must find another way of reconciling with her past. Leaving Clearview wasn't the answer.

"Isn't it amazing up here?" Abigail took Emma's side as they left the car, wrapping her arms around herself against the bluster of the sharp breeze that whipped at her black velvet top. Having an eye for the theatrical, she always dressed to favour style over substance and certainly without the windy turbulence of the Tor in mind.

Arm in arm, they walked past the Tor's large Celtic cross; paused to wonder at the host of straw dollies and palm crosses tied to it. Will had told Emma that it once rested at the main junction into Flammark, but that over time it had become an obstruction and had to be resited, upsetting the pagan community in and around Sandmarsh. She could see why they soon piped down their objections. What better place for it, and their rituals, than on a beautiful, ancient hilltop far away from traffic?

Once more Emma faced the view. She took in huge breaths and, closing her eyes, lifted her face to the newly risen sun. She loved the Tor, the spot where she'd finally come to terms with her decision to leave Ben. For her, it would always be a place of peace and truth.

Abigail shivered.

"You okay?" Emma asked. "I've got a spare cardie in the car, if you want one."

"No thanks. I'm not cold. It's … something else."

Emma knew better than to say anything. Abigail also had an affinity with this place, had honed her psychic senses here as she camped out with Gabby and Michael in their mission to watch and protect the village. To protect her.

With a sudden groan, deep—visceral— Abigail grunted, "Strike that. I feel … I feel sick."

Running to a nearby boulder, she bent over and retched violently. Emma ran after her and put a comforting hand on her friend's shoulder before gently pulling back Abby's hair, holding it away as she threw up.

"Something's been here, Emma." Abigail said, gulping as she straightened up, her fingers, nails varnished black, pressing into the side of the hill. She wiped her mouth on her velvet sleeve. "Something really nasty. Thank God Gabby's not here."

"Gabby? *Gabby?* She left with Michael months ago, just days after Ben died."

"I know that, 'course I do!" Abby made little coughs to clear her throat. "I just got this surge of, I dunno, hatred. Pure hatred. I've never felt anything like it. Not even with the curse." She lowered her voice almost to a whisper, "Not even when we were with Ben."

Emma looked in horror at Abby's stricken face. "And you think it's directed at Gabby?"

"Yeah. It's like her name popped into my head, all in lights, written all over my mind. It … throbbed. Made me sick, like I'd suddenly got a migraine."

"Come on, sit over here," said Emma, taking her clammy hand. "Get your breath back."

"It was her full name," Abby said, querulously. "Gabriel. I

never use her real name, not even to myself. Someone or some*thing* put it there."

They moved away from the tiny pile of slick vomit towards the Tor's vast rocky promontory, edged either side with tiered, flat boulders. Before they could get to one, Abigail pointed a trembling finger at something on the ground ahead. "Emma! Look!"

Following Abby's gaze, Emma took a few steps forward. Dead centre of the ledge she spied a dent, only about six or seven centimeters in diameter, so deeply driven into the stone it seemed only a piledriver could have made it. Perfectly even and circular, it might have escaped attention were it not for the collection of spidery cracks which emanated outwards from the indentation, one so long it led almost to the edge of the promontory.

"My God, Abigail. You were right. Something did happen here."

Not quite succeeding in hiding her triumph despite her nausea, Abby replied, "I knew I heard something, I knew it! It must have been—"

A loud grating noise interrupted her, and the two friends stood stock-still. Arms instinctively out, they locked on each other's eyes, motionless as if on a lake of thin ice. Emma felt and heard the barest whisper of a rumble beneath her feet and could tell Abby had sensed it too. As one, they moved their gaze to the indentation. One of the spider legs had thickened and a new one appeared to be making a run to the precipice. No discussion needed, they pelted towards the car park.

"Shit! That was close!" exclaimed Abigail, taking deep breaths.

"It's not safe," gasped Emma. "You should go. Now. Make your way down the hill and ring someone."

"I can't. I left my bloody phone at home, didn't I? Anyway, we need to go together. Let's take the jeep."

"I'm staying." Emma looked at her watch. "It's nearly seven and the dog walkers will be out in force, not to mention hikers. They'll be taking the roadside trails." She nodded towards one of the two hand-railed paths which emerged from either side of the promontory. "Someone has to warn them to go back. Jesus, the road might even have to be closed."

"No bloody way I'm leaving you. Besides, two trails, two watchers. You can't do this on your own." Abigail stuck out her chin, teenage stubbornness not brooking any arguments. "You've got your phone. Ring someone. Now!"

Chewing her lip, Emma pulled out her mobile. "Okay." She looked uncertainly at it. "Who? Who do I ring? It's too early for the council, plus it's Saturday." She didn't like how her voice had risen, telling the tale of her rising panic.

"Come on, Emma, get a grip. Better still, get Westen."

Emma threw Abigail a long look which the girl returned with a what-are-you-waiting-for stare and an urgent nod. "All right," she sighed, and pressed a single button.

"Hi. It's me. Can you meet me on Seely Tor? There's something you need to see … Yes, I know it's early. That's why I'm ringing you … Because there's no one else we can think of calling at this time in the morning! … No, Abigail's with me. A crack's appeared in the rock and we're sure we felt a tremor … an earth tremor!" Emma, knowing she was red in the face, awkward at having to share a conversation with someone she'd been at pains to avoid, rolled her eyes at Abby. "We're worried you may have to close the Tor, maybe even the road below … 999? We didn't think of that … It was Abigail's idea to call you. I'm fine … No, I'm not leaving. We need to make sure no one comes near it … I'm not being fucking stubborn! … Fifteen minutes? Fine." She was about to end the call when she thought better of it. "Oh, Westen—"

She turned to Abigail and shook her head in frustration. "He rang off. Says he'll be here—"

"—in fifteen minutes. I know, I heard. Oh, and thanks for blaming me, by the way." Her voice went all sing-song, "It was Abigail's idea …"

The sound of dogs barking stopped any further conversation and reminded them why they were still there. Abigail strode over to one of the trails and headed off a bemused woman, out with two lurchers that seemed much crosser at being turned away than their owner did. Emma walked towards the second path, upset that it had to have been Westen she called and fuming that he'd ended the call before she had.

Shit, shit, shit.

As it transpired, they had to wait a little longer than fifteen minutes for him to turn up. Both stood watch over their respective paths, with half an eye on the car park. Thankfully, no more visitors climbed to the plateau, no more tremors, and, as far as they could tell, no more spidering.

"He's here!" shouted Abigail, as a car swung into the grassy parking area. She left her post to walk towards it.

Emma joined her, ignoring an unwelcome frisson of anticipation.

"I still can't get her out of my head, you know," said Abigail.

"You mean Gabby?"

"Yeah. I know she's gone. I'm sure she's gone." She tapped her forehead. "So why is she in here?" She shook her head. "Something really bad's on its way, Emma, I'm sure of it. I'm not going to be able to tell Westen that, though."

"No, you're not. He never met Gabby, remember? Besides, he wouldn't be able to believe you. He's not—"

"—made that way?"

Emma nodded, girding herself to greet the detective.

Except it wasn't the detective she'd expected. Wearing civvies and an apologetic smile, Donna Stirling got out of the car.

"Hello you two. Sorry, but the Guv's been called out. Will I do?"

❧ 5 ❧

WOOD END

Westen could have kicked himself. First, he had to endure that fucking terrible interview with the super, then Emma phones him for the first time since the last awkward date at the Flammark Arms and he'd all but brushed her off. Who's the pecker now? Not that he could have done much about it. If a body had been discovered, what was he supposed to do?

Burrows had sent directions to a caravan site out in Ledbridge. Wood End. Driving along its tree-lined access road, his copper's training clicked in, obliging him to set aside personal concerns. As usual.

The place turned out to be much more than a simple caravan site. After a mile or so, clipped hedgerows and neat verges either side of the road gave way to dense woodland. Beneath its canopy, other holiday homes had been situated, log cabins tucked away in secluded clearings between the trees. Must have cost a fucking fortune to run power lines.

After a mile or so, the first caravans came into view. Not what he had expected at all. They weren't placed in the kind of serried ranks that notoriously blighted coastlines. Though never for one minute would he ever consider staying in one, Westen had to admit their pale green exteriors blended reasonably well into the woodland and were not unattractive —if you liked that sort of thing. They were randomly placed; a few here, some there. Enough to develop the small friendly communities he'd heard about in park life, but without too much forced companionship.

The road wended its way, until he arrived at two stone pillars, topped with brick. Judging by the massive iron hinges fused into them, gates must once have hung there swinging open to the huge courtyard space within, paved with flat cobbles. Ahead, almost dwarfed by the scale of the courtyard, stood a very old stone cottage. In any other setting it would be considered picturesque and 'highly desirable' but as Wood End Caravan Park HQ, its charm had been neglected. Any garden must be at the rear, since the front door butted head-on to the cobbles, its pale green paint peeled and scuffed. Burrows' car rested a few yards away, next to two other police vehicles, including Savage's pathologist's van, though neither man could be seen.

Ugly and incongruous, a huge metal barn had been erected a few yards away from the cottage, its massive sliding doors gaping open. Ever the jobbing copper, after parking, Westen wandered over to it and gazed inside. Tractors, mowers, woodchippers—racks of chainsaws. All the industrial-grade machinery and tools needed to tame the trees which surrounded the park. It would take serious money to keep this place going.

Where the fuck was Burrows?

Westen wasn't about to bang on the cottage door—an absence of activity indicated the body had been found elsewhere—so he strode to the other end of the courtyard, where the road dipped out of sight, presumably leading down to the caravans.

Standing at the rim of the park, Westen raised his eyebrows in surprise at the vista that opened up before him, his gaze following the contours of an enormous, crater-like depression in the land. He'd seen one like it in Scotland, when he took time away from a tedious conference on interpreting crime stats. But that was the footprint of an ancient meteorite; he doubted this was of similar origin. Nestled within shrubby alcoves and byways, random groupings of caravans and cabins rested in a kind of tended wilderness, from this distance looking for all the world like a model village.

His eyes followed the road as it looped down and around, servicing the small patches of gravel in front or to the side of the caravans, where owners parked their cars. At the bottom of the basin, the well of the park, heads bobbed around a large circle of seven large statics, one of which lay on its side.

Everyone was shouting, and he could just make out the long, narrow form of Burrows, gesticulating in his direction, as uniform battled to get a large group of onlookers up the hill and away from the scene.

Time to move. Making his way down, Westen passed through the straggling group, some stopping to take pictures of the scene with cameras or mobile phones, annoying the coppers who chivvied them. Nearing Burrows, he could see his sergeant trying to calm down a wiry, dark-haired man who was too busy shrieking to listen.

Rubbing at his three-day stubble, the man yelled, "How would I know what happened? I'm as much in the dark as you lot are." He stared at the fallen caravan as if the earth had caved in. "I ... I need to clear it all up. Now. There's no time for this. I have to order a crane and get it taken out and replaced." He waved his hands in the general direction of the circle of vans still standing. "Everything has to be put back the way it was."

Something about his eyes, in the way they refused to meet Burrows' gaze, interested Westen. Some kind of internal panic in play that pointed up his fear. Pure and visceral. He could smell it in the stench of the man's sweat. He wore green overalls with a machine-sewn Wood End insignia on one pocket. A site employee, then, and making it pretty fucking clear he wasn't as much in the dark as he'd made out.

"That might be so, Mr … Wyland," Burrows said. Eventually managing to complete two sentences, he pushed the man back. "But this is a crime scene. You won't be craning anything just yet." Spying his boss approach, he managed two more. "Excuse me a moment, sir. If you could wait over there, I'll be with you in a minute." He left Wyland standing outside the ring of black and yellow crime scene tape before ducking under it to join his Guv.

"He's lying." Westen eyed the man as he spoke to Burrows from the side of his mouth. "I don't know what you've got for me, but whatever it is, he's definitely hiding something."

"Agreed, Guv. He's the owner and has been a bloody nuisance since we arrived. Been in all our faces, yet won't tell us a thing."

Westen said, "Have uniform to take him to the station. We won't get any sense out of him here." While Burrows left to give the necessary order, Westen stared at the crime scene for the first time at close quarters, able to survey the full extent of the damage to the fallen caravan, its trailing anchors and chains, windows and door smashed. Where it used to rest he could see the wide rounded back of Savage, hunched over something in the middle of its hard standing. He knew a body had been found, but, on site, Westen struggled to understand the scene. Had the van been turned over to get at it? Unlikely. If they'd somehow discovered someone underneath, it'd still be upright, waiting to be craned away.

He picked his way over the rubble to join him. Since his transfer to Sandmarsh Serious Crimes, Westen had learned to be wary of crossing swords with the pathologist. Not because he was intimidated by him—Christ, no—but the man could be an unpredictable bastard and had a habit of getting under people's skin, a trait Westen could do without when trying to bottom-out a case. Quiet-spoken, six foot two and shaven-headed—a thirty-something gym-rat—there was no common thread between the two colleagues. Westen knew he was bright; very bright. Even so, he wondered how, given his age, Savage had managed the jump to senior pathologist.

At least someone was on the fucking up!

"Come no further, Inspector. This is a crime scene."

No kidding. Rolling his eyes to the sky, Westen reluctantly stopped his advance and stood at the side of the hard standing.

"Morning, Savage. What have you got for us?"

"I'll be with you in a few moments. Stay there, please."

Nothing much Westen could do but fume. Brilliant fucking day this was turning out to be. Still, Savage didn't keep him long, just enough to assume his usual residence under the detective's skin.

The pathologist rose from his squat; an elegant, almost balletic movement from one so tall. Brush in one hand, he twisted the peak of his baseball cap to the back of his smooth head with the other. He fixed an intense, blue-eyed stare on Westen, and gave a rare half-smile as he announced, "You may approach, Inspector. I have completed my preliminary examination."

He fucking did it on purpose! For a split second, before stepping closer, Westen visualised the satisfaction he'd feel at lamping the smug bastard right between the eyes. Luckily, the job took over.

The hard standing to which the caravan had been anchored had completely fractured. Apart from its outer rim, where Westen had been perched, hardly anything of it remained intact. Large lumps of concrete, their jagged edges upturned, bloomed outwards from a central eruption. It encircled a smoother stone exposed beneath, roughly the shape and size of a small watermelon.

"Jesus. What the fuck happened here? And … where's the body?"

"There," replied Savage, a long finger pointing to the watermelon.

Incredulously, Westen exclaimed, "That … stone?"

"It is not a stone. It is a cranium."

Westen let out a long whistle.

"Quite," said Savage. He licked his lips as they turned upwards. "And I believe it comes complete with skeleton. I have been able to dig a little deeper around it. The skull is definitely attached to a spine. We will need to excavate to see the whole picture."

"So, the body was buried—"

"—upright?" The pathologist's smirk widened. "Exactly so."

Burrows, having effected the removal of the site owner, joined them. He said, "So the hard standing had been laid to deliberately hide the body, then? As in, someone dug the hole, bunged it in then concreted over it?"

"I think not," replied Savage, obviously in his element. "First of all, it is incredibly difficult to bury a body upright. It would take a great deal of time. A counter-intuitive endeavour if all one wanted to do was dispose of it. Secondly," the pathologist pointed to the small hill of debris around him, "although there is aggregate and fragments of rebar, as you'd expect, I can see evidence of several soil layers whose origin lies well below the surface." He stooped and grabbed a fistful of impacted earth, much lighter than the rest. "Given the position of the skeleton and the variety of soil layers that erupted from here, I believe we may be looking at a burial that has some age to it. Possibly ancient."

"You seem to know a lot about geology," Westen grunted. "For a pathologist."

"I will confess to an amateur fascination. Beyond the kind of basic knowledge of earth sciences required within my field of expertise."

"So this isn't a murder scene after all?" Burrows put his notebook away.

"As to that, who could say? But if I am right about the skeleton's age, and if the bones do show signs of foul play enacted upon them, I believe that, as a cold case, it is likely to turn out to be positively glacial."

Westen stood in silent cogitation, relaxing slightly as he let the information sink in. Possibly the only expert needed here was a forensic anthropologist, not a detective. Waving his hand vaguely over the area, he said, "What caused all … this?"

"Guv—"

Westen, ruminating, continued, "Obviously something with some welly. A sledgehammer or …"

"Guv—"

Westen stopped talking, looked up at his sergeant who was staring back at him, eyebrows raised, waiting for the light-bulb moment.

"Jesus! So we did have an earthquake!"

"Possibly," Savage interjected. "I've been in touch with the BGS."

"BGS?" asked Burrows.

Savage let out a long sigh. "The British Geological Survey.

There has been no report of any unusual seismic activity hereabouts, so they are sending someone over."

"There can't be any other explanation, Guv. Not for this and not for what Donna saw on the Tor. I've just been on the blower with her. There are cracks everywhere."

"But nothing like what we're seeing here?"

Shaking his head, Savage said, "Had there been a tremor, it would have impacted upon the Tor in a vastly different way."

"What do you mean?" asked Westen.

"Though I am no expert, Inspector, I do know Seely Tor is nearly one hundred per cent granite and, rather like an iceberg, comprises beneath the ground far more than one sees above it. I'd imagine it would need an earthquake of considerable proportions to make anywhere near the same impact we see here."

Shaking his head, Burrows replied, "I don't know about that, but the way Donna described it, Guv, you were right to give her the go-ahead to get Flammark Road closed, at least 'til the inspection teams arrive."

"Shit. That viewing platform is only a few feet thick." Westen's heart sank as he remembered Emma calling him from there, breathless, perched near an outcrop that might give way any minute. Why the fuck had he sent Donna? He'd put her in harm's way too! He should have gone.

"Is it over or are we to expect aftershocks?" he said. "Is the park safe?" He looked above and around at the cosy groups of caravans many with their occupants outside, looking back at him, some with binoculars. "Do we need to evacuate?"

"That's why I contacted the BGS," said Savage. "As I mentioned, no activity registered at their end, and without any data they were reluctant to issue any guidance that might trigger a panic. This may be a fluke, a localised, deeply fascinating fluke, or it may be something more. We will not know until they get here in a few hours. Ultimately, it is your call, Inspector."

Westen sighed. He turned to his sergeant. "Get everyone out, Burrows. Now. I'm not taking any chances."

"Okay, Guv. Will do."

As Burrows left to co-ordinate the evacuation, Westen turned to Savage.

"Do *you* think we've had an earthquake?"

"I have no idea, Inspector. None whatsoever. If not …" His smile widened as he looked in fascination at the ruined bed of concrete, the perfectly smooth skull jutting out three inches from the disrupted surface, "… then it almost looks like the body pushed itself to the surface, does it not?"

❧ 6 ❧

EMMA AND WESTEN

The evacuation in motion, Westen ordered Burrows back to the station to take a statement from the Wyland character before letting him go. The remains would have to be lifted and Savage's theories confirmed. If they were proved right, he'd no idea where the bones should go afterwards. Returned, probably. Not really his problem.

Best not to get ahead of himself. Savage had volunteered to call the forensic anthropology department at Lanchester University. They were sending someone out 'as soon as possible.' Meanwhile Westen had told uniform to post someone at the site, to make sure the remains that were in the ground stayed in the ground until the boffins arrived. No one ever lost money overestimating the need of the average English tourist to swipe a few trophies. Savage had also insisted on liaising with the geological survey people. Fine with him. Westen wouldn't have a clue where to start.

What a fucking day. As he drove away from Wood End, Westen brooded over the two things that pissed him off, the morning's conversation with Pecker being first on the list.

Though he knew Sandmarsh had always been just a step on the ladder to greater things, it surprised him to discover he hadn't been in any great hurry to move on. He liked it there, hence his request for promotion. His rental, a heartless, dingy box of a flat, acted as nothing more than a stopgap. After nearly a year, he'd only emptied half the boxes he'd moved in with. For the first time in his life, he had been harbouring thoughts about settling, buying somewhere—a better flat or maybe even a house. No fucking point, now. Especially after also getting nowhere with the second item on his list.

Emma Blake.

He'd left it until a good few weeks after Ben Cregan's attack before asking her out, but it soon transpired that even that had been too soon. Their dates—or rather their uncomfortable conversations in the Flammark Arms—had come to nothing. She'd been through hell and back with that bastard and he completely understood she needed time, but how much time? How the fuck was he meant to build some trust between them if she wouldn't let him in?

He sighed out loud. None of this was her fault. There *had* been something there, he was sure of it, but maybe their connection had only been fleeting, forged in the heat of the moment he shot Ben Cregan. He wanted her more than he cared to admit, and would be prepared to wait. But he needed a sign; something to hope for. Surely there would be no harm in trying again, one last time?

Which was why he'd decided to interrupt his journey home by making a stop in Flammark.

Westen drew up in front of Clearview Cottage having decided not to ring Emma to ask if he could come round, for fear of being rebuffed at the outset. Her jeep rested in the drive, but that didn't mean anything, since she was still thick as thieves with Will fucking Turner and might at this very moment be over the green at the vicarage, telling him all about how he'd not turned up at the Tor this morning. Though she'd repeatedly told him her relationship with the priest had always been purely platonic, he nursed doubts. Being a sensitive sort, Emma would surely prefer someone who lived more in the mind than he, and that certainly applied to Turner.

What the hell had she done to him? He sounded fucking … insecure!

He tapped on her door. No answer. Tried again, a bit louder. Reluctant to ramp it up into a policeman's knock, lest he scare the living daylights out of her, he kicked his heels for a few minutes, his impatience rising inversely to his diminishing confidence. After another few taps, followed by some aimless rearrangement of the gravel in the path with the toe of his shoe, he made his way back to the car.

Waste of fucking time.

He'd almost reached the vehicle before he heard her door open. As he spun around, Emma appeared, obviously straight out of the shower. She wore a plain sleeveless frock, hastily donned, judging by the pools of damp that had begun to form where they touched her flesh. As she stood in the doorway in the late evening sunlight, towelling dry her wiry red hair, Westen knew he was a completely lost cause.

"I thought it might be you," she said.

"Did you, now?" said Westen, grinning like a teenager as he retraced his steps. "Why's that, then?"

"Because you owe me an apology."

"Do I?" His grin froze at the sharpness of her tone.

"Yes, you do. When I rang you this morning and you told me you'd come to the Tor. Fifteen minutes, you said. After half an hour you were a no-show before along came Donna to deal with everything."

He shrugged. "I was called out. Nothing I could do about that."

"Very convenient."

Digging a deeper hole, he said, "I should have sent a uniform. It was only because it was you that I rang Donna. It's her weekend off, but—"

"Oh. Well, thank you for that. I'm sorry I spoilt her day."

This was going well. Westen's grin had fled the scene and, put on the spot, he chewed the inside of his cheek, hating that he was being forced to justify himself on the fucking garden path. Keeping his voice even, trying to stop his eyes tracing the progress of the slowly creeping dark patches on her dress, with no little amount of concentration, he said, "Again, there was nothing I could do. There was a problem out in Wood End." He went further than he strictly should have. "A body."

Emma sighed. "So why are you here?"

Awkward silence.

Westen's confliction deepened. He wasn't used to offering apologies and he felt both pre-empted and pre-judged. He'd imagined coffee around her kitchen table, maybe on the bench in front of the window, the sun setting, the … Jesus, get a fucking grip, man!

He stiffened and straightened his shoulders. "You're right, Emma. I should at least have phoned you this morning to tell you Donna was on her way. There really wasn't anything I could do about arriving in person. I'm a copper. I go where I'm told." Working hard to keep mortification out of his tone, he continued, "You seem to have got it into your head that I've been trying to avoid you. I can assure you that has not been the case." He couldn't—wouldn't—do anything about the edge that had crept into his voice. "I'm sorry I called at such an inconvenient moment. It won't happen again."

He turned on his heels, walked to his car and drove off.

～

Emma could do nothing but stand on the doorstep, watching Westen leave, tears welling. Why was she being like this towards him? Why? She knew he'd come to apologise. *Knew* it. There couldn't have been other reason why he came. More than anything, she'd wanted to invite him in. What possessed her not to?

She had been upset that he'd left it to Donna to come to the Tor. Either he didn't believe it was worth his bloody time, or he'd just bottled out of seeing her. Not that she'd been unhappy to see the female detective again, and Donna had seen the danger quickly enough. In short order, she'd called out Highways and by the time they'd left, a lorry filled with orange cones and diversion signs had already arrived.

So, he'd been called out, had he? Fair enough. He had no reason to dissemble and seemed keen to put things right between them. She kicked herself. She should have been more forgiving.

Stepping down onto the path, Emma sat on the garden bench, welcoming the warmth from the afternoon sun. She'd felt chilled, having just finished showering when she'd heard the knock on the door. Peeping round her bedroom curtain to see if she could spot a car, realising it had been Westen's, she'd hastily grabbed the first thing that came to hand without properly drying herself. Looking down, adding embarrassment to her confusion, she discovered damp patches that *he must have seen* spreading all over her flimsy nylon dress, sticking to the contours of her body.

Emma bowed her head. She had feelings for this man. Although Ben had been no threat to her at the moment when Westen had killed him, she knew without a shadow of doubt that it had been done in defense of her—and that he had got into trouble for it. She still remembered the strength she took from his arms as they held her afterwards. How they had calmed her. Like nothing else in the world, she wanted to feel them around her again, to let go and give in to him once more, even if only for a moment. Keeping herself so tightly wound was exhausting.

So why treat him like that?

Back to Ben.

Oh, she was getting so very, very tired of this ... circularity. She had made her escape, found a new life, got a job, made good friends. It seemed all that was simply not enough. The nightmare that was Ben refused to go away. As did the memories of her life with him before she came to Flammark, the fear of God he'd put into her; the loss of control. More than anything, this lay behind the problem of Westen, and it rose up to bite her every time she thought of him.

Her gaze turned to the spot where he'd parked his car. She remembered the grin on his face as he came up the path, how it froze at almost the very first thing she said. She'd blown it—again— and he had left.

If he had any sense at all, he wouldn't be coming back.

Emma gazed across the green to the church on the other side of it. Will would most likely be putting the finishing touches to tomorrow's sermon. He'd be open to a visit and a download might be just the thing she needed. And his perspective.

She shivered as the breeze caught her and whipped at her damp, wiry hair. She couldn't go like this. Not wanting to face the rest of the afternoon alone, she dragged herself back into the cottage to get changed.

Will would make her feel better.

7

WYLAND

Sunday bus services being a complete nightmare, Abigail had asked her grandad to take her to Wood End. He hadn't minded interrupting his pint at the Flammark Arms when she came in looking for him. Sam would do anything for her.

As they neared the turn-off to the caravan site, Abigail said, "You can drop me here, Grandad. I'll walk the rest. It's a lovely day and I'm sure you want to get back to your pals."

"You sure? It's no trouble."

She smiled as she shook her head. "No, I'm fine. Didn't I see the cribbage board being taken out?"

"Yes, well, I like a game or two, and a bit of a wager now and then. Doesn't mean you need to go and tell your grandma." He pulled over. "You won't tell her, will you?"

Properly chuckling now, Abigail shook her head. "'Course not. Won't say a word." Her hand on the door handle, she paused before opening it. On impulse, she turned to him. "I'm really proud of you, Grandad."

"Eh? What brought that on?"

"I'm glad you decided to get this van up and running again. I'm not sure what I felt about it at first, when I saw you'd restored all the paintwork."

"Well, retirement didn't suit, and I was getting under your grandmother's feet. After what happened last year, what with you gone and me hardly able to leave my bed, I got so fed up I could've torn my hair out."

"Is the business doing okay?"

Sam nodded. "People always need locksmiths. Might even have to take someone on. It's even busier than before, when I worked with … your dad."

"He would be proud of you too." In silent understanding, they met each other's eyes, then Abigail looked away and fumbled in her bag. "Right, I'll be off then. I'll get Wyland to bring me back, so there's no need for you to bother."

"You and him. Are you … ?"

"No, Grandad. It's not like that. He's only a friend. He heads up the Sandmarsh pagan group I'm in."

"Your mum told me you were getting into all that. I suppose there's no harm in it, if it keeps you out of trouble."

"Me? Trouble?" Abigail chuckled. "Perish the thought! Seriously, though, Wyland's behind the fracking protests. Out in Ledbridge? He's a good man."

"Are they still going on? I thought they weren't allowed to frack no more."

"They aren't, but DeepDrilla haven't packed up yet. Maybe they're hoping the ban will be lifted, I dunno. He's made sure there's always a small group of activists posted outside the site. He says it's important for the frackers to know we'll be back in force if the government backs down and they're allowed to start drilling again."

"I don't like you getting involved in all that stuff. You watch yourself, missy. Be careful what you get into."

Abigail rolled her eyes. "Honestly, stop worrying, Grandad. I know what I'm doing. I'm not a kid any more! Anyway, I'm not here about the protests. Something a bit mad happened on the Tor yesterday. I'm positive there was a tremor. If it's something DeepDrilla might have caused, I need to make sure Wyland knows about it. Plus, I've never been to his place. The park sounds ace."

"A tremor? You mean a bloomin' earthquake? I didn't feel nothing."

"That's because you were fast asleep." She chuckled. "You snore like a giant, by the way."

Sam grinned before letting his face grow serious again. "Well, you be careful. You might be nineteen but ... Well, try not to get back too late or Josie'll worry. You got your phone?"

"'Course. I'll ring Mum to tell her when I'll be back. Promise."

Abigail opened the van door, swung her legs round and jumped down. She banged the door shut and waved as Sam got in gear. After waiting for the road to clear, he made a three-point turn and started his drive back to Flammark, the posh new gold-on-black lettering of 'Chater's Mobile Key Services' glinting in the sunlight.

Abigail turned into Wood End Road, looking forward to the mile walk to Wyland's house. She had a lot to mull over.

Still pained from yesterday's episode on the Tor, it bugged her that she couldn't get Gabby out of her mind. She missed her—and Michael—terribly—and fondly remembered the few months she'd spent with them, under their protection against the curse that plagued them all last year. She loved the nights when they let her join them on the craggy hilltop where they'd set up camp, overseeing the safety of Flammark, anxiously waiting to see how events would unfold.

They'd near-enough become her parents, had supported her as she came to terms with what'd happened to her dad. Her mum had always been the brittle sort, easily broken. Abigail would never be able to tell her the exact circumstances that lay behind her father's death.

Nor could Josie ever understand her gift. Gabby and Michael had seen it in her, though. Had done everything possible to help her develop it.

Since yesterday the ache she felt for Gabby had grown even more intense, beyond simply missing her. Something was very wrong, and she couldn't understand why the name of her friend featured so strongly in the sensation that had made her throw up so suddenly. The crack on the Tor felt like a crack in the world. She'd bet anything Wyland had felt it too, but she wanted to check. He'd a relationship to the land like no other person she'd ever met.

And what a land it was! As she strolled, Abigail took in the hedgerows of hawthorn and dog rose, the abundance of cow parsley and wild campion, cornflowers and poppies nodding beneath. As the trees thickened, she drank deeply of the air, heavy with their oxygen. Lifting her heart-shaped face to the azure sky, delighting in the warmth of the day, she savoured the touch of her long, blue-black hair on the small of her back beneath her crop-top, where a recently inked triquetra tattoo rose millimetres above her black, sequined belt.

She'd originally decided on a five-pointed star, the upward-facing pentagram much admired by the Sandmarsh pagans. Wyland himself favoured it, and sported his own version on his forearm, splendidly augmented with a circle of ivy. But in the end, she plumped for the triquetra. Not only were the past, present and future intertwined; it looked way cooler.

As she neared the caravan park it became obvious something was wrong. Abigail's heart quickened as the highway ended and she neared the two columns, one either side of what looked like a courtyard, a large blue police sign parked in between.

Road Closed.

She sailed past, her attention caught by all the vehicles behind it. A blue and white police car and three small vans. Larger than all of them stood a truck emblazoned with the words: *British Geological Survey.* Its back doors were wide open and a uniformed policeman leant in, chatting to a chap behind a bank of computers, both too busy staring at a screen to notice her.

What *was* going on?

She walked toward the only sign of habitation—a stone cottage—and, knocked gently, hoping not to disturb the men inside the large van.

No answer.

She tried again, and on getting no reply hesitated about what to do next. Deciding on a spot of exploration, Abigail wandered further along until she came to the edge of the cobbles. And gasped.

The ground fell away into a breathtaking tiered landscape. Trees and undulating pathways led to cleverly landscaped hollows enclosing groups of caravans and the occasional log cabin. All with wild gardens too, as far as she could make out. Wow. She wondered how all this could belong to Wyland. Did he actually own it? She would have to find out.

Shouts interrupted her reverie and drew her attention to the bottom of the park. A group of people—mostly men— were huddled there. She recognised one with a mess of black hair as he gesticulated and pointed next at a uniformed copper, obviously mouthing off.

She half-grinned. Typical Wyland.

Not wanting to draw attention to herself, though desperate to get in the know, Abigail slowly started down the hill. She followed a side road till she came to a path that led her to a huddle of caravans within listening-distance of the main event. Pressing her back against the corner of one of them, she craned her neck to hear.

Wyland's words came loud and clear. "You still haven't told me how long this is going to take!"

"I don't know, sir, but by the looks of it, they're nearly ready to transport the remains. You'd do well to calm down. The sooner we can get on, the sooner we'll be out of your hair."

"Why? Why do you have to transport them? Why did you have to dig them up? They've obviously been here for centuries. You still haven't told me why you can't just bloody leave them where they are! I've looked after this place for more years than I care to remember. It shouldn't be disturbed. Not on my watch."

"I don't know about that, sir, but we can't ignore a suspicious death, no matter how old it is. You need to stand back." The copper squared up against Wyland, who'd bunched his fists. "If you don't calm down, sir, I'll have to remove you." Nodding over to the crime scene, he continued, "Consider yourself lucky that Dr Savage there let you watch. Don't push it."

Abigail's eyes widened. Carefully edging around the van, she tried to get a view of the remains they were on about. A really tall man in a cap stood slightly apart from about half a dozen others who were huddled around a gurney. On the ground lay an array of tiny pickaxes and a small pneumatic drill, but she could see no sign of what had got Wyland so riled up.

Moving her position slightly, she managed to catch his attention while the copper was still giving him the hairy eyeball. A few seconds later Wyland gave up the stand-off, shrugged and walked past her, scratching the back of his head, surreptitiously wagging a finger in the direction of his cottage.

Careful not to be seen, she made her way back up the slope, following him to where his front door opened in wide invitation. Hearing Wyland banging about in the kitchen, she made her way down the dingy hallway to join him.

"Abigail! Welcome to the mad house." Kettle filled and on the boil, he opened a half-full jar of instant coffee and threw the lid on the worktop. "How the hell did you get past that lot?"

"Not too hard. I don't think they were expecting visitors, and the only policeman up here was gossiping with the bloke in the computer truck. What's going on?"

"Where do I bloody start?" He scooped coffee into two mugs. Sensing this was not the time to ask for chamomile and ginger tea, she said, "Nothing for me, Wyland, if you don't mind; I'll make do with water."

"Suit yourself." He yanked open a cupboard and took down a glass, blew in it, and, unable to shift whatever resided within, rinsed it out. "It's a violation, that's what it is. A ... defilement."

Wyland handed her the water. "You go through. Give me a minute. I need something stronger than this." He ditched the coffee and opened the doors to another cupboard. He might have been peering inside, had his head not been down and his shoulders heaving. Sensing it best to leave him alone a while, Abigail returned to the hall and 'went through' the only other door.

She'd always been curious about Wyland's place. Although their friendship had begun with the Sandmarsh pagans it had been truly forged more in the eco-protests he organised. She loved the heated discussions in the pub afterwards, where they'd rail against the crassness of politicians and put the world to rights. Occasionally, he would walk her home. He'd been a great listener, and apart from Emma and Will, the only other person in Flammark she'd told about her gift, and encouraged her all he could. He, on the other hand, refused to be drawn much about himself. She never really knew what made him tick.

She wasn't attracted to him—not in a sexual sense. But his personal reserve intrigued her. Made him mysterious. Arcane. Something else for her endless curiosity to fathom.

The room she'd entered reeked of oil and sock, of a man not used to company or the need to keep house, though it had its charms. An old, cracked leather sofa, an ancient throw hanging over its back, sat against a wall facing a window draped with handmade danglies of wood, stone and feather. An assortment of unlit candles rested on a brick hearth.

A large low table, cobbled together with what looked like offcuts, took up most of the space, the surface covered in neat piles of books and maps. She recognised the usual oghams, the works of Gerald Gardner, and her favourite, Ronald Hutton. Others she didn't know, with names like Virgil and Macrobius. More maps, framed this time, took up almost every inch of wall space. She peered at one captioned *Mappa Mundi*. Wow, it looked really old. She'd always thought Wyland a genuine expert on the old ways—a true pagan—but all this looked … academic.

It all took Abigail's breath away. For the first time she understood that someone could take what they believed in so seriously, become so immersed in its ideas, that it became a life's work to gain true understanding, beyond what might come from within. In a flutter of excitement, she suddenly realised she wanted this for herself. Well, maybe not the maps, and she'd want her place to be way less cluttered. No matter. If she really wanted to understand and develop her gift—find her own path—then she needed to take it seriously enough to learn. Nothing like this existed back home. There wasn't a book in the house.

A loud, ponderous ticking added weight to the air. Glancing up at the chimney breast, her eye was caught by the crude iron frame that hung there, with cogs and counterweights and simple fingers, marking time on a set of carved wooden numbers.

Wyland appeared at the door, glass in hand. He looked calmer. "I made that myself. Years ago."

"It's fantastic." She looked about her. "I can't get over this room. Wyland, I had no idea—"

"No idea about what? That I could read? Look at maps?"

Not wanting to set him off again, she said. "No. Well … sort of. That you actually … studied." She waved in the general direction of the table and the bookcases that lined the alcoves.

"Not everyone is what they seem, Abs. You of all people should know that."

"Okay, I get you're angry. I was just … forget it." She glugged some water, set the glass down on the low table and sank into a huge floor cushion next to it. Trying to disarm him with a teasing grin, she said, "Now, if you're over yourself, tell me everything about what's going on out there."

He rolled his eyes and gave an exasperated sigh. "I don't know where to start."

"Did whatever it is have something to do with the earth tremor yesterday morning? About two-ish?"

He raised his eyebrows. "You felt it, too? I've asked around. No one I know did."

"Yeah. Really badly. Not so much the … physical-ness of it. That only lasted a few seconds. There was something else, something more to it, you know, *significant*. It really bugged me. I sensed it started under Seely Tor. My friend

Emma drove me up. There's cracks all over the viewing platform."

Wyland threw himself on the sofa, nearly spilling some of his drink. "Are there, now?" He nodded grimly, as if she'd confirmed something. "As you saw, one of the vans toppled. I thought the tremor might have caused it."

He told her what had been revealed underneath.

"God, Wy. Do they know who it was? How he—assuming it's a 'he'—how he got there?"

"No, they don't. It's bloody obvious he's been there a while, even to that lot. Didn't stop them digging him out and arresting me."

"They arrested you?"

"Yeah, yesterday. Some arrogant bloody sod of an Inspector ordered it. They took a statement then let me go."

Abigail smiled to herself. That would be Westen. Then a sudden realisation dawned. "I saw the gurney. Were the bones on that?"

Wyland nodded.

Randomly, her brain spilling thoughts all over the place, she said, "I'm surprised they didn't use a tent. You know, to stop people like me from gawking."

"There's no one here to gawk. As soon as someone cried earthquake, they evacuated the park. At least the press haven't cottoned on yet, but it'll only be a matter of time before I have to put up with them, too."

"What's that big truck? The one with all the computer screens inside?"

He lifted his glass and took a huge gulp from it then threw his head back and blew out a long, slow sigh. "That's Baldy's doing."

"Baldy?" Abigail chuckled.

His tone edged with annoyance, Wyland replied. "He's the police pathologist. He called in the survey people to check for more tremors. They've put sensors all around the park. I expect they've done the same on the Tor. The people you saw standing near the body are from the university. Archaeology *and* anthropology. I suppose I should be flattered. It took all morning to break up the rest of the concrete and extract the remains. Once they were out, that's when I finally I lost it."

"They'll be gone soon, once they've taken the bones away."

"That's the point. I don't want them to take the bones away. And the survey people will be here a while—the cops haven't told me when I can reopen the park." He swallowed another mouthful from his glass. "*If* I'm going to open it."

"Why wouldn't you? You'll be losing money!"

"I've lost a damn sight more than money, Abs."

"What do you mean?"

He sat up and put his head in his hands. Abby could sense his upset. Reluctant to break the silence, she waited, listening to the heavy ticking of the wall clock.

Suddenly he looked up and said, "What do you know about local history?"

She shrugged. "I was born and bred here. I doubt I understand as much as you obviously do, but I know Sandmarsh and Flammark are special. It's why St Jude's is such a tourist spot. It's got Celtic roots."

"Yeah. See, that's the problem right there. People assume that's where the power lies. In spiritual institutions like churches and cathedrals. To a degree they're right. Places like that seem locked in time as centres of ceremony and prayer. It's true. They're part of our cultural history and do have great power. But that's only half the story."

Abigail settled back into her cushion. She sensed a Wyland lecture coming on.

Seeming to gather his thoughts, he continued. "The old

Celtic tribes weren't religious in the way we think about it today. They listened to the earth, and it told them how its energies worked, so they understood where to put in the required ... protections."

"You're talking about ley lines and standing stones, aren't you?" said Abigail.

He considered a moment. "Some people believe in Ley lines but I'm not sure I do. Actually, they're quite a modern concept, an attempt to explain how ancient monuments and structures ended up being aligned with each other." He leant forward and reached for a book. "This is the chap that started that thinking. Alfred Watkins." He weighed the volume in his hands, then reached for another. It was called, *The Triumph of the Moon*. "This one, though, has a different take. Ronald Hutton—he's a professor, you know—debunks a lot of it. Makes very interesting reading. You can borrow it if you like."

"Thanks!" Abigail took it from him and riffled through the pages of tiny, densely written script. "Obviously we talk about this stuff at the pagan meetings, so I know a bit. I haven't done any reading. Want to, though."

"What we cover at those meetings hardly scratches the surface. Most of the members are tourist pagans with surface interest, toe-in-the-water stuff. There are very few diehards like me. Ones who study looking for deeper understanding." He gave an indulgent smile. "If you're really interested, Abs, that's as good a place as any to start. And borrow the Watkins book, too. It's interesting, to be sure, and there's probably something to his theories, though his focus lies in patterns and connections. Sometimes things more ... fundamental ... are at play."

"Like?"

"Like chaos."

Abigail shot him a questioning frown and put the Hutton volume on the table. "Eh?"

"Some people think the earth is under constant attack. It can come from within—mankind's propensities for self-destruction, and all that—"

"You mean, like with the frackers?" Abigail nodded in vigorous agreement. "They're a right lot, they are. Doesn't matter what damage they do. All they're bothered about is getting at the shale, selling the gas."

He gave her another look, this time laced with irony.

"Oh, sorry. I don't need to tell you that, do I?"

"No, you do not. The land has long been hostage to the forces of ambition and greed. War, boundaries and enclosures, the rise of the factories, more war. Each passing century marks a different phase of change and destruction. True pagans know that the planet wages a constant battle against those who would loot its resources; people who know nothing of our way of life and will do anything to distract us from the only relationship that really matters. Our connection with the sacred earth."

Abigail had witnessed Wyland's fervent outbursts before. At protests and in the pub. Loving his passion, knowing she had way longer to go before she could match it, all she could manage was, "Totally."

They sat in a terse silence; she, mulling over his words and Wyland getting antsy again. He leapt up and walked to the window.

"Sometimes the threat comes from without. That's not happening this time. I think—" he stopped abruptly. "They're bringing him up. Sorry, Abs, I've got to go."

"Don't. You'll only get wound up again. They'll probably take him to the morgue. They won't let you go near him."

"You don't get it, Abs. You don't get it."

"Stop." She put her hand out, laid it on the ivy-encircled five-pointed star on his forearm. "Tell me."

He gave her fifteen seconds before running out of the door. "What we felt the other day ... it wasn't a quake. At least not in the way you think. Something else caused the tremor. And that something ... " he took her hand off his arm, "... managed to unearth a sentinel."

❧ 8 ❧

REBUFFED

Abigail let him go. Standing at the front door, she witnessed Wyland dash to the gurney, shrugging off the heavy hand of the copper who was part of the tiny procession that came up with it. There must have been something in his demeanour that stopped the policeman from ordering him to the house. Instead, he stepped away, allowing the desperately upset man to approach and walk next to the trolley before watching them fold its legs and slide it gently into the pathologist's van.

The muscular form of the tall bloke she'd seen watching the proceedings came into view next. Since she could see no sign of any hair beneath his cap, this must be the 'Baldy' Wyland talked about. Something made him look Abigail's way. Frowning slightly, he held her gaze a few seconds before moving on. Tch. If he dared to kick off about her being here, he could go to hell. None of his bloody business.

Wyland accosted him as he climbed into his van and there followed a noisy exchange. They were still arguing as the other grave robbers, together with the two policemen— nothing to guard now—took to their vehicles. Wyland stepped back suddenly as Baldy drew up his driver's window. Firing up the engine, he drove away.

Game over.

After a few moments, she joined Wyland at the courtyard entrance and stood with him as the van disappeared from view. He said not a word. Broke away from her. Ambled off then down, into the park.

Realising Wyland would probably prefer his own company, Abigail started back towards his cottage. As she turned, her attention was caught by the computer truck, its doors still gaping wide open, with the young man inside sat exactly as he had when she first arrived, only now he was wearing massive headphones and peering at a screen. Shaking back her braids, she took a deep breath and strode up to the truck.

To get his attention she cleared her throat. No response. Absorbed in his work, he obviously hadn't seen her and clearly couldn't hear her either. Bold as anything, using the grab-handles either side of the door, she hoiked herself inside.

"What the—" The man yanked off his gear and seemed about to continue shouting when he stopped, mouth open. Then grinned. "Erm ... you shouldn't be in here, miss. We're looking into an incident."

Elongating the words, Abigail said, "*Are* you?" She took another step further inside the cramped space. With affected wonder she widened her eyes and fingered the long rolls of maps cradled in their wire racks before peering at the bank of computers opposite. "Wyland told me you were here because of the tremor. I felt it, you know." Completely without shame, she sat on a swivel chair and rode on its castors until it came to a stop right next to the poor chap.

His turn to clear his throat. "Did you, now? There's not many that did, and even we didn't believe it at first." Obvi-

ously encouraged by her fascinated gaze and nodding interest, he nerded on. "We've installed sensors and are
monitoring them closely. If it had been an actual quake, we'd
expect there to be aftershocks. Probably nothing you'd feel,
but the equipment would pick them up, for sure."

"And there hasn't been any?"

He shook his head and pressed his lips together. "Nothing
as yet. It was probably just a small tremor. The earth having a
grumble. Nothing to worry about."

Abigail leaned over his desk even further. "What are you
looking at?"

Up close, he didn't seem much older than she was. Not
bad looking, either. Judging by the flush on his face, she
guessed he was thinking along similar lines about her.

"Erm … I'm not sure I should be telling you."

She turned away from the screen and bestowed her violet
gaze upon him. "Why? It's not top secret, is it?"

He considered her for a moment, his grin widening. "If
you tell me your name, I might be persuaded to give you a
look."

Smiling back, a finger twiddling a bead in her hair, she
said, "Abigail. What's yours?"

"Tom, Tom Shepherd. I'm a third-year grad student at
Lanchester Uni. When Mr Savage called, we—that's the prof
and I—came straight over. He's at the Tor. I'm picking him up
when I've done here."

"Savage?"

"Yeah, he's the chap in the cap." Whether it was because
of the unexpected rhyme or the need to relieve some of the
sexual tension Abigail had steamed up, Tom chuckled way
louder than the confines of the van could easily accommo-
date. It made her wince a little. Tapping at points on the
computer screen, he said, "See, these are where we've

planted the sensors. I've been monitoring for seismic activity."

Abigail nodded vigorously. "You've got one on the Tor? I was up there yesterday. Saw some of the cracks form with my own eyes. Emma, my friend, she called the police."

Tom replied, "Wow! I wish I'd've been there. I've never witnessed strata movement actually happening. If it affected the viewing platform, they'll have to reinforce it now."

Tapping the screen, he said, "This is part of the geological map of Sandmarsh and its environs." He pointed to a faint dotted line. "See this? It's called a fault trace. It marks the shift between two blocks of stone. This red line runs exactly from the Tor to here, Wood End. It wasn't there before."

"It's very straight. We're not in any danger, are we?"

"The line distinguishes the point where two blocks of rock sort of ... rub against each other. The blocks of granite like those the Tor came from can be huge formations and tend to run in straight lines. The point is, if something shifts at one end, it affects the other. But no, we're in no danger. It's more like a crack than a fault. When we map this up properly, it'll turn into a minor dotted line. Nothing to worry about."

Abigail looked closer at the screen. "Can you pan out a bit? Show a bit more of Ledbridge?"

He tapped a key a few times.

"Stop. See there? You know what that is, right?"

"We certainly do. It's the DeepDrilla site, a place we've been keeping tabs on ever since they set up."

Abigail's heart leapt. "The crack's there too! It's their doing, isn't it? I knew it!"

"We've a lot of evidence-gathering to do before we can attribute responsibility. We have to be a hundred per cent sure. Whether they caused it or not, once we've put in our report and mapped the new crack, I think it's safe to say it'll put the kibosh on any future attempt to frack in Ledbridge, or, hopefully, anywhere else for that matter."

Abigail clapped her hands. "Yesss!"

It must have been her enthusiasm that spurred him to continue. "I probably shouldn't be saying this, but we advised against the Ledbridge frack. It should never have been licensed. The government keeps threatening to roll back their decision to suspend the activity. This should put paid to all that."

Hearing heavy footsteps outside, Abigail turned towards the open doors of the truck. The looming form of Wyland appeared.

"How long are you gonna stay?" he growled, staring at Tom. "The sooner you lot go, the sooner I can bring things back to normal."

"Sorry, man. The police won't give the green light until we're satisfied things have settled down."

"And when will you know that?"

"A week, maybe. Then we'll get out of your hair. Monitor things remotely."

Not bothering to reply, Wyland moved away. As she got up to follow him, Abigail said, "Tom, thanks ever so much for letting me have a look. It's all been really interesting."

"Fancy going out later?" he asked. "I hear there's a half-decent pub in the village."

Abigail chuckled. "Yeah, there is. Thanks, but no thanks. I'm going to stay here tonight. Make sure Wyland's okay."

"Oh, I get it." Tom switched off his friendly grin.

"No. It's not like that, so don't get miffed. He's a friend, that's all. And he's upset. The least I can do is check he's going to be okay. Maybe we can hook up another time."

Cheered by her suggestion, Tom grinned. "Okay. Give me your number and we'll sort something out."

Fishing out her mobile, she asked for his number, then sent him a text. "There. You've got it now. Ring me."

She climbed out and turned to wave. Tom was okay. A bit bland for her taste, but it wouldn't do any harm to have a drink or two with the guy. You never know what else he might be able to tell her, especially about Godzilla.

Inside the house, she found Wyland sat on the sofa, a diagram of Wood End and its caravans in front of him. He circled the set of seven in the well of the park, neatly placed in an almost perfect circle. He drew a huge cross over one of them.

"One down, six more to go."

"What do you mean?" On seeing that he had no intention to expand on the statement, she said, "Okay, Wy. Time to spill. What's really going on and … what's a sentinel?"

He held her eyes for a while, as if weighing something up, then he shook his head and looked at his map again.

"Wyland?"

"I shouldn't have said anything. It was stupid."

"No, no it wasn't. You never say stupid things."

His voice took on a tone she'd not heard before. "Forget it, Abs. Forget I said anything. I think it's probably time you left. I want to be on my own. I've got stuff to work out."

Abigail couldn't believe it. Could Wyland really be trying to get rid of her? Mild desperation entered her voice, "But—"

"You heard me." He got up and faced her, started shouting. "I want you to leave. Get out. Go. There's nothing you can do here. Nothing. I don't want you around anymore. You're just a kid. You'll be in the way."

Shocked into silence, Abigail didn't move. Not an hour ago, they'd been chatting, looking through his books, talking about the land—the Celts. She'd lapped up every word thinking she'd found another mentor, someone she could share her passions with. Determined he shouldn't see her stinging tears, she gathered her things, thought about leaving the two books, but as she really wanted to read them decided not to. She paused in the doorway. Wyland, still ignoring her, stared with tense calm at his map.

Utterly crestfallen, Abigail left the cottage. She waved again to Tom, but he was too engrossed in a screen to notice. Rummaging in her bag, she grabbed her phone and with relief found it had a signal. As she turned against the breeze to call a taxi, she glimpsed movement from the house. Had Wyland followed her out? Did he want to make things right?

Obviously not, since he strode the other way, to the brink of the park. Then he did an extraordinary thing. Sinking to his knees, then his belly, he laid himself prostrate, spreading out his arms, palms downwards.

Then, turning his head, he pushed his unruly hair away and put his ear to the ground.

✵ 9 ✵

KNIFE

Emma fretted over Westen's visit throughout the rest of the week and the next, their encounter having done nothing to improve her sleep.

On most mornings she arrived at the surgery both cross and groggy. By Friday, she still hadn't decided what to do about him—and he certainly had been keeping true to his promise not to bother her again.

"Just in time," Robbie said, striding out of his office, frown on face, file in hand. "I can't do with being behind today. We've got the monthly vaccination figures to return and the powers that be don't like them to be delayed."

Emma managed a curt nod. Was he accusing her of being late? Her jeep had been playing up; dodgy battery, probably. Even though she'd had to taxi in, she'd still made it through the door on the dot of eight-thirty.

Glancing up at the clock, honing the edge to her voice, she said, "You know, Robbie, I hate it when people say 'just in time'. All it means is I am *on* time." Not bothering to tell him about the car, she slung her bag in the cupboard underneath the counter and plonked herself down. She had no idea what had put him in so foul a temper, and it did nothing to improve hers. "I'm just sick of all this. Sick of it. I give everything I have to this job. I don't have to, you know." Snapping her fingers she said, "I can get a better one any time I like."

Robbie Mason's mouth opened then closed. He stroked his red beard and pressed his lips together, presumably to stop himself answering back. He fixed her with the kind of stare she hadn't ever seen from him before, his eyes flashing with temper. Then his face suddenly melted with concern. "You're right, of course, lass. I'm sorry, I really am. I'm not sure what came over me. I got up in a perfectly good mood." Then, eyes widening as the impact of her words sunk in, he said, "You aren't really thinking of leaving, are you?"

Emma fought the impulse to keep snapping, her temper these days always on edge. She took a few breaths, forcing her frustration down. "Of course I'm not, Robbie." Suppressing a sigh, she booted up the computer. "I'm sorry. I have been mulling over whether Flammark's the best place for me to be, but I hadn't seriously contemplated leaving it. As for what I said about the job … well, my remarks were thoughtless and arrogant. None of it entered my mind until you greeted me like that." With a conciliatory smile she got up. "I need a coffee. Want one?"

Like a lumbering bear he followed her into the little kitchen area behind her desk, his huge frame full of remorse. "I'm not usually prone to tantrums, lass."

She filled the kettle and spooned instant coffee into white mugs. "It's okay, Robbie. You aren't the only one, you know. One or two of the patients have been really short with me, too. It might be my imagination, but sometimes there's an atmosphere in the waiting room. As if I've done something to offend everyone." She shrugged. "I expect it's just paranoia— and I shouldn't have lost it like that with you. Put it down to sleepless nights. You caught me on the raw."

"Are the dreams back?"

"Yep. What about you? Are you … okay?" She had to tread carefully, not really wanting to dwell on her ordeal last year, yet needing to acknowledge his own suffering after what Ben had done to him.

"I still don't remember much. Sometimes I feel an echo of the pain." As if by impulse, he put his hand to his chest, where Ben's scalpel had bitten deep.

"You know how sorry I am about—"

"Ach, I know you are, lass." He leant against the sink unit to face her. "How many times do I have to tell you, stop apologising for him. None of it was your fault. I'd rather you concentrated on yourself. It's damned obvious you're not over it."

Emma slowly shook her head as she poured the boiling water. No, she wasn't. Nowhere near. At the time, getting through the nights had been the hardest part. The Mogadon he'd prescribed had worked well. So well, in fact, that she hadn't bothered taking the full course. Now that the nightmares were back with a vengeance, she'd retrieved what remained and had nearly run out. Maybe this would be a good moment to broach the subject and get some more.

"If you are experiencing a recurrence, I'd be loath to repeat the prescription. Sleeping pills can be addictive, lass. Maybe you need more … specialist help? There's someone I could recommend in Sandmarsh. I can refer you, if you like?"

Damn.

Yet hadn't this been what Abigail had suggested? Although not wanting to take him up on the offer, Emma could no longer deny the extent of her exhaustion. The blue rings beneath her eyes had become increasingly difficult to conceal.

The phone rang. "Let me think about it," she said, taking her mug through to her desk.

The calls came in thick and fast, as they always did before the weekend. Half an hour later, all the day's appointments had been taken and the waiting room filled with its usual limps and coughs and splutters. And sly glances.

Was it her imagination? Ignoring them as best she could, mainly on automatic she worked the reception desk. As the morning crawled on, stretching limbs and suppressing yawns, she looked forward to lunch hour, thinking perhaps she might call in at the salon to see Abigail and take her to their favourite cafe, 'Food for Thought.' Maybe talk through the idea of a counsellor. Her friend had made herself scarce these past weeks, probably stressed by what happened on the Tor—either that or she'd been making a nuisance of herself to Godzilla. Whatever the case, high time they caught up.

At eleven-thirty that plan flew out of the window.

The weather being warm, Emma had hooked open the heavy front door to let in the gentle breeze. She started at the sudden sound of a horn blaring, followed by car doors banging. Two men burst through the entrance. The few patients left stood up in alarm, one of them grabbing her daughter, keeping her close. Two men. One of them, shirtless, had the other's arm around his neck, by which he half-walked, half-dragged the bleeding man inside. "Where's the doc?" he shouted. "Get Mason, now!"

Emma rushed from behind the counter as Robbie pelted through his door.

"What the—Wilby? Jason Wilby?" he exclaimed to the shirtless man, quickly taking the other arm of his injured companion. "Let's get him in my surgery. What's this fella's name?"

"Dunno," Wilby grunted. "He got into a shouting match outside the Flammark Arms. This bloke came out of nowhere and after a scuffle, pulled a knife. Stabbed him before taking off! It was either wait for an ambo or get him here."

Emma followed them through to Robbie's surgery. Once they wrangled him onto the examination table, the doctor took one look at the bloody shirt Jason had tied tightly round the man's thigh and shouted to her, "Ring for that ambulance. Now!"

Three minutes later she was back. "They're on their way. The dispatcher also alerted the police and they're sending someone on to the hospital. What can I do?"

"Get towels." He turned to Jason, "The shirt stays, it needs to keep doing its job, but we could do with more pressure. Lean hard, here." He pointed to an area just above the wound.

Emma ran to fetch towels, then piled them on a chair. Robbie, grabbing one after another, said, "I think whoever did this might has nicked his femoral." He glanced up at Jason. "You did really well to get him here, lad."

Blood continued to soak the towels but, thank God, after a minute or so, its pace noticeably lessened, leaving Robbie space to grab oxygen and a mask. The man, floating in and out of consciousness, moaned incoherently.

"Keep him awake. He needs to stay alert. Where's that bloody ambulance?"

"Bloody here!" shouted a paramedic, one of two men who'd suddenly rushed in. "You were lucky we had a drop-off." With implacable speed and efficiency, they took in the scene. While Robbie staccatoed a situation report they substituted the oxygen with a cylinder of their own, and debated for a few seconds about whether to abandon the tourniquet. They decided loosening it could do more harm than good, and after taking some vitals, lifted him onto a trolley. Then they were out the door.

"Well!" said Robbie, puffing out his cheeks in a massive sigh as they surveyed the mess in the room. "What a way to end the week, eh?"

Emma nodded, picking up the towels and wrapping them in the thick paper covering that had lined the table. "I can't believe it all went so quickly. One minute I'm sitting in reception, the next it's like an episode of *Casualty*. Then they're gone!"

"Aye, lass, paramedics don't mess about." Robbie gave Emma a sidelong glance. "You did well. Didn't bat an eyelid, considering he'd come in with such a nasty wound."

"Had no time to think. I expect reaction will soon set in, though."

She left Robbie to wash his hands while she disposed of the towels. Truth be told, she'd surprised herself at her level of composure. Awful though it might have been for the injured man, she'd felt something close to exhilaration. On her return she noticed the half-naked figure of Jason Wilby sitting in the emptied waiting room, pumping his knee up and down.

"Are you okay? Shall I get the doctor?"

Robbie, already emerging from his surgery, gave him the once-over. "He'll live. Shaken, but not stirred. I think maybe he could do with something to drink. I have just the thing in my office."

Emma knew exactly what that meant. Taking a seat next to Wilby, she grinned as she heard the bottom drawer of his filing cabinet open. "What about your patients?" she said, as Robbie returned armed with a bottle and a cut-glass tumbler. "You're fully booked! All afternoon!"

He put everything down and gave her a look of mock indignation. "It's not for me, Emma—or for you. We can make do with tea." She got up. "No. You stay where you are." He poured a finger of whisky and handed it to Wilby. "Get that down you, Jason." He turned to Emma. "You stay there, lass. I'll sort the tea."

On his return, drinking their beverages, a kind of stunned

silence filled the room. Robbie said, "I'm going to have to ring through to Sandmarsh police. They'll want confirmation of what went on here, and probably a written report. They'll need a statement from you too, Jason. About what happened outside the pub."

"I know," Wilby acknowledged. "I'll finish this, catch my breath and then show my face at the station."

"Erm, you might need to buy yourself a tee-shirt or something first," said Emma, exaggerating the need to keep eye contact.

"Oh, yeah. I forgot about that. Good job it's hot outside."

"Will you be okay to drive? It's all been a bit of a shock—not to mention ..." she nodded at the empty glass.

"Yeah, I won't go straight away. I'll walk it into the village and buy a top. Maybe get a bite to eat."

Robbie changed the subject. "Jason here is a war vet, Emma. Two tours, wasn't it?"

"Three. So yeah, I'm used to a bit of action, though I didn't expect to see it in Flammark!"

"I bet you didn't." His gaze still and deliberate, Robbie continued, "You're sure you didn't know him?"

"Positive." Jason tried to hold the doctor's eyes. "Okay. What happened to that guy had nothing to do with me. I know I used to get into a bit of trouble here and there. But I was just a kid, and never arrested. The army straightened me out."

Robbie's face softened. "Aye, I can see that it has. Without you, that man wouldn't have lived to tell the tale."

Jason gave a modest smile and finished his drink. After placing the glass on the tray and getting up, he said, "Right, well, thanks for the drink. I'll be on my way."

Robbie and Emma saw him out and watched him walk out of the gravel drive, leaving his car where it was. As they went back in Emma said, "What did he mean about being in trouble?"

"Back in the day, our Jason was cock of the walk hereabouts. A troubled lad. Had a habit of stirring things up—lots of fights. Andrew Wilby nearly tore his hair out over him. He couldn't have been more delighted when his son told him he wanted to join the army."

"Do you think he had anything to do with the knife attack?"

He shrugged. "I don't know, Emma. Possibly."

They moved inside. The relative shade, though welcome, brought her back to the traumatic events of earlier. For some reason, she started yawning and wanted to sit. She felt hungry too—ravenous—but with the afternoon's surgery about to begin, they'd lost their lunch break.

Her body must have been sending out smoke signals, for Robbie said, "I'm starving. Why don't you ring Bella's and get them to send round a pizza PDQ. We'll set it up in the kitchen and graze when we've each got a gap. The first patient's due in ... ?"

"Ten minutes."

"Right. If I could, I'd close the surgery but—"

"I know, the vaccination figures."

"Sorry, lass. I'd send you home—I can see you're exhausted, it's just ..."

"I'll cope, Robbie, honestly. I don't feel much worse than I have all week."

"Right. I'm going to ring that colleague of mine. See if we can set you up with an appointment. How about it, Emma?"

Reaction setting in to all that had happened during the last hour, she didn't have the will to put up a fight.

"Okay."

❧ 10 ❧

CHANGES

An hour before surgery finished, having managed to upload the vaccination figures, Robbie let Emma go home early. "I'll manage the rest of the patients. There's only one or two more to come. You get off, lass. I'll cope."

She didn't argue. Not that she was that tired—she could have happily stayed—but it occurred to her she might like to drop in on Will; et the day's events off her chest and maybe chill out a bit. She hadn't seen him since the day Westen visited. She supposed they'd both been too busy, though it wasn't like him not to follow up.

She took the taxi straight there and, having paid the driver, crunched her way up to the door where she pressed the large brass button of the porch bell. No answer. Surprised at being kept waiting, she tried again. Nothing.

Odd. Sure that Will was at home, Emma turned and scanned the large expanse of gravel that fronted the vicarage. Once a huge garden, it now acted as a car park, so big it could take a small coach. St Jude's pagan roots, reflected in its unique Romanesque architecture, attracted hundreds of visitors each year. Just as she thought, Will's VW rested in its usual spot, so he must be in. She rang a third time and was about to turn away when the inner door opened. Not Will. Though she recognised the handsome, cassocked figure who came out to greet her, she struggled to remember where she'd seen him before.

"Hello!" the priest said, friendly but earnest. "I'm sorry but the vicar is ... Don't I know you?"

For a few moments they stared at each other before mutual recognition dawned. "Peter!" said Emma. "Peter Martin! We met last year at the cathedral library. I was doing some research into the Blackstone family. Do you remember?"

"Of course! I remember everything. As I recall, you didn't tell me your name, though."

"It's Emma. Emma Blake. I'm a friend of Will's. Also, his tenant. I live over the green, in his cottage. Clearview."

Peter didn't budge from the door, but nodded his head as if remembering some past conversation. "Oh, yes. He's told me a lot about you. And about your discovery."

Emma cocked an eyebrow.

"... That you are yourself a Blackstone."

She wasn't sure what she felt about Peter knowing her business. She knew Will had been Peter's pastoral mentor—he'd mentioned that in the library—but she know they met regularly enough for Will to gossip about her.

Still processing last year's events, Emma hadn't yet come to terms with the knowledge of her noble—or rather, ignoble—ancestry, though she knew it must be contributing to her deliberations over whether or not to stay in Flammark. In one sense it was where she truly belonged. Where her roots were. Probably time she acknowledged it and not worry who knew about it.

The second time today she'd got cross about nothing!

"Are you visiting, Peter, or on retreat?" Perhaps he and Will had been deep into some kind of counselling session which might have accounted for the long wait at the door. But that wouldn't explain why Will hadn't greeted her instead. And why was she getting the distinct impression that Peter didn't want to let her in?

"Actually, neither of those things." His face clouded over for a moment before it cleared with a faint smile. "I've been … I've been asked to give the vicarage some support."

"Support?" The idea surprised her. She knew the tourist side of things had got busier, but Will had wisely developed a small team of volunteers who helped with the church tours. The Friends of St Jude's kept the building and its environs in spotless condition and the church warden lent a strong hand in some of his parish duties. After one of the vicarage wings had been converted into a conference centre, the diocese also employed a part-time secretary to help with bookings and retreat residentials.

There'd been a curate, once upon a time. But he'd left under a bit of a cloud and no replacement had yet been found. Will hadn't been fazed. He always seemed absolutely in control of things and not in the slightest bit stressed-out by his workload. A born manager, he enjoyed the work. From her conversation with him in the cathedral last year, she knew Peter did not.

"But … what about your precious library? You gave the impression it was the love of your life!" Emma remembered his eidetic knowledge of each shelf, of every book.

Again, his face grew serious. "Not quite, that." He paused, a troubled thought flitting across his dark eyebrows. "But the cathedral does mean a lot to me. They've … allowed me to split my time between here and there so I can't really complain. Will's quite flexible about it all, though it isn't really what either of us want."

Curiouser and curiouser. Emma nodded, taking it all in, pondering what could have made their circumstances change so quickly. She had the definite feeling that something wasn't sitting quite right with him. Before she could ask any more questions he said, "I'm sorry, Emma. Will is in, but I don't think he's taking visitors at the moment."

Even as he said the words, Peter seemed to plant himself more firmly at the door.

Awkward. Unable to fathom the issue and not wanting to argue the toss, she was just about to give up the impasse when the inner door slowly opened and Will appeared. "It's okay, Peter. I'll take it from here."

Emma was completely taken aback by his grim expression. Peter gave her a quick smile and bowed his head slightly as he faded back into the house.

"Hello, Em."

"Will! What's wrong?"

He sighed and stepped back to let her into the large porch, but not before closing the hall door behind him, as Peter had done. "Sorry. All this must seem really odd." He lowered his voice. "I expect Peter's told you of my change in circumstance. It wasn't my idea to take on extra help. You know me, I'm more than capable of bearing the workload."

"I didn't doubt it for one minute. So why is Peter here?"

"The bish insisted, and we had to go along with it. The last thing Peter wanted was to be parted from his precious books but, apparently, there wasn't enough for him to do at the cathedral library. As you know, he isn't cut out for—"

"—parish life. Yes. I remember you both saying. Not much of a people person."

"He's trying to make the best of things. He's looking forward to sorting out the office and has already reorganised my entire filing system. The diocese has also decided upon a few alterations, pending planning permission, of course. There's going to be a lot of disruption. Not only am I priest in charge of St. Judes, I also have a new title. Heritage Co-ordinator!"

"Wow," said Emma, eyes widening. "It's all a bit sudden, isn't it? You didn't say anything about this the last time we met!"

"Tell me about it! I was summoned to Sandmarsh last Monday to be met with a *fait accompli*. Apparently, there's a new dean in town. A diocesan consultant on parish affairs." Will couldn't stop himself from curling his lips. "I haven't met him yet, but he's obviously got the wind up the bish. He doesn't usually act so precipitously. It honestly couldn't have come at a worse time."

Emma noticed a pulse throbbing in his temple, his face pale. She'd rarely seen his even temperament stressed out and it worried her; made her suspect something else in play. Glancing at the closed door behind Will, she wondered who else might be inside. Someone he didn't want her to see?

Will caught her glance. "Em. I want you to come in—I really do—but I have to talk to someone first. Can you give me a moment?"

She said nothing, only raised her eyebrows and nodded before he left her to keep company with the porch's leggy pelargoniums and perspex racks of tour guides.

After a good five minutes, and still no sign of Will's return, Emma stepped outside. The late evening sun still shone strongly, and she'd begun to sweat in the glassy entrance. She walked to the edge of the gravel and sat on one of the benches that had been placed to view the vicarage. A photogenic listed building, it still impressed her as she took in its rambling dimensions and pondered over how it had originally been built to provide the parish living for the lesser sons of her ancestors. A restlessness stirred within her; a kind of dread. Maybe their remnant spirit hadn't yet done with her.

Will emerged from the house and crunched his way over; at next to her on the bench. "It's okay. I've had a chat. She wants to talk to you."

"She?" Emma racked her brains. "Who is it, Will? Someone I know?"

"You must promise not to tell a soul she's here—especially not Abigail, though if I know anything about that girl, it won't be long before she catches on."

"Catches on?"

"And watch what you say to Peter. He's met her but he doesn't know who she really is." He put his head in his hands before turning to her, giving her a long look. "It's Gabby."

Gabby? Jesus. Emma's thoughts immediately flew back to the top of Seely Tor; how she held back Abigail's hair as the girl threw up, her mind taken over by Gabriel's name. Will called it right; she had caught on, though much earlier than he imagined. And she'd picked up something else, some danger. What was it the girl had said? *A surge of hatred?*

"She's back? But … but we got rid of the curse. She and Michael were convinced it was gone forever. That's why they could finally leave."

"Don't you think I know all that?" Will sat back for a moment, resting his elbow on the arm of the bench. "She arrived last night. I found her sitting right here, waiting for me to come back after Evensong. Oh Em, I wish you'd turned up to the service and had come back with me for our usual chat. It would all have been so much easier."

"Easier? How?"

"Because now the story has to be told all over again. She doesn't want it recounted for her. Frankly, I'm not sure she's up to it, but there we are. I must warn you, though ..." A worried frown furled his brow. "She's in a terrible, terrible state and not the person we remembered."

"What do you mean?"

"Simply put, Em? Her heart is broken."

❧ II ❧

GABBY

Emma followed Will into his living room. A private space, out of bounds to visitors, Will hardly ever used it, always preferring to spend his down-time in the library, whether any of the retreat residents were there or not.

Comfortable would not be the word to describe this room. Sparsely furnished, its original oak floor was smothered by a large threadbare rug of faintly oriental design which, at one time, had been rendered in shades of green. A vintage, dark red, bulbous sofa rested on one side of the hearth. Opposite, in a matching chair, slumped a sad, small, defeated figure. An untouched cup of tea and a box of tissues rested on a side-table next to her.

The Gabby Emma remembered had been both larger than life and full of it. She had been there for Emma from the very first day she arrived in Flammark—which turned out to be no coincidence, of course. She had not known then that Gabby would prove to be a neighbour, confidant, friend and … an imposter, keeping her secret from everyone who knew her. Now she sat as a pale shadow of former herself, her spirit—

her essence—all but gone. Her dirty-blonde hair, longer and stragglier than Emma remembered, framed a face etched with desperate sadness.

As if she'd lost the world.

"Gabby?" said Emma quietly, seating herself on the edge of the sofa.

The figure returned no response, except for the faintest move of her head, sunken eyes fixed on a point somewhere on the floor.

Emma turned to Will. Though he hadn't offered, she said, "How about that coffee?"

Will wasn't daft and knew he'd been sent packing, so he played along. "Can I get you anything, Gabby?"

No answer. No movement. Giving Emma a sidelong 'see-what-I-mean' glance, he shrugged slightly before leaving the room.

No stranger to despair herself, Emma understood the need not to probe, not to question. Occasions like this required solidarity, and she could give that in spades. So she sat with her friend and waited, hoping she would eventually want to open up.

Except for the ticking of a mantel clock, quiet filled the room. No sound from elsewhere in the vicarage broke the peace of their solitude—which suited Emma too, considering the day she'd had. Matching her heartbeat to the rhythm of the timepiece, it seemed as if an age passed before Gabby let out a tremulous sigh and whispered through lips that barely moved.

"I'm glad you're here."

"Always, Gabby." Emma paused before continuing, "Do you feel up to telling me what's happened?"

Another monumental pause. Then, eyes welling, clearly struggling to keep back sobs, Gabby murmured,"I went … I went too far." More words tumbled out. "I got too close to

Abigail. Wanted to protect her too much. It was because of me the curse became untethered and found you. If you hadn't defeated it, it would have gone out into the world and ..."

That damned curse.

They might have defeated it, but its aftermath was still with them. Shaking her head, Emma gently replied, "I don't believe that, Gabby. The Blackstone curse belonged to Flammark and only Flammark. That's why I was lured here in the first place. And I am a Blackstone too, remember? It looked for its own."

"Yes, but—"

"And we overcame it together. Without you, I couldn't have done anything."

Breaths catching in her throat, Gabby replied, "Michael didn't agree. Said all along I was getting too attached. If you hadn't outwitted Ben—outwitted the spirit that possessed him—its evil would have been unleashed into the world and—"

"But—we—*did* outwit Ben, and the evil didn't escape so ... ?"

Another moment of silence.

"But it could have. It could have all gone terribly wrong. Because of me."

"So this is about guilt?" Emma knew about guilt. Understood its destructive power. She tried a smile and said, "I didn't realise angels could feel this way, and have ... crises."

Gabby remained still, her face a multitude of expressions all vying for control.

She swallowed. "I'm not an angel anymore."

Emma caught her breath.

Then tears came thick and fast, huge droplets of despair that stained the fabric of Gabby's chair.

"There was a Reckoning and ... and it was decided that

since I was so 'fond' of humans, as Michael put it, that I should be made one of them. I am as mortal as you are."

"But … but …" Emma struggled to understand. "You're Gabriel. *Gabriel*, for God's sake!"

With a snicker Gabby replied, "No, I'm not. Was not, I should say. I explained this to you. I'm merely a replica, just as Michael is, too. How else are we supposed to do our Father's bidding; be anywhere and everywhere at once?"

Not quite believing what she was about to say, Emma slowly framed the words, "And where is … God … in all this?"

Gabby's eyes welled up once more, and in even lower tones she continued, "God is unknowable, even to us—to them. All I know is I can't feel him anymore. His Presence is gone."

"Presence?" Emma's curiosity got the better of her. Even in poor Gabby's straightened circumstances, she couldn't help but pry into a realm she'd always thought belonged in a biblical fairytale. Until last year.

"It's how we get our instructions. His Presence fills us, and we, well, we just know what we have to do. I have—I had —complete clarity about who I am and what my purpose … was. That's gone now, and all I can feel is its opposite: a terrible, terrible absence. Emma, I've lost who I am."

Then the sobs finally arrived; huge violent beasts that forced Gabby's head down into her arms, wracking her body as she folded forward.

Emma shot up and knelt beside her friend, placing an arm around her shoulders as the storm took her. "I am so sorry," she murmured. "So sorry. I don't know what to say. I cannot comprehend the pain you must be feeling." Leaning into Emma's awkward embrace, Gabby's sobs increased. Got louder.

"Shh … shh … It's okay, I'm here. Will's here. We'll do everything we can to help."

"Help? How on earth do you believe either of you can h-help?"

Ignoring the rebuff, Emma continued her shushing and strengthened her hold. Eventually, Gabby's wails subsided a little. Emma grabbed the tissue box and put it on the crying woman's knee.

"What am I supposed to do now? Where am I supposed to go?"

Emma had no answer. She remembered again what happened on the Tor. How relieved Abigail had been that Gabby had left Flammark, because she'd sensed an evil towards her so violent it had made her retch. Something 'worse than Ben'. Now Gabby had returned and in greatly reduced circumstances. If something *was* after her, something … other … she would have neither strength nor resources to fight it.

"You're not lost, Gabby. It might seem that way now, but you are amongst friends. Good friends. Robbie will be delighted to see you again, and Abigail too, of course." She paused for thought. "I don't know much about this sort of thing—who does?—but I'm sure you haven't been abandoned. Isn't that why you ended up here?"

Gabby shrugged. "I don't know how or when I arrived. After the Reckoning I found myself sitting on that bench outside."

"There you go. That had to be Michael's doing. He's put you where he knows you'll be loved." Digging deep into what little cod-theology she knew, Emma said, "Isn't that what it's all supposed to be about? Love? And your situation might not be forever. Maybe you'll be …"

"Forgiven?" Gabby scoffed. "It doesn't work like that for

us. We can't afford to make mistakes. I'm done for, Emma. I'll never get back."

She retreated once more into despair, eyes fixed on the same spot on the carpet as when Emma had entered the room.

After a while, seeing no sign of any further outburst, Emma said, "Can I leave you for a moment? I should go and find out what Will's doing in the kitchen. He's taking an age with that coffee."

No answer.

Emma left, blowing out a sigh as she went in search of Will. Failing to find him in the kitchen, the sound of unusually raised voices told her he might be in the library.

"When?" Will, flushed and angry-looking, sat at his desk under one of the mullioned windows. Looking up at Peter, he was saying, "When are we supposed to get this … visitation?"

"Next Friday. I'm sorry, I understand you've got a lot on, and I know you're worried about your friend." Peter jerked his head sideways in the vague direction of the living room. "The bishop was adamant. The dean's coming and there's not much either of us can do about it."

Will rapped his fingers on the desk. Emma had never seen him so angry. Actually, she'd never seen him angry, full stop. Looking her way, fury etching his voice, he said, "Just to add to our problems, we're to get a visitor. This … dean … has seen fit to make us his first port of call for his parish 'consultation'. Having already suggested I'm not up to the job without some help—sorry Peter, you know it's not personal—there's now a rumour that he wants to shake things up even more."

Emma bit her lip. Awful though his situation sounded, she was more concerned about Gabby. Will saw it too, and looked crestfallen. "I'm being selfish, aren't I?" He sighed, twisting his lips in a smile that never once reached his eyes. "I suppose we should get a room prepared, Peter. How long does he want to stay?"

"He's told the bishop he'd like to make Flammark his base. Something about not wanting to be affected by cathedral politics. Also, it's closer to a number of other parishes he wants to visit. By the sounds of it, I think he's going to be here for several weeks."

Will sighed. "All right. I don't suppose we can do anything about it. Can you make the necessary arrangements?"

"No problem."

As the Peter moved towards the door, Will called to him. "Peter … I'm sorry all this is happening."

"So am I," he replied, turning again to Will. "I think the bishop is too. This new chap seems very connected, though. Won't take no for an answer."

As Peter left, Will gathered himself and turned to Emma. "So, Gabby. What do you think?"

"Poor thing. She's inconsolable."

"I agree. She won't budge an inch, not even to go to her room—or the loo, for that matter. And she doesn't sleep. To be honest, I'm not even sure she knows how to sleep."

"Her body will teach her. She won't be able to hold out against it for much longer." Emma shook her head for the pity of it all. "And as if this isn't enough, you're getting another visitor?"

"Yes. Dean Anthony St Saviour. Bloody mouthful." He swivelled violently in his chair and looked out of the window. "I shouldn't be so cross about it all. But he's the one who told the bish I needed Peter here, and I don't. I was coping perfectly well without him. It's complicated everything, especially now, with Gabby."

Though Emma didn't want to add to his woes, there was nothing she could do about it. "That's not all, I'm afraid, Will. We've got to tell Abigail about Gabby, and quickly."

"Why? Gabby might not want to see her yet. Mixed feelings, I think. She believes that it's because she got too close to her that, well, you know …"

"Remember what I told you about when we were on the Tor a few weeks ago? That Abigail threw up because—"

"Oh, yeah. I'd forgotten all about that. Didn't she have some kind of premonition."

"She wasn't sure what it was," said Emma. "Only that she felt so much hate directed at Gabby, it made her sick."

"And now she's here." He sighed. "It's not over for us, is it, Em? Something's up again."

"If there is, Abigail's the one we need to ask about it. She's the one with the Sight. And I must admit to more than a passing curiosity as to why it all seems to be happening here again, in Flammark."

"Maybe it has something to do with the curse. When it left, perhaps it created some kind of, oh, I don't know … a vacuum?"

"What, for other crap to take its place?" She stared at him. He couldn't be serious. She could feel the thump of her heart. Please, God, let it not be true. "Will, I … I don't know if I can go through all that again."

"Let's not get ahead of ourselves, shall we? We're going to have to talk to Abigail, see if we can tease any more out of her. And she'll have to be told about Gabby."

"I know." Emma rolled her eyes. "Leave it to me. I'll call her. Meantime, Gabby will be fine here, with you. Do you think anything can be done for her? You know, about her getting her … power back?"

"Don't ask me," he snickered "I haven't yet joined the ranks of the angels and have no intention of trying. Not after I've finished murdering a certain dean. Seriously, though, I don't think there's much anyone can do—except to offer the usual platitudes—and they can't begin to speak to the scale of her loss. I'll sit with her." He sighed and grimaced, "The irony is, thanks to Anthony Saint Bloody Saviour, I have the time." He frowned. "Now Peter's here."

"I thought you got on with him—Peter, that is."

"Oh, I do. I'd ... I'd simply prefer that he wasn't here. It's made everything so much more ... difficult. I don't feel the bishop trusts me any more."

Emma waited for elucidation, but received none. Sensing they'd exhausted their conversation, she made to leave. "Okay, I'll be on my way. I'll pop in to say goodbye to Gabby on the way out and will let you know how things go with Abigail."

Will left his desk and joined her. Never had a man looked so in need of a hug. Before she knew it, and with an easy familiarity that surprised her, Emma put her arms around him, offering the comfort he so obviously needed. She could feel a sigh catch in his throat. "I'm sure it will all come right, Will. At least I hope it will. Everything's just happened all at once."

He let go, eyes glinting with a sudden moisture. "Go. I'll be all right. Speak to Abigail."

She left him to find Gabby. Finding her once more unresponsive, staring at her spot, Emma knelt by her chair for a few minutes. Garnering the distinct impression that Gabby wanted nothing else than to be left alone, she briefly squeezed her friend's hand before taking her leave.

Head in turmoil, Emma made her way over the green to her cottage. It was all going to hell again, and once more she was right in the middle of it.

Shit, shit, shit.

❧ 12 ❧

CATCHING UP

A s soon as she got back from the vicarage, Emma rang Abigail. Since the girl didn't pick up, she had no choice but to leave a message asking her to call back as soon as possible. Important, but nothing to worry about.

An hour later, having heard nothing, she decided to try her at home. Josie answered.

"I'm sorry, Emma. She came in about six and went straight out again."

"Oh, I left her a message. She usually gets right back to me."

"Yeah, well …she's been really off these past few weeks. Not her usual self at all. I keep asking her what's wrong, but she just snaps at me."

Abigail never snapped at her mother. Emma frowned as Josie babbled on.

"She's friendly with the man who owns a caravan park in Ledbridge. She called him Why or Way … or something—I can't remember. She went to see him a fortnight ago and hasn't been the same since. I think there must have been a falling-out."

"A fortnight ago? Not like her to nurse bad feelings."

"No, I know. But she won't be drawn."

"Okay, I'll have a go when I see her. Can you ask her to ring me as soon as she can?" Emma racked her brains to think of something that would signal the urgency without spelling it out. "Tell her … tell her Will needs to speak with her too."

"I'll let her know as soon as she gets in. I wouldn't hold my breath about her getting back to you tonight, though."

Emma wondered what could have happened. Fiercely protective of her mother, Abigail was never moody or funny with her.

She rang Will.

"Em! Did you get hold of Abigail?"

"Not exactly." She got him up to speed.

"I wonder what's got into her? Back in the day, she used to cause Josie all manner of worry, but nowadays she's very careful not to."

"My thoughts exactly. Hopefully I'll be able to get to the bottom of it when—if—she rings back. How's Gabby?"

"Much the same when you saw her earlier on. Still in her chair, though I think she managed to doze off once or twice. As you said, there's only so much a body can take. The poor woman's exhausted."

"Shall I come over? Talk to her again?"

"Don't be offended, but I think … not. We need to give her time and space to adjust. Besides, if Abigail rings you later, what's the betting she'll hare it over. I'm not sure Gabby'll be able to cope."

"I've been thinking about that. I might not tell her over the phone what's actually happened. What are you doing after lunch tomorrow? I could ask her to come here, break the news, then walk over to yours."

"Splendid idea. The next coachload of visitors isn't due until Monday. We've only two other people in at the moment—new ordinands—so we should get some quality time to ourselves."

"And Peter's there, of course, if anything comes up."

"Well, no, actually. He only stays here Tuesday to Friday. The rest of the time I'm being allowed to fly solo. In my own bloody vicarage!"

Emma offered a charity laugh. "Ah well, it might not be for long. Peter's not happy with the situation, either."

"You … you don't think he's going to leave, do you?"

"Isn't that what you want?"

The line fell silent for a few moments, then Will replied, "Mixed feelings. I certainly don't want him to feel he has to leave the diocese, and certainly not on my account. He's been so settled, and he loves the cathedral library." His tone changed. "This new—" Will almost spat out the title, "—dean is arriving. I'm very glad Peter will be here to help sort him out. I'll be avoiding him as much as humanly possible."

Her laugh was genuine this time. "Okay, you get back to Gabby. I'll deal with Abigail and hopefully come over some time tomorrow afternoon."

Poor Will. Emma felt for him. As priest-in-charge of St Jude's he'd proved conscientious and popular. The villagers loved him. The rise of the vicarage as an attraction for both academics and tourists had been managed sensitively and efficiently and its growing importance to the diocese as a place of research and retreat had been entirely down to his hard work. She could see how Peter's appointment made him feel undermined. Possibly even threatened.

Wondering when Abigail would deign to call, she decided not to wait around stressing about it. Probably best to get a bite to eat; maybe spend the cool of the evening doing a bit of weeding.

After soup and a sandwich, donning a pair of gardening gloves and carrying a plastic trug, Emma stepped outside and knelt with a hand fork over one of the tiny flower beds. She loved the small patch of land which fronted the cottage. Though calling it a garden might be an understatement, it offered the only control she had over her landscape. Aside from a small access path, the rear of the cottage backed onto open fields. How different to the three-bedroomed terrace her parents had left her. After her mum died, and the broken-hearted Josiah not long afterwards, she'd enjoyed setting about a renovation that included its two large gardens. But that was before Ben came on the scene.

She shuddered; regretted, now, that she hadn't sought counselling earlier. Robbie had rung his colleague in Sand-marsh and learned she'd have to wait at least a month for an appointment. The way Ben kept invading her thoughts had to stop. She *had* to move on.

She was startled away from her thoughts by the creak of her garden gate.

"Abigail!" she exclaimed, with some relief. "I rang your mum. She—"

"I know," she replied, her face like thunder. "She told me. What's up?"

Wow. Josie had been right. Abigail was not a happy pudding. This was going to make things even more difficult.

Clambering to her feet, Emma replied, "Let's have some-thing to drink first. I presume you walked it here since you look a bit ... hot. Tea? Chamomile? Lemon Grass?" She grinned. "Why not push the boat out and have a go at Straw-berry Serenade? You haven't tried that yet."

Abigail's frown deepened. "No thanks. I'm not in a straw-berry mood." Then, as if sensing she'd overdone the moodiness, she relented slightly. "I might be able to go with peppermint."

They walked into the house together, Emma mentally orientating herself to breaking her news in such a way that it wouldn't upset Abigail any further. She didn't want her running across the green to poor Gabby, especially in this temper. Their reunion would need to be a carefully controlled explosion.

Once she'd installed Abigail at the kitchen table, Emma said, "So … Josie tells me you've been a bit low this week. Was it because of what happened on the Tor?"

"No. Not really."

"She said you'd been to see a friend?"

"I wish she'd keep her nose out of my business."

Emma bit back a retort. Whatever bugged her friend, criticism would only make it worse, though she couldn't let the comment go completely. "Bit harsh?"

Abigail sighed. She nodded as she flicked back her hair to take a sip from the steaming cup. "Yeah. You're right. Not her fault."

"Whose fault, then?"

She huffed and shrugged. Rolling her eyes in acquiescence, she began, "His name's Wyland. I've known him for ages, and I thought he was a good friend. He lives out in Wood End and is in a bit of trouble. Got in Westen's bad books, actually."

"Westen?" Trying to ignore how her blood surged at the unexpected mention of his name, Emma frowned before remembering. "Oh, yes. He said something about having gone out there. Something about a body?"

Abigail nodded but, retreating back into herself, refused to say any more.

Emma tried something else. "You *thought* he was a good friend? Come on, Abby. You said this happened a while ago.

It must have been something major to have stayed with you for this long."

"Yeah. It was. I went to see him the day after the thing on the Tor but … oh, it's a long story."

"I've got the time."

The girl blew on the steaming liquid and took a sip. As if she'd been asked to pull out all her teeth, she told Emma about the gruesome discovery at Wood End, and how it might have happened because of the tremor. She described the caravan park and Wyland's cottage, which had this amazing room with books and maps and things, and how they'd talked for ages about stuff.

On a roll now, Abigail continued, "It's as if he knew me, Ems! You know, really *knew* me … what I wanted to be. He lent me some books."

"He sounds nice."

She must have sensed where Emma was going with this. "He is. But not like *that*. I don't fancy him. He's too old, for a start. He's at least forty."

Emma suppressed a grin at that. "What were the books about?"

"One's by a writer called Hutton. I'm reading it now. It's about how our thinking about paganism has been shaped, by politics and that."

"So, what did this Wyland do to make you so upset?"

"I think the body they found was special in some way. Wyland called it a sentinel. We got interrupted. Bal—the pathologist—took the remains away before I could get him to explain. When I asked him about it later—" Her eyes welled up. "He dissed me. Totally dissed me. Said I was just a kid and that I'd only get in the way." Her chin trembled as her tears spilled over. "I'm not a kid! I'm not! I haven't been able to get it out of my mind. He really upset me."

"Oh, Abigail, I'm sorry." Emma found her friend's hand

and squeezed it. "I'm sure he didn't mean it. Sounds like he'd been having a pig of a day."

"Yeah," Abigail's breath came in hitches. "But h-he shouldn't have said that. I-I'm not just a kid. I was l-learning loads from h-him. Since Gabby left, I've had no one to h-h-help me."

Emma sprung up and tore off a few sheets of kitchen roll.

Sitting down, choosing her words very carefully as she offered Abigail the tissue, she began, "I've got some news for you that may cheer you up, but before I say anything, I want you to promise me something."

Abigail took a sheet and blew her nose, then another, folding it to use the edge to wipe under her eyes. Emma tried not to smile. The damage to her kohl liner was totally irreparable.

"I'll try. W-what is it?"

"When I've finished talking, I do not want you to budge from this table."

It took a few more moments for the tears to dry up and her sobs to subside. Eventually, Abigail said, "Okay. I'm listening."

"Gabby's back."

Abigail froze. Her eyes, still glistening, widened. "Omigod! She's *here*?!"

Emma grinned and nodded. So far so good. "She's not how you remember her, though. She's … changed."

"Changed? Changed how?"

"She's … one of us."

"One of us?" said Abigail. "I don't understand."

"She … isn't an angel anymore. Michael, he …"

"He what?" She swapped her quizzical expression as the truth dawned. "No. No. Don't tell me. He had her bloody desanctified, didn't he? She was worried he might. All along he thought she'd lost her objectivity. What did he call it? A loss of … dispassion. That's it. A loss of dispassion. He was good to me. Well, tolerated me because of Gabby. We never had a … relationship as such. Angels aren't supposed to have relationships." She rummaged under the table for her bag. "I've got to go. Got to see her. Where is she? At Will's?"

"Abby!" The sharpness in Emma's voice must have pierced through. Abigail paused before letting go of her bag.

"I know I promised, but I can't stay, Ems."

"Hear me out first."

Abigail relaxed slightly but held Emma's gaze; a bird about to take off.

"She's been at the vicarage since Thursday night. She was waiting for Will on the bench outside when he returned from Evensong. He wants to keep things as calm and quiet as possible. She's in a terrible state—heartbroken. I agree with him. It was bad enough seeing her this afternoon; God knows what state she must have been in when she arrived."

"I have to go, Emma. I've got to see her. She'll want to see me."

"Yes. We know. Just … not today. She's only just started to learn how to sleep and she's exhausted. She hasn't been eating, either. She's needs to understand how to—"

"—be human." Abigail dropped her bag and picked up her drink. "Has she asked for me?"

"She hasn't spoken very much at all. She's very into herself, Abby. You know, depressed."

Abigail sat still, mulling over the news. "If I hadn't been so into myself, so selfish, I probably would have picked all this up."

"Will and I have been wondering about that. It seems too much of a coincidence that you had that episode on the Tor— so awful it made you throw up—then Gabby arrives. There must be a link, and from what you said she may well be in some kind of danger. I think we should see her together, but before we do, is there any chance you could get your Sight onto it? Maybe find out more?"

"I'll try," replied Abigail, sitting back. "Though it did make me feel really sick that morning—I had a migraine all day. I'll see if I can work the orb. Since I got it at Christmas, I've only managed to squeeze a few faint images out of it, so I know it works. Other than that, it's been a bit pants. I don't know whether it's because it doesn't have anything to tell me or whether I'm just useless at it." Her chin trembled. "I think that's why I've been so upset. As Wyland reminded me, I'm not much more than a kid." Then, straightening her shoulders, she threw her hair back. "I'll have another go with it tonight. What with the Tor, this sentinel thing at Wood End and now Gabby being back, it can't all be coincidence."

"Will wants us to go over tomorrow after lunch."

"Okay. I'll get here about two-ish. Let's hope I'll have something to report."

13

THE ORB

It took Abigail nearly half an hour to persuade her mum to go and meet her mates at the Flammark Arms. Josie had got it into her head that her daughter was in such a moody state that she shouldn't be left on her own.

"I'm terrified you're gonna take off, like you did last year."

"Don't be daft, Mum. I'm not going to do anything silly. I'm sorry for having been such a pain, I've just been a bit fed up, that's all."

"You sure? I don't know what I'd do if you left me like that again. Six months you were gone, Abby! Six months and not a word!"

"I know and I'm sorry again, for all the worry I put you through. But I was younger in my head then. Things are different now. I feel good about myself and you're getting your life back. You should enjoy every minute." She broke into a grin. "Besides, Jiggy's on. It's your favourite folk group. You can't miss them."

"Well, only if you're sure you're okay. I have been looking forward to the band."

"I'm positive. I'm going to have an early night. I've got some … reading to do."

Still looking uncertain, Josie went upstairs. A few minutes later she was down again, hair mussed, lips glossed, flashing her daughter a how-do-I-look expression.

"Wow! Is that a new tee-shirt? That colour really suits you. You look fab. Now … go!"

Josie slammed the door shut, leaving Abigail to herself in the tiny living room, heaving a sigh of relief. Truth be told, she hadn't been totally motivated by the need to make sure her mum got the social life she deserved. She needed quiet. The last thing she wanted was the telly blaring through the ceiling.

Ambling into the kitchen, she made herself a cup of green tea. Good for focus. She needed all the help she could get since concentration had definitely been a problem in the past. After the message she'd received loud and clear from the Tor, it was vital she got her act together now Gabby had returned. After drinking the beverage, she climbed the stairs.

Abigail loved her room and had gone to great pains to have it exactly how she needed it. She'd always loved purple and had pleaded with her dad to paint it all a lurid shade of goth puce. Having returned from her 'disappearance' last year, even she thought it a bit over the top so she redecorated it herself, choosing a pretty shade of lilac. It set off the black metal frame of her queen-sized bed to perfection, and the three framed Glennie Kindred prints she'd hung over it, bought with her very first wage. A small, distressed-white painted dressing table rested beneath the window, festooned with make-up cases, jewellery boxes, bangles and pendant trees. Every inch of the room had been utilised, except for her newest acquisition, a bookcase to the side of her bed. The books Wyland had lent her were its only occupants.

Out of respect for her sacred space, standing at its threshold, Abigail slipped off her shoes. She drew the plain, dark-purple curtains and lit her candles before sitting on the bed, facing the wall between the two deep closets that lined the alcoves. High up, she'd pasted a huge poster of the Goddess. Below this rested another old table, rescued from one of Sandmarsh's many fleamarkets. Its twisted and knotted grain would have won even Wyland's approval. It made the perfect altar.

Dead centre, unencumbered by fuss or decoration, waited the orb.

She remained sitting until her mood calmed and her breathing steadied, as free from mental encumbrance as she could manage. Then, rising from the bed, she pulled out a padded stool from beneath the altar table and sat on it, straight-backed. The orb had been Gabby's gift to her last Christmas, and she'd spent whatever time she could, when the house was quiet, learning how to attune herself to it. Globes like this were usually made of simple glass. Spherical objects used for decoration by wannabe witches. Not hers. This one had been carved and shaped out of pure, clear, ancient quartz that had taken millennia to form. Such was the age of its memories.

Abigail had developed a ritual when she wanted to approach her oracle. Getting it right now, tonight, couldn't be more imperative. She knew in her bones something was wrong. Imminent. A pressure had been building at the base of her skull ever since that morning on the Tor, and it had got worse after Wyland mentioned a sentinel. When she saw him lying on the ground, as if *listening* to the earth, the doomy feeling had intensified further. She'd tried to ring him, left messages …

Now Gabby.

Her nights on the Tor with the two angels had taught her that everything was connected; that deepening her Sight entailed fathoming networks, understanding the forces at work. She knew the orb would help her—*knew it*—but so far it hadn't deemed her a worthy enough companion. She had to persuade it she was not 'just a girl'.

Spreading out her elbows, placing one upward-facing palm over the other, Abigail bent over and rested her forehead upon them. Closed her eyes. She altered her breathing, the out breath longer than the in. Out. In. Out.

Empty your mind.

Calm the chatter in your head.

Listen to your heartbeats.

Hear the silence in between.

In. Out. In. Out.

In.

Out.

In …

Her breath became a metronome. Soon Abigail could hear nothing but its slow beat, soothing the hurt Wyland had caused, calming her fears for Gabby. Heart rate slowed, her breaths like sighs, she existed on a plane of rhythmic silence, her mind quieted, focussed on the crystal sphere.

She'd reached this point before, the moment when she'd lift her head and open her eyes to gaze into the glass. About to do so again, she paused as a pinprick of light appeared within the black. Slowly—imperceptibly—it grew, filling her mind's eye with the orb in facsimile, resting in its place on her altar below the Goddess.

She swallowed, keeping her respiration even, her eyes closed, parking her excitement at the breakthrough next to her dread at losing the connection.

The image continued its expansion, growing towards her until her senses felt its glassy wall.

Then she breached it.

Abigail, in the orb, had become the orb.

She breathed on.

Nothing at first. Then, mist. It came in a roiling circularity, gathering apace, the movement reflecting the curved space that enveloped her—and it. Real mist. Tangible.

Cold.

Then … arms around her. Someone whispering a susurration that swirled deep in her mind's ear. *Keep down. Don't move. Don't look, and for God's sake, don't listen.*

Spirit fingers tugged at her hair, nudged at her flesh, trying to insinuate into her.

Terror raced her heart, ragged her breath. She fought it, tried to keep it at the slow regulation, but it was too strong, her fear, too powerful.

The orb let go. Suddenly she was back to black with not even a pinprick of light. She swallowed, saliva coming thick and fast just as it had on the Tor. She mustn't be sick … mustn't. Eyes tight shut, she tried to stick with it, tried to get back into the orb but it was useless. The connection had been broken.

Fazed, hardly aware of her surroundings, Abigail tore herself away from the real orb just in time to reach the bathroom before the vomit overtook her. Retching, shaking with shock, she hugged the toilet bowl, still feeling fingers in her hair, pushes on her skin.

Gaining some equilibrium, still trembling, she turned on the shower and threw off her clothes, praying the hot water would cleanse her mind as well as her body.

She stayed until her fingers pruned.

Calmed—but by no means calm—she turned off the water and reached for a towel, drying her hair with it before wrapping it around her. Grabbing the edges of the sink underneath the steamed-up bathroom mirror, she smeared it with the back of her hand, half-wondering what kind of image would look back at her.

Still her. Still Abby.

Dismissing her foolishness, still feeling weird but slightly better, she bent down to bin her discarded clothes in the laundry basket.

It took some courage to return to her bedroom. Just as with the mirror, she wondered if it would all look the same. That was some trick the orb had pulled. It had completely messed with her perspective.

Some relief, then, that everything seemed completely normal. Her bed, bookcase, dressing table—all as it should be. Heaving a sigh of relief, she turned to the crystal.

And gasped.

Quietly, she rummaged in her drawers for underwear, then in the closet for an old pair of jeans. She used the towel on her hair again and fingered it through so it would air-dry untangled.

She needed her hiking boots. They'd be in the cupboard under the stairs.

Down she went to find them in their usual place. Did she need a coat? No. It was a warm night, and there'd be a lot of walking. She strode into the kitchen to leave Josie the least frightening note she could think of.

Sorry, mum, had to go out.
I need to help a friend, so I'll be staying over at hers, there's no need to wait up.

I PROMISE you there's no need to worry.

Love you!

Abby xxx

Grabbing the tiny plastic torch that always sat on the hall windowsill, she made her way out of the house, slamming the door behind her …

… leaving the orb upstairs looking for all the world like a cheap snowglobe at rest, displaying a stunning three-dimensional tableau of the overturned caravan at the well of Wyland's park.

❧ 14 ❧

NIGHT TERRORS

It took Abigail nearly an hour to get to Wyland's. There being no taxi companies in Flammark, she'd had an anxious wait for one coming all the way out from Sandmarsh. Finally turning up, it had delivered her both nervy and anxious. Not wanting the driver to drop her in Wyland's courtyard, she plumped for halfway down Wood End's mile-long access road.

"You sure you're okay being dropped here, miss?" he said, turning on the internal light as he took payment.

No. But she didn't have much choice if she wanted to avoid a difficult reception. Going for casual cheerfulness, she'd pointed randomly into the woods. "Oh yes. We're staying in that cabin." The driver had craned his neck past her, presumably to see signs of any kind of light or life coming from the direction she indicated.

"It's all right," she said hastily, as she opened the door to climb out. "They'll be asleep. They must have forgotten to leave a light on for me. See, I've got a torch." She held it aloft lamely, not blaming the driver one iota for the dubious look he gave her, especially as it was only about half-ten. No way would anyone she knew be in bed at this time. Not that he could do anything about it, for, by now, she'd left the car. Giving a shrug and an uncertain "Okay ... " he checked his job menu on the dash, turned off the light and drove off.

She walked the final half-mile without the benefit of street lighting. Normally that wouldn't have bothered her; she liked the dark, and, clear sky allowing, could use the skills Gabby and Michael had taught her to navigate by the stars. This night was different. Already weirded out by the orb, she could have done with something more comfortingly halogen to light her way other than mother moon and a flimsy plastic torch.

The police 'No Entry' sign still stood at the entrance to the park. Wyland hadn't been allowed to reopen it to visitors, then. Desperate not to raise an alarm, she slipped noiselessly past, only to suppress a shriek on hearing a click and finding the courtyard suddenly bathed in yellow light. Damn. Motion-activated security lighting.

As quickly and quietly as her boots would allow, she ran past the stone cottage and headed towards the park and down, veering off the road to hide behind a caravan. Heart thumping, fully expecting to see Wyland come barging out, after a while all she heard was the light clicking off and no sign of him. Maybe he'd gone out.

She waited in the dark for another five long minutes. Deciding the coast was clear, she left the van and wound her way down the narrow road until she came to the spot where they'd exhumed the remains. She could risk the torch now, since she was way out of the sightline of Wyland's cottage at the top of the slope.

Though pretty pathetic, the beam was strong enough to illuminate the scale of the erupted earth and the outlandish image of the turned-over caravan next to it. Odd that Wy hadn't craned it out yet. Despite the heat in the night air, she shivered, all her senses screaming at her to walk away. Yet she could see no movement, nothing that should be causing her so much anxiety. So why had the crystal shown her this scene?

A noise.

Abigail cocked her head, straining to interpret and locate the sound, probing the dark with her silly torch. Nothing. Something. Enough to make the hairs on her arm rise.

To her relief, a pathway caught the light, leading upwards into the woods.

The sound again.

She snapped off the torch and with only the moonlight to guide her, ran up the path and swerved sideways between a bank of hawthorn and a huge tree, partly hollowed out. A perfect hiding place.

Not so perfect. After taking one step forward, Abigail stopped dead. She'd clearly stumbled into a child's favourite spot, for at the base of the tree lay a discarded circle of dolls, no less, complete with tiny eyes fixing their implacably black gaze upon her, daring her to gatecrash their tea party.

No bloody way was she sitting there.

Instead, crouching down, she shuffled towards the hedge and peered through a convenient gap. The hairs on her arms still at full tilt—the dolls behind her not helping at all— Abigail's stomach churned as she strained to hear the noise again. No. *No!* Get a grip, *get a grip*. She must not throw up again.

Out of nowhere something clamped over her mouth. Eyes wide and frantic, she struggled against it, her cries compressed into tiny, futile whimpers. She felt rather than saw a face loom next to her.

"Sh...shhh. I'm not going to hurt you," came a shouting whisper. "It's me, Wyland. What the *hell* are you doing here, Abs?" Though her struggles lessened, Abigail didn't completely let up, and tried to speak through his palm. "Shut up!" he hissed. "You've already made enough commotion. You *have* to be quiet. I'm going to take my hand away. Okay?"

She nodded.

His hand slowly losing its grip, she turned around in fury, crying out, "What the—"

The clamp returned.

"Shhhh! Keep your voice down! I'm going to take my hand away again. Do not ignore me, understand?"

She nodded again and Wyland once more dropped his grip.

Sub-whispering, she mouthed, "Why are you down here?"

Before she got an answer, Wyland jerked his head and, crouching lower, peered through the gap. "Did you hear that?"

She strained to listen and this time heard an almost imperceptible mewling. High-pitched, agonised, tortured. Like a kitten in pain.

Wyland gripped her shoulder. "Get up. Get into the tree hollow."

"I … I can't. The dolls—"

With a cry of frustration he hoiked her up and, crunching over the toys, pushed her down and backwards into the tree. "Get right in. As far as you can. Quick." Without demur, she did as he asked, the wails whining louder, echoing around the well of the park. Eyes glued to the gap, Abigail gasped to see tendrils of vapour rise from the hole in the ground, growing in density as if by fuelled by some raging underground fire.

Wyland threw himself down in front of Abigail, obstructing her view. "Hold my hands," he hissed. "Keep down. Don't move. Don't look, and for God's sake don't listen to the howls. Do you understand?"

Heart battering, the atmosphere charged and brittle, Abigail did as he asked, barely grasping that she was being called to enact in the flesh what had been in her head only an hour or so ago. How was she not supposed to listen? Grabbing hold of him, she took no reassurance as his clammy fingers encircled hers. Cold now, teeth chattering and shaking, she drew in closer.

The atmosphere thickened. Abigail took quick, shallow breaths, determined to keep the smog out of her lungs. The mewling changed frequency, ramping into an orgasm of wailing sighs, loud, louder, so loud as to wake all Flammark. Too terrified to give voice—even if she could—she prayed Wyland knew what he was doing, for every sense she possessed screamed their mortal danger.

The air moved. Slowly at first, then violently. Wyland uncrossed his legs and drew even closer towards her, and without even thinking to struggle she leant-in further to him. As the howling increased, the wind turned cyclonic, whipping and grabbing at their hair, lifting Abigail's above her head; a black sheet of tangled braids. Their grip tightened as, in forced intimacy, they entwined themselves in each other, heads burrowed deep into their chests.

Unable to control her breathing, only managing short, shallow pants, Abigail fought for equilibrium, knowing she mustn't lose control, mustn't let anything in, mustn't listen. *Trust the Orb. Trust the Orb. Trust the Orb.*

It must have been the rhythmic tones of the mantra, for suddenly, in the black behind her eyelids, she saw a pinprick of light grow.

In a heartbeat it expanded, and she was transported next to the fallen caravan, in and of the crystal again, a protected witness to the circling, frantic wind that churned the miasma, roiling and dividing it into a multitude of swirling, screaming shapes. More sucked out from the ground, birthing upwards in hideous abandon. Following the arc of orb that now encompassed the landscape, they dove and cavorted, circling the park, shrieking their delight as they wound around cabins, caravans and trees.

Around Wyland and her corporeal self.

Somewhere she felt her physical, terrified body cling onto Wyland, desperate for protection against the spirit horde. Her psyche felt none of that. Sharing the orb's plane, her focus on the outside manifestations—that by some miracle she had become part of—remained clear and sharp.

Calm.

As if constituted by the very air itself, the shapes began to solidify. Became bone. Skeleton. Hundreds of them, sinking to the earth, taking flesh, hitting the ground naked, as with dancing leaps they scattered into the woods.

After what seemed hours, but probably only about fifteen minutes, the wails finally lessened, the air warmed and the atmosphere lost its charge. The scene disappearing into a pinprick, Abigail reconnected with herself, shocked at the sudden physicality of her breath and the sense of being held. And her fear.

Her diminishing fear.

As her senses returned, she began to relax and could feel Wyland doing the same. Gradually, slowly, they peeled themselves away from each other.

Wyland sat back, propped up on his long arms, face raised to the skies. Abigail tried to stand, but her legs shook too much and she tumbled back down. Despite the returning warmth, she couldn't stop shivering. Tearing his eyes away from the stars, Wyland took off his jacket and wrapped it around her shoulders.

Grateful, Abigail took it, then saw his face in a shaft of moonlight. "God, Wyland. You look as if you need it more than I do. Your face is like a slab of marble."

"Thanks. It feels like one."

"Is it over? Have they gone?"

"Yes, I think so. For now."

"W-what were they?"

"Not sure."

She hunkered into his jacket, staring around for a lurking monstrosity.

"So … how did you know?"

"I didn't. That is, I didn't know exactly what or when something was going to happen, but I did expect an emergence. I've been keeping watch ever since the day you came over."

"I saw you. After you threw me out. You came out of your cottage and got down on the ground."

He said nothing.

"Wyland, tell me! What's going on?"

He gave her a long look. Sighed. "I will. But not now. It's way too complicated and we're both shattered. And you, girl, look in shock. I should take you home. Does your mother know you're out?"

"By now she will. I left her a note." She finally managed to get to her feet. Swaying a little, she said, "I don't think I can go back tonight. I'm too wobbly and it'd scare her. I wrote I'd be back in the morning. Please, Wyland, can I stay with you? You've no idea what I've been through, even before I came. I'll sleep on the sofa."

He sighed. "Okay. You're right, I can't take you home in this state. And yes, you will take the sofa. Can you walk, or shall I carry you?"

"I think I can walk, but I might need to hold your arm."

He scrabbled around and found the torch he must have discarded when the spirits came. It was much sturdier, than hers. Switching it on, he lent her the crook of his elbow as its strong beam found the path that would lead them out of the bushes. As they walked up to the house, Abigail asked, "Why did you say those things to me? The last time I came?"

"Yeah, I've been feeling guilty about that." He pushed in his elbow, giving the arm he held within it a gentle squeeze. I wanted to protect you, get you away. I knew something was coming but not what. I didn't want to get you involved."

"Too bloody late for that. What were those things?"

"Shit. You didn't look, did you? I told you not to look."

"I didn't need to. The orb showed me."

Wyland screwed up his face. "The orb?"

"Yes. A bit like a crystal ball, but turns out its more than that. My friend, Gabby, gave it to me before she went away. I did tell you about it, but that was months ago. It's supposed to help me focus the Sight. I've not been doing so well with it, to be honest, but since the tremor, and ... other stuff ... I sensed something was off. So I had a session with it earlier."

"And it showed you something?"

"With a vengeance! I wanted it to give me a clue about something me and Ems are worried about." Nearly at the top of the path, she got Wyland to stop. Turning, she pointed to the dead caravan. "Instead it showed me that. Clear as day." She looked up at him, trying to gauge his expression in the torchlight. "Are you sure you have no idea what they were?"

"You're not going to let it rest, are you?"

"Nope."

"Truth be told? Like I said, I don't have a clue, but with a sentinel down, something was bound to come through. All I know is that whatever they are, they're out. In our world. On my watch."

"A sentinel? You never explained what you meant by that."

He turned to the house. "I'll explain later. We both need a drink." Pushing stray locks out of her face, he added, "... and a few repairs."

"It's going to be bad, isn't it?"

"Yes."

"You're … different from us in some way, aren't you?"

"… Yes."

"And the park?"

"Basically, a front. Honestly, Abs, let's talk about it inside. I need to get my own head around it all too."

Ignoring him, she looked down at the other caravans. Unoccupied, equidistantly spaced in their circle. Six, seven, including the one on its side.

"There's something special about that group of vans, isn't there?"

Wyland sighed and shook his head her. "Abs, you're the complete limit. Yes, there is. If you must know, and I suppose you absolutely must, they aren't just caravans."

"Come again?"

Another exasperated sigh.

"They're a henge."

🦋 15 🦋

VISITATION

Hardly able to bear her own company, Emma waited for Abigail on the bench under her window, desperate for something other than four walls to look at. She'd taken the last of her sleeping pills two nights ago and was now total hostage to insomnia.

It was exhausting.

As if that weren't enough, memories of the recent past had come raging back, haunting her as she tossed and turned, playing visions of Ben's abuse against the emaciated monster he'd become, and who was finally ended. By Westen. Abrasive, insensitive, arrogant Westen. Assured, centred, steadfast Westen. A man who irritated her to death and yet one with whom she'd never felt so secure. He wouldn't suffocate her or take away her independence. He'd encourage her, make sure she'd live her own life, respect her striving to become.

She needed a partner like this; wanted a partner like this. Could love a partner like this.

Did love?

"Gawd, Emma, you look worse than you did yesterday."

"Abigail!" Emma started from her reverie. "You made me jump." Surprised by her friend's pale face, she said, "You don't look so good yourself. Are you okay?"

"Yeah. Just tired. I had a hell of a night. Believe me. I'll tell you about it later. I'm not up for it now." She took a seat next to Emma. "You were miles away. Have you spoken with Robbie yet? Got more pills?"

"Yes and no. I followed your advice and agreed to take some counselling. He thinks the insomnia is probably caused by ... you know ... trauma, though he thought it unwise to prescribe any more sleeping tablets 'til I've seen someone."

"Tch. Have another conversation with him. You can't carry on like this. It'll be a while before you get an appointment, I bet."

"He hoped his colleague could squeeze me in this week. No go. The world's suddenly gone mad, apparently. He's fully booked for the next month." She quivered out a sigh. "But you're right. I'm going to have to talk to Robbie again, though I'm not convinced pills are the answer. They still make me feel tired. I'm really crabby at work. The patients have started to notice." She frowned. "They give me funny looks."

Abigail sat next to her, draped an arm around Emma's shoulders, and tried for a chuckle. "Paranoid too! Poor you. If there's anything I can do to help, you know, talk stuff through? Have you seen any more of Westen?"

Emma rolled her eyes. "Nope. He's not been here since he came over that day. He won't be back. I've blown it."

"Maybe you can go to him? Ring him. Arrange something."

"I might do. When I've got the energy." She smiled and then frowned again at Abigail's paleness. "I have to say, you really don't look a hundred per cent. You said you were going to spend last night working with the orb. Did it go okay?"

"Long story, Ems, long story." Twisting her head to glance at Emma's wristwatch, she continued, "Way too complicated for now, and you've enough on your plate. Let's go. It's nearly two."

Emma took a few minutes to get her bag and lock up, then arm-in-arm they strolled over the green. She got Abigail up to speed with what was happening with Will and Peter—this dean—and they chatted on about it, the lewdly carved corbels on the roofline of the church watching them as they rounded the back of the building.

Changing the subject, Abigail said, "I'm nervous. Do you think Gabby will want to see me?"

"I think so. I talked to Will this morning. She managed some sleep yesterday—lucky Gabby—though he thinks she's still very depressed. He hasn't been able to get her to eat anything. Maybe you can help with that."

"I hope so. I'll do my best."

Lulled by warmth and companionship, they walked through the church's ancient graveyard, its massive headstones mossed and leaning, some planted centuries ago. Emma loved it as she loved everything about St Jude's—which seemed an irony. Her ancestors were buried in this beautiful place; a line dominated by males, afflicted by the Blackstone curse that had subjected their wives and daughters to unspeakable horrors and which had wanted the same for her, through Ben. Terrible people they might have been, but they were *her* terrible people.

Despite her tiredness, as they strolled to the vicarage Abigail's idle chatter soothed and refreshed her. It left her completely unprepared for the murderous look in Will's eyes as he met them at the door. He must have been looking out for them, appearing before Emma had the chance to ring the porch bell.

"Thank God you're here. Everything's all gone to bloody pot."

"Why?" Emma replied, a gentle scoff in her tone at Will's tendency towards overstatement.

He looked behind him and shut the door. "He's here. Saint Bloody Saviour. He came to Sunday Eucharist. Said he'd decided to come early because someone had cancelled on him. Rather than twiddling his thumbs until next week when Peter could deal with him, he descended on us early."

With a grimace of a smile, he turned to Abigail. "Sorry Abby. I'm being unconscionably rude. It's great to see you. Sorry I'm in such a flap."

"Oh, don't worry. Everyone seems to be cross lately, even me! It's been a while. Great to see you too." They gave each other a brief hug and a huge double air-kiss. Emma chortled. When had they started doing that?

"Emma got me up to speed with what's going on with you. This dean, he's bad then?"

"Awful. Bloody awful. I shouldn't say this as a paid servant of Christ, but he's creepy as hell. 'Someone cancelled on him,' my left foot. He wanted to catch me unprepared, find my measure, trip me up. Slimy b—"

Abigail interrupted. "Ems was telling me about him. He wants to change everything?"

Will nodded and plunged his hands deep into the pockets of his black trousers. He usually changed into civvies after the service unless anything else was in the diary. St Saviour had obviously kept him too busy for that.

"He's been here less than half a day and already I can't stand the man."

"This isn't like you," said Emma. "He can't be that bad, surely?"

"You're going to have the pleasure of meeting him, so you

can judge for yourself." He huffed. "Come on. Can't put it off any longer. He's in the library."

"How's Gabby?" said Abigail. "I can't wait to see her."

"You might have to. I haven't told him about her."

Abigail looked surprised. "You're *hiding* her from him? Why? Surely he couldn't object to you having a personal friend to stay? The vicarage *is* your home, isn't it?"

"Of course, it is! Having friends staying is no issue. But it'll become one if she stays long-term. We've no idea how this is all going to pan out. Having met him, something tells me he'll know there's something up. He's got a nose for trouble, and I don't want her upset by prying questions. She's a bit better, but not that much better."

"What will you do if their paths cross? Lie?" asked Abigail, half-teasing.

"Absolutely. Through my bloody teeth. I've asked her to stay in her room upstairs while he's here, but I don't think that's good for her." He sighed and shook his head. "It's a problem. She needs a sanctuary, and I'm not sure this is it."

"Hopefully he won't be here for long," said Emma.

"I wouldn't count on it. He wants to use us as a base, remember? The first thing he asked for was the books. He wants me to account for every conference, visitor, expense— you name it. He's thorough. *Very* thorough."

Glancing at each other with raised eyebrows, the two women followed him inside. As usual, the faint, familiar scent of church incense greeted them. Will never used it in the house, but years of High Anglican services had ingrained it in his clothes. It had become part of his scent. Today, Emma detected something new. She couldn't quite place it. Something like oil, or tar.

Sniffing, Emma said, "There's an odd smell in here. Have you picked up on it?"

Will lifted his nose and shook his head. "Not now. It'll be

him, though. Caught it as soon as we met. Sounds a stupid thing to say, but he smells like … war."

Passing the sparse living room, Emma peeked round the door. The vintage armchair lay vacant.

"She's upstairs. It's conference season so we're strapped for space. We had an old study on the second floor. Peter sorted it out for her, bless him. She's well out of the way of —," he jerked his head in the direction of the library and lowered his voice, "—the Prince of bloody Darkness in there."

"I could go up, if you'd let me." Abigail's eyes widened, as they always did when she wanted to get her own way. "I promise, promise I won't upset her. Please, Will. I can't wait to see her."

He chewed his lip for a few seconds and took in Emma's almost imperceptible nod. "Go. She had a reasonable night. She knows you're coming and didn't say she didn't want to see you, so yes. Second floor, remember, at the end of the hallway." She'd turned towards the staircase when he called her back. "Abby! Do not upset her!"

Abigail nodded and scurried away, taking the stairs two at a time. He turned to Emma. "Ready? This isn't going to be pleasant."

"Can't wait," she said, as he opened the door to the library.

Abigail stopped at the top of the stairs, partly to catch her breath, but mostly to prepare herself. She'd spoken the truth when she'd said she couldn't wait to see Gabby, though less so after last night. Something apocalyptic had entered the world and, by all accounts, her friend and mentor was in no shape to help her deal with it or confront the dangers ahead.

Thank God she'd managed to grab a bit of sleep last night. Wyland had insisted she drink a finger of whisky first. They'd huddled in his living room, trying to make sense of what they'd seen. Try as she might, she'd failed to wring out of him any more details about the sentinel and how it got there, and when she asked him about the henge he got even more evasive.

To be fair, Abigail had also been selective about what she'd revealed. He'd asked a few questions about the orb and about Gabby. She didn't tell him who she really was, nor did she disclose the whole story of that morning on the Tor. How she'd felt the raw malice, directed towards her friend, so bad it caused her to be sick.

Then, the next minute, Gabby's back! She did not like the coincidence.

She walked down the small hallway and shrugged. What lay ahead would be a juggling act. On the one hand, Will expressly forbade her to mention anything that might upset Gabby. On the other, Abigail desperately needed to tap into her friend's knowledge. It would help her understand more about Wyland and what had happened last night. Gabby may have lost her superpowers, but she still possessed aeons' worth of insight. They couldn't have taken that away from her too. Could they?

She may have promised Will not to upset Gabby, but he hadn't been at Wood End last night. Didn't know the stakes. At the very least, shouldn't Gabby be warned?

Quietly, she tapped on the door.

No answer.

She tapped again and, heart thumping, turned the handle, not really knowing how to play it, guilty because she had an agenda. The door opened into a pleasant, sunny room. As she crept in, not sure what to expect, she glimpsed a still and slumped figure sitting on the window seat, staring out of the mullioned glass.

"Hi Gabs, it's me. Abigail." She went over to the bed. Sat down. "Emma's told me what's happened. I'd have come sooner, but they said you needed some time, to—"

"Adjust." Gabby's voice was flat, the eyes she turned on Abigail, dark as the void. "That's what they told me, too."

She turned back to the window. Was she … angry?

Abigail had been prepared to see her friend depressed. In her line of work, many people came to the salon to be brought out of themselves by a chat or a hairdo. She knew the platitudes, had rehearsed some of them for today. She hadn't expected the fury behind Gabby's eyes. Not at all.

"Do you want anything? I could bring up some tea, something to eat?"

Gabby, slowly shaking her head, continued to stare out.

"I was over the moon with your Christmas present. You know, the orb? You'd left before I could properly thank you."

Still no response.

She carried on talking—what else had she to do? So much to tell her, so little she could! Abigail decided to make it all about herself. Gabby'd be used to that.

"I started at the salon after Christmas. They made good on their promise to take me on as a junior. I'm training on the job and can already style most bobs. I'll have a go at your's, if you'll let me. I need the practice."

Still nothing.

"So … I have been trying to develop the Sight. Like you and—" God, should she even mention his name? "Erm … like you and Michael taught me. I really miss our nights on the Tor, keeping watch. And I'm trying with the orb, trying hard. Had a session with it yesterday, actually. I had a … breakthrough."

She needed another breakthrough with Gabby. Still silent, stubbornly gazing outside.

Taking a deep breath, mentally apologising to Will, she continued, "And things have been kicking off a bit here, again. Did they tell you we had a small earthquake? Just a tremor, apparently. It came from the Tor. Emma and I went to have a look. Cracks everywhere. Then they found a body at the caravan park in Ledbridge. Wyland—"

"Wyland?" Gabby spun around, even grabbed Abigail's arm. "What about Wyland?"

Such was the force of the interjection, Abigail wondered if she had been altogether too hasty in mentioning recent events. If Gabby got upset, Will would never forgive her.

"Er—"

"Come on Abigail, tell me. Everyone's pussy-footing around, and I understand it, I do. But it makes me feel worse. I know Will thinks I'm fragile—he told me I should stay up here and take another day to rest." Having looked away from the sunny window, her pupils were like pinpoints, her eyes piercing Abigail as she growled, "I'm sick of it."

Her outburst exploded so vehemently, so unexpectedly unlike the friend she remembered, it made Abigail's jaw drop. She looked down at her arm. "Gabby, please let go. You're hurting me."

She kept her grip a moment longer before relaxing it. Abigail frowned, craving the old Gabby, wanting to hear her say, in her usual cheerful way, 'I'm really, really sorry.' But no apology came. Not a word.

"Tell me what's happened to Wyland."

"N-nothing. Nothing's happened to him, but one of the caravans turned over just after the tremor and—"

"—was it a caravan at the bottom of the park well?"

"Y-yes. How do you know? Are you feeling better? Are you … you know … back?"

Gabby slumped, as if remembering her situation anew. "Hell will freeze over before that'll happen. No. But I know about Wyland, and I know what he protects." She searched Abigail's face, saw her chewing her lip. "There's something else. Tell me."

"I-I don't know if I should. I didn't expect you to react like this. Will told me not to—"

"I don't care what he told you. Tell me what you know and tell me now."

The odd smell intensified as the door to the library opened, Emma suddenly understanding what Will meant when he described it as being like war. Metallic, with a blend of woodsmoke and tar. Emma avoided the impulse to screw up her nose as she scanned the huge room. All the sets of chairs and tables were unoccupied save for one, in a dark corner next to the massive glass-fronted cabinet that housed the rolls of old parish documents. A few of them were on the table, together with what looked like open ledgers. Accounts, no doubt.

She looked questioningly at Will. He rolled his eyes and nodded to the back of a nearby armchair, from which rose a grey semicircle. As Will loudly cleared his throat, it jerked. Long-fingered hands slowly grabbed its arms, hauling up a surprisingly heavy-set figure.

Anthony St Saviour.

Emma hadn't really known what to expect. Some fussy cleric, perhaps. Bespectacled. Possessing an OCD eye for detail. The man in front of her shocked her out of that delusion. Before he said a single word, her stomach gave a familiar lurch. He intimidated her.

Late fifties. Tall—about six foot. Buzz-cut hair. Granite

face. Handsome. Over-assured. Thrusting.

Animalistic.

Wearing a thin smile that never reached his steel-blue eyes, he let her—no, he *expected* her—to come towards him. To hold out her hand in greeting. A hand which he didn't accept, giving her nothing but a simple nod of acknowledgement.

This man chose the *priesthood?*

Everything about him shrieked entitlement. He stood proud and still—commanding—feet planted apart as those eyes bored into her. Emma had the feeling of seconds slowing, elongating, as if time itself demanded she stood still for his inspection.

He wore an immaculately cut black suit, his black leather shoes so reflectively polished they reminded her, randomly, of tinted windows. His black shirt looked straight out of the packet, a gap in its pleated neckline displaying a glimpse of the white band clerics preferred nowadays, instead of a full collar. He crackled with arrogance; owned the space.

"Aren't you going to introduce us, William?"

Will pressed his lips together and threw a see-what-I-mean glance at Emma. Obviously irritated, he replied, "I was just about to. Dean Anthony St Saviour, this is Emma Blake. She is the tenant of Clearview, my cottage, over the green. Emma is also my closest friend."

"Good afternoon, Miss Blake. Have I got that right?" He stared pointedly down at the empty ring finger on her left hand. "You are single, I presume?"

Jesus.

"Er—"

Will must have caught the impropriety of the question too. "Dean, you asked to be introduced to key members of the parish. Her marital status is not relevant."

"Calm yourself, William," St Saviour replied. "Though I

can see why you might leap to her defence. I expect she gives you plenty of …" a scintilla of a pause, "… support."

Emma thought Will would explode.

She thought she might, too, had not something—thankfully—caught her eye. "Is that a walking stick next to your chair? I've never seen one like it before. It's very unusual."

"Erm … that's my cane." Quickly he strode back and picked it up, turned it horizontal and balanced it in his hand. "It has many admirers. I don't need its help to walk, you understand. It's merely a valuable heirloom. I keep it with me at all times." His abruptness oppressed her. It signalled an absence of empathy she found extraordinary for a man of his calling. His tone softened, however, as he caressed the wood of his cane. "It's precious to me. I cannot be parted from it."

The cane was indeed admirable, not so much for its obvious age and elegance, but for the curious finial that topped it. Its thick glass reminded Emma of Abigail's orb, but much, much smaller, not quite the size of a tennis ball, and a different colour.

She said, "Is that amber?"

His smile became uncertain as she questioned him. Narrowing his eyes slightly, he replied. "It is indeed."

"Isn't there something inside?" she asked, peering closer. "May I look?"

He drew back, eyes like flints. "Amber is a fascinating material. It catches the light remarkably. I'm sure you know all manner of creatures get caught in its resin. It preserves much that is part of our past."

"The setting is, I'm sorry, Dean—" She struggled to find the right words to describe the two black, long-fingered hands between which it had been mounted. "The setting is … unconventional."

"It is, and not particularly befitting for a man of the cloth, I know. But what can one do? As I said, it is an ancient piece and the amber has been fused into its setting. It cannot be altered without damaging it."

Obviously wishing to change the subject, protecting the amber within his palm, he stepped with the cane back to his chair, using it to indicate the seats opposite. "Do join me, both of you. Miss Blake, as you can see, I am deep within the bowels of William's accounting system. It is taking some time for me to make sense of it all."

"I can assure you, Dean," said Will, further dialling up his irritation at the implication, "you will find nothing untoward. We are audited every year and never had anything more than one or two minor queries."

"Yes. And I have unearthed one or two concerns myself, though it would be inappropriate to voice them here. Not in front of your … friend." This man was an absolute master of pausal innuendo.

Will took the captain's chair next to her, his knuckles white as he gripped its arms.

"Emma. Emma Blake, you say, William." St Saviour, cane tucked away, steepled his hands as he locked her in his steely gaze. She could have sworn there was a hint of defensiveness about him, as if for some unfathomable reason he thought her a threat. "Splendid name. Not dissimilar to the patrons of our village. The Blaxtons? Formerly known as the Blackstone family? An interesting line. A very interesting line indeed."

Emma shot an unnerved and questioning glance at Will. How could he have known about her ancestry? She couldn't imagine Will would have told him.

St Saviour, continued. "Don't worry, my dear. I make it my duty to ferret out every last piece of information I can about the people in my parishes. I don't care for surprises."

Preferring to avoid his eyes, Emma stared at his hands instead. His nails shone like tiny slabs of marble, expensively manicured and buffed.

"Yet that is exactly what you are," he glozed. "An interesting surprise."

Slowly, her hackles rose. Surely, surely he wasn't … ?

Will snapped, "What do you mean by that?"

St Saviour turned hooded eyes to him. "I thought you were … unattached. I'm pleased for you, that's all."

"There's nothing of a … romantic nature between Emma and myself. Nothing. And even if there was, it would be no business of yours … Dean."

St Saviour's full lips curled. "I meant nothing by it, William. Nothing at all."

She'd had enough. Fully up to speed with exactly why this man had got so far beneath Will's skin, Emma said, "Excuse me. I came with a friend. I think she might be waiting for me outside." She glanced at Will, and, as one, they rose to leave.

St Saviour got up too. "Thank you for your time." Jesus! He was acting like this had been some kind of interview. "This has all been very … illuminating."

Tch.

They left the man standing, a sardonic half-smile twisting his lips. Once outside the library, they blew out identical sighs of relief, Emma saying, "I'm sorry, Will, I had to leave. I can't stand the man."

"I know, right? Didn't I tell you? He's a complete piece of work."

"That cane!"

"I know! Those carved fingers are vile. Totally inappropriate. I wonder if the bish has seen it."

"Oh, I'm sure he will have. I don't think that man possesses an ounce of shame." She shuddered. "I'm sorry, but I don't think I can offer much in the way of support. He made me feel uncomfortable. He's foul."

"Yes, he is," replied Will. Then he chortled, "For what it's worth, I think you made him just as uncomfortable, though

God knows why. I'm sorry you can't stay a bit longer but, no worries. I'll pop upstairs and see how Abigail's getting on. She should go with you. If he's wound you up, it's a sure thing he'll do the same to her, then there'll be fireworks."

Will bounded up the stairs only to return a minute later, alone, a piece of paper in his hand. He gave it to her, eyebrows skyward.

"They've gone."

16

UP TO SPEED

Abigail left Gabby looking out into the park, as she knocked on Wyland's door. It took a few more taps before she raised any response.

When he eventually appeared he seemed more than ever to be filled with nervous energy. Or just plain nerves.

Without offering any greeting, his brow furrowed as he growled, "I said this morning before you left, you shouldn't come here again, Abs. It's not safe. After last night—" His frown deepened as Gabby joined them. "Who's this?"

"Hello to you too, Wy. This is Gabby. The friend I told you about."

A glint of recognition. "The one who gave you the orb? You told me she'd left! Gone for good."

"Believe me, Wyland, that had been my intention." A wry smile played on Gabby's lips as she spoke, almost like her old self. "But it was not to be. I'm back now, and I need you to tell me what you know about recent events. Preferably not on the doorstep."

He stared at her. "Why should I tell you anything? Just because you're a friend of Abs …"

"Wyland," said Gabby, fixing him with a stare. "I really, really think you need to let us in. We've no time to hang about."

He opened his mouth as if to argue, then obviously thought better of it. Without a word, he let go of the door and left it to hang as he retreated inside.

They found him in front of the brick fireplace in his living room. Abigail made for her usual seat, on the big cushion next to the low table. Gabby took a quick glance around, seeming to approve of what she saw. Without being invited, she sat on the cracked leather sofa.

Apart from the ticking of the homemade clock, the room went quiet. Wyland, refusing eye contact, stood shoulders hunched, hands in pockets. Gabby's presence had obviously created some kind of tension. Abigail wanted to ease things, but she hadn't much of a clue what to say, not really being sure why Gabby had wanted to come. Nor did she know how much she should reveal about her friend's origins—or her current situation.

It didn't really matter, because, acting more and more like her old self, Gabby broke through the awkwardness and got down to business. "I understand we've had an emergence, Wyland. Has there been any more activity?"

The question obviously floored him. Jaw dropping, he said, "What did you say?"

Abigail intervened. "It's okay. Gabby knows what's what. She'll be able to help."

"Will she now? And just how's she going to do that? Apart from being your friend, I don't know a thing about her."

"Oh, there's not much to know any more," said Gabby, a hint of irony lacing her tone, "Only that my kind has been in this world much longer than yours."

Wyland's eyes widened. "My ... kind?"

"Oh, don't be coy. I've come across many Guardians in my time, dearie."

Abigail's eyes glistened with excitement. She was going to find out what Wyland had been keeping from her. She'd tried to pry out of him how he had predicted—what had Gabby called it?—an emergence. Everything he'd kept back was about to come out. Poor man. He'd no chance.

Wyland staggered towards the window, leant on the wide sill. "How … how could you possibly know?"

Unable to help herself, Abigail breathed, "Gabby's an … an—"

"I'm a Messenger," said Gabby. "Or … was. You'll understand me better within the terms of your own mythos."

Wyland visibly swallowed. "A Messenger? Wow. I've heard of your like but have never encountered one. I believed you were just a phony legend." He blew out his cheeks and hoiked himself away from the window. "I need a drink."

"We all need a drink," said Gabby. "You sit down. You had a lot to deal with last night. I think I can manage to sort us all out."

Without waiting for permission, Gabby rose from the sofa and walked out of the door. A few minutes later they heard the banging of cupboard doors.

"She's a force of nature, your friend."

"She certainly is," beamed Abigail.

"Why didn't you tell me?"

"It's not as if you haven't been keeping stuff from me, Wy. Besides, I couldn't exactly broadcast it, could I?" She grinned. "Guardians and Messengers, eh? What makes Flammark so special? It's like mythic central."

Wyland took a deep breath as he perched on the arm of the sofa. "In a way it is." He paused, his brow clearing. "If she is a Messenger, it'll be such a relief. She'll understand …"

"Understand what? Come on Wy, you've got to tell me now."

He sat a while, obviously pondering, flinching as he heard something smash in the kitchen.

Ignoring it, he said, "There are things that make Flammark—and Sandmarsh, for that matter—different from anywhere else in Britain. For a start, most of it is lowland—except for the Tor, obviously. The well of the park here is below sea level and, believe it or not, the lowest point in the country. That's why it needed special protection. But we're not unique. There are other henges, some just as hidden as ours, guarded by people like me."

"Are you ... mortal? I mean, do you ... die?"

Despite himself, Wyland chuckled. Gosh, Gabby had definitely worked some kind of magic on him! "Yes to both. I'm just like you, really. But as a young lad I got drawn to the place and it sort of took over. Possessed me. Told me what I really am. I suppose it's a kind of earth energy. It attracts people and puts them where they need to be. You just have to go along with it."

A sobering thought. Could the same thing apply to her? Maybe she'd never been called to discover her path. Maybe the path had chosen her.

"This cottage used to be a smithy," Wyland continued. "Our 'kind', as your friend refers to us, has—had—an affinity with travellers. We gave them food and shelter to see them on their way and tended to their horses. Most of us live in or by one. Until the highways were modernised and petrol replaced beast. Soon the old routes were forgotten." He grinned wryly. "Everyone prefers a faster, flatter world! Guardians can't really move with it, though. We're tied to the land. We're called to protect it with our lives."

"And a great job you made of that!" Gabby had appeared at the door with a tray. With it, she offered a glass of whisky for Wyland, a cup of hot water infused with a sprig of mint for Abigail and took a mug of coffee for herself. Abigail rejoiced at her smile—and her ability to rustle up fresh herbs. Maybe Wyland grew a patch outside.

He slid down onto the sofa's leather cushions as Gabby returned to her place next to him, setting the empty tray on the low table. The ancient clock ticked on as they took a moment to drink.

As she did so, Abigail peered over her cup at her companions. It was impossible to miss the transformation that had taken over her friends. Gabby seems like her old self—as if she now had a purpose— and Wyland looked so much more at ease. As he'd said, relieved.

"Ooh, that's better," said Gabby, smacking her lips. "Such a pity you had no biscuits, Wyland. Situations like this always look better with biscuits. Now, tell me everything."

Glass in hand, Wyland relaxed back into the sofa. "Well, no doubt Abs will have explained about the tremor. She was on Seely Tor when she and her friend felt another. I think it dislodged one of the peripheral caravans and turned it over. I'd have been able to sort it, had one of the visitors not blown the whistle. When the police came, they took it out of my hands. Dug out the sentinel's remains. I still haven't had the go-ahead to order a crane. I suppose they still think it might be a crime scene."

"And the emergence?"

"I'd known it was coming. Been on the alert for it since they took the bones away. Ear to the ground, I could hear it getting nearer—hundreds of spirit voices."

"It must have been terrifying," said Gabby. "There's only been one other at Wood End, but that was centuries ago. The nearest to our time happened in Serbia. About a hundred and fifty years ago." She looked at Abigail's bewildered face and flapped her palm. "Roots of the First World War, dear. Don't worry about it."

She turned back to Wyland. "*Hundreds* of voices, you say?"

"Yes. Huge event. Couldn't believe it when Abigail turned up." He cocked an eyebrow at her. "If she'd arrived ten minutes later, they'd have been on her."

"Wyland told me to close my eyes. Tight," said Abigail, ignoring the admonishment. "I connected with the orb when my eyes were shut. Honestly, it was amazing, Gabs. I could see everything. It put me right in the middle of the action."

Gabby grinned. "I expect that came as a bit of shock."

"You're telling me! You could have warned me, left me a note or something. I've been trying to work it for months."

"Orbs of that ilk choose their own moments. I expect it controlled your fear?"

"It did. Bit like watching telly. Rough coming out of it, though. I'm still feeling a bit zonked."

"You're young," said Gabby. "You'll cope."

Abigail rolled her eyes and put out her tongue. "Where are they—the things that came out of the ground? What will they do?"

"Put simply, dear, they will 'do' whatever evil comes their way. Once they're in the flesh, they subvert. They'll start gradually, perhaps begin by turning friends and families against each other. Then tempers will flare. Everywhere. Unwise political decisions will be made, then the violence will start. Once they've properly attuned to the beat of our social rhythms, they'll get into our power structures. Expect corruption, uprisings, fascism. Death camps."

Her frown deepened. "Sometimes emergences happen as random events. Hellish spirits joining together, out for mischief. That it happened here, again, disturbs me." Her face clouded over. "I'm hoping it's not what I think it is."

Suddenly Abigail felt tears prick her eyes, her childish excitement suddenly fading away at the terrifying prospect Gabby had painted. A hard lump formed in the back of her throat as she contemplated what she needed to say next. She tried really hard to swallow it down, but failed. She'd promised, promised Emma and Will she wouldn't say anything about what really happened on the Tor, but she couldn't keep it from Gabby. Not now.

Gabby noticed. "What's the matter?"

Tears rolled. Abigail stammered, "G-Gabby. I have to tell you something. They told me not to, but I don't think I can keep it from you. It's not right."

"Come on, out with it."

"When I went up Seely Tor with Emma I felt ... I sensed something, some kind of presence. Pure hate ... so strong it made me sick. Like, so bad I actually threw up. It—" She stopped, genuinely conflicted about whether she should carry on.

Gabby frowned, "Say it, dear. Say it all. It'll be all right."

Abigail shook her head. "Can't."

Wyland intervened. "We have to know everything, Abs. It's the only way we'll be able to fight this thing, whatever it is."

She swallowed again, struggling hard against that lump. "It ... it gave me your name."

"My *name*?"

Abigail nodded, wiping her nose with the sleeve of her velvet top, leaving snot trails all over it. "Gabriel."

"Gabriel?" cried Wyland. A puzzled expression grew on his face, turning to astonishment as he put two and two together. "Of course! Messengers and angels. Same thing, different worldview."

Ignoring him, suddenly a child again, Abigail clambered out of the oversized cushion and, holding out both arms staggered towards the sofa, knelt at Gabby's feet. She leant in, putting her head on Gabby's lap, sobbing.

Bending forward, Gabby hugged the girl as best she could in that awkward position, rocking her gently as the old clock ticked.

She glanced at Wyland. "This settles it. No way was the tremor caused by natural disturbance. This was no *accidental* release of a bunch of disturbed spirits."

Abigail looked up, nodding vigorously. She burbled something about Godzilla.

Puzzled, Gabby looked at Wyland.

Rolling his eyes, he explained, "Nothing to do with Japanese sea monsters. It's what they've called DeepDrilla, the fracking company out in Ledbridge."

Gabby smiled, "Ohhhh." Then she looked down at Abigail and shook her head. "Evil though fracking might be, that too is not the cause of our current situation. There's a mind behind this." She put her finger under Abigail's chin. "Thank you for telling me. You did the right thing. And it's really moved us forward."

"Has it?" said Wyland. "How?"

"Because whatever's behind this, knows me. If I'm right —" She chewed her lip. Her face had grown pale. "I need to think. Long and hard." She tapped her forehead, then sighed. "My head feels fuzzy. Is this what exhaustion feels like?"

"You need to sleep," said Abigail. She brushed away her tears and, turning to Wyland, said, "Gabby isn't an angel. Not any more. And she hasn't slept for days."

Wyland shrugged. "I've a park full of cancelled caravans, I'll open one up for her." Turning to her friend, he said, "Gabriel, it's an absolute honour to have you here. Please, stay as long as you like."

17

FRACKING HELL

Westen detested hospitals. Hated everything about them: their smell, their manufactured calm, their containment. He'd only ever been admitted once, after his appendix burst on a stakeout. At first he thought the nausea had been triggered by the stinking takeaway his partner had brought for them and which they ate in the car. If only. Worst fucking night of his life. The pain had long since been forgotten, but not the look of sheer horror on his partner's face as he threw up his guts in the steering well.

He'd been gurneyed into the hospital—not this one, but they all look the fucking same—semi-conscious and babbling, apparently. Complications having set in, he'd had a protracted stay. Couldn't get over the ward politics. Having to make conversation, needing help.

Trying to explain why no one came to visit.

With a nod to how he'd felt during the whole of that period, he sniped at his sergeant. "Have we found him yet, Burrows?"

"Guv," said the man in question, clearing his throat as he reluctantly pushed himself off the reception counter. His enquiries with the young woman behind it had taken a decidedly flirtatious turn. "It's this way."

"I didn't think she was your type," grunted Westen.

"Any woman who takes the time to talk to me's my type, Guv. They're thin on the ground, given I'm such an ugly sod."

Weste glanced at him. He never got personal with people he worked with, and he certainly never gave Burrows' allure a minute's thought. But the remark brought him up short. Was he an 'ugly sod' too? Had that been Emma's problem?

Get a fucking grip.

An elevator later, they alighted at a men's surgical ward, and before long stood before the bed of a bespectacled, dark-haired chap in his mid-thirties.

They flashed their warrant cards. "David Walker? Morning. I'm Detective Inspector Westen and this is my sergeant, Burrows. We're from Sandmarsh police, Serious Crimes."

"They told me to expect you, Inspector. I've been waiting."

Pocketing his ID, Westen said, "How're you feeling?"

"Oh, you know. As well as can be expected. Have you found him yet, the man who did this to me?"

Westen grimaced. "Not yet. We have the brief statement you made when you came round from your surgery. The ball's rolling."

"And we've got a description from Jason Wilby," added Burrows. "He's the one who got you to the doctor in Flammark."

"Oh, yes. Sorry. I don't remember much about that."

"Do you mind?" Westen drew up a chair, one of those blue plastic jobbies, high-backed with wooden arms. Leaving Burrows to stand, he said, "If you wouldn't mind going over what happened again for us, it's possible you might remember something more. Let's start with what you were doing outside the Flammark Arms."

Wincing as he shifted in the bed, Walker replied, "I'm a journalist—the science correspondent for the Lanchester Herald. I've been trawling the hostelries in and around Ledbridge, acting on a tip-off about something that's going down at the fracking site. You know, DeepDrilla? There's nothing like pub gossip to see the way the land lies." Walker licked his lips. "Do you mind handing me that cup?"

Burrows sidestepped to the bedside cabinet, refreshed the man's plastic cup and handed it to him.

"Thanks." Walker took a sip. "I left the pub just before twelve—a quarter-to, I think. I remember hitching my laptop over my shoulder. That's not an automatic thing, Inspector. I always check I've got it whenever I leave anywhere. My whole life's on it." He grimaced. "Then this bloke came out of nowhere and tried to grab it. I'm not much of a fighter, but no way was I going to give it up without a struggle. It was only when he flicked it open that I realised he'd been carrying a knife. Tried to cut the strap with it. I hung onto the case and managed to pull free, then my leg kind of buckled. That's when I knew the knife must have slipped and caught my artery. He grabbed the laptop and ran off."

Burrows opened the thin file he'd brought and whipped out a piece of paper, an A4-sized image printed on one side. "Here's what Mr Wilby managed to come up with. This the man?"

Walker concentrated. "I think so. I didn't pay much attention to his face," he rocked his head sideways, considering. "Yes. It's definitely him. I won't forget those eyes in a hurry."

"What's the story with DeepDrilla?" asked Westen.

Giving the picture back to Burrows, the journalist looked

around the ward, as if worried the other five patients might overhear. "Do I have to go into the details?"

"Yes, you do," Westen growled. "If the attack had something to do with it, we need to know." Seeing the uncertain expression on Walker's face, he continued, "I shouldn't need to remind a man of your profession that withholding information is a very serious matter."

Walker chewed his lip and moaned again as he tried to move his leg. Lowering his voice, he replied, "My source told me they're massaging their data. Not reporting as they should."

"Isn't fracking over?" asked Burrows. "I heard the Ledbridge site was packing up."

"Change of tack," said Walker. "Though the government wants out of fracking, they're all-in on carbon capture. Tenders have been invited. There are two main players on that front. DeepDrilla is one of them—as I'm sure you know, they own all the UK fracking sites—the other is based in France."

"France?" Westen's heart sank. After hospitals, European politics came a close second on his avoid-at-all-costs list. Organising arrest warrants and data-sharing had suddenly become a whole new cruelty.

"But carbon capture is only theoretical at the moment, isn't it?" said Burrows. "I mean, it's not been done on any sort of scale."

Westen, eyebrows raised, rounded in his seat to give his sergeant a surprised stare.

Burrows looked sheepish. "One of those very brief relationships we spoke of earlier, Guv. She was an environmentalist."

Westen grunted and turned back to the Walker. "Go on."

"It's more than theoretical. Carbon capture has been around for decades. Power stations are now either built or retrofitted with filters that allow CO2 to be caught. Trouble is, it doesn't go anywhere near solving the climate crisis since the process emits almost as much crap as it saves. It needs machinery, fuel for transport, storage and so on."

Westen dug himself deeper into the hospital chair. This was going to take some time.

"But your sergeant's right. It's nowhere near scaled-up enough to make much difference. Until now. Now they want to suck the stuff directly out of the atmosphere. Scientists always knew it was possible, but there's been no money in it. Things have suddenly changed now governments are seeing their forests burn and their cities flood. They're beginning to take climate targets seriously."

"Yeah, right," Burrows muttered. "Not seriously enough. They wouldn't have to suck the stuff out if they stopped putting it there in the first place."

Wanting to get out of the place sometime before fucking midnight, Westen curbed his sergeant's enthusiasm with an irritated sideways glance. "Where's this going?" he said, shifting on his chair. "What's this got to do with your tip-off?"

"DeepDrilla has earmarked Ledbridge as the first of its sites to convert to carbon capture. If it wins the tender, of course."

"I suppose it makes some kind of sense," Burrows said. "They'll be using the same gear, won't they?"

"This girlfriend of yours was very well informed," Walker replied. "Yeah. All they need to do is blast the C02 solution down the shaft they've already drilled before pressuring it back into the rocks. It's basically a reverse frack. If Deep-Drilla's bid wins, they'd be able to hit the ground running." Despite his pain, he grinned. "If you pardon the pun."

"You do know we had a tremor in these parts?" said Burrows.

"Of course! It's one of the reasons why I'm down here."

"Come on, Walker," said Westen, impatiently. "Time to get specific. There's been nothing untoward in what you've said so far."

"Do I have—"

"Yes," snapped Westen. "You do!"

With a reluctant sigh, rolling his eyes, Walker said, "Something to do with DeepDrilla falsifying the mining data to enhance their tender. My source had the serious wind up. Really scared. Wouldn't tell me more. Enough for me to have a sniff about, though."

As Walker paused to ask Burrows to pour more water, Westen asked, "Enough to warrant your attack?"

After taking a few more sips, Walker shook his head. "Not the initial tip-off, I don't think. Too non-specific. But after I visited the site someone sent me a flash drive. Anonymously, of course. It contained emails."

"About?" Westen said, wanting to get on.

"They're between the head of DeepDrilla and the site manager. A chap called Drew, Angus Drew. They're very exercised by a crack that seems to have developed. Runs from Ledbridge to Seely Tor and beyond."

Burrows let out a low whistle. "Jesus!"

"Yeah, big stuff," said Walker. "Worse still, seems a fissure has opened up. A gap in the earth. Supermassive, apparently. It would make the carbon insertion uncontrolled and unstable. DeepDrilla would lose the tender if the government found out about it. They're planning to doctor its submission, maybe try to seal the fissure."

"No way," exclaimed Burrows. "No way would they get away with that."

"They might, once their tender's been accepted. Apparently, it's impossible to prove they were actually responsible for the fissure. All they have to do is keep shtum and sit on the info, then once they've won the tender, if they can't rectify the problem—they're talking about injecting some kind of medium into it—they can close Ledbridge and use another site for the carbon insertion."

"They've got to report, especially if it makes everything unstable," said Burrows. "Can't get out of it."

"That's their plan."

"We're talking about fraud and criminal negligence—to the whole freakin' planet." Burrows grew red in the face. "My ex was into all this, Guv. Proper doomster. She tried to convince me the likes of DeepDrilla were conspiring to end the world." He gave a little laugh. "Maybe she was right after all."

"Do you still have the flash drive?" asked Westen.

Walker shook his head. "I could kick myself. It's in the laptop case."

Westen chewed the inside of his cheek, not convinced the stabbing had been as accidental as Walker maintained. You don't catch an artery with the slip of a knife, not when there's serious money involved. The mining industry was worth millions—trillions! Whoever stole the laptop might have also have wanted to shut the journalist up for good.

Walker said, "There's something else."

Westen leant forward.

"This fissure. The geology doesn't add up. Earth fissures can develop fairly quickly at a certain level. But the one they've discovered under the Ledbridge site is miles deep. Near the earth's crust. Something that far down would have to have formed within what they called 'geological timescales'. That's millions of years."

Westen glanced at Burrows. "We've heard nothing about this fissure from Lanchester, have we?"

"No, Guv. Their report isn't in yet, though even if it was,

I'm not sure it would come to us. Not exactly a police matter."

Seeing Walker's puzzled expression, Westen explained, "The quake caused some damage at Wood End. Know it?"

Walker shook his head.

"It's being investigated by a team of seismologists. They're checking for aftershocks."

"Don't know anything about that, but if that was the extent of the remit, their equipment is unlikely to detect the fissure. That'd require a really deep sensor and engineers to sink it." Walker, obviously beginning to tire, rubbed an eye. "One thing's for sure—had it been there when they first surveyed the Ledbridge site, DeepDrilla would never have started the work. That's what Drew said, in one of his emails. It's bloody obvious they're scrambling like mad for an explanation—and a solution. They don't have a bloody clue how it could have happened."

"Okay," said Westen. He heaved himself up from the chair. "I can see you're getting tired. I think we've got enough from you for now. If we've any more questions, we'll get in touch."

"Yeah. I can't seem to keep my eyes open. Must be the painkillers. Let me know when you catch the bastard that did this to me, will you?"

The two detectives left Walker to rest. Once outside the ward Westen said, "Get uniform to post someone, Pete. I don't want to take any chances that Walker might get a return visit. Then we'll pay a visit to DeepDrilla. Put the wind up."

"Okay, Guv. Are we going for their computers? Get to these emails at source?"

Westen shook his head. "We don't have enough evidence for a search and seizure, but we can get them another way." He took out his phone. "I'll brief Pecker. Our worthy superintendent informed me that fraud is his bag now. We can use his clout to get DeepDrilla and its data properly investigated. It's pretty fucking obvious where the attack on Walker came from." He threw the car-keys at Burrows. "You drive. I need to make some calls."

❧ 18 ❦

DEEPDRILLA

Thirty minutes later they came to a dead stop half a mile out from the DeepDrilla site. Hundreds of people had gathered in the lane adjacent to the entrance, chanting slogans, blocking their access.

Westen glowered through the windscreen. "What's going on?"

"Hang on, Guv."

Before Westen knew it, Burrows had left the car and plunged into the mob. After a while he came out, followed by a scowling young woman, flaming orange hair piled-up within a red bandana, obviously chewing his sergeant's ear off. There was a loud but indistinguishable back and forth, then she slapped Burrows in the face before flouncing off to be swallowed once more by the crowd.

Face flushed either with heat or embarrassment—or possibly passion—Burrows returned to the car. "Sorry about that, Guv. That was Jasmine. My ex."

"I thought it might be," Westen replied, a sardonic smile playing on his lips. "Gentle sort."

Burrows chuckled as he rubbed his cheek. "Oh, yes."

"So, did she explain this lot?" Westen asked, waving an impatient hand at the marchers. "There's fucking hundreds of them!"

"They've always had a small presence here, just to keep giving the frackers the finger, so to speak. A taste of what's to come if the suspension gets lifted. Apparently, a fleet of vans arrived this morning spewing white coats, which they think is odd, seeing as the site's supposedly mothballed. They think something's up, so they've ramped up their numbers. Uniform's here, up front."

"Are they, indeed?" Westen said, shaking his head. "One day we'll learn to let one fucking hand know what the other is doing."

Burrows reversed out of the access road and parked the car out of harm's way. As they returned, a police utilities truck pulled up, piled high with portable barriers.

With none of them deployed as yet, the two men had no choice but to shove through the crowd. As he pushed nearer to the front Westen could see a line of police officers, feet apart, arms folded. No shields, no riot gear. No intention to scare the horses. So, a holding brief. Westen hated that they'd been called out. He'd nothing much against activism—he could see the point—but he detested it when politics used him and his own as lackeys, putting them in harm's way to keep the peace for dodgy corporations.

Badge at the ready in case any uniform had the ill-judgement not to recognise him, he burst through their ranks and walked across the fifty-yard no-man's-land towards the gates.

Burrows whistled. "That security fence, Guv. It's easily, what, two hundred metres wide?"

Westen nodded. Still having to raise his voice over the hoots and jeers of the protestors, he said, "And probably twice as long. No wonder the green brigade is acting up.

They must have got rid of some pretty decent woodland to make room for all this."

"Morning," said Westen. As they reached the fence, a heavy-set security guard lumbered into view, the sleeves of his pristine white shirt folded nearly to his elbows. "We're—"

"I know who you are." The guard scowled at Westen as he parked himself behind one of the double palisade gates. "You nicked my nephew a few years back. His whacko girlfriend accused him of assault. You broke his fucking wrist."

Westen furrowed his brow for a few seconds, then pressed his lips into a grim line of recognition. "Broady, was it? Charlie Broady? I remember now. You're George. You had to be removed from court at one point, as I recall." Eyes never leaving the man, he leaned in. "When triple nine gets a terrified call from someone who orders a fake pizza to give an address, we don't hang about. Nasty piece of work, your nephew."

"You shouldn't have laid hands on him. You've got rules about that, nowadays."

"We do. And we have rules about knifepoint rape. I had no problems breaking a bone to get his blade away from her." Westen's lip curled further as he pushed his face even closer to the fence. "Some people might blame his values. Family values."

The guard balled his hands, widening the snarling mouth of the pit-bull he had tattooed on his forearm. He tried to stare Westen down.

"Open up, sunshine," Burrows called. "We don't have time for this."

Seething, Broady moved away from the fence and into the security hut where he began talking into a two-way. A few minutes later the cantilevered gates slid open a few derisory feet, leaving the two policemen to squeeze through the gap.

"Wait there," Broady shouted from the hut. "Someone's coming for you."

Two men in expensive suits approached. Both wore smiles and one held out his hand. "Inspector Westen? I'm Angus Drew, the head of operations here. This is my legal associate, Paul Cram."

Westen nodded to them both. He stared at the proffered hand without moving.

Drew's smile faltered as he lowered his arm. "If you follow me, we can go somewhere more comfortable—cooler. Then you can tell us what all this is about."

As they followed the two men, Westen drank in his surroundings. He'd been mildly curious about what a fracking operation might look like. He'd imagined a mess of water tanks, pipes, cylinders—heavy machinery—so it came as some surprise to find a neat, well-ordered landscape of huge static tanks, stacked portable offices, cranes and winches, all positioned around a narrow, perpendicular drilling rig. Its iron frame towered upwards, dominating the scene.

Men with hard hats and white coats scurried about, clipboards in hand, some bending over theodolites or chunky field laptops. A great deal of activity, considering that drilling had been suspended. He could see why the protestors had thought something was afoot.

The four men entered the largest of the offices. It contained little more than a huge table, a stack of plastic chairs and a presentation screen above which hung a projector, bolted to the ceiling. Drew unhitched four chairs and set them at the end of the table near the door and indicated for them to sit down.

"Now, Inspector," said Drew. "What can we do for you?"

In that psychic connection born of a well-honed partnership, Burrows started the ball rolling, knowing that Westen liked to watch reactions. The sergeant took out his notepad, slowly flipping the pages. "We understand you're in the process of tendering for a new project, sir. Care to tell us about it?"

Drew shrugged. "There isn't much to say, other than what's already on public record. Fracking has been suspended and the decision on that is unlikely to be reversed. We're ... diversifying."

"Into carbon capture. That right?" asked Burrows.

Drew nodded. Donning a puzzled and impatient frown, he said, "Sorry, why is this police business?"

Westen couldn't resist a pop. "It's police business when you need us to keep that lot at bay." He jerked his head in the direction of the distant chanting crowd.

Cram intervened. "May I ask what lies behind your visit? Our business is, well, our business. As for policing protests, that's surely a uniform issue and one under the remit of the chief constable. With whom we have a very positive relationship, I might add."

"Relationship?" replied Westen, cocking an eyebrow. "What do you mean, you have a relationship?"

Drew shifted in his seat. Cram said, "Nothing untoward. We are merely pointing out that our business plan has been formulated and shared with the powers that be and our security requirements, going forward, are agreed at the highest level."

"That's why the white coats are out in force?" Burrows nodded at the window. "Out there?"

"Yes," replied Drew. "There is considerable work to do if we are to repurpose the site for capture."

"Like what?" asked Westen.

Exhaling loudly, Drew replied, "Surveys, geophysical monitoring, et cetera. We also have to keep the shafts clear and open, so we have to perform the occasional chemical sluice."

"Is that all?" asked Westen.

"Is what all?" snapped Drew, loudly.

Westen sat forward and nodded to Burrows to dig out the sketch of David Walker's attacker. "Do you recognise this man?"

Drew took the sheet and gave it a cursory glance. "No. Should I?"

"You tell me," replied Westen. "In fact, why don't you study it for a bit longer than a split second. Maybe a lightbulb will come on."

Drew slapped the sheet down on the table and pushed it back to Burrows. "I don't know the man. What's he done, and what's he got to do with us?"

Westen eyed Burrows again. This time he handed over a photograph of Walker. "Do you recognise *this* man?"

"N—hang on, yes. He's a reporter. He was here early last week—Monday, I think. Sniffed about, asking questions about the tender. Much the same as you are, Inspector."

"How long was he here for?" asked Burrows.

"We're trying to facilitate a more positive relationship with the media. If we're successful, the CSS project—the carbon capture tender—will be a huge win for us, and the country, of course. Jobs, green tech, and so on."

Westen put his palm up. "No need to sell it to us, Drew. Just answer the question. How long was he here for?"

"After the interview we gave him the tour. So ... what ... an hour? Bit more, maybe." He breathed out heavily. "Enough now. What's this all about? Has something happened to him?"

"Yes, something 'happened' to him. Someone tried to kill him."

Cram stood up. "Don't say another word, Angus."

Turning to Westen, he said, "I think this interview is over, Inspector."

Westen didn't move. "I'm sure the chief constable would be more than interested to hear of your lack of cooperation, Mr Drew, seeing as you're so friendly with him. Cram, why don't you sit down?"

Drew nodded to his associate. The lawyer, reluctantly returning to his seat, fished out his mobile and pressed the record button. "So that we can avoid any future misunderstandings, Inspector."

Westen shrugged. "We know Mr Walker visited you last Monday. A few days later, someone sent him a flash drive containing a series of emails between yourself and your CEO regarding some kind of underground anomaly. You've a problem, haven't you, Drew? It could compromise your tender."

Drew didn't move. His expression never wavered, yet Westen sensed his fear, palpable in the silence that filled the room. Not so Cram. He threw a puzzled glance at his colleague. Then he tapped off the recorder.

Westen continued. "Someone tried to snatch Walker's laptop, and in the process stabbed him in the leg. Nicked an artery."

The tension held for another few seconds, then suddenly Drew reddened. He leapt to his feet and sidestepped to the window, turning his back on the two detectives. "Shit. I can't believe this has got out."

Cram's bewildered expression deepened as he stared at his colleague.

Suddenly swinging round, Drew said, "You think I found out there'd been a leak and sent someone to take out a reporter, don't you? That's … that's preposterous."

"Stop talking. Now," said Cram. "They're on a fishing trip." He flashed his eyes at Westen. "Aren't you, Inspector?"

"No. I am investigating a very serious attack, clearly motivated to protect your organisation from embarrassing and costly exposure." He sighed. "Look, we know about the fissure. If what Walker has told us is correct, your goose is cooked. You have no idea how it developed or how serious it might be, yet you're keeping the lid on it. DeepDrilla is over."

Drew's two-way crackled. Broady's aggressive tones rattled over the airwaves. Something about a minister wanting to book a Zoom meeting. Cram turned it off. "This your doing?" he asked Westen.

"Yes."

"We're finished. *I'm* finished," cried Drew.

"Yet I'm not finished with you," said Westen. "We still have an active investigation. A man nearly died."

Silence.

Finally, Drew said, "I have no idea who attacked your reporter. I had nothing to do with it. I didn't even know the information had been leaked."

Westen got up. "Whether you did or not, a world of pain is about to descend on this place. If I were you, I'd come clean about the data you're withholding."

Drew wouldn't look at him; stared instead at a spot on the table.

"And I need a list of all employees on site last Monday during Walker's visit. Mark it with all those who had access to your computer network. I want to know who gave him the flash drive."

"I'll have to consult my CEO first," said Drew

"Consult away," replied Westen. "We'll take a stroll around while we wait."

❦ 19 ❦

THE CALL OF ST SAVIOUR

L oud banging on Emma's door.

Not a hand-knock. Something much harder. It came again. Insistent. Whoever it was either didn't know or didn't care that it made her throat throb.

Slowly, she made her nervous way downstairs. She *had* decided on an early night. Patients' attitudes towards her had not improved and she'd had to field some really dirty looks as she worked behind the reception desk with no clue as to why. They'd never been awkward with her before. If they'd thought her snappish, all the more reason to steal a march on the insomnia. Fat chance now.

She glanced at the alcove clock. Nine-thirty. Late enough to wonder who on earth it could be. Certainly not Westen. He'd never knock like that.

At the door, Emma put her eye to the peep-hole. Instantly she pulled back. St Saviour!? What the hell was he doing here?

She jerked the ties of her thin kimono. After making a cursory inspection for signs of any wayward flesh, she turned the locks and key. Judging by the way the dean held that awful cane of his, she'd obviously opened the door seconds before he intended to use it a third time.

Nothing about him made her want to smile a greeting at him. So she didn't. "Dean!" she said, abruptly, "what brings you to my door at this hour?"

"It's not that late, is it? And I don't believe it's your door. May I come in?"

Jesus!

Hardening her tone, she replied, "I've had a difficult day. If you don't mind, perhaps we can leave whatever you have to say for another time?"

"No. It really can't wait. Nor is it something you'd want me to talk about on the step."

Every instinct screaming 'keep him out,' a familiar knot gathered in the pit of her stomach and her mouth watered, nausea threatening. She swallowed it down. She would not let another man affect her like Ben had done. Besides, what could be the harm in letting him in? Though she found St Saviour loathsome in the extreme, he was a priest, for God's sake.

She took the time to breathe slowly in, out, then in again, keeping him waiting. "Very well. I suppose you'd better come in. But not for long. I'd planned an early night."

"So I see," he said, his steel-blue eyes sweeping over her as he stepped over the threshold, making her wish she'd closed the door on him after all. "You're not sleeping well, are you?"

Her eyes flashed. "What has Will been telling you?"

"Enough. Though it's plain for all to see, my dear. The shadows beneath your eyes, your general air of exhaustion. William really ought to take better care of you."

"Excuse me? What has my well-being got to do with Will?"

"Despite William's protestations, I rather thought you

two were, what do they call it nowadays … an item. Am I wrong?"

"Not that it's any business of yours, Dean, but yes, you are."

She wanted to get this over with. Get him out. Priest or not, something … primal told her not to trust St Saviour. It might have been his stench: Eau de Woodsmoke with top-notes of tar.

Inside the living room she stood in front of the fireplace, hugging her arms. She did not ask him to sit. Not that it bothered him. He lowered himself anyway, onto the cream, shabby-chic sofa, placing his cane carefully against the arm. Again, something within it caught her eye. A movement?

St Saviour saw the glance. Narrowed his eyes, appraisingly.

"Please, Miss Blake. Emma. Sit. Be comfortable." He patted the cushion next to him.

Resisting the urge to shudder, she sat on the edge of the armchair opposite. "You said there was a matter of some sensitivity you wanted to discuss?"

He chuckled softly as she recoiled. He sat back and rested his elbow, one leg crossed wide over the other as he twirled an ankle.

"Very well, Emma. I shall be straight with you. You are renting this property from William?"

"Yes," she replied. "As you rudely pointed out earlier."

"I think it only fair to warn you that he may require you to leave sooner than he intended."

Emma's stomach lurched. "Oh? And why might that be?"

"I have discovered some … anomalies in the church accounts. I really don't believe I can keep them from the bishop. He would be most disappointed in William."

"Anomalies? Like what?"

"It seems fewer residentials and conferences have taken place than he has declared. His expense claims, on the other hand, have increased. Significantly. In short, he has falsified his declarations on the Parish Returns System."

How dare he. How bloody dare he accuse Will of being a thief. "I don't believe it. Will doesn't possess a dishonest bone in his body."

"Really? I know he lies. He lied about having someone staying this past weekend. Didn't he, Emma? There is no record of any bookings and he specifically told me he had no personal visitors staying over. One wonders what he's got to hide."

"If there are no records of any residents, what makes you think there were any?"

He was referring to Gabby, of course. But Abigail had been in contact. Told her she'd whisked her away to Wood End and that she had now been safely ensconced in one of Wyland's caravans. So how had St Saviour picked up on her? And what was the big deal?

"Do not be disingenuous with me! Two days ago, you said you arrived at the vicarage with a friend. Where did she go if not to visit someone else? My remit is to ensure the diocese is being served by the best possible stewardship. I don't like being lied to."

"Again, why assume there's some mysterious guest, if you haven't seen her?"

"Her?" St Saviour's lips curled, his eyes suddenly darting to his cane.

Emma could have kicked herself. "Slip of the tongue, Dean. There's no reason to read anything into it." She followed his gaze and started. Definitely a movement within the amber sphere; a sudden swirling. This time she was sure of it. Seeing it had her attention, he let it lie for a few minutes while she stared at it, then wearing an expression of grim satisfaction—as if something had been confirmed—he snatched up the cane and laid it next to him, hiding its sphere from view.

St Saviour smiled. "I have the distinct impression you too are hiding something from me, Emma. You're quite the dark horse, aren't you?" He shrugged.

"I have no idea what you're talking about. I think it may be time for you to go."

Instead of moving, though, he nestled further back in the sofa, surveying the room. "This is a nice place. Cosy and yet roomy at the same time. I think you will miss it, yes?"

Emma frowned, her heart suddenly racing. What game was he playing now?

"You'll have plenty of time to look elsewhere," he continued. "Once William gets out of prison."

He could not have chosen a better bombshell.

"Prison?" Emma stood up. "What the hell are you talking about?"

St Saviour shrugged. "It seems William has been a very naughty boy. On the face of it, a plausible character whom the bishop tells me is very popular in his parish." His mouth curled into a sneer. "A clever front. Who'd have thought him capable, eh?"

"What are you talking about?!"

"Fraud, Emma. Embezzlement. Thousands of pounds involved. *Thousands*. Gone! Gone in the tweak of a spreadsheet."

He smiled.

Slowly she got his drift. Her mouth went dry. "You bastard. You're ... framing him for something, aren't you? You want him out."

"Actually, I don't. I think that milksop is doing a passably good job. No Emma. It's you I want out. Out of this house, out of the village and out of my way. As soon as possible." He smiled. "Or I press the button on my 'discoveries'."

"You're *blackmailing* me to leave the cottage? For God's sake, why?"

"I have my reasons."

"Well, what are they? Why do you want me to leave?"

No reply. He simply tapped the side of his nose as if the purpose behind his bombshell were none of her business.

"I'll tell Will. It's his house. He can choose who he wants to live here. And don't forget the bishop. He'll never believe Will capable of stealing!"

"Won't he? Oh, I am very thick with that gentleman. Our relationship, though brief, has been very productive. I can assure you he will accept anything I find it convenient for him to believe."

Emma's jaw dropped as she collapsed back into her seat.

"But, tell away, I really don't care. If you do, I shall immediately overwrite Will's accounts and call the police. The bishop won't stand by him, not after I tell them about the affair you've been conducting, both here and at the vicarage. There have already been complaints, you know. Wagging tongues."

Heart sinking, all Emma could come up with was a weak, "I don't believe you."

But Westen might.

"Oh, you should. I've spoken to many people. The village is rife with gossip about you both."

Light dawned. The hostile glances in the surgery, the stand-offish attitude from patients who used to be so friendly. So they'd been talking to St Saviour, had they? Or, more accurately, he'd been winding them up. Twisting facts.

"Why?" she said again. "Why do you want me to leave? What do you mean about me being in your way?"

Not bothering to answer, he rose. "I'm going now. I'll give

you a week to move out, Emma. A week. Or I press that button."

He picked up his cane.

"No need to see me out, my dear."

❦ 20 ❦

AFTER THE SLEEP

What the hell just happened?

Emma could hardly process the substance of St Saviour's visit, dumbfounded at the sheer malice he displayed in coming up with such a web of lies. Could he get away with it?

What had she done? What did he mean when he said he needed to get her out of his way? Did she present some kind of threat? If so, what?

She should tell Will. *Could* she tell him? Should she risk St Saviour pressing the button if she disclosed the threat? She had no doubt the dean was a man of his word. If he did manage to get people to believe him, Will's work, his reputation, his whole life in the world he grew up in, would be in tatters.

She should go to the police. Pre-empt everything. But that would only serve to bring forward the discovery of these so-called accounting anomalies. She could have a quiet conversation with Westen, though. Or not. Though she had faith in his integrity, he'd always thought there'd been more to her relationship with Will than friendship. He might choose to believe St Saviour, especially as he'd been well aware she'd kept things from him in the past, things he would never understand.

Now they were not on good terms, approaching him for help didn't seem any plan at all.

It all hinged on the plausibility of St Saviour's accusations. If he really did have the skill to falsify Will's accounts, then yes, he could get away with it.

Adding the dilemma to her already troubled mind rendered sleep completely out of the question. In fact, Emma hardly budged from her chair all night, fretting and mulling over the priest's visit. Why did she threaten him so much? He'd gone on about her ancestry. Could it have been something to do with that? If so, how? All the weirdness in the family came through the male line. She was nothing out of the ordinary.

Not for the first time in her life she felt stuck in an unfathomable web, manipulated and unable to move forward. The more she struggled to make sense of it, the greater her dread.

And she could be homeless in a matter of days.

Where was she supposed to go? What reason could she possibly give Will for leaving, and at such short notice?

As dawn broke, with no end to here quandary in sight, only one course of action occurred to her. Go to Wood End. Find Abigail and Gabby.

She rang Robbie as early as she dared to tell him she hadn't slept and was too exhausted to come in. Not a word of a lie.

"I've been expecting something like this, lass," he said. "It's Wednesday. Take the rest of the week. The agency will send someone. I just hope they have a pulse."

Emma stared at his name on the screen as she ended the

call, feeling terrible at letting him down. She'd find some way to make it up to him.

Eager to get going now she'd made her decision Emma left the cottage. It took two stomach-churning attempts to start the jeep —that damned battery—then she left it to idle as she looked up Wood End's postcode and tapped it into the satnav.

Half an hour later she arrived at the caravan park.

Seeing as a body had been discovered, she'd half-expected Wood End Road to be closed, but she encountered no obstruction until she got to the park entrance, where a police sign had been placed between two pillars. She parked at the verge and climbed out, stretching and arching her aching back, exhaustion now completely setting in. Eyes watering with the massive yawns she was suddenly making, Emma knocked on the door of an old stone cottage she assumed was Wyland's.

A tall, wiry man with the makings of a beard opened up. He gave her a polite smile. "I'm sorry, but we're closed for business at the moment. We should be open again in a few weeks if you'd like to enquire then."

"Are you Wyland?" asked Emma.

The man nodded. "Yes, I am."

"Very pleased to meet you. My name's Emma Blake, I'm a—"

He put up his palm. "Say no more." Holding out his hand he rolled his eyes and grinned. "You're a friend of Abigail's. The girl doesn't go one sentence without mentioning your name."

Emma attempted a return smile, but with another yawn threatening, couldn't pull it off. She must have seemed truly pathetic, because he said, "Come in. I'll put the kettle on. You look done in!"

As she dragged herself over the threshold he put a hand

on her shoulder—she had no clue why she didn't object to his touch. It affected her. Calmed her.

He nodded towards a door. "Go through. Make yourself comfortable. The sofa's best."

≈

"Emma! Emma dear, I don't like to wake you, but it is getting late."

Emma opened her eyes, and, startled, looked around the unfamiliar room. Though still strong, the sunlight had a different, late afternoon quality. As her senses returned, so did her recollection. "I'm at Wyland's, aren't I? Sorry, I must have dozed off."

"You are," said Gabby, perched next to her, fingers hooked in the handle of a large mug of coffee. "Wyland has a way with weary travellers. He said you looked shattered."

"Did he … drug me? I don't remember drinking any—" In a sudden movement, she sat up. "You didn't … mess with my head. You know, like you did last year, when you—"

Gabby interrupted. "Not one of my better moments. I had hoped time would lessen the upset we caused when we got you to talk to us." She squeezed Emma's arm and smiled apologetically. "To get back to your question, though. No. No drugs. No messing with your head. Wyland has more subtle gifts. This is a place of sanctuary. Natural rhythms take over. He merely amplifies them. He has a very healing influence on all sorts of travellers." She handed Emma the mug. "This is for you. Coffee just as you like it. While you drink it, I'll tell you about him."

Emma sat, rapt in Gabby's words. Wyland, a … Guardian? Suddenly she flashed back to when Gabby had confirmed her research about the Blackstone curse. Their conversation in Clearview's kitchen all those months ago had filled her with the same mixture of awe and dread she felt now. What kind of a place had she ended up in, for God's sake? Where curses were real, and angels lived side by side with Celtic legend.

After the past few days—hell, the past year—she had neither the energy nor the wherewithal to do anything but accept it.

It was the world she lived in.

Instead of questioning it, she simply said, "You look good, Gabby. Better. Are you—"

"Back, as Abigail calls it? No dear, I'm not. I feel better— some of it's Wyland's doing, of course, and as long as I don't dwell on things, I'm okay. Michael was very … unforgiving. I think that was the worst part about it, really. We'd worked together for centuries." She gave a wan smile. "I thought he'd be more on my side."

"You're the reason why I came," said Emma. "You might have lost your wings, but you still have your wisdom."

"This is a good place for me. A healing place. Wyland's letting me stay for a while. It's already done me no end of good, and the caravan he's let me stay in is lovely."

Abigail came in and waved. "Yay, Emma! Finally! I thought you'd never wake up!" She threw herself onto a huge floor cushion in front of a similarly oversized low coffee table, covered in books.

Wyland followed, immediately making the room seem crowded, carrying a beautiful wooden chair, obviously hand-made. After placing it under the window, he sat on it and grinned. "You look a great deal better, Emma."

"Thank you. I feel better. I'm sorry I dozed off."

Abigail snorted. "Dozed off? Coma, more like. Oh, and you snore. Worse than grandad!"

Emma chuckled. Goodness, she really was feeling better! Then the reason for her visit came flooding back, and her mood shifted. The others must have sensed it. They grew quiet. Expectant.

"Tell us why you came," said Wyland. "It'll be all right. It's safe to talk here."

As if his words opened a floodgate, words came tumbling out, as Emma told them about St Saviour's visit, his threats about the church accounts and her impending homelessness.

"Right. Before we go on, let's get that stresser out of the way," said Wyland. "If it comes to that, you've no need to worry. I have plenty of caravan space." He grimaced. "There've been cancellations."

"Anthony St Saviour," Gabby said. "This is the man William didn't want me to meet, isn't it? The reason why I ended up in that poky garret?"

Abigail tutted. "Don't be daft, Gabs. It wasn't that bad. The view was fab. Will'll be gutted you saw through him, though. He didn't want you to know he was getting you out of the way."

"I'm right though, yes?" Gabby turned to Emma, who nodded.

"Once he'd met St Saviour," Emma explained, "Will was determined to keep you out of his way, what with you being so … depressed. Have to say, it was a good call. I don't know how you would have coped. He seemed to sense you were at the vicarage, though—or at the very least that someone was being kept from him. Hidden."

Flaring her nostrils as she inhaled, Gabby asked, "Hmm. What's he like—other than being an evil so and so?"

Emma sipped from her mug. "He's … strong-looking. Heavily set but I'd say more with muscle than fat. Grey hair cut really short, almost like an army cut." Emma shivered. "Carries himself more like a soldier than a priest." She shuddered. "I can't begin to tell you how loathsome he is. He reeks of power. It fills the room."

Gabby leant forward. "Go on."

"An intimidating man. Seemed very interested in my ancestry—oh, and my relationship with Will." Emma shivered, her hand flying to the cross around her neck.

"Your *ancestry*? What, the Blackstones?"

She nodded. "I have no idea why he wants me out of the cottage or, as he said, out of his way. He's gone to a lot of trouble, and he's obviously more than capable of carrying out his threats," said Emma. "I should tell Will, but daren't take the risk. If I say something, he'll tell St Saviour to go to hell, then I'm sure the button will be pressed on those accounts and the police involved." She remembered what the dean had got up to with Robbie's patients. "Even if he's proved innocent, word'll get round. He'll make sure of it. Flammark's a tight-knit community. Will would lose everyone's confidence."

"Can't you go to the police yourself? Trust Westen?" said Abigail.

"What could he do? St Saviour has fabricated proof. He wouldn't be able to stop an investigation into Will based on my say-so alone. Anyway, I don't know where I am with him. You know we're not getting on."

Abigail rolled her eyes as Gabby said, "Tell me more about St Saviour. Anything, no matter how seemingly trivial it might be."

Emma blew out her cheeks as she tried to think. "He smells."

Gabby chuckled. "Smells? Like what?"

"Will called it war. He stinks of fire and smoke and metal —really hard to describe."

"What else?"

Emma shrugged. Then it came to her. "He has a cane. It's really unusual. Carries it everywhere with him."

"A cane? What's unusual about it?"

"Erm. It's black with an amber sphere on the top. I noticed it as soon as I came in the room. He showed it off to me."

Gabby froze.

Cupping her hands together, she said, "It wasn't, by any chance, this big? Set between two hands, like this?" She slapped the base of her palms together, and bent her hands outwards to forty-five degrees, curling her fingers inwards.

Emma nodded. "Exactly like that."

Gabby blanched. Pressed her lips into a pale line.

"You know him, don't you?" said Abigail.

The clock ticked on interminably before she made her reply.

Eyes closed, her breathing shallow, she nodded. "Yes."

A few more ticks.

"I've met this St Saviour of yours before, a very, *very* long time ago. We're in a world of trouble." She seemed reluctant to continue, leaving the rest of the friends looking at each other uncertainly.

Eventually, Wyland said, "Long though the tale might be, Gabby, I think we need to hear it."

She opened her eyes and stared at him. Then nodded. Sinking herself more deeply into the embrace of Wyland's sofa, she began her tale.

✣ 21 ✣

THE LAST SYNOD

You'll need to take a massive leap of the imagination, to a time when Britain bore no resemblance to the country we live in now. We're talking about the very beginning of the common era and the start of the Roman invasions.

Between them, powerful tribes had carved up the land. There were still terrible battles over territory, but tribal leaders had begun to prefer the stability of peace to the churn of war. You were a resourceful lot. Not only good in a fight, you had traders and artisans, fertile land and plentiful food; the makings of a great civilization.

Britons have always had a sense of what we might call 'the other'. Eventually, a priestly class developed, comprising those with perception acute enough to sense the existence of my kind. When the Roman threat became imminent, having already endured persecutions abroad, these priests understood they would need our protection.

I'm talking about the Druids, of course.

One of Rome's most successful emperors was Claudius. No Julius, that man. Not pretty or very strong. What he lost in stature, though, he gained in intelligence. Goodness me, he was astute! A consummate politician, he scanned the globe for quick wins, proving himself time and time again. The Romans had known for a while about Britain's existence, and there'd been a few incursions to get the lie of the land. Their reconnaissance discovered it to be rich in lead—they were really good plumbers—and gold, and tin. Plenty of forest wood for ships. The country had hundreds of thousands of sheep, too, so they could add wool and hides to their loot. Well worth the effort of a full-scale invasion.

They made one mistake. They thought Britain a divided land, their population unsophisticated, making it easy to play one tribe off against the other. They couldn't fathom that a balance existed between communities; a glue that held it all together.

A belief system.

Now, I'm not talking about religion. That was a later construct. But we're definitely in the ballpark. This is the age when myths were made, those cocktails of fantasy and experience that point to deeper truths which make meaning of life and land. The Druids were front and centre of all that. Intelligent, creative, articulate people—mostly nomadic—they might be used as judiciary, to settle disputes, to make laws. Did you know that some were even soldiers? All of them knew the power of ritual, especially when enacted within stone cathedrals already ancient in their time. They fed and developed the culture.

The Romans loathed them. They'd already killed thousands in pogroms across the continent. Take my word, nothing undermines an invasion quite like belief. The Romans needed their world view to stick. Where they couldn't assimilate the old ways, they eradicated them. Once they found the country to be 'infected' with Druidic influence

—one that refused to give way to the Roman insurgents—getting rid of it became one of their prime missions.

They brought in a chap called Paulinus. Suetonius Paulinus. Ugly so and so, wide as he was tall. Pity that poor horse of his! He teamed up with a lieutenant who'd already been posted here—or so the Romans thought. A warrior called Numenius.

Numenius had zeal.

Take what happened in Anglesey.

The Druids used it as a spiritual centre. Though they travelled far and wide, they'd retreat there every now and then. Touch base, as it were. Hold a synod or three. There were natives too, of course, and other travellers who'd come in by boat. Traders, mostly.

Numenius and his thugs chose a holy day to sail over from the mainland. Paulinus should have led the invasion, except dysentery had laid him low, so the task fell to his lieutenant. He nearly overplayed his hand by feeding his men superstitious nonsense about the Druids they would find there. Maybe it had been because they'd been so oppressed by their fears—or Numenius' threats if they didn't set off—but when they landed, something snapped. All hell broke loose.

Imagine ancient villages, kids playing, women pounding dough, men hunting or praying, thinking their island a safe haven. Then picture the leather-strapped army, half a cohort—that'd be about two hundred men—jackbooting over the grassland. Six men abreast with sword, javelin and bow. Oh, and a standard-bearer, of course. They sent ahead to slaughter watchmen and lookouts, surprising villages as they broke ranks to run amok.

Soldiers grabbed children and threw them into fires or broke their necks before—or worse, after—tearing off their mothers' clothes and raping them. They rounded up the men and if found to be Druid, put them to the sword or tortured them for information.

That was just the start. Day after day, our kind heard Druidic cries from Wales, in Ireland, as well as across the water in France. And beyond. Within a month after the Anglesey massacre any communities suspected of harbouring a priest were routed, sacked and slaughtered.

A complete annihilation.

Then suddenly Paulinus left Britain. The records say his time here had been a triumph. Not so. Numenius spread rumours about a dalliance between his commander and the daughter of a tribal king, effectively turning the general into a political liability. None of it true, but that didn't matter. With Paulinus out of the way, his path to power had been cleared.

But we got him in the end. Brought him here, in fact.

Emma could hardly take it all in.

Apparently, neither could Wyland. "What, really here? To Wood End?"

"Yes."

"I'd've thought you'd know all about that," said Abigail, "What, with all your books—and being a Guardian, of course!"

Gabby replied for him. "He wouldn't. Guardians find themselves attracted to a place then bond with it in a way they don't fully understand." She turned to Wyland. "It's all instinct with you, isn't it?"

"That's right." Wyland shrugged. "It's like a calling, an … imperative … to stay here and make sure the sentinels are protected. That … instinct … tells me to keep watch and to listen to the earth. How they got here—the history surrounding their burial—is a complete mystery to me." He made a wry grin. "I expect that's about to change."

Smiling, Gabby replied, "Specifics do get lost, though your purpose, and that of those who will eventually take your place, remains."

"Carry on, Gabs," said Abigail, not wanting to lose the thread of the story. "I want to know what happened to Numerous."

"Numenius!" Gabby tutted and shook her head in mock crossness. "I'll get you there, but there's more I have to explain first."

Her voice once more serious, she continued, "Though Anglesey had been a huge base for the Druids, as I've already said, their ministry was nomadic, rooted in their individual missions. Their network could only be described as … esoteric. Hard to pin down. They didn't leave trails because they only rarely communicated with each other. Yet time and again the Druids were found in ways quite beyond the resources of the Romans. Impossible, since by definition the invaders were strangers to the country. They did not know the sacred pathways."

"They'd have had informers," said Emma.

"No doubt about that," Gabby agreed, "but something wasn't right. Thousands of priests had been found in their hiding-places over an astonishingly brief period of time. A month—less. Sometimes hundreds in the course of just one week. Not possible, no matter how sophisticated the spy system. Long story short, it became obvious to us that Numenius was not all he seemed. The man had knowledge of men's hearts no mortal could possibly have. And he had help."

Abigail started. "I know where this is going. There'd been an emergence, hadn't there? Here, again?"

"An emergence?" Emma sighed. What had she missed?

"Oh, I forgot," said Abigail. "That was the long story I was on about. You know, before we went to see Gabby at the vicarage."

"Might be an idea to tell me now!"

Abigail held the floor, describing the night she and Wyland sat huddled together in the hollow tree, terrified out of their wits by the beings that emanated from the ground.

"Oh no," groaned Emma. "Please no."

"Abigail's quite correct," said Gabby. "The lie of the land hasn't changed in the last two thousand years. What she and Wyland saw was, in effect, a re-enactment of the earlier emergence, from when Numenius and his acolytes rose into the world and, like chameleons, merged with humanity." The frown she wore deepened. "They bond to their entry-points, which is why we posted the sentinels, so that they may never return."

"Yet they did," said Wyland.

"Yes. From what Abigail told me about her visit to the Tor, I think that's where he found his way out. I don't know how—it should never have happened. Then from there he somehow managed to raise the sentinel and undermine the integrity of the portal to let his minions through."

Emma let out a little moan. She couldn't bear this. Not again. "More spirit possession? Seriously?"

"No, dear." Gabby chuckled. "I rather think this is more an incarnation. Ironic though that may be."

"What do you mean?" asked Abigail. "Why ironic?"

"That something with such a burning hatred of priests, should this time choose to take the form of one."

Turning to Emma, she said, "As soon as you started describing him, I had my suspicions about who he really was, but your mention of the sphere clinched it. Numenius had one just like it, though he didn't carry a cane. In that era, it was the pommel of his sword. He could not be parted from it. I'm positive. Numenius is back. He's your St Saviour."

Emma's hand clutched the cross around her neck as Gabby's talk of priests hit home. She felt a surge in her stomach, a hint of bile at the back of her throat. "He hated priests so much he hunted them down. Will's in danger! We've got to warn him!"

"I think he's safe for the moment. I fear he has a more ... immediate victim in mind."

"You?" said Wyland.

Gabby nodded. "Me. I officiated at the ritual of Removal, here at the original emergence site." She called forth what must have been words from the ceremony. "To Compel Him Back from Whence He Came." She shook her head at some terrible memory. "Wood End makes a natural hidden amphitheatre. As they say nowadays, it was a tough gig for all concerned, particularly the audience, having to face the murderer that had decimated their kind. The ceremony became their final synod, the last thousand or so Druids left on earth, summoned to bear witness to his leaving it. I was in my full power—and little match for Numenius. That, combined with the prayers of the Druidic witnesses, enabled us to end his body by the taking of head and hands—and his sword—which were consumed in the ceremonial fire. Once we'd freed it from his corporeal flesh, we consigned his spirit to the underworld."

Wyland blew out his cheeks. "Wow. As you're talking about it, I see it now. As if I was there."

Gabby smiled at him. "One of the Druids stayed and began the guardianship. It has since formed a long and unbroken line. You'll be picking up his echo."

Her face grew sombre. "I'll never forget that night. On the removal of Numenius, his consorts joined him. Doomed to follow wherever their master led, they came as an army of airborne skeletons, their flesh scourged as soon as the fire had taken his. A few at first, then hundreds. Shrieking, they coursed and circled the amphitheatre in vain attempts to frighten the wits out of their audience. They too had been instructed to keep their eyes tight shut. Then, as little more than vapour, the spirits followed their master."

Her remembrance seemed to force a sigh. "Elder Druids brought in their dead, their most revered comrades, to act as sentinels against the wicked one, guarding the lowest point— the well of this park—where the spirits had descended. We buried them upright, facing inward, then I sealed the henge. We wanted it hidden in plain sight, so we built dwellings on top. The more innocuous the better, to avoid grave robbers and ..."

"Forensic archaeologists," finished Wyland, grimly.

"Quite so," said Gabby. "The caravan park carried on the tradition. Genius, really, until this happened."

Emma could barely control her creeping fear. No one seemed to get the bloody obvious problem that stared her in the face. "Fascinating though this history lesson might be, it says naff-all about what we're up against now. What it means for us. Me. I want to keep my home. I want Will to be safe."

Gabby left the sofa, blew out a sigh and stared out of the window at the sun beginning its decline behind the wooded edge of the park.

"For now, I don't think you need worry about Will. As I said, it's me he wants. He'll have taken hundreds of years to claw his way back. More. Fuelled by revenge, no doubt." Chin trembling, she turned around. "He might even have sensed it was me Will was hiding at the vicarage all along. Perhaps it was my presence that made him want to stay there, get his hooks into Will—you. Thing is ..."

Emma, ashamed of her outburst, said gently, "You have no protection any more. No ... power."

Gabby could only manage a tearful nod.

"Can't you tell Michael? Get him here to help?" Emma's eyes were gentle. "Pray?"

With returning sorrow for all she had lost, Gabby whispered, "I don't know how."

Emma got up and joined Gabby at the window. She gathered the woman in her arms and took her back to the sofa.

"Wy," said Abigail. "Go and get her a drink. What you're having."

No one said a word as Gabby gave in to sobs. Abigail too came to sit with her, solidarity the only gift she could offer. Wyland came back and placed a glass of golden liquid on the table, together with a roll of kitchen towel.

Emma ripped off a sheet and gave it to her friend, who blew her nose so loudly the noise broke the tension. "Sorry," said Gabby.

She picked up the glass, took a gulp from it and spluttered, coughing loudly. "My goodness," she said, still sniffing back tears not wholly caused by distress. "That packs a punch. Will it make me drunk? I've never been drunk."

"If you neck much more of it like that, yes." Wyland smirked, sensing a shift in the mood.

So did Abigail. "These spirits don't half choose stonking names," she quipped. "Numenius. Wow. And St Saviour. What's all that about?"

"In themselves, they don't mean anything. He picks up on whatever cultural vibe he's riding. We ascribed one to him, though, at the Removal, so he would forever see himself for the base character he truly was. Being in the Roman era, we used that vernacular. Its meaning changed over time and I have to say has collected quite a few odd attributes along the way."

"Go on, Gabs," said Abigail, "Say it. Say his name."

"Normally I wouldn't, lest it be a conjuring. But since he's already here I suppose it couldn't do any more harm."

She closed her eyes; took deep breaths, as if girding herself.

"Animus. We called the spirit, Animus."

22

SUMMONED

"**A**nimus?" Emma frowned. "Isn't that a Freudian term?"

"I think it's Jung, actually," said Abigail. "Remember when I suggested you see a counsellor, or a shrink? I did a bit of research. They follow different schools of thought. There's a Jungian psychologist in Sandmarsh. Interesting stuff. Deals with archetypes, apparently, you know ... Like we have guardians and sentinels and..." she nodded to Gabby, "messengers. They have their own labels, which are all about the patterns created by ..." lowering her voice to a doomy level, " ... the Collective Unconscious."

Gabby wiped her nose with yet another piece of kitchen towel and sniffed. "Hmm. 'Created' being the operative word. That lot still believes mankind makes everything up. It doesn't seem to occur to these 'experts' that for every archetype there's a prototype."

She gave an impatient shrug. "I'm always amazed at how the human race can pick up a word, twist its meaning and make it signify whatever it wants. We couldn't have been clearer when we chose the name. *Anamos, Hnnu, omma, anmie.*

In every possible language it incorporates notions of breath, wind, spirit—drive." She lowered her voice. "Wrath. Hate."

"Wow," said Wyland. "Very biblical."

"We thought so. As a name, the word encapsulated all that he was. All that he is."

"I am so sick of this," Emma burst out. "Bloody sick of sitting here, calm as anything—" She threw a recriminatory grimace at Abigail, "—excited even. Gabby's in danger, Will's in danger, the whole world's in bloody danger, and all you can do is talk about … words." She took a breath. "It's just words. Evil is here. In Flammark. Again. And I'm in the middle of it all. Again. I'm nowhere near over what happened last time. I can't cope with another onslaught."

When Gabby tried to put a comforting hand on her knee, Emma made an angry swipe at it. Her voice rose. "You've lost your powers. You tell us you can't contact Michael, so there'll be no help from the bloody angels. Abigail is still young in whatever gifts she has, then there's you, Wyland. No offence, but you don't have a flaming clue what's going on, apart from whatever remnant vibes this place chooses to throw at you." She waved her arms randomly around the room, glaring at everyone and no one. "Then there's me. I have no home, my best friend's in trouble, and I can't confide in the man I lo—"

Emma shut down, shocked at her outburst, speechless in the face of what she'd been about to admit.

A dumbstruck silence followed.

Abigail broke it, as only Abigail could. "You were going to say it! You were talking about Westen. You *do* love him!"

Though Emma's face crumpled, she made no specific answer, only, "Did I really just say all that? I am so sorry. I have no idea where it all came from."

"Animus, Emma," said Gabby. "It came from Animus. His influence is growing. It's in the very air we breathe. You see now why it's a name well chosen. He turns your primal instincts against you. Against us. You—we—must guard against it. We must not let him in."

Though her rage subsided, Emma's fear had not. She rocked back and forth, assimilating, remembering how she'd treated Westen that day, Abigail being at odds with her mother—even Robbie had been difficult at times. Then there was the psychologist he'd referred her to. No appointments for months.

She said, "We've got to tell Will. He—and Peter, of course —are both living with him in the vicarage. We've got to get him out. And I don't know what to do about his blackmail threat. For some reason, St Saviour—he—it—Animus, wants me out of the way." Glancing at her host, she continued. "He'll get his wish, too. I can't risk Will's reputation."

"It interests me that he wants you out of the cottage," said Gabby. "There's a reason behind it. You clearly present some kind of danger, but I have no idea what it is."

Emma slumped back, shaking her head with frustration.

"What's his plan?" asked Wyland. "What can we expect?"

Gabby fell silent for a while, her brow furrowing as she gathered her thoughts. "After breaking into the world, Animus has acted very quickly in freeing his minions. At this very moment they'll be scouring the land, sowing discord and disruption." She paused to look at Emma as a case in point. "For some reason, he's making his base here and already has his hooks into the church. It won't be long before he uses the influence it gives him to inveigle himself into more corridors of power. It might take years, decades even, but he is well-versed in how easy it is to break a civilisation, undermine its faith, destroy its totems. One minute there's the rule of law, the next, the order of the jackboot. He'll sleepwalk humanity into chaos."

At her words, Emma looked around the room, at Wyland's books, maps—even his carpentry. A harmony of peace and erudition. She remembered St Saviour's twisted smile as he delivered his threat against Will. There would be no room for a Wyland in his realm. Or a Will, or a Peter, or an Abigail.

"We have to stop him," Gabby continued, passion threading her voice, "before everyone is consumed with ... well, Animus. I just need to think up a plan."

"You'll come up with something," said Abigail. "*We'll* come up with something."

"Will I?" replied Gabby. "I don't even know how I'm going to protect myself, let alone the whole bloomin' human race!"

Stunned contemplation in all their faces, silence fell once again.

Emma's mobile chirped out a notification, then another and another. She fished it out from her pocket and read the text messages as they came in, each one stacking above the others.

In a sudden movement, she stood up. "I've got to go. It's Will. He's been trying to ring. He wants to meet." She looked around at the others. "I think there's something wrong."

She speed-dialed his number, but got nothing. Texting back, she glanced at Wyland and said, "Is there a signal problem here?"

He nodded. "Yeah. It's intermittent."

"Do you want us to come with you?" asked Abigail.

Frowning with indecision, Emma replied, "I don't know. Yes. Not you, Gabby. If these texts have anything to do with St Saviour, we can't risk you going anywhere near."

Nodding at Abigail to follow her, she cried, "His texts sound really urgent. We need to go. Now."

∽

On the way to the car, in deep twilight, nerves on edge, Emma jumped as the security light burst into life. How had it got so late? Out of the courtyard, hurrying onto the verge where the jeep was parked, Emma bleeped open its doors.

"God, it's hot out here. Wyland's living room is a fridge compared to this," said Abigail, flapping the front of her top. "Must be those thick stone walls. You okay?"

"Not really. I'm bothered that I can't get hold of Will. While I'm driving, will you try to, you know, use your Sight thing? Try to get a sense of what might be wrong?"

"Okay."

The engine churned for a few seconds before firing. Damned battery! Kicking herself for not getting it sorted, she left behind the glare of Wyland's courtyard. With a heavy heart she switched her headlights to full beam. Flammark's lanes were windy and unlit. They'd drain her power in no time. She couldn't shake the awful sense of dread on receiving Will's texts. Why her alarm bells were ringing, and not Abigail's, she had not the faintest idea.

Ten minutes out of Wood End and hanging on to her seat-belt with both hands, Abigail said, "I know we're in a rush, but can you slow down a bit? I hate travelling at night at the best of times."

Suddenly a vision of a locksmith's van, careering into the night much like she was doing now, burst into Emma's head. Had Abigail just projected? She hadn't the time to fathom it, but decelerated slightly to adjust for the nervousness the girl had about speeding vehicles. Like the one her father drove to his death.

"Anything?" she asked, hoping Abigail's Sight hadn't failed them.

"No. I'm getting no vibes about Will at all." She peered out of her window, "Why are you going this way? It takes loads longer."

"Will doesn't want to meet at the vicarage or mine. Prying eyes, apparently." Emma resisted an urge to bang her fist on the steering wheel. "I'd bet my bloody life St Saviour's told him about the gossip that's going around the parish about us. He wants me to go to the ruins."

"The ruins?" said Abigail, incredulously, "What, the old Blackstone chapel?"

"I know, seems odd to me, too. He never liked it there. He'd never go unless he had to."

"Totally," Abigail nodded, "he's done a few weddings there over the years. Ones he couldn't wriggle out of. I can see the appeal, though."

"You would! The place gives me the creeps."

"It's a favourite with my pagan group. They like the atmosphere. Seely Tor's great for Samhain—you can work up a brilliant bonfire without getting complaints—but the ruins have a different vibe altogether. Good for rites of passage. I asked Will if he wanted to join us for one of them."

Driving posture stiff, nose closing in on the windscreen, Emma was in little mood for conversation. Abigail's idle chatter soothed her nerves, though, so she encouraged it by saying, "Oh? He didn't tell me about that."

"Yeah. Mary Pullman wanted him there for her Croning Ceremony. She doesn't go to church, obvs, but she'd known Will's parents and had really wanted him to be there."

Emma took a corner too hard. Muttering an apology, she shifted the gearstick but couldn't help whacking up the speed again as the road straightened. "Croning Ceremony? Seriously?"

"Not what you're imagining," said Abigail, white-knuckling her seatbelt. "It's about reclaiming female stereotypes—can you slow down just a bit?" The speed barely dropped, but Abigail spoke faster, as if trying to take her mind off her anxiety. "You know, old women being seen as a bit mad, past-it or just plain wicked. We think the opposite. Crones are experienced and wise. It's another phase of life."

Abigail chirped on, her words fading as Emma's thoughts grew darker. Why *did* Will choose the ruins? She'd visited them only once—the only physical remnant of the Blackstone family that existed after their family home, Blaxton Hall, had been razed.

It had been an impulsive attempt to connect with her ancestors. Despite their monstrous past, and what their curse had tried to do to her, she couldn't resist the temptation. Emma shuddered at the memory of the smoke-blackened remains of the chapel on that cold spring morning. Deserted. Bleak. Grim. She couldn't bear to stay any longer than ten minutes, after the briefest of meanderings amid their columns and crazed brickwork. She'd felt nothing.

"Are you listening to me, or what?"

Emma glanced at Abigail as she stopped at a junction. "Sorry, my mind wandered." There being no traffic, she made the turn. "I've got a really bad feeling about this. I think you're right. The ruins are the last place Will would choose to meet."

Abigail grew silent. A few moments later she said, "Are you absolutely sure the texts were from him?"

Emma started. Heart thumping, she peered into the rearview mirror and pulled over. Hazards on, she switched on the internal light and, leaving the engine idling, reached into the back seat for her bag to rummage out her phone. "It's his number," she said, scrolling through. I didn't think twice about it." She stopped and searched in Abigail's eyes. "I'll ring him again. I've got a signal." She slumped. "But not a lot of charge."

Abigail shook her head. "I wouldn't bother. If Will didn't send the texts, whoever did must have his phone—or some kind of access to it. Plus—" She chewed her lip, her eyes not leaving Emma's.

"Shit. You're thinking St Saviour—Animus." Emma's voice rose, "He might have started. Might have done something to Will!" She shook her head. "But that makes no sense. Why would he text me?"

"I don't know."

Scared, indecisive—hostages to conjecture—the two women locked eyes again, scrabbling for ideas.

Emma breathed, "I don't know what to do."

"Ring him. Go on. Ring him. If St Saviour answers, then we'll know."

Emma speed-dialed again. Straight to voicemail. Then another text swooped in.

- Sorry I missed your call. I'm okay. I'm here at the ruins. Waiting. Hurry. W. xxx

Showing the message to Abigail, Emma said, "It doesn't read like something Will would write." Another notification arrived. Reading it, she exclaimed, "Shit. Damned batteries! It's saying I'm down to five per cent. One phone call and it'll be completely useless. You've got your mobile, right?"

Abigail bit her lip and shook her head. "I gave it to Gabby. Her caravan doesn't have a phone line." She heaved out a sigh. "Can't see we've much choice but to carry on. If Will didn't send the texts, yeah, we can guess who did." She balled her hands into fists. "I'm being totally useless. I can't feel or 'see' anything. I don't *think* Will is in danger, but I can't really be sure."

"Okay. Let's get moving." Emma put the car in gear and, about to set off, thought better of it. She put the handbrake back on. Started texting.

Abigail looked at her oddly. "What're you doing?"

"Requesting backup."

✷ 23 ✷

RUINED

Emma drove on in silence, fretting over whether Westen would pick up the text, wondering if she should have risked calling triple nine instead. But that would've entailed describing the exact nature of the emergency, and she hadn't the will, words or battery power to get into that.

She could only pray he'd received it and wouldn't be too busy—or asleep—to respond.

- Meet me at the ruins in Flammark. Asap. I'm in trouble.

Relief and dread building in equal measure, Emma turned into the drive that once led to Blaxton Hall. Now a narrow, tree-lined public road, it offered the only vehicular access.

After a quarter-mile, they swung round an elevated curve, Emma's headlights illuminating ranks of columned arches—the only bones left of the old Blackstone family chapel. Broken walls, their charred brickwork tumoured with creeping moss, leered at her under the ribcage of rafters that formed the outline of the church's vaulted roof. In the gaze of its black, glassless mullions, Emma stared it back, coming to a halt, revving the engine to keep it charged.

She peered through the windscreen for any sign of Will's VW.

Nothing. She glanced down at the phone in Abigail's lap. "Anything?"

The girl shook her head. "Not yet. Shall we get out? Take a look around?"

"No. If the texts were Will's, he'll come to us."

"And if not?"

"Let's jump off that bridge when we come to it."

Then for no reason in the known universe, Emma sat back to wait and switched off the engine.

"Shit, shit, shit!" Closing her eyes in silent prayer, she turned the ignition. The engine gave a sickening churn. She tried again.

Click.

Now what?

Suddenly enveloped in black, moonless night, neither of them spoke.

Emma couldn't bear the tension. "What the hell made me do that?"

"I don't know, Ems, but if Will's in trouble, it's made it much harder to find him."

After drumming her fingers on the steering wheel, Emma muttered curses. "Damn. I can't stand it in here. I've got to get out."

"Okay," replied Abigail. "It might be a bit lighter outside."

They opened up and jumped down from the jeep, letting the doors hang. Emma felt no relief. The night seemed even darker, the silence thick.

Beset with anxiety and indecision, Emma worried at her necklace. At the sound of an incoming text, she almost fainted with relief.

"It's him!" exclaimed Abigail, her face briefly lit by the phone screen. "Westen." She handed the mobile to Emma.

- On way. Be there in 20.

"Oh, thank God! If everything's okay, I'll take the hit and apologise. No harm done."

Perhaps to lighten the tension, Abigail chuckled, "Yeah. You could take him for a drink."

"Honestly, don't you ever give up?"

Their attempt at jocularity lasted for as long as it took Emma's phone to die.

With no sign of Will, no inkling of a moon, they were caught in a conspiracy of dread and dark. It quickened their pulses, closed their mouths, forced them to find each other's hands.

Emma started. "Shh. Listen."

Nothing.

Abigail whispered, "Are you sure you heard something?"

"Yes. It came from up there. From the ruins. Sounded like a cat."

The noise repeated. Some kind of mewling. Faint. High-pitched. Definitely maybe a cat. Something in pain, for sure.

Hands flying once more to her pendant, Emma breathed, "Oh, pray God it's an animal. Pray God it's not …" Unable to utter Will's name, she gulped, "We've got to find out who—what it is. I need to be sure."

They stood still, getting their bearings, peering into the dark for some following light. She could just make out the deeper shadows of the treeline on one side of the road and the elevated outline of the ruins on the other.

Mewling again. Louder this time, agony in every cry.

Not an animal.

With joined hands oiled by the sweat of their fear, they

started forward to the grassy incline, feeling their way to the wide stone steps which led to the entrance.

"Ouch!" Abigail exclaimed in a shouty whisper. "I've stubbed my toe."

"We can't stop now. It's Will. I know it."

Emma cried out as her feet touched something hard. The steps!

They started up them as fast as the dark—and their dread —would allow, climbing the wide stone sleepers until the darker hue of the arched entrance loomed, the atmosphere around them hardening with the onset of brick and stone, amplifying the pitiful, pain-ridden whining within.

Let it not be Will. Please God, let it not be Will.

They crossed the threshold, the transition marked only by a colder ambience. Some mutual instinct made them drop each other's hands as they raised their arms, moving forward in tiny painstaking steps, pressing the air for obstructions.

"Over there," Emma whispered. "It's coming from that direction." In a gesture Abigail couldn't possibly see, she pointed somewhere to her right and called, "Will? Is that you? We're coming."

Whimpers.

Abigail holding onto the waistband of Emma's jeans, they inched over the uneven ground, feet scouting each step, Emma's arms outstretched like a sleepwalker, following the sound of pain.

"Damn," whispered Abigail. "It's more overgrown here. I still can't see where I'm treading."

Emma made no reply, but gasped, hit by a sudden stench.

Musky, metallic.

"Blood. I can smell blood. It's strong. There must be lots of it."

One faltering step further …

Emma slapped into something heavy and warm.

Wet.

Hanging?

Almost falling, she stumbled back and screamed. Abigail screamed. The mewling intensified, the sudden cacophony echoing around and around the shattered walls. Heart in her throat, every nerve on edge, Emma closed her eyes, digging deep to collect herself. She took a deep breath and held it. Lifting her arms once more, she moved forward.

A second slap.

Ready for it this time, keening with revulsion, she caught and slowed the swinging mass. Touched flesh. Broken flesh.

A torso.

Barely able to summon the word, she whispered, "Will?"

"Nnnnnn … Hhhhheeelll …"

A man, for sure. Not Will!

"Abigail, go. Fast as you can. Westen can come only one way. Run to meet him. Flag him down. Get him to send for medics."

The girl stumbled away. Emma took a moment, over-whelmingly relieved that the bleeding body she held did not belong to her best friend, devastated that it belonged to someone—some *person*—else. Carefully, she let it go, terrified of the damage she might already have caused. "Shhh. Sh… shh. You're safe now. Nothing else can happen to you."

Gently, oh so gently, she touched here—there—making sense of the naked flesh … the body's orientation. Gaps in the skin, wide and raw, what felt like rags hanging down.

A penis. Wet and with the viscosity of blood.

She jerked back her hand, wanting to run. Needing to stay. Feeling his head sway into her waist.

Crying—babbling—Emma said, "I'm sorry. I'm so sorry. I … want to get you down, but can't. Your foot is too high for me to reach. Help is on its way. Won't be long now. Probably no more than five minutes …"

Collapsing onto her knees, she reached for his hands. They dangled no more than a few inches off the ground, scratched and scourged, but, as far as she could feel, intact. As if it were the most precious of objects, she slipped one of them into hers, the slightest comfort she could offer amidst the atrocity of his torture.

She sat. Lost all sense of time. Made his hand the centre of her being as she prayed this man might live, and that Westen would get to them soon.

She couldn't move, couldn't let go, not even at the blare of a siren, still chirping as it reversed in the road and suffused the ruins with its headlights, bludgeoning her with its awful illumination.

"Stay there. Do not follow me," Westen shouted at Abigail, as he jumped out of his car.

Guided by its full beam, he pelted up and into the ruined chapel, scanned its silhouetted columns, its broken brickwork randomly exposed in the variegated light. "Emma, Emma, I'm—"

He stopped in his tracks.

"Jesus fucking Christ."

Westen was no stranger to death. Used to bodies. Slaughtered, tortured—his mind flew to the gruesome discovery of Stephen Holbrooke last year, part of Cregan's spree. Even his evisceration paled against the tableau that confronted him now.

Creaking rope, hung from a high rafter, a single foot looped in its end. Male victim. Naked. Bloody ribbons of flayed flesh dangling from upper thighs to chin.

A man dressed in skin rags.

Raw flesh glistened in the brutal light. The other leg, bent at the knee, foot tied to opposing thigh, posed him like a reverse fucking jester.

A Hanging Man.

Westen's eyes were drawn to his genital area. A penis, part severed. White flower shoved into the cut.

The scene turned his stomach, but what caused his heart to burst was the sight of Emma, bloody, sitting, holding the victim's hand, like some kind of terrified fucking Magdalen, mouth encircling a silent scream as she stared up at her upside-down, mutilated fucking Christ.

Rushing to them, he flung one arm around Emma's shoulders while he pushed the fingers of his other hand against the victim's neck, feeling for a pulse.

He sagged. Gently prising the victim's hand out of her iron grasp, he whispered, "Emma. Love. He's gone. Let him go. Let me get you out of here."

He lifted her in his arms and she sank into him, her body wracking with silent sobs. He took her outside and placed her gently on the grass, blindly nodding in the headlights for the girl he knew was waiting.

As Abigail came tearing up, he said, "I want to stay with her, but—"

"No. Go. Do your job." She sat and put her arms around her friend. "She'll be all right. She'd want you to."

"Don't go inside, Abigail. It's a scene I wouldn't wish on anyone."

As he turned, she reached up and caught his arm. "Just answer me this." Lips trembling, eyes welling, she asked, "Is it Will?"

Westen shook his head. "I don't know who it is."

A minute later, Burrows arrived and, with a puzzled glance at the two women on the grass, joined his boss at the entrance.

"Good. You got here fast," Westen said, unable to hide his

relief. He leant his arm against the iron-black archway and spat on the grass, heaving in gobfuls of air. "It's not good. Prepare yourself."

Still guided by the beam of his headlights, he went inside, his sergeant on his heels and carrying a torch. Burrows let it probe the slowly spinning, hanging body. Letting out a low whistle, he exclaimed, "Jesus Christ Al-bloody-mighty."

"Do you recognise him?" asked Westen.

Burrows shook his head. "Never seen him before, Guv." He pointed at the little white flower. "What the hell?"

"We're dealing with a sicko," said Westen. "What is it about this fucking village? Fifteen years on the job, the worst I've seen has come from here. Cregan last year; now this."

Raised voices outside. What now? Abigail and someone else. He could hear her cry, "No. No! You mustn't. Don't go in. Westen's inside. He won't want you to—"

"Bugger Westen, he can't keep me out."

The Inspector groaned. What the hell was Will Turner doing here?

Westen turned to face him as he ran into the chapel before stopping, mid-stride.

"No. Please God, no ..."

The priest made a run at the hanging man. Burrows nearly had him but, with surprising strength, Turner lashed out and caught him on the chin. Westen leapt at him, but was thrown by a lucky punch and the detective jerked back, affording Turner precious seconds to get to the body. He grabbed at it, tried to heave it off the rope as he tore away that blasted, fucking white flower.

Sobbing, out of his mind with despair, Will shouted, "Why are you leaving him like this? Help me. *Help me*, damn you! *HELP ME GET HIM DOWN!*"

Together, they managed to yank Turner off the victim but he showed no sign of calming. Westen planted himself firmly and pulled the distraught man back into a body hug, restraining him while nodding at Burrows to keep his distance.

"Turner … Will. I'm sorry but this is a crime scene, and you aren't helping. We can't get him down. Not until forensics are done. You can't be in here."

Will, ignoring him, leant forwards, arms outstretched, straining against Westen's hold. "Peter, Peter! I'm so, so, sorry."

Suddenly, a female voice pierced the air. "Will! Westen's right. We shouldn't be here. Let him do his job."

Emma! Thank Christ, she'd talk sense into him.

"You know him?" he shouted over to Emma. "This … Peter?"

"Yes," she called, obviously not wanting to come any nearer. "It's Peter Martin. He … he's working with Will."

At the sound of the name, Turner increased his struggles, trying to wrest himself from the detective's grip.

"Come on, man," Westen huffed, pulling him up and away. "Easy. You can't do anything for him now."

"Let go, Westen. I'm all right." Then defeat entered his tone and he slumped. "I won't try anything again."

After waiting a few moments to test the water, the detective relaxed his grip and Turner slid to his knees. With pleading eyes he looked up at Westen and said, "I want to hold his hand."

Westen shook his head. "I'm sorry, Will. Not even that."

Turner shifted to look at Peter's ravaged face, his wide, dead eyes staring back.

"Forgive me," he cried. "Forgive me. You're safe, now. At peace. Where you know for sure, that I have always … will always … love you."

❦ 24 ❦

WILL

Will and Peter? It took a while for Emma to process the information. Despite the depth of their friendship, she'd never asked Will about why he wasn't with someone. She'd thought it a boundary too far, perhaps concerned that asking the question might lead him to believe she wanted something more from him than friendship.

Westen too, seemed taken aback. Eyebrows raised, he locked his eyes on hers in a silent exchange of meaning as he once more gathered up the distraught man. With a firm grip on Will's elbow, and his other arm around his waist, he walked him towards the entrance.

"Sh … shush, Will," Emma said, taking over from Westen. "I've got you." She nodded Abigail towards them and, threading their arms around his waist, they led their friend outside, shielding their eyes against the lights and sirens of arriving police cars.

Raising his voice above their noise, Westen said, "He's in shock. Burrows will put him in an ambulance." He peered down the road and muttered, "Once they fucking arrive."

Eyes wild, Will cried, "I'm not going to a hospital. I want to stay with Peter."

"Will, love, that's not possible. Why not come back with me to Clearview? You can have the spare room. And we can talk." The last thing she wanted was for him to go back to the vicarage. Where St Saviour would be waiting. Emma had no doubt he'd been behind this. Had probably picked up some sexual tension between Will and Peter that had evaded all of them. Now she thought about it, hadn't he been behind his Peter's transfer in the first place? Had he planned all this, even then?

For spite?

How was she supposed to tell him about Animus now? She hadn't even told him about the blackmail. It might send him over the edge. For a wild moment she considered spilling it all to Westen, but again, where would she start?

With not a hint of irony, Westen said, "If he won't go to the hospital, I think taking him back with you is a very good idea."

He gave her that raised-eyebrow look again, its meaning not lost on Emma. If he'd imagined Will to be an impediment between them, he thought so no longer. He continued, "I have questions, but they'll have to wait until he's in a fit state to answer them."

"Can someone give us a lift—and drop Abigail home too?" Emma asked. "Josie'll be out of her mind."

"I'll organise a squad car. I'd take you but—"

"I know," she replied. "You have a murder to solve."

Ambulances began to arrive. Westen said, "I still want him checked out before you go. You too."

She acquiesced. With Abigail's help, she walked Will down the steps and onto the road. Paramedics leapt out of their vehicles and opened their back doors. After Westen briefed them, blankets were found and wrapped around them before Will and Emma were led to separate ambulances. Westen sat with her as they wiped blood from her hands and face and put on a blood pressure cuff.

"This Peter Martin," Westen said. "Who is he exactly? Where does he live?"

She looked down to find her free hand in his. She didn't take it away. "Erm … Will's heritage work has been upgraded. The bishop brought Peter in as added support."

"Was he living at the vicarage?"

"Some of the time. Tuesday to Thursday, I think. I'm not sure if he was there tonight, though."

"Right. That's where we'll start."

Emma couldn't resist. "You'll be meeting St Saviour." As casually as she could, trying to point a finger without making it obvious she knew more than she let on, she said, "He's a piece of work. Will doesn't get on with him."

Once they'd dropped Abigail off, Emma had second thoughts about taking Will to Clearview. He'd begun to shiver. Silent tears rivered down his cheeks.

Shock.

Other worries assailed her. If she took him home with her, he might decide to make the short walk to the vicarage across the green from her cottage, and she might not be able to stop him. She couldn't risk him going back there. Back to St Saviour.

She leant forward and asked the driver, "Can you take us to Dr Mason's surgery? It's on the Flammark Road. I'll show you."

The constable nodded. "No problem, miss. I know it well."

"I hope you don't mind, Will. I think it's the safer option

all round. Robbie'll be happy to put you up. Good that he's a friend as well as a medic."

Will replied with a thready sigh, and a single word. "Okay."

Five minutes later, the squad car swung into Robbie's gravel drive, its headlights strafing the familiar ivied walls of his Dickensian villa. Having been unable to phone ahead, she asked her driver to let Will stay in the car while she raised the doctor.

Emma had the keys to the surgery in her bag—thank God she'd had the foresight to rescue it from her dead car—but somehow it didn't seem right to use them. It would feel like an invasion: letting herself in, shouting upstairs to wake him. Better to let his heavy lion-head knocker do the job for her. She crashed it down three times and waited. About to start the next triplet, she heard the doctor's heavy footsteps thundering down the stairs.

A few seconds later the door opened, revealing the tousled Scot in a tee-shirt and shorts. Unfazed, though. Not his first rodeo.

"Emma!" His horrified expression as he glanced over her prompted her to look down at herself; her first proper realisation that her clothes were covered in blood. "What the hell's happened? Where are you hurt?"

"Not me. It's Will. There's been an incident. He isn't hurt either, but I think he may be in shock. He's refused to go to the hospital, though he's been checked over by a paramedic. I'd thought of taking him to mine but—"

He'd already started to stride towards the police car. "No problem. An incident, you say?"

"Yes. At the ruins, you know the Blaxton chapel? Someone he's very … close to. He saw the body."

"Right."

Barely acknowledging the uniformed copper, Robbie carefully opened Will's door and took a few moments to make a visible assessment. Gently but firmly, he said, "Now then, Will. I can see you're in a state. We need to get you inside so I can give you the once-over. Maybe a sedative."

"No,"Will managed to say. "No sedative. I'm all right. I need to be able to feel."

Robbie took an arm and gently helped him out of the car. He offered no resistance, even leaning into the body of the doctor. After thanking the driver, Emma followed them inside.

"Lead on to my living room, Emma. I always leave the woodburner good to go."

Emma ran up the stairs. Familiar with his living quarters, having shared many an evening meal there, she lit the fire and pushed one of two large leather armchairs closer in, grabbing a throw which rested over the other. She played at its hem as the two men came in. Will, still shivering, face white as death, slumped into the chair and without a word stared at the woodburner's early flames.

"Right," the doctor said. "The paramedics will have taken his blood-pressure. I'll just check him over, for my own peace of mind." He shone a pencil light in Will's eyes, then gently felt his wrist. "Heart rate slightly elevated, but nothing untoward."

He took a moment. "He'll be okay. Shocked, I think, but not in shock. He's alert and lucid. We can probably do without a sedative. I'll make some tea. Hot and sweet."

While he left for the kitchen, Emma tucked the throw around Will then, remembering that the chair reclined, gently pushed down the lever. "I'm going to help Robbie. I'll be back in a minute. Will you be okay?"

"Of course," Will said, still staring at the fire. "You go."

Seeing Robbie already at work with the tea things, she

leant on his massive pine table, the centrepiece of his equally massive kitchen.

"You need some rest too, Emma. You're almost in as bad a state as Will!"

"Not quite, Robbie," she replied. "I haven't lost what he lost tonight."

"Tell me what happened."

As with Westen, where to start?

After a moment she murmured, "I'm not sure you know Peter Martin? From Sandmarsh Cathedral? He and Will were working together. He was also his ... close friend." She lowered her voice to almost a whisper. "He'd been ... tortured."

Robbie's eyes widened as he mouthed, "Tortured?"

Emma nodded, her eyes welling at the memory.

"Jesus, Emma. And you saw it?"

"Yes. Abigail and I ... we discovered his body." Saying the words brought everything back. She fought back the nausea, stopped herself from swaying.

Robbie must have sensed her struggle. His face a picture of sympathy, he walked over to her, opened his arms and drew her into a hug. Grateful for the comfort, she leant into him, borrowing his strength. "It was dark. I had to feel ... his skin was—". She shuddered, and Robbie held her tighter. "When Westen came he turned on his headlights and ... I saw ... Robbie, it was ... "

He held her until her quiet sobs subsided, asking no questions, letting her cry it out.

"You should be in bed yourself, lass," said Robbie. "We're being all about Will, tonight, when we should be about you, too."

Coming to herself, she stiffened. "I'll be all right." She had Will to look after; his suffering must surely be deeper than hers.

"This Martin fellow, he's … special to Will?"

Another nod, acknowledging Robbie's drift.

The doctor fell silent. "Stay with him, lass. For as long as it takes. The agency has sent someone marginally competent, so no worries there. Will's needs are greater than mine."

"Thank you, Robbie."

He smiled. "I'll take the tea through, then I'll find you both something clean to wear."

As she returned to the living room she heard the grandfather clock downstairs strike twice. Had it only been this morning—yesterday morning—she'd knocked on Wyland's door? She'd slept so little and learned so much; had experienced so much tragedy it took her breath away.

Robbie poured the tea and handed him a cup. Will's hand trembled only a little as he took it and he seemed to be a lot calmer.

As Robbie left to find some clothes, she asked, "Do you want to talk or would you prefer to sleep?"

"It's hard to keep my eyes open, but yes, I think talking might help."

Robbie returned carrying a small pile. "I think it best Will stay here, with the fire. I've made up the bed in the spare room for you, Emma—unless you want to keep him company, of course. Anyway, you know where it is. I'll to my own bed."

"Great," she replied, "thank you, Robbie." Will murmured something similar.

"Not a problem. Try to get some sleep, now, both of you."

She smiled as he left. She noticed the empty cup on Will's lap and took it from him, asked if he wanted another. He shook his head.

"I'm staying here with you," she said. "It's okay if you want to talk."

He bowed his head. Emma waited. No rush.

She began to lose track of time, her thoughts going over the events of the evening. Desperate for them not to wander into the depths of the ruins and Peter's swinging body, she tried to fathom why she'd got those messages. Why she'd been brought to the place. Was she meant to be some kind of witness? Was it another attempt to scare her off, make her run away?

Suddenly she sat up. Peter's wounds had been fresh, unclotted. How fresh? Could the murderer have still been there, waiting for her? Had her decision to bring Abigail deterred him from making a move?

All sorts of possibilities racked her brain. Was it St Saviour? Had he decided that getting her out of Clearview wasn't enough? What was it that made her such a threat? Should she tell Westen? She shivered, reliving a world of fear all over again.

When Will chose that moment to talk, she could barely hold herself together. Her mouth had gone bone dry. No way would she move, though. Not now her friend chose this moment to pour out his soul.

"Peter and I met while he was an ordinand. The bishop had assigned me to be his pastoral mentor." He grimaced. "That was the first issue. Mentors are not supposed to fall in love with their charges." He caught his breath. "Peter is—was —a lovely man." The words choked off.

Still struggling with her own thoughts, Emma kept the silence. Waited for him to try again.

"He was a little too ... structured ... for parish life. He told you about not being a people person, I think? He loved his books, was a bit OCD about them."

Emma remembered her visit to the cathedral library last year. How immaculately dusted the volumes were, even in the section she'd been interested in, where visitors would have been few and far between.

"The second issue was his parents. His father—ex-army—never accepted Peter's calling and on the rare occasion he visited them, it always ended in a row. His mother loved him, but his father was a bully. Pure and simple. She couldn't stand up for her son."

Eyes glistening as he gazed into the flames, Will continued, "Peter had come out to her but not to his father. When priesthood called and he applied for seminary life, she did all she could to encourage him to go. Not only for his sake. She said it would be better for everyone and, of course, she made him promise never to tell anyone about our dirty secret, lest it got back to Mr Martin." He looked over at Emma. "That's what she called it. Our 'dirty secret.'"

His chin trembled. "It all seems so petty now. He wanted to end it between us. Said our relationship couldn't go anywhere and that I should find someone else. I disagreed and said we should meet his parents together, openly. I was so sure I'd be able to bring them round." He sighed. "He refused and we had a blow-up. I said some terrible things … accused him of being ashamed of what we had." His voice trembled, "I called him weak …"

His tears spilled over, Will an utterly heartbroken man. Empty. Bereft. Emma could hardly bear it.

"That was five years ago. Peter loved the cathedral, adored Sandmarsh, and didn't want to leave. I was wedded to Flammark—it's always been my home. But we couldn't be together, so instead we opted for a kind of near-distant friendship. It worked, up to a point. Until St Saviour came along."

Emma got up and knelt beside him, taking his hand as he fought for control, almost overcome herself by the wealth of human misery crass prejudice could cause. And Animus. Living up to his name. What had Gabby said he'd do? Start by turning families and friends against each other?

Somehow he'd found out about their relationship. That was why Peter had been transferred to the vicarage. A cruel foreplay to an even crueller death.

"How did you know where to find him? How did you know Peter would be at the ruins?"

He frowned. "He left a note."

❦ 25 ❦

PARTY ANIMAL

No sooner had Emma left with Will than Savage arrived at the crime scene. Taking him inside the ruins, Westen felt no satisfaction at the look of horror that replaced his normally supercilious expression. It's not often that pathologists let their work get to them. Maybe for once he might be able to complete a conversation with the man without wanting to punch his fucking lights out.

"You don't have to tell me the cause of death," Westen said, "I just need an estimate for how long he's been here."

"As to that, I am not sure I can be of much use to you, Inspector. Until we get him on the table, I cannot say whether he has been hanging for a few hours or a number of days. However, I can tell you the flaying is fresh work." Eyes probing, he circled around the body. "Clever, too. Preserving just enough skin for him to have exsanguinated slowly. Poor man."

"So?" Westen could hardly contain his impatience. "How fresh?"

Savage swallowed hard, shaking his head as he made another circuit. "Again, I can offer no accurate estimation."

"So give me an inaccurate one!"

After a seemingly endless moment of cogitation, Savage replied, "I would say these wounds are no more than an hour old."

"*An hour?*" Jesus, the murderer might have been on or near the scene when Emma discovered the body. She could have been next—and the Chater girl! And he might still be here, skulking near the treeline.

A watcher.

"Burrows, get the woods searched … and request air support. I want lights and cameras on this whole area. If they spot anyone, bring them in. No one takes a walk in a place this remote at this time of night."

His phone chirped. Westen turned his back on Savage, who'd started his team on photographs. His heart beat a little quicker when he saw Emma's name flash on his screen.

Holding the phone to his ear, softening his voice, he said, "Emma. You okay? Mason's? Good call … Yes, we'll be over in the morning with questions … A note? … Okay … Thanks, we'll find it. I have to go. Good to know Turner's getting some sleep. Try to get some yourself."

Burrows, too, had just finished a call. "All done, Guv. Uniform are sending two teams and the copper chopper'll be up in five."

"Right," replied Westen, pocketing his phone. "Was that Donna I saw arriving? Take a minute to brief her and get her to co-ordinate. I need you with me. I've just spoken with Emma Blake. She's taken Will to Doc Mason's. We'll interview him first thing. He's told her Martin left a note."

Burrows cocked his head. "What sort of note?" He glanced at the swinging body, then just as quickly looked away. "Suicide doesn't work here, Guv."

"I know. We need to see it, though. It's a start."

~

Ten minutes later, they drew up in front of the huge vicarage.

"Blimey," said Burrows. "Someone's having a good time."

Lights from the house blazed onto the gravelled forecourt, its stone window sills strewn with empty bottles and half-filled glasses. A few decidedly unclerical figures languished amongst an assortment of chairs, specially brought outside. One of them warbled tunelessly to a jazz refrain streaming through the open windows. Another pointed listlessly up at the lights of a low-flying helicopter. A third chap, buttocks bare, had taken up residence between the legs of a young woman, both enthusiastically in the process of redefining the word 'unfrocked.'

As the two men left the car, another female approached, alcohol legs wobbling for purchase on the gravel. Slurring, she said, "Hellowww, you're a bit late to the party, aren't you, boys?" She tripped and fell against Burrows, who put his arms out to steady her. "Ooh," she giggled, gripping one of them above the elbow as she twiddled a strand of bottle-blonde hair round a finger. "You're a strong one. Let's have a drink."

The sergeant, side-glancing his amused disgust to Westen, walked her to one of the chairs and sat her down. "You need to get some coffee, miss. And a taxi home."

"Jesus!" muttered Westen. "This is supposed to be a fucking vicarage."

Both the porch and inner door hung wide open. Burrows banged on the open door and loudly announced their presence. They strode into the brightly lit, oak-panelled hall. Westen had only been here once before—last Christmas. The atmosphere couldn't have been more different. Instead of the faint, comforting smell of incense, he wrinkled his nose at the stink of alcohol and cigarettes. And something else he couldn't quite place.

Like gunpowder.

Whoever controlled the music must have heard Burrows' shout as it suddenly stopped. Seconds later, through the library door appeared a square-set individual. Heavy. Offering only a glimpse of a clerical collar, his black shirt was filled with a bulging musculature that seemed both inappropriate and alien for a man of the cloth. Maybe he went to Savage's gym.

Yet he carried a walking stick. The most ridiculous fucking thing Westen had ever seen. Like a theatre prop. He couldn't see a man so obviously built like a brick privy needing help to walk. Nor did he seem the sort to brook affectation.

Westen took an instant dislike. Impressive features, no doubt. Rugged, as if he'd seen some action. Cruel mouth, full lips, steel in the eyes that bored into his. Not that Westen would look away first. He'd met his sort before: men who'd turn any encounter, no matter how casual, into a pissing contest.

How could this man be a fucking priest?

Words clipped and arrogant, tone deep and sonorous, with a twist of his lips the cleric said, "I don't think we've been introduced."

Still eyeballing, Westen felt for his warrant card and flashed it. "Inspector James Westen. This is my sergeant, Burrows. You are?"

"Dean Anthony St Saviour, parish consultant to Frederick Thomas, the Bishop of Sandmarsh." He curled his lip some more. "Why are you here, Inspector?"

"We understand a Peter Martin is resident here."

St Saviour's gaze slid to the library door before returning

to Westen. "Yes. On a part-time basis. The bishop has asked him to support William Turner in his capacity as Heritage Co-ordinator." He frowned. "He left before our gathering began. What has he done?"

A guffaw of laughter, followed by loud shushings, emanated from inside the library, something else Westen couldn't associate with the large, scholarly space he remembered from last year.

Burrows asked, "Have you been here all night, sir?"

St Saviour didn't bother looking at him. "Yes."

"What time did Martin leave?" Westen tried to read this ... dean. So far nothing. "Did you see him go?"

"No. I did, however, see William Turner leave. He seemed ... distressed."

"Do you know why?"

St Saviour pressed his lips into a line and shook his head. "I do not. He ran down these very stairs and out without saying a word. About an hour ago. Rude, given we have visitors."

"And you didn't think to go after him, sir?" asked Burrows.

"Why on earth should I have done that? Rumour has it William is a fully grown man. I had guests to look after."

Westen jerked his head towards the door. "I see you've been looking after them very well."

"That's enough, Inspector. Get to it."

Arrogant fucker.

Westen, matching St Saviour's tone, said, "We need to see Will Turner's room. Can you show us the way?"

"His room? Oh, you mean his bedroom!" An odious smile snaked between St Saviour's cheeks. "What on earth can you want there, I wonder?" He shrugged. Inhaled, loudly flaring his nostrils. "If I'm honest, I'm not sure where it is, but I do know it's on the second floor somewhere. No visitors are staying, so feel free to hunt. I considered tonight's reception important enough to cancel this week's residentials."

"Reception?" Westen mused, sardonically. "That's one word for it, I suppose." He nodded Burrows upstairs. Turning to the dean, he said, "Now … sir … if you wouldn't mind introducing me to your other guests?"

For the first time, St Saviour hesitated and gripped that ludicrous cane as he chewed the inside of his cheek. Eventually he decided to comply. "Very well."

The library had lost most of the tables and chairs he remembered; deep indents on the carpet speaking to their pimping-out for the party. Save for those in one corner where a group of individuals, all male, suited, sat round with drinks in hand, talking quietly, looking everywhere but at the door.

"My apologies, gentlemen, for interrupting the gathering," St Saviour said, approaching them. He walked in front of Westen, stepping with his cane. "The police are here. This is Inspector Westen. He is keeping his cards very much to his chest, but I believe it has something to do with Peter Martin. He has asked to be introduced to you all."

All the men bar one put down their drinks and stood as the visitors drew near.

"Detective Inspector … This is Jonathan McKewan, the CEO of Forward Electronics." Westen nodded, as he did at Philip Ackroyd, MP for Sandmarsh and Flammark, then Charles Athill, the head of GreenStar Energy. Angus Drew, from DeepDrilla, he already recognised. He didn't bother nodding to him.

"And of course," said St Saviour, "you'll be more than well acquainted with this gentleman."

The man in question, his back towards them, sat motionless at first, then, reluctance etched within every movement, he put down his brandy glass and rose from his winged armchair to join the others facing Westen.

Superintendent Peter Pecker.

The silence that followed was thunderous.

Pecker broke it. "With me, Westen."

Without a glance at his fellow guests, the red-faced and fuming officer strode out of the library. To irritate him further, Westen stayed a few moments longer to hold the gaze of each man standing. All but Anthony St Saviour looked away.

With a curt nod, Westen turned on his heels.

He found Pecker outside, well away from the lounging riff-raff, pacing the gravel, face incandescent.

"What the bloody hell was all that about, Westen? How dare you? How bloody dare you embarrass me like that!"

"Sir. There has been a brutal murder not two miles away from here." He pointed up at the lights of the copper chopper still circling above. "I'm surprised you weren't paged."

"I told you a few weeks ago." Pecker glanced towards the wide-open vicarage windows and lowered his voice. "I'm winding down in Serious Crimes. I'm joining the Corporate Fraud Task Force, for Christ's sake."

"Joining? So you aren't actually on the job, yet. Sir."

Pecker, looking as if a heart attack would take him any minute, snarled, "Are you interrogating me, Westen? I'm warning you, if your future with this force was ever in question, it's teetering on the brink now!"

Implacable, expressionless, Westen stood his ground, waiting for the defence he knew would follow.

"I-I've been attempting to get ahead of the game," Pecker started, " ... trying to infiltrate a network of major players. It's taken me weeks to get accepted into their cabal. All now down the bloody drain, thanks to you."

"Not necessarily. My intervention may give you more ... credibility. I go where the cases lead me, and this one brought me here. To you. Sir."

Still seething, Pecker glared at his Inspector. Then, perhaps deciding to cut his losses, he visibly calmed, and took a deep breath. "You didn't tell us who the victim is. This Martin is it, or Turner?"

Unwilling to give him an inch, wanting to keep Pecker off-balance, Westen replied, "You know Turner, sir?"

"We were introduced. He was here earlier. Seemed personable enough."

"And this St Saviour. He's part of your ... network?"

"Westen, I don't like your tone." Through gritted teeth Pecker said, "It is not *my* network. And, yes, St Saviour *is* on my radar. He's new on the block, but seems to have a lot of influence."

"Influence?"

Pecker tightened his lips. "It's none of your business. Can't say any more."

Westen lost it. "None of my business? None of my fucking business? I've just come from the old Blaxton ruins where's a man's been strung upside-down, with most of his skin torn off. We came to retrieve a specific item of evidence and surprise, surprise, we found a vicarage turned fucking Sodom and Gomorrah, hosted by Sandmarsh's nomination for fucking priest of the year! Who, I may add, is now a person of interest and, as it turns out, seems to have a highly questionable association with a senior police officer."

"There's no need to sw—"

"No need? No need?" Westen sucked in air between his teeth and balled his fists, thrusting them in his pockets lest they lost the plot and cost him his job.

Pecker took the fucking biscuit. Westen didn't know what

to believe. Part of him understood his attitude, seniority being hardwired into the police psyche. He never expected the superintendent to take his questions lying down. But alarm bells were ringing all over the show, and not just in relation to the Martin case.

He couldn't get beyond seeing Angus Drew amongst the group of individuals in the library, remembering on his visit to DeepDrilla, how the man had boasted of some kind of pull with the chief constable. Just how far did this fucking 'network' extend?

He needed to keep sharp.

Steadying his breathing, Westen said, "I am going to require a statement from you, sir, since you've been here, in relatively close proximity to the crime scene throughout the murder window. You will tell me anything out of the ordinary you might have observed, specifically relating to the movements of either William Turner or Peter Martin."

Pecker growled, "I don't know this Peter M—"

"Furthermore, you will also disclose full details of the 'network' you've 'infiltrated.' It is in your interest to disclose whether it has anything to do with the suppression of certain geological data by your friends in DeepDrilla, as reported by myself to the Ministry of Business, Energy and Industrial Strategy."

"My friends! Now you just hang on a—"

"In our interview with Angus Drew, *with whom you have shared an evening*, he revealed DeepDrilla to have links to a senior police officer other than yourself. I want to know if you were aware of these links and, if so, whether you are investigating them as a matter of record. I'm sure I do not need to remind you of the consequences if you cannot confirm your legitimate involvement with any of these matters."

Westen let the accusation hang.

An expression of relief flitted across Pecker's face as a flustered Burrows appeared from the vicarage entrance, casting about for his boss, a piece of paper in his gloved-up hand. He began to hasten forward when Westen, palm upraised, stopped him in his tracks.

"Are we clear … sir?" Westen's eyes once more locked on Pecker's.

"Yes, Inspector. We're clear. I will have to make a few calls. Check in with the task force. You'll have whatever statement I am cleared to offer, after which time, make no mistake, we will be having quite a different kind of conversation."

With that, he wheeled around and crunched his way over the gravel, back to the house.

Westen nodded Burrows over.

"What took you so long?"

"Sorry, Guv," Burrows said, handing over the note he'd found. "Thought since I was there, I'd take a general butcher's, lie of the land and all that."

Westen reached into his pocket and fished out a pair of latex gloves before taking the note and reading it.

My dearest Will

I can't do this anymore. Having to work here, so close to you and yet unable to BE close to you, is killing me.

You were right about me all along. I am weak. Stupid and weak and ineffectual.
You'll find me at The Ruins. I couldn't think of a more appropriate place to end it all.

Forgive me. None of this is your fault. It's all mine. All of it.

Peter.

"Jesus," said Westen.

"I know. Guv, it may read like a suicide note, but strikes me as more of a cry for help. As if he was going to try something and expected Turner to rescue him. Like, save the day."

Westen chewed his lip. "Then what? Someone reads it and decides to follow him? Do him in then? Strike that. This was planned. They'd need equipment—the rope—and there must have been at least two of them."

"Yeah," agreed Burrows. "Definitely would have taken more than one to hoist him with the rope, and he'd be struggling—assuming he was conscious."

"Oh, I think he was conscious, all right," muttered Westen. "This is the work of someone who very much enjoys his calling, and a killer who knew about Turner and Martin."

And Emma. He'd have to get to the bottom of why she'd been there.

"What if Martin didn't write it, Guv? What if the intention was to grab him, do him and leave him for Turner to find. You know, for a touch of the sadistic."

Westen perused the note again, desperate for inspiration. Seeing Angus Drew bugged him, caused a connection to spark that hadn't quite fired yet.

Then suddenly it did.

He said, "Find out if Charlie Broady's still inside. His girlfriend'll attest to how handy he is with a knife. He must be due out soon, if he behaved himself."

"Broady?" replied Burrows, his eyebrows curling into matching question marks. "Oh, right, the nephew of the thug we met at DeepDrilla. George Broady. Will do, Guv, though I can't see it myself. Why him? And why would he be interested in a couple of God-botherers?"

"Other than for the fun of torturing one of them, no

reason at all, but aimed in the right direction, he'd make the perfect assassin for someone who was. If Charlie got his Uncle George involved, there's your help right there. And there've been two attacks, remember."

"Yeah. You're right, Guv. David Walker!" Burrows whisked out his phone.

As his sergeant talked, Westen strolled away, watching the guests outside trickle away. Pecker's lot hadn't emerged yet.

Pecker's lot …

Light bulbs flickering in his head, he strode back to Burrows, who'd just finished his call.

"Charlie Broady, Guv. He's out. Paroled a fortnight ago."

"Bring him in. George too."

"I still don't get it. How … why would those two be involved? I can't see the connection."

"Guess who our chief superintendent is hob-nobbing with tonight? Along with a few other big hitters—two CEOs and a fucking MP—Angus Drew from DeepDrilla is in there. Broady works at DeepDrilla. Only two degrees of separation."

Burrows' phone chirped.

"They've pinged over Charlie Broady's mug shot." After taking a few moments to look at the screen, he handed it to Westen. "His hair's longer but he's a dead ringer for Wilby's description." As Westen scrutinised the image, Burrows scratched his chin. "Drew's here? Why? What's the connection to the church?"

After handing the phone back to Burrows, Westen stared into the middle distance; at the vicarage entrance through which his senior officer had disappeared to join his chums. Undercover, or under a thumb?

"I have no idea, Burrows. But there is one. I can smell it. Like I can smell the biggest rat of them all."

Westen fished in his pocket for his car-keys. "Once you've

picked up the Broadys, get Tony Stamford to dig up everything he can on Anthony St Saviour. Personal life, work history, financials, the lot. I'll bet the fucking farm he's at the bottom of it."

❧ 26 ❧

QUESTIONS

As her eyes opened to the sound of Robbie drawing back the living room curtains, Emma stretched and tried to rub away the crick in her neck.

She'd intended to stay awake and keep her eye on Will, but after he'd fallen into an exhausted sleep she too had succumbed. So much for insomnia.

"Westen called," said Robbie. "He'll be here in half an hour. He's bringing a detective constable with him. Someone called Donna?"

"Donna Stirling. She's good. She helped me a lot, you know … with what happened last year."

A kindly smile emerged out of his huge red beard. "Lass, I keep telling you, don't worry about mentioning that. What that man did to me was not your fault, and I barely remember anything about it."

She nodded. "I know. I can't help but think twice before I mention it. You wouldn't have had to go through it all had I not decided to come to Flammark. Now we've another situation."

"Nothing to do with you this time, though?"

"No. At least I don't think so!" She gave a wan smile as she changed the subject. "Donna's ... nice. She'll be good with Will."

"There's a pot of coffee in the kitchen. I'm off to start surgery. I'll leave it to you to wake the man."

Will stirred as Robbie left, blinked and stared round, quizzically.

Then his face clouded over.

"Westen's on his way," said Emma, gently. "Donna's with him. I know this is going to be hard but ..."

Eyes desolate, he replied, "I know. I'm going to keep it together for Peter's sake." He tried to control the tremble on his lips. "At least I'm going to try."

"Good. I've got time off, so I'll be with you all the way. Robbie's made coffee." She pointed to the pile of clothes the doctor had brought in last night. "He's given us something to change into. I'm going to take a shower. Maybe do the same? I'll let you know when I've finished, then I'll rustle up some toast."

"Coffee sounds perfect. I'm not sure I can face anything to eat."

Emma picked out the clothes that were meant for her and disappeared upstairs. Only when she dressed did she realise they must have once belonged to Joanie, his wife, dead these three years. He must have kept some, if not all, of her things. The thought oppressed her as she made her way downstairs. Loss never goes away.

She popped her head round the living room door to let Will know the shower was free, then headed for the kitchen. Despite Will's protestations, Emma cut some slices off a hand-baked bloomer Robbie had left on a cutting board in the middle of the table, next to marmalade in a gingham-topped jar and a butter dish. She didn't find comfort in the prosaic. It made the horror of the previous night even worse.

Minutes passed. Not enjoying being alone with her thoughts, Emma was just about to find Will when he appeared, hair damp, still pale-faced. She wondered where Robbie had found a pair of jeans that fit him.

She poured a steaming cup of coffee and, ever hopeful, placed a slice of bread in the toaster for Will. It popped up at the same time that she heard voices and footsteps coming up the stairs.

Robbie brought in Westen, Donna following. Seeing him, the details of last night—pushed to the back of her mind while she looked after Will—returned like a blow.

God knows how her friend must be feeling.

Brave-faced could hardly describe his obvious efforts to keep himself together. With a quiet tremble, Will said, "Have you found who did it, yet?"

"Not yet," said Westen, "but we have something to go on."

"Sit down, detectives," said Robbie. "I must go to my surgery. Help yourself to coffee."

"Thanks, Mason. Nothing for us. We have a few questions, then we'll be on our way."

"As you wish. Emma, you know where to find me if I'm needed."

She smiled as he left, her hand moving over the table, enclosing Will's.

"I'll try to keep it brief," said Westen, softening the expression on his otherwise grim face.

Will, unable to offer any sustained eye contact, squeezed Emma's hand as he fixed on a point somewhere north of the butter dish.

"Tell us about Peter's note," Westen began.

"Did you find it? Have you read it?" Will asked, looking up.

Westen nodded. "Emma rang me after you told her about it. It became the starting point for our enquiries."

Will swallowed, eyes fixed back on the table. "S-St Saviour told me he and Peter had what he called 'a heart-to-heart'." He scoffed. "Heart to bloody heart, my foot. Peter told him he didn't think the transfer to the vicarage was working, and could he please return to the cathedral."

"Who organised this ... transfer?" asked Westen.

"St Saviour. Somehow, he's got the ear of the bishop and wants to effect some kind of diocesan restructuring plan. I've spoken to other parishes. They're upset too. Everything was working fine until he came on the scene. Now he's everywhere." He stared at his spot, grasping his cup as if it were a lifebelt. "He refused point-blank to talk to the bishop about reinstating him full-time at the cathedral library. Said Peter needed to learn humility and to accept the wisdom of his betters. He planned to create the position of Heritage Secretary for him, making it both permanent and full-time. He'd never be able to return to his old post."

"Would that have been such a terrible thing?" asked Donna.

"Absolutely. He'd been working on a book—a biography of the cathedral's patrons. Working here, away from the library, he'd never be able to complete it. It would have broken his heart to leave the cathedral." His hand shook as he raised his cup. He put it down again.

"Take your time, Will. You're doing really well," Donna said, earning a smile of gratitude from Emma.

"We found his note crumpled on your bed," said Westen.

"Did you? I screwed it up ..."

"Where had Peter left it?"

"On my dressing table. In one of our envelopes."

Donna followed up, "Can you remember when you found it? What time?"

"Erm, around eleven-ish? St Saviour had decided to hold a reception for the local MP and his cronies. Peter refused to come. Said he was going back to have it out with the bishop, once and for all. He'd also found something wrong with the Parish Returns System."

Emma froze.

"Peter's always been a bit of a techie," Will continued. "Meticulous, too. He said he'd found some kind of anomaly and the bishop would want to know about it. I begged him to stay. Bish is a good chap, but if you cross him, you're out. Peter would have had to leave the diocese and I'd never see him again."

He stopped, obviously fighting for control, tears massing in his eyes. "I've been so selfish. I knew all along working at the vicarage wouldn't work. We'd got used to being apart. I should have done more to oppose the decision. I'd been totally on top of my job. But when he moved in ... well, I didn't want him to leave. Ever."

After a few moments, Donna asked gently, "After your argument, did you see him leave?"

Will nodded.

"And this would be ... what time?" asked Western.

"I'm not sure. About six o'clock?"

"Okay, that leaves four hours between the time he left and when you found the note." He turned to Donna. "That's not long ..."

Turning back to Will, he continued, "You said Peter had a room at the vicarage during the time he worked there—to save travelling expenses. He didn't have a car, then?"

"He never learned to drive. Roads frightened him."

"So when he left the vicarage, would he have called a taxi?"

"For a twenty-mile trip? Not on your life. He'd have walked into the village. Caught a bus."

"Did you see anyone hanging around before he left? Any strange vehicles?"

"By then the world and his bloody wife had started to arrive for the reception, so yeah, lots of strange cars."

Westen changed tack. "Did you go up to your room after Peter left?"

Will's face crumbled. "I should have followed him. Persuaded him to stay until we could petition the bishop together. None of this would have happened if—"

Concerned the dam might break, Emma tightened her grip on his hand.

"It's all right, Em, I've done crying. It won't help Peter, will it?"

Westen, compassion written all over his face, pressed again. "I'm sorry, Turner, I need an answer to my question. Did you go up to your room after Peter left?"

Fighting for self-control, it took a moment for Will to answer. "Erm … yes. St Saviour found me. Said he needed me … ," his face suffused with disgust and shame, "… to look after our guests."

"Was Peter's note there at that point?"

Will's face paled even further as the reason for their line of questioning dawned. "No. No. I'd have seen it, definitely. Oh my God, do you think someone other than Peter put it there? Did he even write it? It looked like he'd penned it. It was so personal—the details. I didn't think …"

Donna's answer confirmed the suspicion. "We need a specimen of his handwriting. An expert will be able to tell."

"I'll get you one. We can go now."

Almost in unison, Emma and Westen said, "No!"

"I don't think that's a good idea, Will." Emma, pleading, tried to catch his eyes. "It's too soon. And the last person you want to see is St Saviour."

"I met him last night. Admirable fellow," said Westen, sardonically.

Will scoffed. "He's ... vile. God only knows how he got so far in the church, and I have no idea why a man such as he would be tolerated by the bishop. He hates arrogance, and St Saviour is its epitome."

"Had you heard much about him—before he arrived in Flammark, I mean."

"Never heard of him before. That's what makes all this so bloody inexplicable."

Raising his brow, Westen gave Donna a silent nod. She said, "We'll go back to the vicarage and find the sample. No need for you to be there. I gather you won't object if we take a good look around?"

"Of ourse not."

"Where did Peter do his work?"

"Erm, we created an office next to the conference room. He always kept a handwritten diary. It'll be in a desk drawer."

"Getting back to the note," said Westen. "It refers to finding Peter at the ruins and that you'd know the reason why. What did he mean?"

Will sighed, taking time to gather his thoughts.

"After we first ... got together, I asked if I could meet his parents. That's when he told me about his father. Absolute piece of work. Peter point-blank refused. That's when I first realised he hadn't come out to them—well, to his father. We walked up to the old Blaxton estate to talk it through. By the time we arrived at the old chapel we were in full-blown meltdown. It's where we broke up. I've hated going there ever since."

"How long ago was this?" asked Donna, lowering her voice, matching Will's.

"Five years ago, almost to the day."

Emma saw where this was going. "Will, who knew about

this? Assuming Peter didn't write the note himself, who else would know what the ruins meant to you both?"

He shrugged. "I honestly don't know. I've never told anyone about it."

"I think that does it for now," said Westen. "Just one last thing, and it's a question for Emma." He turned his eyes on her. "How come you were there?"

"I got some text messages. From Will—at least we thought they were from him at first."

Will frowned. "They weren't from me."

"What made you think they weren't?" asked Donna.

"I don't really know. Maybe because it had grown so late and that Will wouldn't want me to go there alone and in the dark—it was a fluke that I'd been with Abigail and asked her to come with me. I rang but never got an answer, just another text. It's why I messaged you. To be on the safe side."

"Thank God you did," said Westen, eyes unflinchingly on her, full of unspoken meaning. Then to Will he said, "Do you have your phone with you?"

"Er … no. It's at the vicarage."

"Does anyone else have access to it?"

"I leave it around all the time. Anyone could have used it. I find passwords annoying. Peter always used to go on about it."

At the mention of Peter's name, Will's entire body seemed to sag.

Westen stirred as if about to get up. "You need to get some rest, Turner. We're done for now. If there's anything else, we'll let you know."

Squeezing her friend's hand, Emma said, "Will you be okay if I see them out?" Will's nod was barely perceptible. "I'll only be a minute."

She led the two detectives down the stairs and outside.

"There's something I need to tell you."

Her eyes slid to Donna then back to Westen.

"Donna. Give us a moment, will you?"

With a quizzical frown, she said, "No problem, Guv."

Once sure that Donna had made it out of earshot, Emma said, "I don't want this mentioned to Will. Not yet. He's not up to it."

Westen frowned. "Go on."

Taking a gulp, she told him about St Saviour's threat, realising, with a little leap of her heart, that it had now been neutralised. The police would seize Will's computer and his accounts and come to their own conclusions.

"Why did he want you to clear out?"

"I have no idea. He wouldn't tell me anything other than he had his reasons. I-I've been racking my brains as to what to do. Who to tell."

"And that didn't include me?" His eyes drilled into her. "Didn't you trust me?"

She shrugged, trying to find the right words. "It would be my word against his. Besides, we haven't exactly been on speaking terms."

"Well, we're talking now. Is there anything else you're keeping from me?"

Eyes fixed steadily on him, she slowly shook her head.

"Would it be inappropriate to ask what that was all about, Guv?" said Donna, as Westen neared.

"St Fucking Saviour. He's threatened Emma. Told her to leave her cottage and get out of Flammark. Cooked the books against Turner as leverage to get her out."

"Eh? Why? Seems pretty extreme."

"She doesn't know why, apparently." Western kicked at a

piece of gravel. "You've not met him. Comes over as the kind who'd stop at nothing to get what he wants. And whatever that is, it involves Emma Blake. What is it with that bloody woman?"

His phone chirped. "Burrows! What've you got for me?" He swiped his screen. "You're on speaker. Donna's here."

"Still no sign of Broady's nephew and George hasn't turned up for work, either. Looks like your instincts last night were right, Guv."

"Okay, you know the drill, get a BOLO out. What've you got on St Saviour?"

"Nothing, Guv."

"What do you mean, nothing?"

"He has no financials—no bank accounts, no plastic. We can't find any assets, either. Nada."

"Not possible. Even if he lives off the church, they'll be paying him a salary. And he must own something."

"Not according to any database Tony's been through. Unless he uses burners, he doesn't have a phone either. No call records."

Westen let out a low whistle. "Un-fucking-believable."

"There's more. Tony got permission from the church commissioners to search their employment database. Didn't need a warrant. They're very keen on transparency at the moment. Too many scandals for them not to co-operate, apparently. Turns out there's no employment record for him, either."

"He's a fucking dean!" said Westen. "I may not be a pillock of the church but even I know he'd have had to work his way up."

"Agreed, Guv. Then Tony got on to HMRC. There's no National Insurance number attributed to that name."

"So ... we're talking identity theft?"

Donna chipped in. "That doesn't work either, Guv. If he's

this new on the block the bishop would have done some kind of background check before giving him any sort of responsibility. He can't have come from nowhere."

Westen took a moment to weigh the information. "Right. Burrows, go to the cathedral. Take Donna with you. I'm dropping her at the vicarage so she can find this handwriting sample. You can pick her up there. Get an audience, or whatever they call it, with this bishop, Thomas something or other. Find out what you can about where St Saviour came from. While you're at it, try and find out if he knows why his dean would be cosying up to the likes of DeepDrilla and the Right fucking Honourable Philip Ackroyd. And see what he has to say about Peter Martin."

"Will do, Guv. You've finished with Turner?"

"Yes. We're pretty sure Martin didn't leave the note—or even wrote it, but it needs confirming, so we're getting a handwriting sample. The Broady's are involved too, I'm sure of it."

"St Saviour?"

"Progress. There's been an accusation. Emma Blake. For some reason he's got it in for her, and I think he was behind her being there last night, but I don't want to act on anything just yet until you've finished at the cathedral. We'll get him in tomorrow. First thing."

He put the phone to his chest and nodded Donna over to the car. "I'll be two minutes."

Safely out of earshot and with speaker off, Westen lowered his voice and continued, "Get Tony Stamford to raise a warrant on Pecker's financials and have him lift his phone records. This is between us three, Burrows. The last thing we want is word to get round we're investigating one of our own. Not yet, anyway. Make sure Tony's aware."

"Jesus. Understood, Guv."

✖ 27 ✖

FULL DISCLOSURE

After the police left, knowing Will to be clearly exhausted—and she not much better—Emma made up the bed in Robbie's spare room for him. Once he'd settled in, she stayed until he fell asleep, then wandered downstairs, back to her chair in the living room, though not to rest. Too much chaos in her brain.

Her heart broke for her friend, so overwhelmed by grief and the burden of guilt he carried. And poor, poor Peter. How she'd managed to keep her head together after the other night, she had no idea. She never doubted St Saviour had been behind it, much more so now she'd learned Peter had uncovered an issue with the accounts. It didn't explain the viciousness of the attack, though. It hadn't exactly kept him under the radar.

St Saviour starting his power play by inveigling himself into the church was a genius idea. Great cover. One which poor, conscientious, Peter had been about to blow. Surely he could have found a subtler way to deal with him? A faked suicide would surely have served the purpose better, kept the lid on things.

She shuddered. Too big! All of it, too bloody big. Mind-numbingly complicated. She couldn't think straight, couldn't see any way forward, couldn't keep her eyes open.

Emma felt a touch and jumped awake. "Abigail? You're here? Has something else happened?"

"No, you can chill. The surgery's closed for lunch and we're all in the garden, including Wy. I filled them in about what happened at the ruins and Gabby said we should come, now. She thinks Animus has started." She waited while Emma visited the bathroom, then led the way down. "You should have seen Robbie's face when he saw Gabby! He ran over and picked her up! Swung her round! I knew they'd been friends, but I didn't realise they were that close."

"Didn't you? She got him through the death of his wife, you know. Used to take him on bus tours, of all things. They explored the old routes, letting him talk and come to terms with his loss."

"Wow. Does he know about ... you know, her powers?"

"No," replied Emma. "He never knew she was special in that way. To him, she was just a good friend." She slipped her arm through Abigail's. "Is Will still asleep?"

"Yeah. Robbie bobbed up to check. Out like a light, apparently. He thinks it best to leave him. It's glorious outside. The doc's sorted us out some sandwiches and coffee. He's only got half an hour before he has to get back to work. Then we can all talk."

Once outside, greetings over, Emma sat with her friends. It almost felt like normality: the sun beating down as they gathered round Robbie's handmade picnic table, laughing, joking, all but one pretending it was all about catching up.

"So, how's the family, Gabby?" Robbie asked. "Are you on a short visit? Will you have to go back?"

"I don't know yet," she replied. "I thought I was needed,

but now I'm not so sure. As I'm … away, they may miss me, but I'm not holding my breath."

"Well, their loss is our gain. I think you let your cottage go, didn't you? Where will you stay?"

"At the moment, I'm in one of Wyland's caravans. It suits me really, really well. At the moment, anyway."

"You sure? You can always stay here. I'll have plenty of room once Will—"

A pall suddenly fell on the company. Robbie looked at his watch and heaved his giant frame upwards. "I should get back. Stay as long as you like and, Gabby, you must come round again soon and have a proper chat."

"Yes," she replied, with a grin. "Maybe we'll catch a bus."

Once he made it inside and safely out of earshot, Gabby said, "How is the poor lad?"

"Devastated," said Emma. "Abigail said she'd got you up to speed with everything. Did you know about Will's relationship with Peter?"

"I suspected. Back in the day the two of them were thick as thieves. Then they had a falling out. He didn't share the details with me. No reason why he should, since we weren't particularly close. But with someone as beautiful as William —both inside and out—with no hint of a partner on the cards, it didn't take much to put two and two together."

"I thought you angelic lot were privy to everything," quipped Wyland.

"No. Our involvement tends to be on a need-to-know basis only. Which can be very inconvenient. And, of course, in one respect, I'm like Animus. I need people to give me information."

"How does that work?" said Emma. "You know, how does he communicate with his spirit army?"

"Not sure. Some kind of psychical connection. They go out into the world and do his bidding, and they report back."

"Sounds like a hive mind," said Abigail.

She smiled at their bemused faces.

"Sorry, I'm a *Star Trek* fan. Animus sounds like the Borg Queen. She'd use her mind to send her soldiers out to … what did they call it? Erm … assimilate other races. Once overcome, their knowledge became the Borg's knowledge."

"Goodness me," said Gabby. "Very apt. I really must start watching television. It's obviously going to teach me a lot." She smiled before growing serious once more. "What did the police say, Emma?"

She related the gist of the interview, then said, "They've got some leads, apparently. Peter had left a note for Will to find, but I think they've concluded it was bait to get him to the ruins. They're going to check it was his handwriting."

"I don't understand why he wanted us there," said Abigail. "I suppose he was behind the text messages? What was the point?"

"Animus is a sadist," said Gabby. "If he can find an opportunity to terrorise, he'll use it. Look how he's destroyed Will." She furrowed her brow. "For some reason, he wants to do the same to Emma. I haven't fathomed why." Eyes on Emma, she continued, "Nor do I know why he wants you out of the way. We all know he's behind what happened to Peter. He went to extraordinary lengths to cook up a blackmail plot, too. It would have been easier to—"

"Kill me?"

Gabby deepened her frown. Nodded.

Emma let that sink in for a while, then shrugged. "Well, as to the threat, Will told the police that Peter had been on his way to the bishop when he left. Mentioned he'd found an anomaly in the accounts. It's all in the open now, and I told Westen about the blackmail. I won't need to leave the cottage and I won't need to tell Will."

"Good," said Gabby. "And if the police are onto him, it'll

add pressure. Animus is adaptable and strong, but he may not yet totally understand the way this world works. He'll certainly find the rule of law a challenge. The severity of the attack on Peter did surprise me. It maybe that he's not in full control of whoever did it for him." She popped a biscuit in her mouth. Crunching it, she said, "I think you're wrong about not telling Will, by the way. I think he'll be perfectly capable of—"

"What?"

A stunned silence hung over the group. Unnoticed, Will had come upon them.

Gabby got up. "W-Will. How are—"

Stony-faced, he stood in front of her. "Tell. Will. What?"

He surveyed the rest of them and said, "What have you been keeping from me? And who's this?"

Wyland's turn to rise.

He introduced himself and held out his hand, but Will refused to take it. Returning it to his side, Wyland said, "I own the caravan site at Wood End—out in Ledbridge? Gabby has been staying in one."

"Has she now?" said Will. He glared at her. "And when was she going to tell me?"

Emma had never seen her friend like this before. Outwardly calm but radiating anger.

Gabby clearly felt its heat. Her face crumpled and she slumped back on her seat.

"*Et tu*, Emma?" He turned his gaze onto her. "I thought we understood each other. How *could* you? If you knew something that might have prevented all this—"

"I ... I didn't, Will, I promise."

He found a chair, pulled it away from the table, set it apart and down.

"You'll have to let me be the judge of that. So, make a

start. Tell me everything from the beginning. Then I'll hear what the rest of you have to say."

Like a set of transgressive teenagers, each sat in silence until it was their turn to speak. If any of them thought to hold anything back, Will's expression prevented it. Even though it had only been the previous night that he had beheld his lover's tortured body, he stared at them calmly, unblinkingly, as in random order he learned of the blackmail threat, of the true purpose of Wyland's park with its broken circle of sentinels, the emergence, the Druids, Numenius and, of course, St Saviour.

After nearly half an hour of their shamefaced explanations, Will finally made his only comment. "The sentinels didn't work, did they? This Animus and his followers, they're in the world."

An uncomfortable silence descended, Will having got to the nub of the problem. If he was bonded to the original emergence site, how was Animus able to push into the world from the Tor?

Suddenly, Abigail sat up and looked at Gabby. "They *did* work. They did! But when you formed the henge you didn't take into account twenty-first century greed." She turned to the others. "When I first visited Wyland, I managed to wheedle my way onto the geological survey van they'd parked there. I talked to the person inside. He was checking for aftershocks. A crack's formed in the earth, running directly from the Tor all the way to Wood End and the fracking site. I knew it. I bloody knew it. Godzilla must have opened something up and it messed with the henge's seal. I'll bet you anything, that's how Animus broke free from his link to Wood End."

Wyland rolled his eyes and groaned as the truth finally dawned. "Of course! Resonance. He emerged via the crack and onto the Tor, then somehow tapped into the fault. Sent a shock wave to Wood End and displaced the sentinel, so as to get his followers out. He's what caused the quake."

"Why did he bother?" asked Emma. "Couldn't the rest of them have followed him out from the Tor?"

"No," said Gabby. "Unlike him, in spirit form, his acolytes are completely without intelligence, programmed to a single pathway. He arrives first and sets up his base before calling them. They emerge as blank pages, ready for his will to be imprinted. If Abigail is right, and DeepDrilla created some kind of fault line, they gave him his solution on a plate."

Will sat, coned within a dreadful calm.

He said, "Animus as St Saviour ... Had he felt Gabby's presence at the vicarage?"

"I think so," Emma replied. "Gabby thinks he might have sensed her arrival from the start, and that's why he chose the vicarage as his base."

"Well, there's your answer, Gabby."

"I don't follow?"

"You need to lure him to Wood End, don't you? As you did during his time as Numenius. Do another Removal and seal the henge again. Though it seems to me there's only one way you'll get him there."

Tears welled in Gabby's eyes as his drift dawned on her.

"You want to use me as bait," said Gabby.

"I don't see why not," came the devastating reply.

"Will! You ... we can't—" said Emma, grabbing Will's hand. "We have to talk this through."

He slid away his hand and, holding her gaze, said, "Have you a better idea?"

He gathered himself and started to rise when Abigail burst out, "It won't work. He won't go to Wood End. Ever. He's bound to know it's a trap."

Gabby nodded her agreement. "And a pathetic one at that. At the last Removal, I had my full strength. Combined with the power of Druidic prayer, we were strong enough to banish him." She frowned, desperately chewing at her lip before continuing, "You also have to remember we're a sentinel down. We can't reseal the portal."

She beat her forehead with the butt of her palm. "Think, think!"

Abigail said, "There's the crack, too. If he used it to come out of the Tor, he could use it again and re-emerge at any time and anywhere along it. It stretches for miles."

Wyland chipped in. "Yeah. I expect he could reprogram his followers to avoid the portal, follow him anywhere."

Will intervened. "I don't know what we can do about this … fault line or crack, or whatever, but I know how to seal the old portal so it can never be used again."

"Hey, man," said Wyland. "Not possible. At the last ceremony, the Druids brought their dead. We don't—"

"Yes, we do."

Time didn't stop. The sun still shone, the birds carried on singing, and a pleasant trickle emanated from the rusted old bike wheel that formed part of Robbie's quaint, recycled water feature.

While Will offered up his dead.

Silence descended.

Implacable, with no sign of tear or tremble, Will said, "Though forced to be apart, Peter was my soulmate. I know … *I know* … he'd have wanted this. He loved Sandmarsh and everything in its vicinity. He'd have found it the greatest of honours to be chosen to guard it for eternity." He gave the faintest of smiles. "I envy him."

Jesus.

"Will," Emma whispered, "are you sure?"

"Yes. Just make it *matter*. Find a way of mending this crack. Close that too."

"We'll try," said Gabby.

"How … how would you work it? With Peter, I mean?" asked Abigail. "People will expect a funeral."

"They'll get one. Leave it to me. I'll be in touch when I've worked out the details."

"The police will be holding onto the bo—to Peter," Emma said, trying to catch Will's eye. "I'll ring Westen. I need to talk to him after last night. He'd expect it. He won't mind me asking him about when he'll release …"

Will nodded and got up.

"You're going?" asked Emma.

"Yes, I'm going," said Will. "I need to have a conversation with a certain ancient spirit."

"No," said Gabby, horrified. "If you mean St Saviour, don't. We can't lure him anywhere until we know what's what." She turned to the others. "Though not without its dangers, I agree that Will should go back. Someone needs to keep tabs on St Saviour, since he's obviously on the move, but we need to keep our counsel. If this crack is as big as you suggest, we don't know if or where we can unbid him, let alone seal it afterwards. Will, you *can't* let him know we're onto him until we've a plan."

He shrugged. "I'll be on my way, then. I won't give anything away to St Saviour, and I'll do my utmost not to murder him. Give my thanks to Robbie, will you?"

Emma stood too. "Will …"

Unbending and still, to no one in particular, he said, "I realise you hadn't put it all together about St Saviour until yesterday—probably at the same time Peter was taken. But you all kept me out of the loop long before that. This is my turf, for God's sake! Abigail, I needed to know what happened that night at Wood End and I should have been introduced to Wyland earlier." To Emma he said, "I cannot believe you didn't tell me about the blackmail threat. I thought we trusted each other."

"And me?" asked Gabby. "What did I do wrong?"

Revealing the depths of his anger, Will replied, "You know full well. You disobeyed Michael and had your wings clipped. Were you still in your full power, we'd have got a handle on this long before now. You'd have picked up on St Saviour and would at least have half a bloody inkling about what to do about him."

Emma's hand flew to her mouth. This couldn't be her friend. "Will—"

"Between us all, we'd have got there earlier. Maybe not by much, but enough to have saved Peter from ..." His eyes welled. He swallowed, loudly. "His suffering is down to you. All of you."

He stared round, holding their gazes one by one, until his rested once more on Gabby.

"I'm going back to the vicarage, where no doubt the estimable dean will offer his sympathies. I'll play. When you come up with a decent plan, make sure you let me know. For a change."

Emma made to follow him.

"Not now, Emma." Will turned and raised both arms, palms towards her. "I'm angry, and it's a righteous anger. I want to keep hold of it. I hope we'll be able to have a reasonable conversation in the near future, but not now, maybe not ever. We'll have to see."

"Okay," said Emma, "I'll see you later, then."

Turning his back on her, on all of them, he walked away.

"Possibly."

❧ 28 ❧

IMPASSIONATA

After Will left, Emma returned to the devastated company still slumped around the picnic table.

"It's like he's a different person," said Abigail. "The old Will would never have talked to us like that."

"But he's not the old Will, is he?" said Gabby, fishing out a piece of old kitchen towel from a pocket. "Like it or not, he's in the world of Animus now. The love of his life has been killed in the most horrendous way imaginable and he's right … had we put our heads together earlier—had I not gone against Michael's wishes and lost my wings—Peter might still be with us."

"He's got to come back from it," said Emma. "Got to. I can't imagine my world without Will. I owe him everything. He holds me together."

"I'm sure he will," said Wyland. "I don't know the man, but I know the sort. He's traumatised—who wouldn't be after what he's been through?. I doubt it'll last for long. The dam will burst, eventually. You just have to make sure you're there when it happens, or—"

Gabby finished his sentence. "Or there's no telling what

he might do." She blew her nose, destroying the last vestige of integrity the squished tissue could offer. "Though it breaks my heart to say it, we can't allow ourselves to think about that now. Will is on his own mission. We can only leave him to it."

"That's a bit harsh," said Abigail. "Do I detect a hint of mortal spite? After what he said about you?"

There was a pause before Gabby answered, furrowing her brow. "Is that what I'm feeling?" She blushed.

Abigail smiled, ironically. "Another human trait. Have to say, you're picking all this up swimmingly." Turning to Emma and Wyland, she asked, "So, what now?"

"I wish we knew more about this crack," said Wyland. "If we could map it properly, we'd at least know what we're up against."

"I could talk to Tom," she replied. "He's the chap from Lanchester Uni. You know, the one in the van that was parked outside your cottage? He showed it to me on his computer. I don't think I'll have much trouble wheedling a hard copy out of him. We exchanged numbers and he's already rung me twice, wanting to go for a drink, but I've been too busy."

"Can you also ask for a survey map from before the drilling started? It'll be useful to see how the geology's changed."

"Okay."

"I'll talk to Westen," said Emma. "Find out when Peter's body is likely to be released. I might be able to find out more about where things are with St Saviour."

"And I'll get my thinking cap on," said Gabby. "We've got to solve this. Wherever we decide is the best place from which to send Animus back, the last Removal challenged all my skills. I have no idea where we'll get the power to perform another."

~

As it happened, Emma hadn't needed to ring Westen. After leaving the others and giving her thanks to Robbie—and another hug—she ordered a taxi home. She waited for it on the pavement outside his villa, going over and over Will's last words.

Her phone rang.

Westen.

Yes, she was all right. Yes, it would be good idea to talk and, yes, she could be at the Flammark Arms in half an hour.

Heart lifting a notch, Emma cancelled the taxi, deciding the walk to the pub would give her space to think.

She completely understood why Will needed to hold onto his anger. It crowded out his despair. In a way, it was to be welcomed, because despair can cause people to do terrible things to themselves. There'd been a hint of that, when he talked of how he envied Peter his role as a sentinel.

A job for a dead man.

She had to break through the rage, help him find a way forward, as he had for her when she'd closed herself off after leaving Ben. If Will did something stupid, she wouldn't be able to forgive herself.

She stopped in her tracks. Maybe that's why he'd decided to go back to the vicarage. Not so much to keep tabs on St Saviour, but to be his next target.

Suicide by Animus?

No, no, *no*. She mustn't go there, *mustn't*.

At least Westen had the scent, now. Could run some serious interference with St Saviour's plans—whatever they were. She couldn't help but feel relief that one of them—the blackmail—had come to nothing.

She could stay!

Emma stopped walking, rooted by the thought. Despite

her past and the heartache she had borne and would have to bear, she suddenly realised where her future lay. She loved Flammark and had committed to remain there, whatever it had in store.

As she turned a corner and strolled into the pub car park, she spied Westen bleeping the lock on his car. She must have caught his eye, too, because he broke into an easy smile and walked towards her.

It could have been the awful events of last night, or Will's terrible reaction to them, or maybe simply because she had settled her future. Or it could have been the fact that Westen had become a compass-point in her life, ever true and unwavering, no matter what the circumstances.

And someone who would never—ever—deliberately hurt her.

Whatever the reason, she quickened her pace. Stopped in front of him. Searching his eyes, smiling at their quizzical gaze, Emma reached up and, tenderly holding his face between her hands, kissed him, hard and with passion, open to all his possibilities.

Matching her intensity, he folded her in his arms.

Deciding not to bother with the Flammark Arms, they floored it to Clearview. They would be safely alone. No one would come banging on her door.

As the shadows lengthened, they finally took a breath. "Westen … " she began.

"Why do you always call me that?" he grinned. "I have a first name, you know."

"I've always known you as Westen. Jamie feels … alien."

"Okay," he laughed, gently stroking her breast. "You can call me what you like, providing we can do that again."

"What, now?"

"Well, in a minute—maybe ten. You're exhausting!"

Emma laughed. Laughed! Something she hadn't done in a very long while and perhaps shouldn't do now. Not while her friend was hurting. Not after last night.

Then a different voice spoke to her. One thing—*one bloody thing*—that was pure and perfect had come her way. Why shouldn't she embrace it, find joy in it? Make there be a point to all her past and present suffering. Will's suffering. What just took place with Westen felt right.

She would not ruin it for the world.

But they had to talk. There could be no avoiding it.

"I'll make us some coffee while you ... recover."

She kissed him before carefully extricating herself and grabbing her kimono. Propped up by an elbow, covers on the floor, Westen beamed as he watched her wrap it round her nakedness. He stretched. "I'll come with you. Let's sit outside. We could both do with some air."

Coffees in hand, she found him on the bench in front of her window, sitting with his arms outspread along the back of the seat, chin up, face to the late evening sun, shirt open. Emma had never seen him so relaxed. The perpetual knot in his forehead had disappeared; his hard-nosed attitude suspended. What had she called him last year? Inspector Snark? She almost laughed when she thought about his touch, to the wonder she felt at its gentleness. How could she have so underestimated him, this layered, complex man?

On seeing her, he sidled up the bench and took the proffered mug.

"I'm assuming black, no sugar," she said. "It's in every crime procedural I've read."

He chuckled. "Normally I like a splash of milk, but I'll let you off." He took a sip and gave her a sideways glance. "Out with it."

"What do you mean?"

"I'm a detective, Emma. Questions are breathing off you!"

"Do you mind? I mean, I know you can't say much about the case, but last night, at the ruins, was …"

"Yes. It's why I rang you earlier. I'm surprised you're even on your feet, let alone … what we just did." He took another sip. "I hope it wasn't, you know, reaction."

"No. Well, in one way, perhaps." She visibly shuddered at the memory of Peter's hanging body.

Westen's arm came round her, and he held her to him. "I know. No need to explain. I feel it too. A need for … comfort, I suppose. This evening has made me realise how much I've missed."

"What do you mean?"

"I've seen a lot of horror in my life, Emma. I've had relationships, but none of them lasted. You know how it goes; it's a tough gig being a detective's wife or partner. There's no one to share the emotional stuff with," Westen tapped his temple, "so I carry it all in here." He cleared his throat. "Whatever it is you want to say, or ask, go ahead, I understand. Some things I can't answer, part of the job, but you need to come down from what you saw last night and if I can help, I will."

Could a man be any more perfect? She said nothing at first, savouring the moment in the crook of his arm.

"I'm worried about Will. Really worried about him. He … he wants to organise Peter's funeral but doesn't know when you'll release his body."

"I'd be worried about him too, after what I saw this morning. Tell him soon. It's not like the old days. After he's taken every scrap of evidence he can, the pathologist will probably sign the release in a week's time. Does Will know he won't be able to claim the body? I know he has a special interest, but he isn't next of kin."

"I don't know what he intends, but I'll let him know about the timing."

"What next?"

"Sorry?"

"What else do you want to know?"

"What did you think of St Saviour?"

"Nasty fucker."

God, she loved this man! Westen's turn of phrase cut through the mystic pall of the last few days. It made her laugh. Again.

"Are you going to arrest him?"

"I can't talk about that aspect of the case, Emma," a faint echo of his knotted brow appearing. "We're going to need … boundaries."

"Okay. I understand."

"I'm sure you do. You have them too."

"What do you mean?"

"You've kept things from me in the past, haven't you?"

She bowed her head. Couldn't deny it.

He gave a little sigh of exasperation. "We're bringing him in tomorrow."

"Who, St Saviour? Really?"

He nodded. "I can't tell you the details, but I don't see the harm in you knowing that. Does it make you feel better?"

"Yes. Relieved. Will's at the vicarage."

Westen tensed. "He's what? I thought we all agreed that wasn't the safest place for him. Turner's vulnerable. St Saviour's—"

"A nasty fucker. I know. But, later on, we'd all gathered at Robbie's. He … changed his mind." Try as she might, Emma couldn't hide her distress.

Westen raised his eyebrows. "Fallen out with the Scooby Gang, has he?"

"What do you mean by that?" she asked, trying to be offended.

"Nothing … " he grinned. Then his face turned serious. "Couldn't he stay here? We don't know the extent of St Saviour's involvement. Things might get dangerous."

Here we go again, keeping Westen in the dark, unable to tell him that it wasn't to St Saviour Will had returned, but to Animus. "We tried to persuade him to stay at Robbie's but he wouldn't have it. He won't want me to check on him, either. He isn't himself."

"Try not to worry. There's a limit to what you can do in situations like this," Westen replied, giving her another gentle squeeze. "Grief takes everyone differently. It has stages. He'll be angry." He smiled gently before changing the subject. "Would it make you feel better if I got someone to call round? See if he's okay?"

Her heart lurched. First with relief, then gratitude—and not a little awe—at the extent of Westen's sensitivity. He left her to find his phone. Minutes later, she was grinning at the change in his voice, filled with authority as he spoke down the line. Assertive. Borderline aggressive.

Arousing.

She heard him put his phone down. Next thing, he was at the door, peering out at her.

"Done. Burrows is off to the vicarage now. We've a few more questions, so Turner won't suspect you've had a hand in it. I've told Pete to let me know if there's anything to worry about."

"Thank you," said Emma, under lashes. "I hope I've not crossed a boundary …"

He grinned. "No, but I'm going to. Right now." He pointed upwards. "I'm good to go if you are …"

❧ 29 ❧

A PICKLED PEPPER

As Westen climbed the stairs to his office, he found Burrows hovering on the landing. His sergeant jerked his head in the direction of an empty interview room. "A moment, Guv?"

Once the door closed, Westen said, "Problem?"

"Yep. St Saviour. We've not been able to bring him in."

"Come again?"

"It's the super. Says we've nothing on him. Wants to have a word. Soon as."

"Does he, now." Westen nodded grimly, as if something had been confirmed. "He'll have to wait. Did Donna get that handwriting sample?"

"She did, Guv. Martin kept a diary and a journal."

"A journal? Interesting?"

"Very. Poured his heart into it. Including the day he broke things off with Turner. Donna said you'd be interested."

"I am. Links up with the scene of the murder and points to St Saviour's involvement again. He must have gone through his things. How did you get on with the bishop?

What's his name … ? Tell me we've got enough to pull him in."

"Frederick Thomas, Guv. And he gave us plenty. Took Donna, as you suggested. We broke the news about Martin. He wanted us to leave it to him to inform the parents. I thought it fair enough." Burrows hesitated. "We … er … took the liberty of telling him about Turner's reaction at the crime scene. Thomas is going to close the vicarage to visitors until our enquiries are finished. He's also considering a temporary replacement for Turner."

"Good. And what did you dig up about St Saviour? Did the church carry out any background checks? Are we any nearer to finding out where the fucker came from?"

"Yeah, you'll like this, Guv. The bishop was gobsmacked at St Saviour's lack of history. Showed us his paper file. Full set of documents, employment records, the lot. He couldn't explain it. Tried to get his assistant on the blower, but no one could find him. His desk had been cleared, too."

"AWOL?"

Burrows nodded. "Looks like it." He scratched his head. "This St Saviour, Guv … What I can't work out is, why? Why go to the trouble of impersonating a clergyman? And why the interest in the super?"

Or a Member of Parliament, or a CEO, or the head of a mining company and fuck knows who else.

Shaking his head at the question, Westen lowered his voice. "About that. Did Stamford pull Pecker's records?"

"Came through first thing, Guv. You're not going to like it."

"Go on."

Burrows handed over a slim file. "There've been some cash withdrawals in the last three weeks. Substantial ones."

Westen let out a low whistle as he scrutinised the high-lighted documents inside.

"I see what you mean. There's one for twenty grand, then another last week for thirty. All cash. Difficult to imagine our DS sidling into a bank, stuffing wads of money into a briefcase."

"Tony checked the history. Before these transactions, everything's pretty much as you'd expect. The usual store cards and a credit card, but he settles them each month. Judging by the statements, I'd say they were for Mrs Pecker's use."

Such large amounts stank of something suspicious. Blackmail? Westen noted they'd taken place within the past three weeks—soon after St Savior appeared on the scene. A man he knew from Emma, enjoyed turning the screw. And what the fuck had Pecker been doing at that reception? If St Saviour had him in the frame for something, unlikely he'd be there of his own free will.

"And the Broadys?"

"Still no sign. We visited Uncle George. His wife answered with a real shiner. She was in bits, Guv. Said it's the first time he'd ever laid hands on her. We knocked on the door of every known friend, relative and associate; no one's seen either of them since the night of the murder. Or so they say."

"Okay, thanks, Pete," Westen said. "Double the efforts on finding the Broady pair and get onto Savage. See if he's got the forensics on Martin yet. Did you call on Turner?"

"I did." Burrows frowned.

"What?"

"He's a changed man."

"Well, he would be. After going through what he did the other night."

"Yeah. I don't know how I'd react if it had been one of mine. But ... I dunno, Guv. I'd have expected him to be out of his mind—you know, with grief and all that—but when he opened the door, it's like he was empty. Know what I mean? Nothing behind the eyes."

"I'll talk to Emma—" he cleared his throat. "Emma Blake. See what can be done. I agree the vicarage isn't the best place for him, especially with St Saviour there. Was he in?"

"Yep. Nasty piece of work."

Westen curled his lips. "We need him in."

"Agreed, Guv. What about the super?"

"Leave him to me. Hang fire until we've had a conversation. I'm going up now."

He visited his office to check his desk. Pecker's expected report had not landed. Holding onto the file Burrows had given him, he climbed another flight of steps to the turquoise and steel suite of offices that housed the upper echelons of the Sandmarsh police. Half the floor had also been allocated to the county's Police Anti-Corruption Unit.

Fucking ironic.

Pecker's harassed-looking secretary leapt up as he strode past her. "Er, you can't go in there, Inspector, he's tied up."

"Don't worry, Marjory, I'm damned good at knots."

He grabbed the door handle and barged his way into the office. Faced with the back of Pecker's chair, he could only see the crook of the man's elbow as he yelled into his phone.

At the noisy entrance, the man swung around. Mobile cupped to his chest, he barked, "I'm too busy to see you now, Westen. Come back later."

Westen shut the door and stood in front of it, hands together, file dangling, a pulse throbbing at his temple. "I'll wait. Sir."

The super rose from his chair. "I said—" Seeming to change his mind, with a deepening frown, he snarled, "I'm sorry, Philip, we're going to have to do this later." He ended the call.

"Would that be *the* Philip Ackroyd, our erstwhile MP?" asked Westen.

"None of your business, Westen." He put the phone down and shuffled the papers on his desk. "Right. You wanted to interview St Saviour. Out of the question. Not until I know why."

"Why do you think? Sir."

Pecker's face reddened.

"Don't take that tone with me, Inspector. You'd better sit down. Time we had a conversation."

"I'd rather stand. Sir," replied Westen. He took a step forward. "I don't seem to have your report on my desk, explaining your presence at the vicarage reception."

"You're not getting one. I don't have to justify myself to you. Who I socialise with is none of your business. If I hadn't had one too many whiskys that night, you'd have got the reprimand you deserved. A mistake that won't happen again."

"Socialising? I thought you were, if I can recall your exact words, 'infiltrating a network of major players'?"

Pecker glared at him, cheeks laced with puce. "That too. The fact of the matter is, I am not accountable to you, and I cannot see any probable cause for you to interview St Saviour. When I loaded up the briefing notes this morning, I couldn't believe my eyes."

"I sympathise, sir. Had a bit of an eye-opener myself."

Westen walked towards the desk and, opening the file, spread it out before the superintendent.

If Pecker's face had flushed red before, it could have lit a fucking bonfire now.

"What the hell, Westen? You've gone into my financials?"

"It's normal procedure in an investigation, sir."

"You're investigating *me!* Jesus Christ, have you got some kind of death wish?"

"No. What I *wish* is for you to explain about the money." Westen took a step forward and leant over the desk to point at the highlighted sections. Stepping back he continued, "Or shall we take a walk down the corridor? Get ACU involved?"

The super threw himself back on his chair. Eyes locked, neither of them said a word.

Pecker broke first.

Slumping, he took off his spectacles and held the bridge of his nose between his fingers. "You win, Westen. I suppose it had to come out sooner or later. You're right. St Saviour has me by the balls."

"What's he got on you?"

Pecker's eyes slid away from Westen's. "This assignment to the Corporate Fraud Squad—my bloody swansong, the last stretch in an otherwise spotless career. I can't believe I was such an idiot. On my last visit to London, I ended up in a bar with someone on the CFS team. He was telling me about a merger they had their eyes on. Hadn't happened yet but—"

"You bloody fool," said Westen. "You bought some shares, didn't you?"

"I should have known better. Chap got his laptop out as soon as I said I might be interested and before I knew it, I was in for twenty grand …"

Westen frowned. He picked up documents he'd put in front of Pecker and stared at them for a few seconds. "It was the cash withdrawals that alerted us. There's no record of an electronic transfer here. Where did that money come from?"

Pecker shifted in his seat. "Not a UK account."

"Caymans?"

Pecker nodded. "I'm old school. Worked hard. Saved all my life and been able to grow a decent legacy from my father who did the same, so I've got more than a few bob. An investment manager told me where to tuck it away."

"Conveniently out of our jurisdiction." Westen sighed.

"You stupid bugger. Tax avoidance won't go down well, either."

Now Pecker had opened up, Westen sat in the chair opposite the desk, pulled it closer. "So, after the transaction in the pub, I suppose you got a visit from that fucker St Saviour, something that mentioned insider trading?"

"I did. I have no idea where he came from or how he found out about it. He seems to have people everywhere. He knew I was about to start on the CFS, too."

"You've told him things?"

Pecker nodded.

"What other tunes did he have you dancing to, apart from money? What brought you to the vicarage?"

"He's developing his own network. From what I can make out, he wants to build a kind of Opus Dei Fourth Reich. That's what the money's for. Ackroyd's on the hook too. St. Saviour targeted us for our contacts. You saw some of them at that damned reception. I didn't want to be there, didn't want to have anything to do with him, but he insisted. He's after influence."

"You said you didn't know where he came from?"

After Pecker shook his head, Westen clued him in on St Saviour's details—or lack of them.

"Unbelievable. And you think he's connected to the Martin murder?"

"Yes. We've other suspects. One of them works at Deep-Drilla for your Angus Drew. We haven't joined the dots yet. It's one of the reasons we want him in."

"Westen, he isn't my Angus Drew. I—" Pecker stopped talking. He let out a bagful of air. "I'm falling on my sword. Resigning." He looked over to the ACU offices. "Is there any chance I can persuade you not to walk down that corridor?"

Slowly, Westen shook his head. "My advice to you is to take the walk yourself. You never know, the force may accept a resignation. It won't want the very public revelation that a senior officer has succumbed to fraud and blackmail. You may save your pension, if not your reputation."

Pecker said nothing.

"This man you did the trade with. What's his name?"

"Erm … Booker. John Booker." Shame etched itself all over Pecker's brow. "I made a few enquiries myself, after the fact. Went back to the CFS team. He'd disappeared."

"Seems to be a habit with St Saviour's associates."

Clambering up, Westen inhaled, surveyed his superior possibly for one last time. "I think we're done, sir. Burrows will be bringing in St Saviour." It was Westen's turn to nod down the corridor. "They'll have my report before I interview him this afternoon. Use the time wisely."

❦ 30 ❦

FAULTS AND FISSURES

True to her word, Abigail rang Tom Shepherd. She'd met up with the seismologist a few times but not since he'd returned to Lanchester Uni. There'd been no spark on her part, though she suspected he didn't feel the same. He took no persuading at all to meet at the Flammark Arms for a few drinks.

"Great!" Tom had said, his words coming breathily down the phone. "I can do the weekend. If we met up in Sand-marsh, you could show me the sights."

"Actually, I wondered if you could come down tomorrow?"

"Tomorrow? I suppose I could. It's Friday, I'd have to miss a tutorial, but I think I could get out of it. Yeah, okay."

"Oh, by the way, did your team manage to map that crack you showed me in the van that day? If you've charted it, don't suppose you could possibly manage to bring it with you so I could have another look? I want to tell the anti-frackers about it and need to be sure I've got the facts straight."

Even over the phone, she could sense tension. "Is that why you rang? For a freaking map?"

"Of course not! It's you I want to see. If it's an official secret, or something, forget I asked."

After a few beats Tom said, "I'm not sure this is a good idea, Abby. I shouldn't come. Something—"

"What?"

"Can't say. The readings have changed since we last spoke. There've been … developments."

"Developments? What? Has it got worse, or something?"

No answer.

"Hang on, you aren't suggesting things have got dangerous, are you?"

Again, nothing.

"Look, Tom, I live here. My friends live here—my mother. You're beginning to frighten me. Please can we meet up? Please?"

After a few more seconds of reluctant silence, Tom said, "I suppose I could bring my laptop. You could take a peek." As if unable to help himself, he blurted, "I told the prof we should probably go public but he closed me down."

"Now you've really got me worried. And it sounds like you'd like to talk."

Abigail could almost hear his indecision.

"Okay," he said, "I'll come. But I won't be staying for long."

Abigail was only a bit late in arriving. Scanning the place as she entered, she spied Tom, ensconced in a side booth, hugging a pint of ale. After chatting to Joseph behind the bar, she bought a Fentimans and wove through the lunchtime crowd to join him. He gave her a worried half-smile as he stood up to greet her. Putting on a huge grin, she air-kissed him and said, "Tom! Great to see you again. How've you been?"

He tried to widen his smile, then wrinkled his nose at her glass. "What's that?"

"Dandelion and burdock." His scowl deepened and she laughed. "I don't do alcohol."

They sat down, awkwardly silent. Tom drew from his pint and looked everywhere but at her. Yikes, stressed! Girding herself against his response, she said, "I've asked Wyland to come, if that's okay? You know, from the caravan park? And another friend. Gabby. They'll be here soon."

Tom opened his mouth and closed it again. Shook his head. "No, it's not okay. It's unbelievable, actually. I don't know why I agreed to come. I'm sorry. I have to go."

Fortunately, Wyland and Gabby chose that moment to arrive at their table.

Wyland stood next to Abigail's seat and Tom flicked his eyes from one to the other. Desperate to keep him on board, she said, "It's not what you think. We're only friends." Then, alarmed by a sudden thought, she said to Wyland. "I am right, aren't I? We are just friends?"

Wyland smiled. "Yes, Abs. I'm not boyfriend material." He winked at Gabby, "and definitely not the marrying kind."

"Phew, that's a relief," she laughed.

She hoped some jocularity would settle Tom. It didn't work. The new arrivals seemed only to make him even more defensive.

"Nice to meet you. I'm not staying."

He drained his glass and was about to get up when, thwarting his exit, Gabby scooched in next to him. As Wyland sat next to Abigail she said, "Come on, Tom, what's all the secrecy? Where's the harm? You weren't like this when we first met."

Tom, radiating belligerence, didn't move. After a difficult silence, Wyland jerked his head at the laptop on the table. "Come on. Let's have a look."

Abigail felt a bit sorry for Tom. He was older than her, but not by much—a bit on the immature side, which is probably why she hadn't fancied him—and certainly no match for the steady glare of a Guardian.

Reluctantly, Tom lifted the lid of his laptop. The file having already been loaded, he turned the screen right angles so they could all view it. Bowing to the inevitable, he said, "I think you'll find this the most interesting."

They leaned in. Wyland said, "Thank you, Tom. I've been looking forward to this. I've never seen the land from this perspective."

Abigail knelt up on the seat, tucking her legs beneath her as she cocked her head to look at the screen, locating the familiar jagged line that ran from the Tor all the way to Wood End and the rest of Ledbridge.

"See, everyone, this is the crack I've been on about." She threw Tom a quizzical glance. "It's a thicker line. And what's this rectangle?"

"As I said when you called, things have developed since we talked in the van." He took a deep breath. "It's not a crack any longer. It's become a fracture. There's been more earth movement." He zoomed in on the rectangle. "We put these over faulted strata to show the level of displacement."

"That looks like a lot," said Gabby.

"It is. And the speed of the movement is unusual." He chewed his lip. "I can't say any more."

They all turned their eyes upon him.

Tom sighed. "All right. But you can't repeat any of this."

They all nodded enthusiastically. He glanced around the pub and, lowering his voice, continued, "Someone reported a potential problem at the fracking site and the ministry got onto us. We were ordered to send in a team and sink a probe. We obviously didn't need to drill because we could use the well. It's two miles deep."

Wyland whistled.

"I know!" Tom said, unable to mask his enthusiasm despite himself. "That's how deep they have to drill to reach the shale. Anyway, we got the probe in place quickly and the results came in straight away. It's not been mapped up yet." He looked again at their encouraging faces and shook his head as he clicked a few buttons. "But I have this."

As if by magic, another map flew in from the side to overlay the one they'd been looking at.

"Clever," said Wyland. "What's this black area here?"

Gabby paled. "My God …"

Almost whispering, now, Tom said, "It's only just appeared. The prof thinks it might be a fissure. If it is, it's massive. The team's still at DeepDrilla, trying to assess the level of risk."

"Risk?" said Abigail. She took her legs out from under her and sat down. Grabbed Wyland's arm.

Tom explained, "Fissures are quite common and crop up all the time, but at this depth—the probe picked it up at another two miles down, so we're almost at the earth's crust —they take thousands … millions … of years to form. We've never heard of one this deep develop so quickly. We're worried."

"It is huge," said Abigail. "It's not only under the fracking site, it's under Flammark too, and stretches nearly to Sandmarsh. That's, what … forty-ish miles as the crow flies?"

"You have to square it. If it's as wide as it's long than we're talking sixteen hundred miles. We know how far down it is, but we don't know it's volume, so it'll even bigger than that once the mileage is cubed," said Wyland, grimly.

Tom looked desperate. "You know, I *really* have to go. I'm only a postgrad. They'd throw me off the programme if they found out I was telling you this." He reddened as he looked at Abigail. "I thought this was only going to be between the two of us."

Wyland's response was sharp. "The fault is on my land, under my home. All our homes. We need to know about anything that threatens it. Exactly how dangerous is this fissure?"

Tom looked longingly at the exit as he brought a finger to his mouth, started biting its nail. "Evacuation dangerous. We don't want to start a needless panic, but we'll know for sure by the end of the week, possibly tomorrow."

"You mean, Ledbridge might ... what, collapse?" said Abigail, her mouth open.

"Not just Ledbridge. If the fissure has made the land above it unstable, the effect would be wider. Much wider. There'd be a massive earthquake. You may be ordered to leave."

Wyland swallowed. "I'll not be going anywhere."

"But I will," said Tom. "Look. I shouldn't have come, but when the dust settles, I'll probably be glad I told you. You're right, I do think you need to know, but I'm not ... strong enough to go against the prof—I daren't go public with the info on my own. What you do with it is your business, but remember, if you do leak it, there will be a panic, and we aren't yet certain what it is or how dangerous it might be."

He gathered up his laptop. To Gabby he said, "Please move. I'll make a scene if you don't."

"Of course," said Gabby. "I—we're very glad you came. I promise you, we have our own reasons not to say a word to anyone."

With no more words, Tom left.

Abigail let out a long sigh. "That went well. Not."

"Poor lamb," said Gabby. "We were rather harsh on him."

"Good call getting him here, though," said Wyland. "It's moved us on. He took a big risk. We know where we stand now."

"This fissure is terrifying," said Abigail. "What do you think caused it? How could Godzilla be responsible if they take so long to form?"

"That, I'm afraid, is easy to answer," said Gabby. "It isn't a fissure."

"Not a fissure?" said Abigail. "W-what do you mean?"

Gabby looked around her. The lunchtime crowd had mostly left, and the pub had quieted. "I think Animus is planning another emergence. The first-century affair showed him what he'd be up against should he return. I think what you witnessed a few weeks ago was just the advance party. He's been planning an invasion."

"So, you think the fissure is ... ? What?" Wyland said.

"Spirit legions. Thousands and thousands of them. They'll have been crawling up for centuries, and the earth has finally given way to them. They're waiting below for Animus to find a way of letting them through. It all makes sense now. He must have planned for them to emerge at Wood End. He couldn't have known we'd planted the sentinels. He managed to displace one of them, but with the others still on guard, the portal would have been much too small for anything other than the advance party. It would have taken years."

"Sixteen hundred square miles, Gabby," said Wyland his expression battling between wonder and terror, "and that's a conservative estimate of how large the fissure is, considering we don't know its depth. That would contain a hell of an army."

"A hell indeed," said Gabby, pondering as she talked. "A

hell on earth. That's what Animus has in store, and he doesn't want to wait."

Gabby gave them all a grim smile. "Don't ever again take notice of anything I say. It is clear to me now that Animus never intended a gradual takeover. Bonded to his emergence site but barred by the sentinels, as we surmised, he followed the fracking fault and found a way out." She gave a mirthless chuckle. "Once fleshed, I can only imagine his delight when he realised idiot humanity had drilled a bloomin' great hole, ten thousand feet into the bowels of the earth! A new entrance into the world waiting right next door!"

Wyland frowned. "So, he gathered his minions under it." Then his brow grew perplexed. "But they aren't bonded to it. They're in spirit form. They've no brain … no intelligence. How are they going to know they're supposed to come out there? How does Animus communication with them?"

"I have no idea," Gabby replied. "Abigail may well be right about the hive mind thing, but I can't be sure." She sighed. "I don't know how he got them there or how he intends to get them out. The only thing I'm stone-cold certain of is that Animus will have a plan. I'll bet my life he has contacts at DeepDrilla and will have found out the fissure—and the earth around all of us—is in danger of collapse. He'll know the authorities are involved too—as represented by the likes of Tom. I think he's had to act more quickly than he originally planned."

A confused silence fell upon them.

Abigail whispered, "We're going to have to go there, aren't we? To Godzilla. We're going to have to find a way to stop it."

"And soon. Today,"nodded Gabby. "I have no doubt that the seismologists have called it right. Animus has a very narrow window to get his army out. Once he does, well … apocalypse."

"I can get us into the site, past its security," said Wyland, "but once Animus sets the ball rolling, we have no plan. No clue how to stop him."

"… and no angels to help us," said Gabby.

She stood up. "Yet we have no choice but to go."

MISSING

Westen had been a wonderful distraction. No. Wrong word. An interlude; a break from the catastrophe Animus had brought down upon Will. Upon Peter. Their night together had shored her up. Had centred her. A line had been crossed and she trusted him.

Emma would never have to explain the dark times. Those moments when memories of Ben sailed in to ink her mind and terrify her all over again. Westen knew her damage—he'd been the one who brought it all to an end. Thank God there was one part of her life she didn't have to keep from him.

Leaving early, needing to get back to his flat for a quick shower and change of clothes, Westen kissed her on the doorstep as she saw him off. She took a lone breakfast and wondered if St Saviour knew if his blackmail game was up yet. No matter. It wouldn't be long before he found out.

Should she return to work? Deep down, she knew Will still needed her—needed someone—but his anger was too deep for him to admit it, and she understood why he wanted to nurse it alone. Not the best of situations, but she trusted in his true disposition, both as a priest and a friend, that he'd eventually find perspective. Maybe she would be better off at the surgery.

On the other hand, if Will did decide to come over, she'd never forgive herself if he knocked on her door and she wasn't there.

At around ten o'clock her jeep arrived, followed by a squad car. A young PC parked it on the road and climbed out, assuring her the vehicle had been checked over and the battery replaced. After wishing her well, he joined his colleague and they drove away.

Emma spent the rest of the morning agonising, watching for Will's loping figure to come through the garden gate. By lunchtime she'd had enough. She had to see him.

Grabbing her bag, she locked up and made her way over the green …

… to find the vicarage car park crammed with police vehicles.

Westen's was there too. Breaking into a run, she scanned the scene, looking for him. On the her way out of the house, Donna saw her and came dashing up.

"Emma! I'm afraid I'm going to have to ask you to go home. You shouldn't be here."

"What's happened? Oh my God, I can't breathe … is Will OK?" Emma's mind flew to the sight of Peter's body, then to what Will had said about not minding being a sentinel and how angry he'd been and how they'd left on such bad terms and …

"Try to calm down, Emma." Donna looked about. "There's a bench over there. I'll sit with you before you go back."

"I'm not going anywhere until you tell me what's happened."

"I … I can't. We're in the middle of an investigation."

"You have to tell me! Is Will okay?"

Donna chewed her lip for a few seconds before answering. "We don't know. He isn't here. The place is empty."

"Then why are there so many police cars?"

Emma caught her breath as she suddenly saw two men in front of a navy-blue van put on white forensic suits. "Jesus, why are they here? What have you found?"

"I ... can't tell you Emma. It'd cost me my job."

"Get Westen."

"The Guv?" Donna looked at her uncertainly. "He's in the middle of—"

"I don't care. Get him. He'll want to see me."

"I'm not sure—"

"*Get him!*"

"Okay, okay. I'll find him. Promise me you'll stay here?"

Emma nodded and, chewing her lip, watched Donna bustle back inside. She dragged her little cross back and forth on its chain as she fixed her gaze on the front entrance. Five minutes later, Westen appeared, found where she was sitting and jerked his head to the side of the church, out of sight.

She ran to him. Shaking, eyes welling, she said, "Talk to me. Donna said Will's not here, yet I can see you've brought in a forensic team."

Looking about, checking they were alone, he took her hand and pulled her in closer to the wall. In a low voice he said, "Okay. Try to keep calm. Nobody's here. Nobody. But there are signs of a struggle. There's ... blood." He squeezed her hand. "It's not a lot, Emma, but enough to give us cause for concern. We're putting everything we've got into finding him."

She leaned back against the stone. Though her lips trembled, she tried to keep it together. "St Saviour's got him."

"He might have, but we don't know that. We don't know anything about him. Where he came from, where he might go …" Then his shrewd eyes locked on hers. "But I expect you do, don't you?"

"What do you mean?"

He sighed. "I don't know what I mean. But I recognise that look on your face. You're miles ahead of me, aren't you? Thinking about possibilities that for some reason you can't clue me into. Am I right?"

She gave him a long, tremulous look. "You're not wrong."

He raised his eyebrows. "Well?"

"I honestly don't know where they are. I don't know where St Saviour would go." He stood there, saying nothing, waiting for more. She bit her bottom lip, a case-study of indecision. Finally, she said, "I need to talk to someone. I need to make a call."

Shaking his head slowly, he let go of her hand and folded his arms. "Clock's ticking, Emma. But I'm staying right here while you make it. Put it on speaker."

She could barely hold the phone, so terrified for Will and the possibilities of what St Saviour might at this very moment be doing to him, not to mention the minefield that her next conversation would present. Eyes never leaving Westen's, she speed-dialed Abigail's number, not certain who would answer.

"Emma! It's really, really—"

"Gabby! Will's disappeared and so has St Saviour. Westen's here … he's listening. He agrees with me that St Saviour has probably got him somewhere. Have you any idea where that might be?"

"Just a moment."

Emma rolled her eyes. Agonising as she waited, she could hear Gabby relay her news to the exclamations of Abigail and —was that Wyland? She picked up background chatter, too. Where were they?

Half a minute later, Gabby was back.

"Tell Westen to go to DeepDrilla. If Will's anywhere, it'll be there. We've just met with someone and they have frightening news about the fracking. With a bit of luck the police might be able to get Will out before it starts."

"It? What?"

Silence. A sigh.

"*Gabby!?*"

"It's too complicated to explain now. If An ... St Saviour's made his move, Will's running out of time. I expect you'll want to follow the police out there. Whatever you do, don't. Let them do their job. If they can get Will out of the picture, that's one thing less we have to worry about. We need you here. We need to come up with a plan."

"Where are you? Wood End?"

"No, we're at the Flammark Arms. Meet us here."

She rang off and Westen looked at her long and hard. "DeepDrilla. Okay, I don't know the how or why of it, but in the absence of any other fucking clue we've no option but to give it a shot. I don't know who this Gabby is, but what she's saying does fit in with our enquiries." He shook his head, impatiently. "Go to your friends. We'll find Will. Follow Gabby's advice. Do not attempt to follow us!"

As she started after him, he spun round. "Emma, no. *Go to your friends*. This is important. I'm not telling you as the person you were with last night. Am I clear?"

The change in him, like a slap in the face, stopped her in her tracks. With no choice but to let him go, all she could do was watch from the sidelines as he pointed here and there, signalling, marshalling. He strode over to the white suits and barked at them, hastening their entry to the building, then beckoned to a puzzled-looking Pete Burrows, who'd just come out of it. Seconds later both men joined in the cacophony of car doors slamming and engines starting, before each vehicle, wheels crunching the gravel, turned and waited for Westen to take the lead. Soon five cars were in convoy, lights flashing, sirens blaring, a constabulary army primed on a campaign to find Will.

To save Will.

An uncanny silence enveloped her as Emma stood alone on the gravel. She took a deep breath then speed-walked her way home. Ten minutes later, climbing into the jeep, she prayed to God they'd find her friend, and that she'd be able to dream up something plausible in the reckoning Westen would demand about what she and her friends hadn't told him.

That would come later. After she followed him to DeepDrilla.

❧ 32 ❧

NO PLAN

T he afternoon heat bore down on Emma as she put her foot down along the Flammark Road, speeding past lorries and daytrippers, tailing the convoy. She didn't have a clue what she'd do when she caught up with them, except to keep out of Westen's way. The last thing she wanted was to distract him. Will would need all his help.

Twenty minutes out, she slowed. The banks of blue flashing lights were stationary, despite still being a mile out from the fracking site. Why had they stopped? She pulled up about a hundred yards behind and leaned out of the window to hear faint sounds of chanting and jeering. Craning her neck, she could see the convoy trying to edge forward, but gain little ground, as gradually it became consumed by a crowd of placard-wielding protestors.

Thunder. Ominous grumblings coming from the east. Black clouds striped the sky, making the light weird, almost green.

Emma jumped out of the jeep, climbed on the bonnet and onto the roof. Balancing on tiptoe, she strained to see the extent of the crowd. The road was rammed. There must be hundreds—thousands—if it stretched all the way back to DeepDrilla.

Two minutes later, back in the driver's seat, she attempted a U-turn, but the traffic she'd passed had caught up, drivers beeping their horns as they overtook her, only to be held up again as they joined the gathering crowd. She was getting hemmed in.

Grabbing her phone, she dialled Abigail's number.

"Emma!" Gabby again. "We've been waiting for you! Are you going to be much longer?"

"I'm not coming. I'm on the Ledbridge Road. Sorry, but I had to follow Westen."

"I wish you'd waited. We're already intended to come and we could have gone together. You shouldn't have attempted it alone."

"You won't be able to get through. There's hundreds and hundreds of people here. Protestors. I've stopped well behind Westen's lot and we're still a mile out from the site. They've surrounded him." She waited for a massive lorry to pass, but still had to shout over its engine noise, "They won't be able to get anywhere near DeepDrilla, and we won't be able to meet up."

"Hang on."

Almost screaming with frustration, Emma drummed her fingers on the steering wheel as another hasty confab took place.

"Emma, are you still there?"

"Yes, I'm still bloody here. What's the plan?"

"Wyland knows another way in. Wait a second, I'm giving this thing to Abigail. She's going to send you the location. You're going to have to leave the car and walk."

The text flew in as Wyland's voice came down the line. "Hi Emma. You'll have to cross fields, so you'll need to use a satnav app. We're detouring to Wood End first to pick up some tools, then we'll head your way. I know a shortcut from there."

"Understood."

"The location we've sent you takes you into the back of DeepDrilla. Don't try to get in yourself. I mean it, Emma. It's really dangerous. There're all sorts of powerlines to navigate. Wait for us there. We won't be long."

"Okay. I'm leaving now."

Outside the car the air had grown clammy. There were fewer gaps in the cloud and the atmosphere palled thick and dark. Sweat running in rivulets, Emma picked her way through the traffic jam and across the empty lane, holding the phone as she ran. Having found the general direction of travel—towards the crowd—she peered at a long stretch of hedgerow looking for an opening, praying she would find one before the screaming horde of protestors enveloped her.

There! Guarded by nettles, a gap appeared. Small, but enough for her to wriggle through. Bending her knees, she edged forward, legs immediately on fire, flesh and fabric catching on snapping twigs of hawthorn and bramble. She pushed and struggled, shouting her frustration as the hedge caught at her hair.

Through!

Knowing the torture she'd be in for if she didn't find a patch of docks, Emma scanned the ground and grabbed at the largest leaves she could find, rubbing her legs as she started her run over what turned out to be a barley field.

Quickly—but not quickly enough—she heaved her way through the knee-high crop. Ahead of her, patchwork acres of barley stretched as far as she could see, a sickly beige in the viridescence. Thunder growling, she peered at her phone and adjusted her direction, every moment doubting the pulsing blue dot would ever meet the bulbous yellow arrow.

She must have managed a slow half-mile before the map

told her to leave the fields and join a section of woodland. Emma remembered Abigail mentioning that DeepDrilla had done some tree-clearance and wondered whether the site had once been part of the woods that surrounded the caravan park. Familiar territory for Wyland.

Beneath the canopy of trees the air felt a degree or two cooler. The undergrowth was kinder, affording her the occasional run. After fifteen more minutes, she slowed as her dot closed in on the arrow. Through the trees ahead a dark shape loomed. Slowing her pace, she drew up to a massive metal fence built along the treeline, twenty feet high at least, topped with a fringe of razor wire.

The noise of the crowd had returned. A distance away, but enough to confirm she'd arrived at the right place. The protest must be truly massive if it extended from here to where it had swallowed the police convoy. She leant against the fence to get her breath back, wondered if following it round would bring her to some kind of entrance. No matter what Wyland said, if she found one, she'd use it to get to Will.

Instead, Emma slid down. The heat had got to her and she needed to get her breath back. She stared skywards at the louring clouds. A double blink of sheet lightning made her jump. Great. On top of everything, there was going to be a storm.

God knows how long she sat there until she heard voices and rustling ahead. She rose to her feet at the sight of her friends, two of whom had come dressed in what she could only describe as Charity Shop. What Gabby wore for trousers was a pair of men's shorts. Though just about fitting her ample waist they ended well below the knee, the khaki shirt she'd tucked in making her resemble a dwarf scoutmaster; an image further clinched by a pair of hiking boots, the only things that almost fitted. Where on earth had she got it all from?

Abigail had fared better—of course. One of Wyland's red checked shirts, corners tied above her own jeans, set her blue-black braids off to a tee. A pair of cute red wellies completed the ensemble, seamlessly overlaying her black, skin-tight jeans.

Emma almost laughed. When Wyland said he'd detoured to Wood End to get tooled up, she'd expected them to bring chainsaws, axes—drills. A slasher version of *Ghostbusters*. On exiting from their side of the woods, they cantered over to her armed with nothing but spades.

"Are you okay, Emma?" asked Gabby. "You look exhausted."

"I am. And hot."

She stared at what they were carrying. "When you said tools, Wyland, I didn't think they'd be of the garden variety. You've got a barn full of heavy machinery, and this is the best you can do?" She stood up and banged the metal fence. "It's solid. It probably goes down another ten feet. We'll never dig under it."

"Wrong. It isn't ten feet, it's fifteen. And we won't need to dig under it." He grinned. "There's a tunnel."

"A what?"

He grimaced. "When DeepDrilla first set up, we knew we'd be in for the long haul. If the protests weren't going to work, we'd have to resort to sabotage. My activist group has connections to a very famous tunneller. Remember Marshy? Took them months to find him, and weeks to extract him from one of his creations. His lot came out and set us up, just in case. We've brought the spades to clear the entrance and exits and in case there's been a collapse."

"A collapse?" said Gabby, worry suddenly all over her face. "Ohhh. You didn't say anything about a collapse."

Abigail handed Emma a plastic bag. "You can't go tunnelling in a sundress and sandals. This is all we could find in Wyland's lost property pile. You'll have to roll up sleeves and stuff."

While the others worked on uncovering the tunnel entrance, Emma got dressed, fishing out from the bag another checked shirt and a pair of torn jeans. Luckily, they'd thought to include a leather belt. She cinched the pants at her waist and pushed the bottoms into a pair of thick socks so the size eight wellies they'd brought had some chance of staying on.

They were ready.

Obviously in his element, Wyland took the lead. Handing them each a head torch, he said, "I'll go first. The tunnel's only about twenty feet long, but there's a steep slope to start with and we're going in head-first. Once we've bellied through, leave the torches. If we get caught, they'll know how we've got in and they'll collapse it." He took some deep breaths and indicated for them to do the same. "Ready?"

No, she wasn't ready. No, she didn't want to go into a bloody tunnel of earth. No, she didn't want to discover the beaten-up body of her friend on the other side of that blasted fence.

"Yes," she replied.

About six feet away from the perimeter the turf had been rolled back to reveal a set of thick wooden boards. Wedging his spade between them, Wyland prised them up. "Okay. So, remember, steep slope down, then only twenty feet before it slopes back up again."

"What about the collapses?" said Gabby, eyes fixed on the hole that gaped before them. "I don't want to get stuck behind a collapse. Collapses would be very upsetting. I've never been under the ground. It's not what I'm used to."

"I'm sure it isn't, Gabby," said Wyland, firmly. "But go we must. You'll be okay. I'll be right in front of you."

"Do you think I'll get in?" pressed Gabby, head still shaking. "I'm a bit wider than you lot."

"You'll be fine. If you get stuck, I'll pull and Emma can push."

"Thanks," said Gabby, rolling her eyes.

"I'm going last, then?" said Abigail. She too looked uncertain.

Thunder rolled. Even nearer. Shouts came from inside the fence, then a surge of cheers.

"Something's going on," said Emma. "Whether we want to or not, we have to go in."

"Oh my God!" exclaimed Abigail, looking around her as they switched on their head torches. "Look how dark it is! It sort of creeps up on you until you put a light on." She peered at her watch. "It's only five to three!"

Wyland replied with a grunt. He got on his belly and stretched out his arms as if about to take a dive. Gabby teetered at the edge for a minute before giving out a long moan and getting on her hands to follow suit. "I'm not going to fit, I'm not going to fit."

Emma could just hear Wyland's impatient, muffled reply, "Yes you are, stop moaning; it's wider than you think."

Her turn now. Switching her brain off, she lay down at the edge of the hole before thrusting herself into it. Muttering to herself, "Only twenty feet … only twenty feet … only twenty feet … Emma pushed her palms against the earth. All went well at first, as she let gravity do its work, but levelling out meant a change of position and a harder going. Tucking her fists beneath her breasts, head up, she elbowed along. She could see okay—the light worked well—what she hadn't factored in were the gobfuls of earth Gabby paddled at her.

Emma had expected a tunnelling distance of 'only twenty

feet' to take, what ... ten minutes? She couldn't have been more wrong. A shuffle equated to half a step, sometimes a quarter. At times it seemed they'd made no headway at all, as even with the headlamp it became hard to judge progress. It was tiring—exhausting—work, their bodies totally unused to the exercise, their minds stressed by the unknown of it. All sense of time lost, it seemed to Emma that hours had passed before Gabby's stopped kicking soil in her face. Relief overwhelmed her, when, at last, her light picked up Wyland's strong arm reaching down the final, upward slope. Gratefully she made her way up a few yards before grasping it to let him whisk her topside.

Spitting out earth, her exertions causing her to sweat more than ever, Emma yanked off her headlamp and joined Gabby in shucking off their wellies, emptying them of tunnel. They might not have been underground that long, but bits of earth got everywhere.

"I really don't like the look of that sky," said Wyland, joining them after they'd restored themselves. "It's getting cyclonic."

Gabby looked up too and nodded grimly, her mouth a taut pencil line in her ivory face. "Animus. I can see his plan now. He's going to create a vortex. He means to suck his army out of the fissure. The stronger he can make it, the greater its pull. His minions'll be out in no time."

The noise of the crowd felt much nearer now, and Emma heard the sound of a lone voice shouting, followed by surging roars. She couldn't see a bloody thing, her view obstructed by a stacked rank of portable offices.

"Will's here. I know it." She bit her lip. "And God knows what's happened to Westen."

"Yes, Animus has been clever," said Gabby. "He must have summoned the advance party. They've blocked the roads. The police won't be able to get near."

"Follow me," said Wyland.

He led them round the perimeter. Two, maybe three hundred yards away from the main action, it seemed unlikely they'd meet anyone unless Animus had posted guards. But Wyland wasn't taking any chances.

Quietly, they slipped past cranes, tractors and loaders—wide, with tank-like track wheels. Ranks of industrial gas canisters and rolls upon rolls of pipe followed, eventually giving way to another row of stacked cabins. They looked empty, probably not needed since the suspension of fracking. The roaring crowd had grown deafening and Emma left the group to scurry into a gap. Craning her neck, she got on tip toes in a futile attempt to get sight of the event that so obviously pleased the mob. She prayed it had nothing to do with Will. Unable to see anything, she returned to her friends.

"I can't see a thing," she cried. "We have to get closer."

"No chance," said Wyland. "We'd be buried in the crowd. Hang on."

He stopped them at the end cabin, in front of a flight of metal steps that led to the top storey. He climbed them crouching, head down, his long legs still able to take them two at a time. At the top he gradually unfurled, obviously feeling no longer in danger of discovery. Nor did he worry about being heard, since he felt safe enough to exclaim, "Oh my dear God."

"What is it?" cried Emma. "What do you see? Any sign of Will?"

White faced, he turned to them.

"It's useless. There's nothing we can do."

❧ 33 ❧

ANIMUS REVEALED

Shielded by the noise of the crowd, Emma shouted, "What do you mean, there's nothing we can do? What's happening. What can you see?"

"Wait!" Wyland stepped away from his viewing platform and cupped his eyes to peer through the cabin windows. "It's empty," he called. "I'm going to try and get us inside."

He tried the door handle. Locked. Gripping it with both hands, placing his foot underneath for leverage, he yanked. Pulled the damn thing off altogether. After throwing it away in frustration, he returned to the window and reached into his back pocket, whipping out what looked like a Swiss Army knife. Taking a moment to swivel out some of its options, he chose one and got to work on the base of the pane, taking off the plastic trim. Two minutes later, he'd inserted a blade and yanked up the plexiglass. He threw it inside and signalled the women to come up.

Abigail went up first. She looked over the handrail, out to the crowd, and put her hand over her mouth. Wyland chivvied her away and lifted her so she could put her legs through the window. Gabby presented more of a challenge, but, with Abigail's help, Wyland managed to get her through without injury.

Emma next. All four inside, they rushed to the window that faced the crowd, offering an elevated and panoramic view of exactly how much trouble they were in.

Through the heavy, green-tinted atmosphere, they stared out at the hundreds that had pushed their way into the site, its gates wide open. Hundreds more jostled in the access road, all pushing, singing, chanting, jeering—some men stripped to the waist in the broiling heat.

Some hundred or so yards away from where they watched, at the edge of the mob, barricaded off, stood the iron rig that surrounded the fracking well. Like a skeleton rocket, its crown rose perpendicular to the tightening circle of roiling clouds. A ring of men, muscles rippling within black, long-sleeved tee-shirts—high necked—stood with arms akimbo, facing the crowd. Black trousers, their belts in matching silver-buckled leather, gave way to calf-length jack-boots, ruthlessly deployed in kicking errant onlookers off the barrier.

Emma's attention strayed to a platform erected about a hundred yards away from the rig. Another barrier—more thugs—with burning oildrums either side, their smoke and flames twisting skywards. A massive banner attached to long poles screamed:

DOMINATION AND DOMINION

Bizarrely, strings of large bulbous garden lights edged the banner, popping gold against the unnatural, green-tinted world. Mesmerised and appalled, Emma almost missed the dark figure to the side, head bowed, tied to a post, flanked by two blackshirts.

Will.

Abigail grasped her arm. She had seen him too! The pair turned heavy, desolate eyes to each other. It was hopeless.

Wyland, practical as ever, opened all the windows. "God, it's hot." Joining the women, he said, "We're safe here for now. That lot aren't interested in us. They're too busy gawping at that stage."

"Yes," said Gabby, grimly staring out. "He's planning to give them a performance."

"We've got to find a way of getting to Will," Emma cried. "I think he's alive, thank God, but—" she swallowed the hard lump in her throat, "—but for how long? Seeing this, I'm worried about Westen too! He mustn't have been able to get through." She gave Gabby a desperate look. "By the time I left the road, they'd been completely overwhelmed."

"The cops'll be okay," said Wyland. "They'll be waiting it out. Police vehicles are virtually impregnable nowadays, save for being set on fire, and they wouldn't do that. They'd be too close when the cars blew. They'd go down with 'em."

"Wyland's right," added Abigail. "They'll just be holding them. Westen won't know what's happening here. He'll probably wait it out for now, rather than risk calling out the water cannons. He'll think he's got caught up in a protest march."

"To some of them, it still is," said Wyland. "I recognise a few. They're part of my cell, though God only knows why they're going along with all this."

"This isn't getting us anywhere!" Emma nearly screamed, anguished eyes tearing as they locked-on across the crowd to her friend slumped against that awful post. "We've got to get to Will!"

Agitation within the crowd. All eyes had turned upwards to the crown of the rig. Bending her head, crouching slightly to follow the arc of their gaze through the cabin's window, Emma saw movement right at the top. A figure! It must have been sitting there all the time, for now it gradually unfurled before their eyes, slowly standing upright on what seemed the tiniest of eye-wateringly high platforms.

Abigail gasped, "Is that St Saviour?"

"No," replied Gabby. "That's Animus."

Swaggering hundreds of feet above them, arms outstretched, chest to the sky, the miniscule figure rotated. Once, twice, three times, slowly raising his hands as his acolytes screamed their excitement.

Heart in mouth, Emma gazed, praying he would fall, knowing he would not.

Amidst the mob's screams and shouts, he slowly bent at the waist and got on all fours. Head between his arms, he took his weight and curled up his legs, knees bent. For a heart-stopping moment he rested there, before stretching the handstand full length. Body as pennant, rising dizzyingly dead-centre from the crown of the high rig.

"Don't the crowd just love it," scoffed Gabby. "Give them a circus and they'll belong to anyone."

Whoops and roars continued as he broke the handstand. He swung his legs onto the iron framework, and with a twist of his torso, grabbed on. Apelike, he climbed down, slowly, assuredly, every foot a new show of strength. The mob surged as he touched earth, the onlookers finally seeing more of their idol, dressed in the same garb as his henchmen, strutting his stuff. His guards leapt into action, jackbooting and punching at any attempt to breach the barrier.

Slipping out of view, Animus left them to it, and ten minutes of mayhem followed until the crowd ran out of steam. Suddenly, reinforcements arriving, the thugs left their positions and pushed and parted the mob, opening up a corridor to Will's platform. Emma could see nothing of Animus, except for a brief appearance as he walked in their wake, his grey buzz-cut bobbing along behind them. Amidst bellows and ululations, he once more emerged, making an agile leap over the barricades onto the makeshift stage.

Almost in unison the three friends gasped in open-mouthed disbelief at the emblem circled in white on the back of his shirt.

"Isn't that ... a Nazi emblem?" said Abigail.

"Resting on a Roman wreath," nodded Gabby. "And also his initials in this incarnation. He couldn't be clearer what kind of world he envisages."

As if by some monstrous orchestration, thunder rolled, nearer than ever before, and as lightning forked overhead, the circling clouds coiled into a marbled nebula, roiling together as the vortex swirled and tightened. Animus, head bowed, turned to face the chanting crowd.

They quieted.

Emma could almost taste the anticipation.

Slowly he lifted his eyes and stretched out his arms. In a voice so unnaturally loud they had no difficulty hearing it, he began:

My people. My ... people.

Today, after many centuries of banishment, our time is at hand. Never again will we succumb to the forces that would

oppress us, would rob us of our right to exist on this earth,
would deny our strength.

We can Become!

The horde roared.

Emma's eyes moved back and forth from Animus to Will, hope diminishing at every terrible word. Yet something stirred in the back of her mind.

Animus waved his palms downwards and the noise quelled.

This land is ours for the taking. Since my emergence, I have
been watching, while you have been infiltrating. You report
nothing but weakness. A world terrified of itself, of using its
resources, of marshalling its strength.

OF WIELDING ITS POWER!

The crowd went wild.

The earth is on its knees!

Its leaders listen to the deficient and eschew the dominant.
They follow purveyors of false beliefs and consider the likes of
us a pestilence.

It hears only fear.

NO LONGER!

Emma racked her brains as Animus gazed at the turbulence in the skies, raised his arms and spread his hands palm-upward to the vortex, a picture of evangelistic fervour.

Something's missing.

Even the skies have answered my call, ready to speed my waiting legions on their upward journey.

My people, together we will form the greatest movement the planet has ever seen. We will purge the earth of its shortcomings. We will seek out the worthy. We will eliminate the frail.

I say death! To the great prevaricators. Death! To the politicians. Death! To the priests ...

Gabby groaned. "Here we go. Vintage Animus."

What do you say?

As the crowd began chanting, "*Death ... death ... death ... death ...*" Animus nodded to the two henchmen. They moved in on Will and untied him from the post, dragging him to the edge of the stage. Grabbing him by the hair, the monster kicked the back of his legs so that Will crunched onto his knees. Then Animus theatrically wiped the hand that had held him on his crisp black trousers. Calming the audience again, he continued:

I speak of puny individuals like this. Men whose purpose it is to undermine your path to power, whose mission is to plant seeds of doubt and strip you of your will. Who tell you what to think, who fill your mind with lies. Those who preach sin while practising depravity ...

"No. No," said Gabby, uselessly covering her ears. "Don't say it, don't do it, not to Will ..."

Those who consort with their own sex!

A collective gasp quivered through the onlookers, including the four friends. Though obviously weak, hardly able to keep upright, Will managed to raise his head in an obvious attempt at defiance.

"The *bastard!*" Abigail ran to the door, but Wyland's long legs overtook her. "No, Abigail. No! You'll be noticed, killed. Outright."

"We've got to do something! We can't just … watch!" She held onto Wyland, face screwed up in despair, as they returned once more to the window. Watching indeed, the only thing they could do.

Gabby wore the same expression. "I can't help him. I don't know what to do. I'm no use. It's … it's all gone."

Emma couldn't cry. Her brain, fuelled by Will's humiliation, racked doubletime for the missing piece.

Look at the penitent!

The crowd screamed.

Do you want me to kill him?

- Kill him … kill him … kill him…

Animus replied with a thunderous chuckle.

Patience, my people. Patience.

I am a generous man. I am a kind man. I am a just man. Today we celebrate an emergence the like of which has never been seen. This sinner will kneel before my assembled army before I rip out his perverted heart.

Disappointed by the loss of their sport, the crowd jeered and booed. Mystically amplified, tied to the rhythm of the raging clouds, Animus' voice deepened and boomed over them.

Fear not! Our mission has hardly begun! Soon my legions will come, and the earth will be purged of scum like this. Are you ready?

- Yes!

Are you ready?

- Yes!!

ARE YOU READY?

The crowd heaved and raged. Someone started: "Death … death … death … death …" and the mob followed, feet stamping to the monobeat as Animus joined in, fisting the air to the pulsing chant.

Then, to the friends' utter dismay, he tore his gaze from the crowd and, laughing, twisted his head in their direction.

As one, the horde turned too, gazing at them mindlessly, sinisterly lowering its tone as they took the lead from their master:

We see you … We see you … We see you.

Sweet Jesus.

Heart hammering, Emma said, "They're coming for us."

"I don't think so," said Gabby. "He wants us to know he's spotted us. We're *his* Druids now. *His* witnesses."

As Animus resumed his ranting, the crowd turning back, Abigail exclaimed, "Why? Why's he bothering? If this lot's the advance party, the ones that came out at Wood End, they'll all be converts! Why put on this show?"

"Not all," said Wyland, grimly. "I've told you. I recognise some of our lot down there. Activists, progressives. It's disgusting."

"It's the power of rhetoric," said Gabby. "And they're massively outnumbered. Even the righteous need to conform; some of them will just be scared to death. As for Animus' real followers, this is the first time they've seen their leader. He's showing them his strength. They're in the flesh too. He's lifting their morale, doing a spot of corporate advertising."

Suddenly Emma shrieked. "His cane! That's what's missing! His cane."

Gabby frowned, then hitched her breath as she processed Emma's words. Suddenly energised, she said, "Oh, my goodness. You're right. Where is it?"

Eyes frantically scanning, Emma cried, "I can't see it anywhere. He doesn't have it!"

"Maybe he left it somewhere," said Abigail. "Is it that important?"

"He never went anywhere without it," Emma replied. "Will said so. When I first met Ani—St Saviour at the vicarage, he either carried it or had it next to him, I ... thought I caught something move inside."

"You saw something inside?" said Gabby, sharply. "What do you mean?"

In her haste to explain, Emma's words tumbled over each other. "As soon as I set eyes on it I was positive I could see something move. He said something to do with amber catching the light. Thing is ..."

"Spit it out, Emma," said Abigail, hardly in control. "Tick, tock."

Emma, hastily collected her thoughts. "When he came to the cottage to deliver his blackmail threat, he quizzed me about who Will had staying at the vicarage. I let something slip that confirmed his suspicions. It … excited him." She paused for a beat to catch her breath. "His cane caught my eye. I'm positive I saw something move inside it again. He realised I'd twigged because he picked it up and put it next to him, hiding the amber from me."

Gabby's frown deepened as again she asked, "You're sure you saw something move, actually *move* inside? Not a trick of the light?"

Emma nodded, then shook her head.

"Then it can't be amber."

Then, as if the dawn of the world had suddenly unfurled, Gabby's expression cleared. "Emma, I could kiss you."

"What is it Gabs?" said Abigail. "What's inside?"

"If he has to have it with him all the time, it must be some element of him—of his spirit. Something that can't be incorporated into flesh. An essence. I'm wondering … no, I'm sure. It's our missing link. The thing that connects him to the underworld, to his minions." She shook her head, irritated. "I should have put it together earlier—when he came here the first time. We knew then he wasn't a magical creature or had psychical energy. He relied too much on his followers to feed him information and do his bidding. But we never put it together how he worked the connection. It's not your hive-mind thingy, at all, Abigail. It's the amber sphere."

She stared at Emma, studiously, meaningfully.

"What?"

"At his Removal, we never saw any movement within. We cast his sword into the fire with him, thinking its pommel mere ornament. Will never spotted anything either, did he?

But *you* did. *That's* why Animus wanted you out of the way." She smiled. Wide and wondrously.

"What?" Emma repeated, utterly baffled by her friend's ramblings.

"I'm not sure what, exactly, but Emma, I think you may have a gift. You're an exciter of spirits."

Emma looked askance, cocking her eyebrow. Despite the exigent circumstances, she spluttered. "G-go away. There's nothing special about me!"

"St Saviour disagreed. He wanted you as far away as possible. The quicker the better."

"Sorry, Ems," said Abigail, "but Gabby, why couldn't he just have, you know—"

"Killed her?" A smile played on Gabby's lips. "Because he didn't know how that would affect the essence. If it made a connection to Emma, it might not take kindly to it being cut off."

"This is ridiculous," said Emma.

"Really? You vanquished an ancient curse, didn't you? I wonder … ?" She shook her head. "Anyway, there's no time to get to the bottom of that. Later. What matters now is that we have a way forward. If the sphere does indeed contain his essence, which I'm positive now it does, if we can destroy it—"

"We can destroy Animus!" Abigail patted her hands together making tiny, gleeful claps.

"We've got to find it first," said Gabby. She bit her lip as she stared out of the window once more. "I'm not sure how much time Will has."

Bewildered, but just about hanging on to the thread of things, Emma said, "Seeing how attached Animus is to it, I don't think it'll be far away. Westen told me he even had it with him when he turned up at the vicarage to ask questions the night Peter died."

"I agree," said Gabby. "As I said, it used to be part of his sword. My betting is, he'd be averse to showing it off on that stage. Canes are not a symbol of strength. He wouldn't want to parade it in front of his New Model Army."

A crack of thunder rent the sky and the eye of the vortex tightened, pulsated. With a terrible, jagged intensity, lightning forked into the murky viridescence instantly ceasing the chants of the lurching crowd. Someone screamed as the air began to swirl. Emma could feel it through the open windows.

Abigail gasped, "I think it's started."

Wyland wrinkled his nose. "You're right. Can you smell that? It's coming from the well, from the toxic juice they throw down to enable the frack. It's rising to the surface."

Emma started to scramble up. "We need to get out. Now. We've no choice; we've got to get Will."

Wyland grabbed her. "Emma, no! Focus! He's safe for now. You heard Animus, he's saving him until his spirit army arrives."

"Yes," said Gabby. "Our best bet is to find this cane."

"He must have it nearby," replied Wyland. "One of the cabins, maybe. He'd surely have one as his base."

"No," said Gabby. "I don't think so. He didn't have it with him on the stage, and he wouldn't risk leaving it unattended. Or attended, for that matter. It'd be like putting his entire being in someone else's hands." She drummed her forehead with her fingers. "He's also going to need to address his legions. He won't have it with him then, either, for the same reasons. I think he'll have buried it. Somewhere only he can know."

"Shit, shit, shit," said Emma, eyes desperately souring the crowd. "How the hell are we going to find it amongst that lot!"

Thunder crashed again and the chemical stench strengthened. Lightning hit a power cable connected to the rig, sending it hissing and sparking down, spasming onlookers on its way to earth.

Suddenly, amidst the chaos, Abigail exclaimed, "I can't stay here. I've got to go."

"*Go?*" said Emma, incredulous. "Go where?"

"The tunnel." Abigail threw Gabby a meaningful look. "It's what you just said about making a connection. I can't concentrate here. I have to go somewhere quieter. I'll text." It took only a moment's puzzlement for Gabby's face to clear and return a nodding smile.

Emma cried, "But—"

Abigail took no notice, almost screaming at Wyland to help her through the window. Seconds later, she'd disappeared.

Utterly exasperated, not understanding, Emma held out her hands as she stared at the others. She cried, "What the hell does she think she's doing?"

Gabby's face looked calmer than it had for a long time. "She's going to work with the orb, but to do that properly, she needs quiet."

"But—"

"Trust her. She has the makings of a powerful witch. The orb I gave her is no ordinary crystal ball. The connection, once made, never leaves her, and that happened the moment it showed her Wyland's caravan. I think it will tell her where he's buried the cane."

34

FRACKED

inutes after Abigail left, pandemonium broke out. Spooked by violent gusts, the crowd stopped their chanting. All eyes flew to the vortex above them: a nimbus halo marbled in green, black and grey.

Animus, needing their attention on him.

Are you ready?

-YES!

Are you able?

- YES!

Are you powerful?

- YEESSSS!!!

He turned to face the rig and the crowd followed suit.

Wind flapped cables, rattled metalwork and shook the trees that surrounded the site. Pointing an arm to the heavens, splaying his fingers, Animus thrusted out his hand in a starburst.

Vertical lightning flashed down catching the rig, taking out a stanchion. The wind surged, rocking the compromised iron frame. For moments it held, then teetered. Metal screeching on metal, it buckled and broke. Unable to keep its integrity, all balance lost, the entire structure crashed to the earth, revealing the well-head it protected.

With a cry, Wyland scrambled out of the window gap. Confused, still shocked at the rig's collapse, Gabby and Emma leant out of it in time to see him holding onto the rail and the cabin's side, taking all the metal steps in two massive leaps before throwing himself onto the path below. Elbows crooked, palms down, he turned his head, ear to the ground. Moments later he was on his feet, shouting as he retook the steps.

"Get out! Now!" Emma pushed Gabby to the window, to little avail valiantly pushing at her ample bottom as she tried to climb out. Wyland grabbed her arms and somehow managed to lift and pull, scraping the woman's belly on the rough frame.

Gabby screamed in pain as she held her abdomen but refused their ministrations, instead making her way as best she could down the steps, leaving Wyland free to turn to Emma. She'd already swung her legs over the edge. All three safely out of the cabin, he ran them as far as he dared away from the stacked buildings before screaming, "Down! Get down! There's been a chemical reaction. I could hear it. The well's gonna blow!"

No sooner had he spoken than a deafening explosion rent the air. Emma's shoulders seized and cramped as she held her hands over her head and ears, bracing herself for more.

The ground shook with impacts, one after the other, as boiling air coursed over them, catching them with shards of whistling debris.

Flinching with every blow—keening, praying they'd come out of this alive—Emma pressed desperately hard against the path. She could hear Gabby cry out in pain and hoped Wyland was okay. At least the tunnel would protect Abigail.

But what about Will?

As soon as she'd reached the bottom of the metal steps, Abigail ditched the red wellies. She'd be faster with her feet unconstricted.

Not fast enough. She'd got within ten yards of the tunnel when the sound of an explosion whumped far away behind her. Instinctively, she threw herself onto the ground, praying her friends were okay. God knows what had happened. Should she go back?

No.

Arms protecting her head from the falling debris, she flinched at a searing pain in the back of her hand. More smoking, flying debris fell about her but she stayed where she was, praying no more would hit. Good call. Before long it had subsided and she felt able to scramble up, brushing herself down, thankful the burning junk had only scorched her garb and not her skin. Apart from her hand. It really, *really* hurt.

No time to linger.

Wyland had loosely re-covered the tunnel entrance. Trying not to think about the blast or the pain in her hand, Abigail tore the turf away before feeling for the set of head lamps he'd left inside for the return journey. Pressing one over her head, she switched it on and, feet first, entered the hole, wriggling down the slope until the world outside became nothing more than a small, oblique, pea-green circle.

She didn't want to see even that. Didn't want the lightning to invade her thoughts. So she wormed further in, rucking up her shirt, her midriff naked to the cold, bare earth. Eventually she stilled, knowing she had her work cut out to gain equilibrium; to eradicate the image of Will on his knees, humiliated in a world gone mad. Not the frame of mind she needed to connect with the orb.

The condition of the tunnel didn't help. Beyond where she lay, the shoring must have failed because, judging by the weight beyond where her feet pushed, there'd been what Gabby had dreaded. A collapse. Above her, soil showered down, forcing her to clamp shut her mouth and squint through half-closed eyes.

Better to close them fully. Her mouth dried as a clench of panic overtook her. It could only be a matter of time before it all came down and she'd be buried, suffocated …

Stop it. *Stop it!* Not helping.

Concentrating, Abigail forced herself to breathe more evenly, allowing the earth to cool and cocoon her, to calm her as she took in its peaty scent. She had no idea how long she battled with herself but eventually, she sensed her heart rate slow and that the earth had stopped falling. She opened her eyes, momentarily surprised by the brightness of her head lamp.

She turned it off, slipped it from her head and dropped it behind her.

Somehow able to squirm around and lie on her stomach, with room enough to place her elbows akimbo, she stacked her hands and rested her forehead on them. Found the rhythm again.

Slowly she lost track of time, letting her thoughts wander a loose trail back to Wood End, to the last vision the orb had given her. Able to let in that terrible image of Will, she allowed it to travel with her, telling her crystal counterpart what she needed from it.

Mist.

Mist swirling. Then greyness ... giving way to a faint vision of skeletons cavorting, dancing on the earth.

Keep the rhythm ... trust the orb ... trust the orb ...

More mist. Green this time. A sense of fullness. Head filled with crowd. Animus staring. Black. Monster eyes, black. Like oil. They widened, expanded, swallowed her in their black.

No light.

Except ... a pinprick. A tiny speck ...

Bigger. Growing slowly ... taking form, linear form. White then yellow ... orange ... amber. A wisp of amber dancing, eddying. Its expansion stopped and the inky backdrop fell to ...

... Animus on the stage and Will, head lolling ... Zoom, to him tied to the post ... Zoom, to the banner ... Zoom, to the string of lights. Zoom, to one light ...

To its dancing filament.

Not a filament.

Not buried.

The essence.

Hidden in plain sight as an outsized fairy light, hanging by the demon fingers of its setting.

From even a short distance no one would ever have noticed it as the odd one out.

With Herculean effort, Abigail subjugated her elation and stayed still, continued resting her forehead, now beaded with sweat. Desperate though she was to sever the psychical connection to the orb, she knew that would only lead to a migraine and sap her of the energy needed to help save Will.

She quickened her breathing until the vision faded and all

had returned to black. Not the demon black. Or the black that lay behind the eyes of Animus.

Tunnel black.

The sound of thunder returned and she slowly raised her head. Abigail drew down her hands. Using her elbows to scramble forward, grabbing the head lamp on the way, she headed for the pea-green circle.

They must be okay. They must have survived the explosion. Emma, Gabby, Wyland—Will. If they hadn't, the orb would surely have told her. At the base of the exit slope she leant against the tunnel wall and reached into her jeans pocket to slip out her phone. Thank God she still had nearly a full charge.

She texted: *A's essence not buried. It's one of the lights on the stage.*

After pressing the send button, Abigail allowed a minute to collect herself and to give thanks to the orb.

Then, filling her lungs with earth-air, she hitched herself out of the hole.

"Is it safe to move?" asked Emma, hopefully her friends were alive to hear her.

Wyland slowly gathered himself up. Nodded. "Are you both okay?"

She nodded. "I am." She glanced across at the squat figure next to her, still flat, face-down on the ground.

Emma struggled to her feet, wincing at her cuts and grazes. Painful, but she'd live. Kneeling next to her friend, she said, "Gabby? You okay?"

The figure moved and muttered, "Is it over?"

"Yes," said Wyland. "For now, at least."

Gabby drew up her bottom, twisted round and sat on it.

Holding her abdomen, she cried, "Will ... Will! He won't have survived it. I ... I can't look!"

"I will," said Wyland. "Stay here."

But Emma couldn't. She squeezed Gabby's arm for a few moments. "I have to go. I have to know."

After about fifty yards through the forced twilight, they could see that the perimeter path ahead had disappeared, blocked by overturned cabins, covered in rubble, pocked and ravaged with detritus from the explosion.

Gabby caught up with them. Holding her stomach, she said, "I had to come too. I couldn't stay there by myself! Have you spotted Will?" As they neared where the crowd had gathered, they stopped.

Bodies as far as they could see, piled two ... three deep on top of each other, some with shrapnel-stripped flesh, others with severed limbs. Wyland cried out as he ran to one from his activist cell, her orange hair spewing out of a filthy red bandana, head cracked open, an eye staring at him, hanging by its optic nerve.

Hardly able to control her dread, Emma raised her head to the stage ...

"He's okay! They're all—"

"Almost exactly as we left them," said Gabby, tight-lipped. "The explosion didn't touch Animus or his entourage."

How was that possible?

Gabby had spoken true. Animus stood just as before, front and centre of the platform, surrounded by blackshirts, a smile playing on his lips as his eyes scanned the devastation before him. His smirk widened as his gaze pinned on Emma. Why her? Why did she peak his interest so?

Next to him knelt Will, hardly moved since she last saw him, save for his bowed head, no longer raised in proud rebellion. Was he alive? Almost as if Animus had read her mind, he jerked a sharp kick at Will's knee. He cried out. She could hardly breathe with the heartbreak of it.

Placing a hand on the cheek of his dead friend, Wyland closed her other eye. Heaving himself up, he followed Emma's gaze. Mouth agape, he said, "Why weren't they killed? And why don't they come and get us?"

Emma lost it. "I don't bloody care, Wyland. If the explosion didn't do it, I'll do it my bloody self." Before he could hold her back, she cast about and picked up a large piece of drilling rig, its end pointed and sharp. Her hand tightened around it as she took a step forward.

Stopped.

The body next to her twitched. And the next.

"Ewwgh!" Repulsed, shuddering with disgust, Emma stepped backwards, nearly flooring Gabby. The broken corpses, now like a sea of maggots, began to stir and to seethe.

Spasming, they rolled off each other, twisting their bodies into sitting positions. Some tried to get to their knees, only to be brought down again by the mass of lurching bodies. Again they tried—and more joined them—necks cracking, bones setting, shattered jaws forming grimaces of delight. Gaining strength, wailing and whining they rose, faltering and unsteady, arms outstretched as they used each other to clamber, slowly and inexorably, onto their torn and bloody feet.

Almost at a run, Wyland grabbed the hands of the two women, dragging them away from the groping mass to shelter behind an upturned cabin. Disgust and fear clenched Emma's guts, bending her double so she could spill them.

Gabby, one hand still holding her abdomen, began rubbing Emma's back with the other. "That's right, dearie, get it out of your system. Best it all comes out now because this isn't over." She called to Wyland, "What's happening?"

"They're regrouping. I think Animus is going to start winding them up again."

Stomach quieted for now, Emma straightened her back. "I want to see. Want to hear."

The three of them came out from behind the cabin, Emma quivering, traumatized by fury and vomit. Any danger from the resurrecting bodies had gone. No point in hiding, since Animus knew they were there, obviously relishing their presence as he addressed the haggard mob.

My friends, it is time. Are you ready?

His zombie acolytes answered …

- We are ready … We are ready … Ready … Ready … Ready … Ready …

Keeping up the chant, low and guttural, they took their lead from Animus. Slowly turning, they faced the exploded well and looked skywards.

Gabby whispered, "That's it. We can't get at Will now they've retaken the flesh."

"My friends aren't moving," said Wyland, puzzled, looking at the hundred or so bodies still left on the ground.

Gabby grimaced. "They were never *of* the spirit, Wyland. They were only caught up *in* it."

"Why is Will still alive?" said Emma. "Why wasn't Animus touched in the explosion?"

The phone in her pocket vibrated.

Emma gasped. "It's Abigail's text!" she stared at the screen. "Oh my God!"

She showed Gabby, who said, "There's your answer. He's standing right next to his essence. It's protecting him."

A deafening whiplash cracked the sky and the eye of the

vortex pulsed. The chant grew louder as the air pressure increased, forcing Emma to swallow and click the muscles in her ears.

The earth rumbled and quaked as a sound like a thousand thundering, deafening trains assailed them. Louder and louder, coming ever nearer, the friends frantically stared at each other then desperately cast about for where the din was coming from and how it would manifest …

… which it did from the devastated fracking well, as the ground around it erupted in a powerful roar, thrusting to the heavens tons of soil and rock and God knows what in a thrashing, escalating, speeding column of earth.

"Animus has triggered the next emergence," shouted Gabby. "He's sucking his army into the world."

35

HELL LET LOOSE

Only as she scrambled out of the tunnel did Abigail notice the state of her bare feet: filthy, caked with soil and blood. Trying to run, but managing only pitiful lunging limps as she held the back of her aching hand, she hobbled her way back to her friends, navigating the altered landscape as best she could in the ever-diminishing light. She only got as far as the debris-strewn ranks of machinery and lorries before the earth beneath grumbled and roared.

Omigod! Eyes wide with disbelief, mouth open in shock, Abigail peered into the greeny murk and watched as a roaring column of earth rose from where the drilling rig once stood, racing to the eye of the vortex like some kind of demonic vacuum cleaner. Even from this distance, the noise was horrendous.

Ouch. Ouch! She grabbed the top of her bare arm as something bit into her flesh. A shard of metal! Without thinking, she pulled it out, and felt rather than saw the ooze of blood. As best she could, she darted to find shelter behind one of the cranes. Wow, that thing must be shredding the crowd!

Maybe not. It would only be Wyland's lot—their lot—that'd be affected. The ones without the power to take flesh again. Animus would need greater protection, though. About to greet his buried minions, he couldn't afford to lose form.

A row of pennies dropped one by one. The function of the essence wasn't only to connect him to his underworld; it insulated him from this one. She pictured him on the stage, next to poor Will, his amber sphere behind him dressed as a puny light bulb. Now she saw that Animus would never have risked being parted from it, not while the bloody Dyson from hell was yanking the guts out of the planet.

Sucking out the next emergence.

How would her friends get to it? The horde belonged to Animus; it'd block their way. Not to mention the stage surrounded by blackshirts. No sign of outside help, either. After the sky had darkened and the vortex had appeared, Westen would get his lot out of harm's way and leave it to the experts to sort it out. Will would be collateral damage—and he didn't know Emma was here. Eventually they'd call in the troops, but not before they'd got air support to do a recon, and with the vortex there'd be no chance of that. Not yet.

Hang on. How could she possibly know all this?

The orb! Deep within her psyche came the certain knowledge that their connection had not been broken. Minute by minute it added to her insight, giving her the lowdown, telling her what to do.

Throwing the image of a lorry into her mind.

She peered through the gloom at the banks of construction vehicles. Hand hurting, feet on fire, every step risking the sharpness of shrapnel, she lumbered over to the low loader: massive—like two-lorries-wide massive.

You have got to be kidding! She couldn't drive, didn't want to drive. Ever. God … she doubted she'd be able to climb up to the cab and definitely not in the state her feet were in. Was there even a key?

Yet climb she did. Tiny Abigail, the whipping turbulence from the monster Dyson making her hair fly everywhere as she struggled up the trackwheels, hands finding holds, toes sliding on blood as they sought niches. Pain gave way to determination. Only one thing mattered.

Save the others. Save Will.

Flinching at yet another pinging near-miss, she scrambled on, processing everything the orb threw at her, trying hard not to waste precious mental energy marvelling at their new-found kinship.

Out of breath, cuts and scratches scarring her arms and legs, she reached the cab and tugged at its massive chrome handle. Open? Of course. Why lock it when there's site secu-rity? Clambering inside, she threw herself into the huge driver's seat.

What now?

She closed her eyes, taking instruction. Okay. Pedals. She looked at her poor feet swinging from the seat. Didn't even reach. Casting about, looking for a lever to move the seat forward, Abigail found one next to the door, and with surprising ease lifted it. Even with the adjustment her foot only just touched a pedal. No way would she able to press it down.

Anyway, how would she start it? She scanned the dash-board looking for an ignition key. Nothing. Damn. She bounced and slapped down the sun visor, feeling all over it, like she'd seen on the telly. Nothing. She got out of the seat and, her tiny frame almost able to stand upright, checked under the passenger visor. Nada.

What now? Can't work the pedals, no key, no bloody clue.

Her eye was drawn to a large red button to one side of the dashboard. Press it.

Boom! With less roar than she'd expected the lorry burst into life, her inner orb mumbling something about noise suppressors. Good to know, what next?

It flashed another picture. Abigail wriggled all her five-foot nothing down the seat until her backside barely touched it; uncomfortable, but she could just about work the pedals—if she could stop her feet from slipping about. They'd gone numb, which was a blessing.

She pressed the left. Nothing. She pressed the right; this time the engine did roar, but without forward movement. The left one must be the clutch thing.

Gears? A handbrake? Yep. Both to her left. Lights? No. No lights. Not yet.

Eyes fixed on the windscreen, mind mystically connected to the video playing in her head, she pushed the brake lever down and grabbed the shift stick. Lying forty-five degrees to the seat, she moved her foot and depressed the left pedal, moved the gear stick to the number one, and shifted her hip to reach the right pedal. She let go of the left as she pushed down the handbrake.

By some miracle of concentration, mind over bloody matter, the mega-truck lurched forward! With her hands white-knuckling the steering wheel, it rolled out from the ranks of trucks and machinery and set course for the Dyson.

And the crazies who watched it.

"What the hell are we supposed to do now?" screamed Emma, as she stared at the shaft of earth rocketing to the sky, the friends sheltering again as stray pellets of earth whizzed past—not that they bothered a crowd able to reanimate. "We're as far away from Will as ever. We can't get to him."

"Or the essence," added Wyland.

"Why is Animus staying there? That thing's going to take out the whole area."

"In time, yes." Struggling to make himself heard over the roar, Wyland gesticulated as he yelled. "It'll hold for a while. The well itself has been reinforced and it's two miles down. It's used to high pressure. Once the lower strata start sucking out, there'll be a collapse—an epic one—but not yet. He'll hold it together until his army's out. They'll probably stay in spirit form during the earthquake. He'll have got air support standing by. They'll follow him."

"What's that?" bellowed Gabby. On tiptoe, she pointed, "Over there! Moving. Something big!"

Wyland craned his neck, squinting into the gloom. He shouted, "It's a vehicle. Big one. Is it? Yes." Puzzlement flooded his expression. "It's that mega-low loader we passed on the way in." Cocking an ear, he strained to hear. "In first gear by the sounds of it, but still going a fair whack."

"It's Abigail," shrieked Gabby. "Has to be!"

Abigail? Driving? Driving a lorry? Emma barely had time to ponder the absurdity of the thought before Wyland, jerking his head to the mob, exclaimed, "She's heading right for them and they haven't noticed yet. She's giving us our chance. After it hits I'd say we'll have about five minutes, tops, before the bodies start to reanimate again. It may be enough to leave Animus exposed. Both of you, get Will. I'll snatch the essence."

Emma and Gabby nodded. No more talk.

Thunder cracking, earth spewing, the world a cacophony of noise. As the mega-truck neared, mesmerised by their chanting, transfixed by the earth shaft, neither Animus nor his acolytes seemed to notice its approach. Suddenly, seconds from impact, the whole scene burst into light as Abigail switched on full beams, scourging the horde with her halogens, blinding it as she ploughed the lorry in and over. Acolytes scattered as the tank tracks furrowed their way in circles amongst them, reaping a deadly harvest as the truck crushed and flattened and ground their bodies into corpses way beyond any possibility of a useful rebirth.

"Nooooo!" shrieked Animus from the stage, his face incandescent as the headlights flashed upon it.

Squelching through carnage, dodging maimed survivors, Waylaid dashed forwards. Flesh clinging to his boots, blood splashing underfoot, he made for the string of lights.

Emma had the makeshift stage-steps in her sights; Will kneeling next to them. She made the first fifty yards without incident, keeping low, trying to minimize her surface area lest a stray rock from the earth shaft hit her. Feet away from the now unmanned barricade—Abigail's driving having scattered the blackshirts—she stumbled, shrieking as she fell forwards, eye to eye socket with a spasming, black-shirted carcass. Sick with revulsion, Emma sprang up, but its arm, tattooed with some kind of snarling dog, shot out and gripped her foot. The body next to it did the same and soon Emma was being dragged down as the creatures grabbed at her calves then her thighs, using her to climb to their feet.

Screaming for her life, losing her balance, she thudded to the ground, bringing the grasping zombies down on her. Gagging, suffocating, retching, she tightened her frantic fingers round the metal shard she still carried. Using all her remaining strength, she thrust her pelvis, sloughing off the writhing bodies enough to scramble clear. Blood up, adrenalin flowing, she kicked and shivved and stabbed, praying she'd done enough to consign their corpses to a final death.

Taking the dripping weapon with her, keening loudly so

she did not have to think, Emma made it to the short set of stairs. Animus had spied Wyland below the barricade and was matching his steps, crouching in readiness for his leap onto the stage. His attention thus distracted, Emma made it to her friend and set the shard to work on his bonds.

"Will!" she cried in his ear, as she cut the last piece of rope. "Talk to me. Are you with me?"

No answer. His eyes only stared to a point in the middle distance, fixed and unblinking. She wouldn't be able to move him. He was too deeply in shock.

As she laid him down, Wyland made his move, bounding over a barricade, taking the stage in a single leap. With a dummy ploy, he dodged around Animus in the direction of the essence. Animus caught up, delivering a sharp punch to the kidneys before grabbing Wyland in a body hug, dragging him away from the string of lights. Wyland whipped his head back into his opponent's face, bone on bone, but despite the blood spurting from his broken nose Animus held on, shifting his grip and crooking his muscular arm around Wyland's neck, squeezing him into a headlock. Like a jungle animal locked on his prey he jerked and tightened his grip until Wyland's body started to relax, giving Animus time to reach into his back pocket and take out something black and polished. With a twist of a thumb, out flicked a blade, on its way to Wyland's neck.

But not before Gabby took the stage.

Planting herself in its centre, hands by her side despite the blood oozing from her abdomen, she screamed, "Numenius Animus."

As if caught in a tractor beam, Animus froze, his knife at Wyland's jugular. Seconds that seemed like minutes later, he let Wyland sink to the ground as he turned slowly round.

"Gabriel?"

Amidst the noise of the thundering earth shaft, zombie shrieks and mega-truck engine—now ploughing its way through the gates of DeepDrilla—on the stage, time seemed to stop. Animus gazed at his old foe. A puzzled frown—deliberating, evaluating—played on his brow. He seemed to sniff the air. Then a smile twisted his lips.

A smile of realisation.

"Where is your magic, oh angelic one! So sad you had to resort to the help of puny mortals?" He jerked his head at Emma and Will and kicked Wyland's unconscious body. "Like them." The corner of his mouth curling, he continued, "I have waited centuries for this moment. Centuries! Crawling through rock and dirt to wreak my revenge on you and the humans you so love. How wonderful to learn that I'll be able to destroy you with nothing but my bare hands."

Gabby tried to run, but he lunged at her. She had nothing. A diminutive, middle-aged woman—injured—her greying, dirty-blonde bob shaking like a ragdoll above the pitiless grasp around her neck. She offered no resistance, no cry. She meant her sacrifice to be a silent one.

"*Stop!*"

Wyland's shriek rent the air, piercing the din from the onrushing column of earth a hundred yards behind him. Still bent over Gabby, now clearly blacked out and on her way to the floor, Animus twisted his head to see Wyland holding aloft his precious amber sphere, fused to its black spidery fingers. Even from the other side of the stage, holding Will's head in her lap, Emma could clearly see the shimmering essence within, performing an ever more frantic dance.

Horror flooded over the face of Animus, as Wyland jumped off the stage and ran towards the column of earth. Favouring his left leg after the kidney-punch, he had twenty yards on his pursuer before he began to slow. Heart in mouth, Emma saw him stop in his tracks and fill his lungs. Animus not ten feet behind him, Wyland drew back his throwing arm, bent his knees and hurled the amber sphere at the shaft.

It was as if the earth held its breath. Emma, Wyland—Animus—gazed at the shimmering globe, traced its trajectory as it arced upwards, its black hands somersaulting wrist over fingers, over and over and over, before swinging downwards towards the centre of the roaring column. As it neared, it picked up speed again until, unable to withstand the mighty suction, took on such velocity that, in a wink, it had gone.

Hurtled to the heavens.

"Nooooo … " Animus roared for the second time. Running past Wyland, oblivious to danger, he sprinted towards the shaft. Then stopped, realising a few steps more would lead him to the same fate as his essence. Defeated, he sank to the ground.

Wyland left him there and ran back to the stage, just in time to see Gabby sitting up, holding her stomach and stroking her neck.

He shouted, "Sorry, Gabby. We haven't much time. Can you stand?"

She nodded and croaked, "Never mind me, get Will."

Suddenly Abigail was there, staggering onto the stage as best her torn feet would allow.

"How's Will?" she shouted.

"Never mind that now," shrieked Wyland. "It's enough he's alive. We've got to go. It's not over."

Wincing and grunting, he heaved Will up, hooking an arm over his shoulder. Emma took the other one. Abigail helped Gabby up, put her arm gingerly around her bloody waist, helping her to follow.

As he took them through the sea of bodies, Wyland cried, "At least there's no sign of another zombie apocalypse!"

Gasping, trying to raise her voice loud enough for them to hear above the raging column of earth, Gabby cried, "They're not waking up. Animus has … lost his link to the spirits. In time, they'll rise from the corpses. We just have to make sure they go back from where they came."

They staggered on, Abigail obsessing over Wyland's words. Not over yet? How much bloody more did they have to do? As if driving a truck over hundreds of bodies wasn't enough! The orb had told her they were demonic and in the heat of the moment, fired by adrenaline-fuelled righteousness, it didn't matter. Now, surrounded by the fruits of her onslaught, their death suddenly became a real-world thing.

And that made her a murderer.

"What's going to happen? What did you mean by it not being over?" called Abigail, as she helped Gabby struggle through the bodies.

Ignoring her, dragging Will as he spun this way and that, Wyland desperately peered through the green-dark, scanning the scene. He pointed to a spot about hundred yards away, near the site entrance. "Get over there, and whatever you do, keep low. All we can do is hope for the best."

After reaching the spot, as gently as they could, Wyland and Emma set down their charges. Though Will's eyes were open and his legs on automatic, his mind had clearly left the building. Not once had he spoken. Not once did his eyes waver.

Wyland tried to close Will's eyelids, passing his palm over them as if the priest were a dead man. But they flew open again, would not be shut. Grabbing a corner of his shirt, Wyland put it between his teeth to make a rent, then tore away a strip with his hands. He placed it over Will's open eyes and then, on all fours, knees on the ground, he curled himself over the senseless man's face.

"All of you, get down. Like this. Now."

A surge of panic took Abigail as she repeated, "What's going to happen?"

Gabby coughed and gagged as she squatted over, trying to give her speech enough volume, "It's his essence. Pure energy. His sphere won't stand a chance up there. Once it reaches the vortex ..."

Abigail had started to kneel. Instead, she got up.

Wyland screamed, "What the hell are you doing? Get down! It's not safe."

"No!" she said. "I don't care! I want to see what happens!"

No sooner had she spoken than a crash of thunder cracked the air and lightning forked the sky, poking the eye of the cyclone shut in a blinding line of brilliant light. Somehow managing to get her ragged feet on tiptoe, Abigail scanned the scene and located the frantic, now tiny figure of Animus, his arms thrusting, fists aloft, starbursting his fingers, as he shrieked at the sky.

As if the vortex had listened, the rush of earth stopped and the world fell gloriously silent.

Time suspended.

For a scintilla of a moment.

Before the earth fell.

Before ton, upon ton, upon ton of earth shat down on Animus. One moment there, another ...

Gone.

Instant burial.

In seconds a hill formed, grew, an ever-expanding slagheap interring both dead and undead.

Abigail, now in full acceptance of the danger, screamed as she threw herself down to mirror Wyland's position. The roaring crashing continued as the rubble piled and the heap slid towards them as she imagined cold, black magma might: first over their feet, then their knees, and began covering their backs. She closed her eyes, praying Wyland had got it right, that he knew how the earth would behave, would understand where the bulk of it would land.

In the blackness behind her eyes a speck appeared, and a picture slowly expanded. No. Not a picture, exactly, more a set of symbols; beautiful symbols shining like neon, golden in the dark.

The crashing earth stopped, and she could hear nothing but the occasional slap as the last of the sky-bound earth returned. The picture zoomed out and her physicality returned. She could move! Barely, but enough to squirm and wriggle, casting off the debris.

Light! Daylight! Sunshine and blue sky. A cool evening breeze!

Abigail could have cried!

Emma had made it okay, and was sitting up, spitting soil. Gabby too.

No sign of Wyland.

She looked over at Emma and, both thinking the same thing, they waded, slipping and stumbling over the loose terrain, to where they thought Wyland must be, for they could see no mound.

With bare hands they dug and parted the earth. They located him quickly enough, ploughing only a foot or so before feeling the arch of his back.

"Wy! Wyland!" shouted Abigail. "Talk to me!"

A moan, then movement. Muffled words. "I … must have passed out. Can you dig round me? I want to keep the dirt away from Will's face."

They managed as best they could, fingernails tearing at the soil and rocks. Eventually Wyland moved away from

Will, revealing his prone body, the shirt rag still over his eyes.

He took it away. They were still open. He waved his hand back and forth over them. No response.

"He needs a hospital, and quick. He's been in shock too long."

"Help will come soon, I think," Emma said. She knelt next to Will, wiping his filthy face with the edge of her shirt, the streaks making it look worse. "Now that thing's stopped and everything's back to normal, the authorities'll treat this place like a war zone."

"Except we're not back to normal yet," croaked Gabby.

Abigail moaned. "Gabby, why do you always have to say that? What now?"

"We've got to seal the site. Before anyone comes into it. We've got to make sure no other spirit can enter this way. If we don't, it'll be an open portal."

Eyes red with a mixture of grit and desperation, Gabby cast about, looking everywhere, as if she'd find an idea growing on a nearby tree. "I-I don't know what to do!"

Wyland shrugged, his palms haven't-a-clue outwards.

Bloody hell, was this never going to end?

Staring from one to the other, Gabby said, "I can't do it. I've lost the power of angelic prayer!"

Very faintly, Abigail heard the sound of sirens.

No time.

Tears flowed down Gabby's cheeks; rivulets of salty muck.

"Won't there need to be sentinels?" asked Emma. "Is praying over it enough?"

"It would make us safe enough for now," replied Gabby. "It would force the spirits to make their way home. If they remain, they'll be hostile and purposeless. They'll attach themselves to any tin-pot dictator. Animus is done for. With the essence destroyed, he's lost his connection to them. He'll be scrabbling down there forever."

"I'm putting in some bluestones at Wood End to consolidate the henge," said Wyland. "And I know the families of some of the dead. I'm sure they'll agree to a green burial here. We could turn the whole site into a memorial if I could persuade the authorities to give us the land."

"I bet they would," said Abigail. "It'd be like Ground Zero in America. You know, the Twin Towers?"

"But that'll come too late to work with the spirits Animus left behind. They'll be long gone before I can get the stones laid. We need that prayer."

Abigail hitched her breath; the neon writing filled her mind once more. She said, "What does angelic script look like?"

Gabby shrugged. "Can't explain it." She gave Abigail a thoughtful look. "It is very, very beautiful, though. Why are you asking?"

"Symbols?" asked Abigail.

Gabby nodded.

"Can you remember the prayer? I mean, you may not have your powers, but can you remember how it goes?"

"Of course!"

"Then say it. Wyland is a Guardian, Will is a priest, and I am not without gifts. I think it might be enough."

"Me too?" said Emma. "I might not be mystically endowed, but apparently I can excite a spirit!"

Gabby nodded. "You saved us yet again, Emma. You found Animus' Achilles heel!"

So, sirens approaching through God knows what carnage outside, they flattened the earth around Will as best they could and, holding hands, formed a circle. Abigail didn't have a clue how this was going to pan out. But she'd learned to trust the orb.

She looked out at DeepDrilla, at the mound where the well used to be, then to where Animus had fisted the air before the earth had overcome him. She moved her eyes to the rest of the huge site, under which the bodies were buried; the bodies she'd killed in the truck she could barely drive. Then bowed her head.

Gabby started her prayer. Low at first, the beauty and sibilance of its alien words catching at Abigail's heart. Then louder as, eyes closed, Gabby lifted her chin and spoke to her maker.

And that's when Abigail saw him.

At the point where the rig had stood, slowly manifesting like a developing photograph, rose the breathtaking figure of Michael.

Dispassionate. Resplendent. Chiselled. Awesome. Glinting gold, rays of light surging from his heart, his luminosity burnished the devastated landscape.

Wings outstretched, he gazed at them, mouthing Gabby's prayer word for sacred word.

And how glorious those utterances were, singing into Abigail's soul, blessing her and lifting away from her conscience the weight of her slaughter.

As her heart swelled in Michael's presence, the ground beneath her began to move. No tremor, this. Not an earthquake. Rather, a gentle vibration that somehow bored deep into the earth. Healing it. Sealing the fissure. Securing the land.

Her eyelids drooped heavily as she struggled to gaze at the angel and sensed rather than saw the tip of his wing move. Scintillating and stretching—no effort involved—his golden feathers traversed the hundreds of yards towards them, past her, past Emma, past Wyland. To the still, half-buried figure of Will.

Touched his forehead.

Then it was over. The shimmering wing retracted and Michael began to disappear. As he slowly faded, only the faintest remnant of an image left, Abigail felt his eyes burn into her as slowly, almost imperceptibly, he shook his head.

Nobody, especially Gabby, was ever to know.

🎇 36 🎇

AN END

The small henge of caravans had been craned out of Wood End, leaving the upright remains of the sentinels to continue their underground watch unsheltered, waiting for their new companion.

At their first reunion after the traumatic events a fortnight earlier, the friends milled around outside the stone cottage, in the cool of its shadowed courtyard. Gabby and Wyland fussed about, in deep conversation about the ceremony as Emma and Abigail looked on. Will stood apart from them all, eyes never leaving Peter's wicker coffin which rested on a makeshift trestle table near the front door.

"Has Will spoken to you yet?" asked Abigail, lowering her voice out of his earshot.

"Not a word," said Emma, shaking her head. "You?"

Abigail murmured, "No. He hasn't even asked how I am." She lowered her voice further. "Wyland said Will would have done all this on his own, if he could've. He doesn't really want us here, Ems."

"He's angry with us. He'll come round, soon." But her

doubtful expression said otherwise, a little frown knotting her brow. "He's getting on well enough with Wyland."

"That's because he needed his help with Peter's body," Abigail murmured. "Will told him that Mr Martin had washed his hands of his son and refused to have anything to do with the funeral. Told Will he could … what did Wyland say, now … ? 'Dispatch him in any way he saw fit, because whatever he came up with they would not be attending.'"

"Hmm. Typical bully," said Emma. "Mrs Martin will regret not having the strength to stand up to her husband. Changing tack, she continued, "How did Will manage to keep today secret from the bishop? He'll have wanted to attend, particularly as he was the one that brought St Saviour down upon us!"

"Will played both ends against the middle," said Abigail. "He told the bishop the family had wanted a discreet ceremony back home, and that they didn't want anyone from the church to attend. He and Wyland then arranged for a memorial stone to be installed at St Jude's. Not a grave exactly, but—"

"Near as damn it," said Emma. "Clever. If the Martins had a change of heart and wanted to pay their belated respects, they'd assume that's where his ashes lay. The locals, on the other hand, can still believe his real resting place is back home with his parents." A thought occurred to her. "They must have signed over Peter's body to Will, then?"

"Yeah. He had it brought to the church yesterday so he could sit in vigil over him." Abigail looked over at him. "All night! That's why he looks so wasted."

Emma followed her gaze to the pale and gaunt figure of her friend, his eyes still set unwaveringly upon Peter's coffin. It reminded her of his awful fixed stare throughout his ordeal with Animus. She'd nearly died with relief once Gabby's prayer had ended and Will suddenly snapped out of his fugue state. All would be restored and their friendship renewed.

She couldn't have been more wrong.

Her eyes welled as she regarded him from the other side of the courtyard, hardly comprehending what he must be going through. He had no idea—and had never asked—how everyone had fared at the hospital. He knew nothing of Abigail's virtual collapse when the ambulance arrived, her hand bleeding and blistered, her poor feet unable to take one more step. How she'd been admitted for three days, until discharged in a borrowed wheelchair into the care of Josie and her grandparents. Nor had he known that Gabby had spent her first ever night in a hospital, her stomach so badly grazed and cut—covered in soil and grit—that it needed sluicing and stitching in places. Not to mention the damage to her throat. She still found talking difficult.

Which, in the past, some might have considered a blessing.

Will, though, had refused point-blank to be admitted. Emma spoke to Robbie about him, begged him to pay him a visit, worried sick that he might relapse into shock.

"No one can force him to stay, lass," Robbie had shrugged. "When I saw him he didn't want to talk much. Assured me he felt okay, and thanked me for letting him stay at the surgery that night and told me I didn't need to worry about him. He seemed lucid enough, if depressed. Remember, he's in mourning. I think you should leave him to come round by himself."

But she couldn't. Encouraged that Will had spoken to Robbie, she'd called on him too.

He didn't answer the door to her. Not then, and not the other three times she'd called.

Gabby and Wyland came out of their confab and she gave a little double clap. Her voice grated slightly as she called, "I think we're ready. Will, are you sure I can't persuade you to officiate? I don't have to, you know. I only need to recite the words of the ritual."

He shook his head, eyes still glued to the coffin.

She sighed. "Very well, then."

Wyland stepped forward and, after tapping Will on the shoulder, the two men took their positions at the head of the coffin, on either side. In silence, they waited for Emma and Gabby to take the rear. Abigail, stick in hand, stood behind. Wyland muttered a one … two … three, then as one the pall-bearers bent, lifting the coffin off the trestle by its woven side-handles.

So began Peter's journey to his final resting-place.

Drenched in mid-afternoon sunshine, its roads and gravel pathways gleaming, Wood End received him in splendour. Clipped hedgerows, their verges abundant with wild daisies, poppies and cornflowers, meandered between the groups of static caravans—much fewer now, since the earthquake had prompted many of their owners to site them elsewhere.

As Emma walked, she imagined how it might have looked in the first century. A place free of vans, devoid of shrubby alcoves and landscaped stands of trees. A more barren setting, perhaps. What had Gabby called it? A natural amphitheatre, upon whose outcrops a thousand white-robed Druids once sat to witness another ending.

Or had it been a beginning? Peter, she was sure, would think of it that way.

Downwards they trod, carrying their precious load nearer the line of the woods, accompanied by no sound other than the gentle susurration of trees, their branches softly swaying in the mellow breeze.

Moments later, leaving the path, they arrived at the burial site and laid Peter gently down before his grave, feet facing it. A circular black chasm, four feet in diameter, a pile of soil and rubble nearby. Given that this was an upright burial, Emma couldn't begin to estimate the depth to which Wyland would have had to excavate. Twelve feet? Fifteen?

Stepping away from the willow casket, Gabby walked to a spot beyond the open grave as the others formed a rough circle around it. She bowed her head. They followed suit.

A minute passed.

Gabby raised her head and straightened her shoulders, wincing slightly as she cleared her throat. In rasping tones, she began the ceremony.

"We gather here to say goodbye to our friend, Peter. We remember his life. We remember his work. We remember his suffering." Less formally, she added, "If anyone wants to say anything ... now would be the time."

Emma shuddered as she brought her mind back to ... that night. At the ruins, Peter hanging, skin like rags. How could Will bear it? Tears rolling, she glanced at him but fathomed nothing. He stood, still as marble, expressionless, dry-eyed and cold.

Silent.

Gabby gave the slightest of shrugs as, without saying any more, she nodded to Wyland.

Slowly and in tandem, the two men moved once again to the casket. They walked it up and upended it. Then, stepping to its sides, they took its weight by the straps and, lifting, gently lowered it into the vertical grave.

Gabby raised her arms and looked to the skies.

"Lord of all lords, God of all gods, bringer of life and keeper of earth, we ask that you bless Peter, your sentinel, as he takes his place within this henge. We pray you comfort him as he keeps watch over this place, that he might guard it forever from the evils that would seek to violate it."

Raising her head higher, voice breaking with obvious pain and sorrow, she began the angelic burial prayer. Despite her hoarseness, her Nephilim words lifted and mystically amplified, rapturously echoing and resonating around the well of the park, as if a thousand Druids had taken up the chant.

As it she ended, even Gabby seemed surprised at the enhancement of her utterance, scanned the landscape as if looking for the cause of it. Nothing. She shrugged and continued her words all could understand.

"Peter. Let no demon trespass, no spirit flow into this, our precious land. Guard it with your love, guard it with your soul, guard it for all eternity."

After the ceremony, Emma arrived home exhausted and spent. She nearly cried again when she saw Westen waiting for her on the bench outside her window.

"You are such a sight for sore eyes!" she exclaimed, as she climbed out of the jeep. "I can't believe you're finally here. You've been so busy!"

He held out his arms and she melted into them. "How did it go? A pity you had to travel all that way for the funeral, instead of having it here. Where do Martin's parents live? Northumberland, isn't it?"

"Yes." The question was straightforward enough, though the fact that her simple reply contained a world of dissembling made her heart burst.

"Sh... shush," he said, stroking her wiry hair. "I've taken the week off. I don't want you to be on your own." He sighed. "I wish Turner would pull himself together, though. Not fair that he's freezing you out. You used to be so close. Times like this, you need each other."

She pulled away. "How can you say that? You know what he went through with Peter. And Anim—St Saviour!"

She nearly spilled out his true name. Was this always

going to happen? Would she always have to be this careful about what she revealed?

"I need a glass of wine. I'll—"

Westen hadn't seemed to notice her slip. He said, "Give me the door-key. You sit here. I'll get it."

Once on the bench, Emma stretched out her legs and stared over at St Jude's. Had Will arrived back at the vicarage? Having stridden off as soon as the prayers were over, he'd left an even worse pall over the company. There hadn't seemed much point in going after him.

Wyland would be sinking seven small bluestones between the graves, where the caravans had once stood, to mark the henge for what it truly was. She doubted Will would go to see them installed.

Returning with her wine, Westen said, "Sorry. I shouldn't have said that about Turner. It's just—"

"What?"

"That whole situation—at the fracking site. It got to me. We knew St Saviour might be dangerous. Though I have to admit, we didn't think he'd start the next fucking apocalypse." He shook his head incredulously. "Who'd have thought we'd be dealing with a terrorist attack, here of all places?" He exhaled slowly, then took her hand. "Why did you follow us there? I asked you to stay."

"Actually," she said, attempting a grin, "you ordered me!" She took a sip from her glass. "I couldn't help it. I had to get to Will." This was what she'd been dreading. The debrief. Oh, she'd been interviewed, as the others had been. But not by Westen. Some special services crew had been brought in to hear their concocted and rehearsed story of kidnap and sabotage and he hadn't been allowed anywhere near.

Except at the hospital. Where he found her. Where he shouted at her for disobeying his instructions.

Where he kissed her better …

... before he was airlifted to some facility in London before he could get her to explain, where the government boffins grilled him about his part in what had happened. Holed up since the DeepDrilla fiasco, he hadn't even been allowed to ring her, but he'd 'fucked that' and done it anyway.

She couldn't help but savour the warmth around her heart while she took a sip from her glass and tried to answer his question. "I had to follow you. Had to find Will. He and I —we're more than just friends, we've a ... a special bond. Since I arrived in Flammark—since what happened last year with ... Ben ... Well, you know ..."

"Yeah. I do," he sighed. "Truth is, I feel partly responsible for what happened to him. We should have kept our eye on Turner as soon as we put St Saviour in the frame for fraud and conspiracy. Jesus, he'd even corrupted some of my lot."

"I heard on the news that Peter Piper had gone. He was your superintendent?"

"Yep. He resigned after what happened at DeepDrilla, but —and this remains between the two of us—he was on his way out before that." He pressed his lips together in a grim line as he muttered, "Stupid bastard."

"Leaves you with an opportunity?" Emma cocked an eyebrow. "If you decide to stick around, that is."

"Possibly," he said, smiling back. "There has been a conversation."

His expression darkened. "Jesus, Emma, if only you could have seen yourselves at the hospital. You looked straight out of a pit. No ... a pit in a warzone! And Abigail Chater's feet— her hand! Christ almighty, what happened to them?"

Emma shrugged and, deflecting, replied, "I was worried too, about you! I saw your convoy get swallowed by the crowd."

"Did you? We couldn't fucking move. No one tried

anything, only held us there, pressed us in. Couldn't see a thing except people and placards. We waited to see if the mob would subside, but it didn't. After half an hour we radioed for backup." His lips curled. "Pecker's last revenge. He ordered we wait it out."

"Pecker?"

"Yeah, it's what we call Piper."

He grinned at her quizzical expression. "Long story." He grew serious again. "It was only after the first explosion and the crowd ran to help their fallen, that we got free and clear. Jesus," he exclaimed, shaking his head, "fifteen hundred innocent protestors, dead and buried! They're still digging up bodies and some, near where the well blew, may never be recovered. Two that have been were known to us. We'd been after them for the Martin murder. Dressed like fucking blackshirts, they were." He drained his glass. "They ordered me out of the place as soon as air support arrived and saw the scale of the devastation. If I'd known you were in there, it'd've been a different story. When Donna radioed in you were at the hospital, I …"

Westen grabbed her hand and squeezed it, shaking his head. He held her gaze. "I nearly lost you."

She smiled as she put her head on his shoulder, breathing in his scent, basking in the security she felt within his arms.

"Emma, how did you know Will was at DeepDrilla? How did this Gabby woman know?"

"I'm not sure. She's living at Wyland's caravan park. They're very close. He's a bit of an eco-warrior and has been behind many of the protests there. Maybe one of his activist friends saw Will being brought there."

"Hmm," he said. "That's a stretch. Am I being fobbed off?"

She put a finger to his lips and shrugged, snuggling into

his arms, beginning an intimate silence that seemed to last forever.

"Take me to bed."

～

Emma's eyelids flew open. The quality of the light told her the sun had barely risen, yet she was sure she'd heard her letterbox drop.

Carefully lifting Westen's arm, she slid from under it. Muttered something in his sleep, he resumed his slow, steady breathing.

Grabbing her kimono, she wrapped it around her and crept down the stairs as quickly and quietly as she could.

A note.

Will's handwriting.

Without pausing to read it, she shot the bolts and ran out of the door. Halfway across the green, aiming for the church, Will was walking. Head down, hands in pockets, shoulders slumped. Barefoot, she sprinted over the damp, dewy grass. "Will! Will, wait!"

He stopped, his shoulders sagging some more.

Catching up, she stood in front of him, barring his way. "Why didn't you knock? Come back. I'll make us some coffee."

He sighed. "No, Emma. I'm sorry. I can't come back with you. I'm leaving."

"Leaving?"

He nodded and started walking again. Once more, Emma overtook him.

"What do you mean, leaving? Are you taking a break? I think time away is a really good idea, it'll—"

"Not a break, Emma. I won't be coming back."

Her lips trembling, she cried, "Are you still blaming us—

blaming me—for what happened to Peter? Please, Will, we didn't know—" She stopped at the hardness in his expression. No sign of him giving way. "Please don't go. I … I need you."

"You don't need *me*." He scoffed, nodding towards Clearview. "Westen's there, isn't he? I saw his car. That's great. I'm really happy for you. Truly. He's a good man, a very good man. You deserve him."

"You're going because of *Westen*?"

"For God's sake, Emma, I thought you knew me better than that. Especially now you know about me and … Peter." He ran his hand through his hair. "This isn't about you. I'm not going because I'm jealous." He sighed, and for the first time in weeks made eye contact, "Nor am I going because I lost the man I love." Eyes hooded, face desolate, he continued. "What happened last week changed me. I can't carry on. It's gone."

"What's gone? Sorry, Will … talk to me … I still don't understand."

He started walking.

A third time she caught up with him.

"Is this a faith thing?"

"Faith? That God exists? Hah! If only it was that simple! He's up there all right, and we know His bloody useless angels walk the earth. But where were they when Peter died? Where were they when Animus tied me to that post? When he humiliated me?" Tears welled and he shook them away. "Absent, Emma. Absent." He drew in an anguished breath. "How can I call myself a man of God when He's made me feel like this? I hate Him. Hate Him!"

They stood, eyes locked, Will an island of torment.

He said, "I'm sorry. I never wanted this conversation. Please don't follow me. I've spoken to the bishop and am leaving in an hour. As I told you before, Clearview is yours for as long as you need it. I've put it all in the hands of the estate agents. They'll be dealing with you from now on."

With no goodbye, he turned away and resumed his journey.

Emma, confused—dumbfounded—let him go, finally realising how useless it would be to follow him.

Stricken by the loss of her closest friend, all she could do was stand and watch in utter desolation as Will disappeared.

Into the morning mist.

ACKNOWLEDGMENTS

I'd like to thank all those who gave me the criticism I needed to improve the story and my writing. The two Dans, Rikon, Leslie, my editor Lee and my grammarians Trevor and, of course, Noel (who metaphorically sits on my shoulder as I type every comma and construct every dangling modifier!)

To Beth who's there for me during all the design stages and Lucy who is always happy to tell me where I'm going wrong, lol.

To Edward, from The Garth in Machynlleth, Wales, the caravan site Wood End is based upon (yes, it really does look like that), and Professor Ronald Hutton, who *does* indeed write very densely written text books on paganism in the *tiniest* of fonts!

WHAT NEXT FOR EMMA AND WILL?

Watch out for the next installment: THE WITCH AND THE FAITHLESS! Available next year, yet another entity threatens the village. Can Will can recover from his trauma and join his friends in fighting it?

News of the release date, as well as other stories, character info and village background, can be found by clicking the links below. (If you are reading this in the print version, my website will lead you to all my social media info, bio, etc.)

- MY WEBSITE (https://pjmordant.co.uk)
- MY NEWSLETTER (for release dates, giveaways, Flammark gossip, etc)
- THE FRIENDS OF FLAMMARK FACEBOOK PAGE (contains posts, extra material, reader discussions - and spoilers!)
- MY FACEBOOK AUTHOR PAGE

Thank you SO MUCH for reading Animus! If you liked it, please consider leaving a review on Goodreads and/or Amazon. Doing this really gives authors the social proof they need to help spread the word about the quality of their work.

Printed in Great Britain
by Amazon